Books by
Dennis McFarland

The Music Room
School for the Blind

BROADWAY
BOOKS
New York

Dennis
McFarland

A Face
at
the
Window

BROADWAY

Broadway Books titles may be purchased for
business or promotional use or for special
sales. For information, please write to: Special
Markets Department, Bantam Doubleday
Dell Publishing Group, Inc., 1540 Broadway,
New York, NY 10036.

BROADWAY BOOKS and its logo, a letter B
bisected on the diagonal, are trademarks of
Broadway Books, a division of Bantam
Doubleday Dell Publishing Group, Inc.

FIRST EDITION

Designed by Richard Oriolo

Library of Congress Cataloging-in-
Publication Data

McFarland, Dennis.
    A face at the window / Dennis
McFarland. —1st ed.
        p.   cm.
    ISBN 0-553-06694-3 (hc)
    I. Title.
PS3563.C3629F3   1997
813'.54—dc20   96-31232
                                    CIP

97 98 99 00 01 10 9 8 7 6 5 4 3 2 1

I'm grateful to Ira Ziering, Don Willis, Greg
Luce, Tellis Lawson, John Traficonte, Joseph
Evans, Acre Lifts, Colin Williamson, Sharon
Sellars, Rosalind Michahelles, Doctor Scott,
Gail Hochman, and Bill Hamilton for their
invaluable   help   and   advice; Lindsay
Knowlton, Janice Parky, and Bruce Cagwin
for their hospitality; Ron McAdow for
permission to cite his wonderful book; and
John Sterling for his friendship and amazing
editing skills. The rubber ball in this tale is
meant to pay homage to the great Mario
Bava. And to Michelle Blake Simons—thanks
for so often showing me the way, especially
through the scary parts.

—D.M.

For Meesh, with love

A Face at the Window

Prologue

A FEW VITAL statistics, my human credentials, a subtext for what's to come:

My name, a compound of my parents' surnames, is an example of how they liked to invent symbols of equality where there was none. The result, Cookson Selway, sounds more like an industry than a person, I realize, and hints quietly of blue blood, though nothing could be farther from the truth. I was born, aptly enough under the sign of the bull, to a family of cattle farmers in the Deep South. I'm known to friends as Cook, and my wife, in bed, often calls me Cookie. (It has a strange, unnameable effect on a postorgasmic man, while he still tingles, to be called Cookie.) My mother, when I was a kid, did not call me Cookie, though she might have. The daughter of lazy, tyrannical people, she had quit school and married my father when she was fourteen, the foundation stone in what was to become a great monument of sacrifice to him and his ways and demands. She very soon gave birth to a boy, not me, then, eighteen months later, to a girl; a hiatus of some sort was struck, lasting eight years, then a new era of feeling ensued in which she gave birth to another boy, also not me; eighteen months after that, I was born, the fourth, last, and youngest child, a mutant, wrong-sexed. I was supposed to be a girl in order to satisfy my mother's juvenile fetish for matched pairs, and already possessed of the deep-cut, heroic will of a virtuoso sacrificer, she wasn't to be confused by the fact of my gender and raised me as a girl anyway. She wanted a girl, you see, and after everything she'd suffered, after giving up her youth, freedom, and figure, was this so much to ask?

Of course, my mother never actually had any freedom to give up. She was an incarnation of the old lines:

Hard is the fortune of all womankind:
She's always controlled, she's always confined—
Controlled by her parents until she's a wife,
A slave to her husband the rest of her life.

In the heart of Dixie, in the fifties, the roles of girls and boys were as avidly defined as those of race (I imagine they still are). While my brothers learned to play football, drive the combine, and operate the feed mill, I aided my mother in the house and studied piano. Eventually, at around the age of eight, I mounted the protest my father had failed to mount on my behalf and began acquiring all sorts of dubious skills proper to a man—how to assemble a forty-foot grain bin from corrugated steel, how to pull barbed wire taut around a creosote post and hammer in a staple, how to cuss out the help. But before that, during the important, formative, pre-school years, something else altogether went on: when the menfolk weren't around, which was most of the time, my mother and my teenaged sister would dress me in a pink organdy jumper, paint my nails, and serve tea in miniature cups to my sister's half-dozen toddler-size bride dolls.

It is probably no surprise that these early experiences resulted in a few trouble spots during adolescence regarding my sexual orientation. I enjoyed a longer than usual adolescence (well into my twenties), assisted by the use of recreational drugs and the general sway of the counterculture, which, it seems to me, prodded all of us in the direction of puerility. For a while in my extended youth, I became what the army recruiting office calls a "practicing homosexual," though I didn't practice enough to get very good at it. Maybe my mother's little games had given me a heightened sense of maleness and femaleness, and though sex with three of my male friends (the mystery of their willingness has earned them each a lasting place in my heart) answered some curious call I couldn't possibly have named, having to do indistinctly with the failures of my father, I met with a recurrent physical awkwardness, a quandary about what went where and when and why. Trying to honor the maxim "If you think you might be, you probably are" required me to ignore the truth that I fell in love with girls at the drop of a hat, a truth I eventually embraced, and with my first, belated step into heterosexual waters (Linda Toadvines, 1974, Mount Tamalpais, dawn, her sleeping bag), I discovered what I suppose the rest of the world took for granted: matters of equipment were entirely self-evident. In any case, because of a weird childhood, I believe I came of age with capacities to be sexual in ways that many men would shun, and that many other men would claim to shun. I mention all this because it will count for something later on. If I didn't mention it, some good nose have survived the grip of our love with a minimum of damage.

Some years ago, Ellen lost her closest friends (one to AIDS, one to breast cancer, both in their thirties), and during the same period, her parents were killed in a car crash, leaving her to disentangle the web of a shabby estate. Lines of chronic worry inscribe her face, and at least half of those lines have my name on them. Though she has grown more interesting, more successful, and more beautiful in middle age, the events of the story I'm about to tell have driven her into retreat—to a place somewhere off the mainland of our marriage. On our finer days, in the finer hours, I think I recognize in her eyes the recognition of our passion and history. But there are other times, and plenty of them, when she looks at me as if a memory of loss and disappointment were all that connected us. I believe that this is temporary. I cling today to hope as doggedly as I once chased after drink and drugs. As if it were all that mattered to me. As if it were my only friend.

Soon, God willing, I'll turn forty-four. I still have all my teeth and a full head of hair. I'm in exceptionally good health (apart from a developing arthritis in my right shoulder), with an exceptionally good cholesterol level. I'm five feet ten and weigh in at 162 on the scale at the Mount Auburn Club, where I swim and torture myself on the Cybex machines. I belong to an all-day/all-night gun club in Dorchester, where I go with a friend about once a month for target practice. I own a thirty-nine-year-old Ruger semiautomatic .22-caliber pistol. I don't believe in hunting for sport, but I do believe most of the Freudian stuff about why men (and some women) enjoy packing and shooting pistols. I read and appreciate poetry, chiefly because it's short and invites contemplation. (I'm the only person I know who reads serious poetry, and I'm careful about whom I reveal this clandestine habit to.) My favorite modern poet is John Berryman, the drunk, though his being a drunk hardly distinguishes him among modern poets. My favorite poems of his are the "Eleven Addresses to the Lord," in which he says, "I only as far as gratitude & awe/

confidently & absolutely go" (he's talking about God) and "Unite my various soul,/sole watchman of the wide & single stars" (also God). I am most at-home at home. Home is where my deepest interests reside—the garden, the kitchen, the library, the bedroom. I have become, and remain, a man I would have scoffed at and secretly envied only a few years ago, a simple, extraordinarily lucky man whose great loves are his wife, his daughter, his house, and his dog.

I've noticed that chronicling the past often makes all things seem fateful. Nothing in my background looks especially like preparation for a tryst with evil, and yet, afterward, some things do begin to glow that way. Before we went to England last year, I thought my future apparent, and I saw myself essentially formed, stationed at its helm, my most flagrant troubles already behind me.

been sedated in just the right way—my personal choice: a bolus of morphine popped into an IV—I could have learned to live with it quite peaceably. I rose from the bed and walked into the bathroom, placing my hand at the pain's nucleus and uttering some low, unidentifiable animal noises. It was not yet dawn, and I had to turn on a light. I was naked, and when I stood before the full-length mirror on the inside of the bathroom door, I was stunned by the extreme list of me. Overnight, I had changed from a reasonably vertical person into someone I hardly recognized—the offspring perhaps of an incestuous union, escaped downstairs from his mirrorless attic cell to view his deformity for the first time.

A half-asleep Ellen pushed open the door, displacing the ghoul in the mirror. She was wearing my favorite nightie, a tiger print. "Oh, honey," she said. "What's happened?"

"I don't know," I said, turning down the corners of my mouth in mock sadness, though I really was sad. "Look at me."

She tried to match the expression on my face and, after a moment, said, "Sweetie, you're bent."

I felt a paradoxical rush of pleasure—despite the grim diagnosis—at having been properly diagnosed.

Later in the morning, I telephoned a friend, famous for his back trouble, who gave me the number of his chiropractor in nearby Lexington. Forthwith, I was examined, x-rayed, and interrogated about my recent movements, which included, by my lights, nothing remarkable. The day before, Sunday, I had raked leaves in the yard for a good part of the morning, read the *Times* for a good part of the afternoon, then Ellen and I had gone for an early dinner of rainbow trout at our favorite wood-grill restaurant, returned home, and made love before falling asleep. This roster seemed to me incriminating only in the degree to which it reflected a life of shameless luxury. But the chiropractor, a man about my own age, who wore the white turban and white tunic of what I assumed to be a Muslim sect, nodded knowingly and smiled at me with just the slightest hint of pity. With no apparent concern for the pain I was in, or for the difficulty I had driving a car, he told me to return the next day and we would look at the "film" (the X rays). He asked me to write a check.

The following afternoon, he put me stomach-down on his table and made a few painful adjustments to my spine—the usual chiropractic techniques—and to distract myself, I asked him some questions about his life. My face rested in a kind of face-size padded doughnut, through which I could study the arrangement of the tricolored tiles on the floor of his treatment room. I learned that the chiropractor had been born and raised in Minnesota, but his peculiar path had led him to become a Sikh. In keeping with the ritual observances of this sect, he'd grown his beard down to his belly button. His Panjabi name meant "tiger." (It was he who introduced me, that morning on the table, to the concept of one's growing into one's name.) All in all, he seemed quite ordinary for someone who was dressed the way he was; his costume and his down-home Midwest way of talking (his garb and his gab) collided comically, as if he were en route to a Halloween party.

When we were finished, he invited me into his office, where we sat across from each other in identical black leather swivel chairs and looked at the X rays, a frontal view and a lateral, which he'd clipped up onto a light box. He told me that my sacroiliac joint on the right side was "all jammed up." He accounted for the extreme deviation in my spine this way: "You are leaning away from the pain."

I thought this explanation logical in spite of its New Age timbre, and though he went on a minute longer, I hardly heard a word: Immediately, I had been strangely moved by the portrait of my errant insides, and what demanded my attention now—all my attention—was the vivid image, in the frontal view, of an infant's face, centered in the cavity of my pelvic girdle, a small face wise beyond its years, serious and purposeful, lips pursed just so, as if, in the moment of X ray, it had been on the brink of articulating some critical truth. I realize how this sounds, and the fact that the child appeared to be outfitted for commedia dell'arte clouded rather than clarified anything—my hip joints the padded shoulders of the child's dress coat, the extravagant wings of my pubis bones a high-starched, bright-white Elizabethan collar.

I interrupted the chiropractor. "Excuse me," I said, "but do you see that face—that child's face—right there in the area of my sacrum?"

It was impossible to avoid the thought of male pregnancy, and from somewhere in the back of my mind I seemed to recall an Islamic belief that Muhammad, when he returned, would be born of a man. I think, in fact, that this is balderdash, insulting to Muslims around the world. I knew Sikhism to be an amalgam of Muslim and Hindu elements, but I didn't know which Muslim elements it actually embraced. I hoped my question had not offended the chiropractor. He looked at me, not in an unfriendly way, but not entirely amused either.

He said, "You're not one of those weirdos who see the face of Jesus in tortillas and such, are you?"

I admired the correct agreement between subject and verb in his question.

"Not yet I'm not," I said, by which I meant simply that, so far, I had not seen the face of Jesus in a tortilla. I suddenly thought of the chiropractor's Presbyterian parents, somewhere in the low green hills outside Minneapolis, still trying to figure out where they'd gone so terribly wrong. And I was fighting an urge to reach across the short distance between us—between me and the chiropractor—and give his long, long beard a little rank-pulling tug.

But driving home—or, more accurately, daydreaming in a bottleneck on Route 2—I thought, I *am* the kind of person who sees the face of Jesus in tortillas and such. That's exactly the kind of person I am.

Over the next three weeks, the mysterious back pain slowly went away. I interpreted it as a rite of passage: in case I hadn't already noticed, I was fully inside the door of middle age. I requested and acquired my X ray (the interesting, frontal-view shot) from the chiropractor. I had already told Ellen about the face of the child in my sacrum, and when I first brought the X ray home and showed it to her, she said, "Oh, yeah . . . I think I see what you mean . . . right there," pointing to a different area entirely. I sometimes hauled the X ray out at Ellen's dinner parties and showed it to the guests, but no one was ever especially taken with it, let alone awed or flabbergasted, as I expected and wanted them to be. I began to develop a sophomoric philosophy around the fact that I could see the face clearly when others apparently couldn't—a philosophy involving questions about "reality" and the nature of seeing.

One night, after we'd had Ellen's publisher and his wife over to dinner, I said to Ellen, "Isn't it amazing that so much of what we see—so much of what we can see—is determined merely by what we're inclined to see?"

We were in bed. She had been reading. I had been thinking, the blank, white-painted bedroom ceiling for a muse. "And so much of what we're inclined to see," I added, "is determined by what we have a talent for seeing."

Ellen doesn't especially like to be interrupted when she's reading. Without shifting her eyes from the page, she said, barely audibly, "Yeah, life's just one big Rorschach test, isn't it."

She didn't want me to bring out the X ray at her dinner parties anymore, I could tell.

I had grown up with a father, a murderer, who made no distinction between religion and superstition, and rejected both as the weak stuff of women. My mother, on the other hand, who also made no such distinction, heartily embraced both. She believed (and still believes, I suppose) in an Orwellian God who sees all our actions, hears even our thoughts, and remembers everything. We will be judged at the end of time and punished for our sins, sin being just what you would think: lying, stealing, cheating, taking the name of the Lord in vain; sex outside marriage; sex inside marriage if you enjoy it; *wishing* to lie, steal, cheat, or take the name of the Lord in vain; wishing for sex outside marriage; wishing to enjoy sex in marriage. She believed very strongly in the devil and explained to us children that my father's powder-keg comportment and his other flaws were the result of his being possessed of the devil. She tended to see signs of the Apocalypse—unusual weather, the conflicts in the Holy

Land—and to be actively waiting for it: not living, but waiting. She sensed vague forebodings and would cancel trips and even brief outings at the last minute because she had a "bad feeling." Once, shortly after my oldest brother had gone off to college in Kentucky, I accidentally knocked his framed photograph off the piano in our living room, breaking the glass. My mother, nearly hysterical, beat me with my father's belt, convinced that "something bad" would now befall my brother—and, as if she'd caught me sticking pins into a voodoo doll, his ill fate would be my fault, the fault at least of my carelessness. To her, the invisible world was something you had to be constantly on the lookout for, something requiring extra vigilance. Most things were a great deal more than they seemed, having two lives: the apparent one and what the apparent one stood for.

This was an easy concept for a child to grasp—I gave myself to it thoroughly—because it spoke to how I experienced much of the world, as very large and layered, and full of marvels and horrors in which there was always more than met the eye. It was a childlike understanding, a newly immigrated understanding (young children are like immigrants), and it was unseemly in my mother only because she was supposed to be an adult. I don't mean to say that a mature person doesn't have religion or believe in the supernatural. I only mean that a mature person is able to distinguish between what's genuinely spiritual and what's hokum, and that the ability to distinguish is one of the things that define us as mature.

There was nothing especially supernatural about my sixteenth-century child of the X ray, my sacral prodigy. He was mainly, as Ellen had so subtly implied, a Rorschachian thing. But in his wake, some strange and forgotten moments from my childhood began to surface. I recalled, for example, a night when I was awakened by my father and told to go sit with my mother; Mother was sick, he was trying to phone the doctor (the only telephone in our old farmhouse was in the kitchen), and he didn't want to leave her alone. Before I reached her bedroom—separate from my father's—I could hear the frightening sound of her moaning. She lay on her bed, on her back, under the covers, her eyes boarded up by fear, uttering an alternately expiring and resurgent wail of pain, not exactly human, not exactly animal, more like a wind trapped in a cave, and every once in a while she would ride out words over it, always the same: "Oh please God don't let me die, oh please God don't let me die, oh please God don't let me die . . ."

It turned out that one of her fallopian tubes had got twisted somehow, a problem that, like a great number of things in the South, led eventually to surgery.

I should say that I was seven years old. I never lost the memory of that night, striking as it was, and recalling it later in life, I reasonably concluded, from the fact of my father's fetching the youngest rather than the oldest child, that she had specifically requested me. But inside the memory there was a moment I had mislaid, a moment when she reached for my hand and I withheld it, a moment when I exploited her extreme weakened state and refused, just this once, to let her touch me. For an instant, her eyes "opened," for they were already open, and I saw, not shock or hurt or reprimand, but something like compassion. The room grew glaring white, we seemed to sit somewhere on a vast beach—white sand, white sky, the sibilance of a distant surf—and I could hear my mother's voice inside my mind; compassionately, it said, *I will not leave you though you want me to*, and then we were back in the room, my father leaning over her, telling her that he'd been unable to reach her doctor and had therefore sent for his own. "I don't want that quack . . . I don't want that quack . . . I wouldn't send a dog to that quack," my mother bawled, and my father, having failed again, said, "Well, what the hell do you want me to do, Frances?" real, historical hatred in his eyes.

When I recalled this night from time to time over the years, it could be that these recollections included the weird transportation to the vast white beach. If so, I probably assumed that I'd dropped off to sleep for a minute on my mother's bed and only dreamed the part about the beach. In my most recent recollection, however, shortly after my back trouble, this did not seem to be the case: I saw the fleeting vision of the beach as linked with the intensity of my mother's pain and her extreme psychic energy at the moment of my refusing her hand; it seemed to me that we'd been pushed by the significance of the occasion into another spectrum, where we were afforded a kind of poetical elaboration of the actual, accessible events.

Then I recalled another, similar experience, in which I was "spoken to" by a young man on a bus. I was probably about twelve and was taking the county bus downtown to the Roxy, which was running a horror film festival, spotlighting Vincent Price, today's bill a double feature of *House on Haunted Hill* and *Horrors of the Black Museum*. Though I had made this trip on the bus a few times with my mother or older brother, this was my first solo flight, and I was preoccupied with the need to signal the driver and get off at the right stop. I wasn't a fan of Vincent Price—frankly (may he rest in peace), I thought he tended to ruin whatever movies he was in by overplaying every scene. I suppose I had already begun to recognize that ghoulishness wasn't truly scary. Scary was the surprise lurking beneath the altogether ordinary surface, the earwigs writhing inside the mailbox. (What I remember of *Horrors of the Black Museum*—which didn't have Vincent Price in it—is the moment when a character lifts a pair of binoculars to her eyes and two tenpenny nails pop out, stabbing her blind.) On the bus, a frail-looking black boy, a teenager, sat several rows behind me; he wore a white dress shirt, buttoned primly at the neck. Near the end of the ride, he and I were the only passengers left on the bus. Secretly, I had begun to panic, for nothing I was seeing out the bus window seemed the least bit familiar to me; I feared that I had missed my stop already, and though I could have simply asked the driver to let me off at the Roxy, some shyness bordering on paralysis prevented me. Several times I turned around and looked at the teenager—I don't know why; I felt compelled in some way—and sure enough, on the fourth or fifth glance, the sound of the bus's engine grew muffled and distant, there was a change in the light as if the sun had gone behind a cloud, and the boy leaned out from the waist, tilting his head toward the center of the aisle. It suddenly seemed to me that I was at the bottom of a well, looking up, and that the sides of this well were lined with shelves; the boy, perched like a bird on one of these shelves and looking down at me, spoke to me without moving his lips. "Next stop, sonny," was all he said—not exactly something to inscribe in stone, but just what I needed at the time—and then everything went quickly back to normal. I pulled the cord to signal the driver. Before getting off, I looked once more at the boy; he was smiling a kind of pointed, naughty smile, as if something taboo had passed between us.

I recalled maybe a half-dozen similar experiences, none any more significant than these two, and I wondered what, as a child, I had made of them. I thought I'd been an easily frightened boy, and yet here, in the memory of the bus, I found myself at the age of twelve going alone to horror movies. It occurred to me that by this time I had made a friend of fear, the way a soldier, thrown by fate into constant, isolated companionship with a captor, will grow to love what he's supposed to hate, his enemy. Fear was, after all, a kind of eternal flame in our house, fueled by my mother's otherworldliness and my father's rage, the abiding promises of doom and disorder. The frayed string between life and death, stretched taut across my daily conduct, got plucked with regularity. Death was as ready as the nearest electrical outlet, the lye beneath the kitchen sink, bluing atop the washer, oily rags in the attic, the mad dog run loose in the road, the drunk-driven truck, lightning in a storm, the escaped convict, the gulf with its undertow and sharks and hurricanes, the pond with its cottonmouths and plain sucking bottomlessness. The supernatural had quite a candle to hold up next to such formidable agents of the natural world, and I suppose those occasions of apparent telepathy didn't seem as noteworthy then, when they happened, as they did when later recalled.

In any case, the eventual result of all this recollection was the development of a personal theory: I came to believe that as a child I had possessed a small gift, an extrasensory capacity, not exceptional, but actual; my drinking and drugging, which began early in adolescence and burgeoned for more than fifteen years, pickled this gift, put it in a preserving sleep; and after almost thirteen years of abstinence, it began to reemerge.

I can tell you the exact moment when the random pitches of this theory formed a coherent melodic line. It was the dead of winter, in Cambridge, early February, eight months before we would leave for England. Just recently, we had finally arrived at the decision to allow Jordie, the following autumn, to enter a private boarding school, a two-hour drive away, in Connecticut. Jordie had been at us for some time about where she would go after graduating eighth grade, her desires advanced to us in idioms of dire urgency. Her two best friends in the whole entire world, to whom she was totally close and from whom she was totally inseparable, were going to the school in Connecticut, she would come home every single weekend if we absolutely insisted, it wasn't as if she were still a baby or something, she would never ever be happy anywhere else, and quite simply, if we didn't let her go, she would be depressed for the rest of her life and die. Of course Ellen and I yielded in the face of such persuasiveness. And about a week later, Ellen said to me, in the kitchen, "Cook, I've been thinking . . ." She didn't look at me as she spoke, but went on rinsing plates in the sink and placing them in the racks of the dishwasher. It was pitch black outside, however, and I could see her face reflected in the kitchen window behind the sink. "By next fall," she said, "Flora will be on her way to London." (Flora was Ellen's character, the young Episcopal priest who did the sleuthing in her mystery stories.) "If Jordie's going to be away at school, I was thinking we might—"

"Go to England," I said, stealing the lightbulb from over her head.

"Well, it would make that part of the story much easier to write," she said.

Jordie, who from an early age had perfected the ability to hear every word of our conversations from several rooms away, appeared from nowhere, throwing open the kitchen's swinging door with a kind of body block. Bare-legged, bare-footed, she wore an enormous black sweater, the sleeves of which hung down about a foot below her hands; keeping her hands inside the sleeves—using them like flippers—she took a glass from the cabinet, opened the refrigerator, poured some orange juice, said, "I think it's a fabulous idea," and left the room.

And thus the plan was hatched for us to go to England. We would take a flat somewhere in London for about a month, Ellen could do research and write, soak up the atmosphere she needed for her book, and my life (of chiefly improvisation) would continue as it usually did, only in a different setting. We both felt excited by the prospect, and yet there was the melancholy signal too—in the fact that we *could* go to England for a month—of our lives changing drastically with Jordie's departure, and sooner than we'd expected.

Later that same night, I dozed off on the couch in the library, where I'd been reading. When I awakened, it was after midnight, the house entirely quiet, Ellen and Jordie upstairs asleep. Spencer, my Dalmatian, slept at the hearth, loyal to what was left of the fire, a few large, still-glowing, still-smoking chunks beneath the grate.

My sitting up roused him, and he quickly executed his yogalike stretches, front and back legs. I let him out the library's French doors into the yard, which was blanketed with a good half foot of snow. The floodlights were on, and I stood at the doors for a minute, watching him sniff around the fir trees at the back of the lot. The quiet of the house, the snow's general insulation, the late hour, my newly wakened state, the dreamy floodlit yard with its long, hard shadows, all combined to make me susceptible to whatever might come along. I could almost say I was meditative—certainly there was that oddness of being poised on the cusp between two worlds, looking from a warm room onto a frozen terrain. Perhaps my eyes drifted away to the dying fire for a moment. Then Spencer was on his way back to the terrace and the windows, and I opened the door a few inches in anticipation.

But was it indeed Spencer, our sweet-tempered Dalmatian, who was headed for the door? The beast trotting toward me in the snow was a dog, no question about that, but larger, taller, rangier than Spencer, and entirely white, without spots. I thought my eyes failed me—in a second, he would look as he was supposed to look—but instead, as the animal gained the terrace and the brilliance of the floodlights, I caught sight of its own eyes, which were albinic pink and trained directly on me. I slammed the door shut and experienced a momentary blankness—my blood had abandoned me, my adrenal glands were running the show now, every joint in my body went weak-kneed—and then suddenly there was Spencer, spots and brown eyes intact, perplexed at my slamming the door in his face, and breathing little foggy aureoles onto the glass panes near my feet.

I allowed him back into the house and gave him many apologetic hugs and kisses. When I went upstairs, my heart was still racing. Ellen had left on a lamp in the bedroom for me and was sleeping with a pillow over her head, to shut out the light. When I climbed into the bed, she stirred, came out from under the pillow, opened her eyes, squinting in the light, and said, "She's out on the ledge. . . ." Then she rolled over, turning her back to me.

"What?" I said. "Who's out on what ledge?"

At the sound of my voice, she turned again and looked at me. "Oh, hi," she said. "Isn't it late?" Suddenly she raised up on one elbow. "Cook, what's wrong?" she said. "You look as if you've seen a ghost."

Lying in the dark a few minutes later, listening to her regular breathing, I would form my theory—or rather, the theory would seem to form in me—of the child's once lost, now rallying gift, small but actual, nipped by drink in its bud. But in response to her question, I kissed her cheek and said, "Nothing's wrong . . . go back to sleep," for though I still trembled from the fright I'd just had downstairs and could have used some comforting, I felt consumed with shame, as if I'd fallen victim to a squalid crime, as if I'd somehow brought it on myself, through negligence or recklessness, and now I needed to keep my part in it a secret.

CHAPTER

Two

IN AT LEAST one instance, I've already misrepresented myself. I've said that I retired at the age of thirty-nine to manage my investments. Technically this is true, but I managed them for only about three months. Very soon I hired two men for this task—Mike Gildenberg, a tax and investment consultant, and Tony Rosillo, a broker. Mike and Tony telephone regularly, go through the motions of conferring with me, and I enact my part, taking time to consider a suggestion one of them has made—sometimes I'm given a multiple-choice question, *a, b,* or *c*—but in the end I do what I'm told. Tony Rosillo lives in New York. We've seen each other, briefly, twice in five years. Mike Gildenberg lives in Seattle. I have never actually met him; I've never even seen a photograph of him. My connection is to these men's voices (to their voice *signals,* actually, bounced off a low-orbit non-synchronous relay station), and I trust their voices in a way I probably wouldn't trust the men themselves, if I can make that distinction. (Putting the emphasis on the first syllable in Rosillo, Ellen refers to Tony and Mike as "Rosillo and Gildenberg"; if I say to her that the time has come for us to upgrade her Macintosh, she says, "Is that the word from Rosillo and Gildenberg?") After these several years, their advice frequently reaches beyond the borders of tax and investment. When I mentioned to Mike that we would travel to London in October, he told me which airline had the most legroom, which restaurant in Chelsea served the best Dover sole pan-broiled with garlic, which tobacco shop near Saint James's Palace had the really good Havanas. When I mentioned the trip to Tony, he told me where we had to stay—a small, quintessentially British hotel near Sloane Square, which had a reasonably priced, full-size flat available if you booked far enough ahead. "The Willerton," he said. "You'll love this place . . . it's like something out of *Masterpiece Theatre.*"

By late spring, all our arrangements were made: passports, airline reservations, house-sitters, and dog-walkers. I booked the flat at the Willerton, mailed in a hefty deposit, and was faxed back a confirmation. The flat, as described to me by the hotel manager, comprised a bathroom, a small kitchen with eating area, a sitting room, a formal dining room, and two bedrooms. It occupied the top floor of the hotel, with northern and southern exposures, and it would be ours for the month of October.

Then a long, slow-moving summer ensued, in which the

most momentous event was Jordie's finally getting her ears pierced. From the age of eight, she had nagged us to let her have it done, and when she turned ten, we consented. Armed with our permission, she confronted for the first time her actual fear of the procedure, and it was another four years before she bravely entered the piercing chair at The Earring Tree in Harvard Square. She had the right ear done in June, the left in July. (That way she always had one unsore ear to sleep on.) By August she was tanned from visits to the Cape, her hair sun-bleached, her eyes intensely clear and bright. She wore a gold hoop in one ear, a crystal heart dangling from a little chain in the other. I could hardly bear to look at her. All of August, there was almost nothing she could do, no way she could be, that didn't seem to break my heart. Midday on a Saturday, I would walk into the library and see her out in the sun on the terrace, white tee shirt and shades, languid in a recliner, book unopened in her lap, lemonade and cordless telephone on the paving stones near to hand; while she lay dreaming, infatuated with her immediate future, I stood frozen, ambushed by loss in my shadowy room with its familiar scents of ash and leather. For the first time I experienced our large house as ridiculously large, profligate; I didn't walk its halls, I roamed them, and everywhere I seemed to encounter the sound of Jordie, singing behind a closed door. Ellen, meanwhile—an alumna of the school Jordie was about to attend—revisited through her daughter's preparations a happy time in her own youth. For about three weeks she and Jordie were inseparable. They shopped for winter clothes, new bedding, new luggage, packed cardboard boxes with books and tapes and CDs, and endlessly, they talked. They went together for lunches in the Square and talked. They went to movies and somewhere afterward to talk. They went swimming in Walden Pond, and to the hairdresser's, and talked. Occasionally, I was summoned and asked to get down something—the old humidifier, a folded garment bag—from a high shelf in Jordie's closet, or sent to the hardware store for more strapping tape. Ellen would beam me a comforting, employer's smile, the smile a woman gives a workman repairing something in her bedroom, and Jordie would say, "Thank you, Daddy," in her new, adultish voice, overly sincere.

I took my misery to the Dorchester Gun Club and shot .22-caliber holes in reams of paper targets, sulking and firing away, exactly like a frustrated kindergartner, but for the actual gun with its real bullets.

Labor Day weekend, the last weekend before we would drive Jordie down to Connecticut, three days of rain set in, torrential, mind-boggling rain that saturated the earth and turned the streets to rivers, rain that continued unbroken for hours, that paused for maybe three minutes midday on Sunday, then started up again, harder than ever. Though we weren't to take Jordie to the school until Tuesday afternoon, she and Ellen had completed their work, bags packed and ready to be carried out the door. The combination of the rain (of being stuck in the house more than usual) and the sight of Jordie's baggage upstairs in the hall put Spencer in an agitated state. He had difficulty choosing a room to settle in, and once he'd chosen, he couldn't seem to find a comfortable position. I suppose I overly identified with him; when our eyes met, it was excessively soulful, and his sharp little insistent complaint (which I thought sounded like a large metal wheel grinding to a halt) might have come from my own pinched voice box. With his chronic circle-turning, his throwing himself on the floor with a thud only to rise and move again to repeat the procedure, he seemed to be acting out my feelings precisely. This made me uneasy, this overidentification with the dog, and I seized on the kitchen as a place of worthy purpose. I spent hours preparing dishes chosen for their difficulty and time-consumingness; Ellen would wander in wide-eyed to find me deveining shrimp, skinning tomatoes, coring artichokes. I focused on details, taking solace in the way a caper tossed into hot oil opens and becomes a perfect little black crispy flower.

The rain continued into Monday night. Around eleven-thirty, unable to sleep, I lay on the glider under the covered part of the terrace. If I hadn't given up cigarettes and booze, I would have been smoking and drinking. Everything about the setting—the time of year, the time of night, the warm air, the sound of the rain—inspired nostalgia, a kind of catchall longing that included cigarettes and whisky and a younger, less levelheaded Ellen, who, instead of saying to me, "Don't stay up too late," would have been there next to me, getting good and messy about Jordie's going away the next day. My longing, which I imagined as a mob of angry men swaggering down a street and growing stronger as they went, suddenly arrived lustily at Ellen's bedroom door, fully focused now and pounding fists. So after a minute, when I heard the terrace door open behind me, I kept my eyes closed and whispered sexily into the dark, "I conjured you," smiling and very pleased with myself.

"What do you mean, Daddy?" Jordie said.

"Jordie," I said, sitting up quickly. "Can't you sleep?"

She walked over and stood directly in front of me. A lamp was on in the library, which provided enough light through the windows for me to see the blue fuzzy bathrobe she was wearing, one of her and Ellen's new purchases.

"Are you kidding?" she said. "I can't even keep my eyes closed."

I patted the glider cushion on my right.

"God," she said, sitting next to me, "I'm just so keyed up."

"Understandable," I said.

She lowered her head and began to push her toe against the stone floor, ever so gently, to start the glider moving. "Daddy," she said after a moment, "my ear hurts." She touched the lobe of her right ear, gingerly. "I think it might be getting infected again," she added in an entirely uncommitted tone.

"You better put some stuff on it," I said.

"Alcohol."

"Yeah."

She stopped touching her ear, bringing both her hands to rest in her lap, and said, "I did already."

The subtler nuances in this little exchange didn't escape

me, its sad attempt at reaching back to an earlier time in our lives, when she had a pain, and I had a remedy she hadn't already thought of. "Jordie," I said, "I'm going to miss you."

"God, Daddy," she said. "I'm not dying, I'm just going to Connecticut."

"I know that," I said. "I know where you're going."

"This rain," she said, "it's unbelievable. Do you think it'll ever stop?"

"Yes," I said.

She looked at me. I thought I saw something like determination on her face.

She said, "That's the shirt I gave you for your birthday."

I hadn't noticed it before, but indeed I was wearing a shirt Jordie had given me in the spring, something called a Chinese Fortune T-Shirt; mine read, "Sing a song, your creative juices are flowing. Lucky Numbers 18, 28, 3, 9, 51, 38."

For about ten years, Jordie had lived with the horror of my singing, lived in fear of my bursting into song in any public place. Walking down a street, I would begin to hum "The Way You Do the Things You Do," quietly to myself, and she would squeeze my arm. "Daddy," she would whisper, desperately. "Shush." Driving car pool, I would sometimes begin to sing along with the song on the radio, mortifying her in front of her friends. When she told me to shut up, I would say in my defense that she was repressing my creative juices. Thus the T-shirt.

"So it is," I said, looking down the front of the shirt.

"And those are the moccasins I gave you for Christmas," she said.

I looked at my feet. "So they are," I said.

She bent down and lifted up one cuff of my jeans. "I don't believe this," she said. "I *gave* you those socks."

I pushed her hand away. "Will you please leave me alone?" I said.

"I don't believe you," she said. "You're wearing practically everything I ever gave you."

"So what?"

"So you're *weird*," she said.

"What's weird?" I said. "I happen to be wearing a few things you gave me. I don't see what's so weird."

"I don't know," she said, "it's just—I don't know—like I died or something. It's creepy. I'm just going to *Connecticut*."

There was a flash of lightning, followed by a kind of slow-mounting thunder that sounded like a giant boulder rolling closer and closer toward us. And someone turned up the volume on the rain. I thought for a moment that I was beginning to get one of my mother's "bad feelings." It occurred to me that if, say, next week, after Jordie was gone, someone should knock her picture off the piano and break the glass, I might beat that person with a belt. I could see myself doing that—not to a child, of course, but possibly to a careless grown-up.

"Jordie," I said. "I've already confessed to the crime you seem to be accusing me of. I'm going to miss you. I freely admit it."

Her eyes clouded over. "But I don't want you to," she said, almost pleading.

"Sorry," I said. "You can't have everything."

Then, suddenly, she was crying and saying what a terrible mistake this had all been, how could she have ever thought for one nanosecond that she could live apart from her mother and me, she'd been foolish and selfish and stupid and totally wrong about everything—all of which caused me to switch sides inside myself and begin to sing the praises of the school, to argue the wisdom of our decision.

"Oh-h-h," she said, shivering, and I held her for a while as we sat listening to the rain—during which time she grew happy again and was soon kissing me good night, cheerfully, eager to return upstairs, where she would lay out her clothes for the next day. She'd only had a spat with her dashing new love, the future—she'd glimpsed him as the heel he might truly be, she'd come to me to complain, and I'd reassured her that he would probably turn out fine; now, restored to her former bleary-eyed infatuation, she couldn't wait to return to his arms, penitent over having doubted him.

The next morning, the rain had stopped. The yard was full of apples of an unknown origin, washed down to us from higher ground. They were Baldwins, I think, scattered singly all around and congregated on the uphill side of trees and shrubs. Amazed, Jordie and I did the only sensible thing we could think to do—we gathered them and made a pie for her to take with her to Connecticut.

The theory of my rediscovered prescience (or whatever), formulated back in winter, lay dormant for eight months. For a while, after the scary incident with the dog, I actively watched for hidden meanings in everything, but even in my willingness to stretch matters, I witnessed no omens or dark happenings of any kind; no new evidence showed up to support my ideas. Eventually, some of the principles of my abstinence from alcohol and drugs—a life of simplicity, a focus on the day at hand, humility, and honest dealing with others— steadied me again, and by the time Ellen and I set foot on English soil (English pavement, actually), I stood firmly in the natural world. Jordie was happily settled at the new school without event. As a parting gift, she gave me a miniature ceramic Dalmatian, saying I should keep it with me for good luck and to remind me of her and Spencer. With Jordie gone, the planned change of venue for Ellen and me was so welcome it almost seemed providential. On the fourth of October, a Monday, we climbed out of a taxi from Victoria Station into a narrow little street and began sizing up the Hotel Willerton: two mid-Victorian brick houses, unified into one facade by virtue of having been painted the same cream-colored trim. A cheerful blue-and-white-striped canopy with polished brass poles sheltered front doors of beveled glass, and above, we could see the windows of our flat, jutting out from a mansard roof of slate. It was about eight o'clock in the morning on a promising, fine day, sunlight already striking the two upper floors of the hotel. I paid the driver, who'd deposited our bags at our feet, and once he'd driven away, Ellen and I looked at each other. She was pale and worn out by the overnight flight, the strange and dreamy passage across an ocean, and yet I could still see excitement in her eyes. She'd braided her hair on the plane, and somehow she projected a simple old-world elegance that appeared suddenly, instantly English. She glanced back at the hotel, shrugged ever so slightly, and said, "Perfect." She bent to lift one of our suitcases and said, "Absolutely perfect."

We were met under the canopy by an eager young Frenchman, who relieved us of our bags. He couldn't possibly carry everything we had, but he insisted we drop it all and proceed into the hotel unburdened. "Go, go, please," he said, motioning us up the steps. "I will follow."

We passed through a vestibule into the entryway, where a flight of stairs, gleaming white, with red carpeting, led down from a balustraded gallery above. To one side of the stairs was the hotel desk, such as it was, a little booth with mailboxes and a door in back, opening onto an office. A pretty gray-haired woman sat behind the desk, and she smiled at us as we entered, though she was busy on the telephone. She held up one finger and mouthed the words "Only a moment . . ." She spun around in her swivel chair and consulted a large chart on the wall behind her; I heard her say into the phone, "Hmm, no, I'm so very sorry. I can only give you a bath just down the hall on those dates. Yes . . ."

To the right of her booth was a corridor leading to other rooms, the same gleaming white paint and red carpet, and I was about to venture down it when the woman got off the phone and greeted us. Yes, our flat was quite ready, she said, and yes, she would have tea sent up right away, and would Pascal kindly show us to the top floor? Pascal, the dark-haired young man who'd taken our bags, then guided us down a narrow passage alongside the central staircase to a tiny elevator. I glanced back at our luggage, and Pascal explained that he would bring it up "immediately when you are settled." We had to step aside for him to open the elevator door; he pulled back the lattice gate and motioned for Ellen and me to step inside. I wasn't at all sure there would be enough room for Pascal to join us. The elevator was mahogany, dimly but pleasantly lit, and a shelf ran along the back of the car, with a stack of clean white linens. Pascal reached past us and removed the linens, then folded the shelf flush against the wall, thereby creating some additional space.

In another moment we were on our way up, riding in silence. I noted that we had begun on the ground floor, which meant that our fourth-floor flat was really five floors up. Wedged beneath the edge of the elevator's panel of push buttons was a business card that read "Lohengrin Lifts." Just past the first floor, a glimpse of which was afforded through a small window in the door, I could hear the muffled sound of a piano, growing louder as we ascended; I smiled at Ellen, who smiled back. The music seemed to be coming from the third floor—it began to fade once we passed the third-floor door.

"A little early in the morning for Schubert," I said, though I wasn't entirely sure it was Schubert that was being played. Ellen looked at me quizzically.

Pascal, whose back was to me, turned his head and smiled pleasantly over his shoulder. *"Pardon, monsieur?"*

"I said it's a little early in the morning for Schubert," I said, nodding stupidly.

Pascal smiled again, but it was clear he hadn't understood my remark and was embarrassed to ask a second time.

Once we'd reached our floor, we were ushered through a brief interval of darkness to a heavy-looking white paneled door; Pascal fumbled with the key for a moment, and then suddenly the hallway was flooded with light. We entered a bright wallpapered sitting room with two tall windows facing the street, and in a matter of seconds Pascal left us. Ellen threw her arms around me, saying, "Oh, Cook, it's wonderful, wonderful, wonderful, now please help me find the bathroom."

We started down a hall, peeking quickly into the two bedrooms. "Look," Ellen said. "Twin beds in both. Isn't that cute?"

"Adorable," I said.

The bathroom was found, Pascal soon returned with our

luggage, and then again with tea and scones and jam, and in an hour or so, we were settled into the larger of the bedrooms, drapes drawn, and we were soon fast asleep in our twin beds.

I dreamed, as I had several times in the last weeks, about Jordie. In the dream, I had been called by the headmaster down to Connecticut to discuss Jordie's spelling problem. The headmaster, who wore the wig of an English judge, was tapping a pointer against a poster-size drawing Jordie had actually done, in real life, in the third grade and that actually hung, in real life, framed in my study back in Cambridge. "The Inside of a Pig and the Outside of a Pig" it was called— just what you would think, with various internal organs visible and labeled: "Brane," "Stumich," "Insestints," "Vains." I was awakened from the dream by Ellen's joining me in my bed, slipping under the covers.

"Hi," I said, flat on my back, reclosing my eyes. I put one arm under her, and she turned onto her side, facing me and sliding her leg up over me so that the inside of her bare thigh pressed against me.

Were I deprived of sight and smell and hearing, I would know this precise warmth, this precise pressure apart from any others; I thought no corruption of life could achieve a gulf so wide it couldn't be bridged by this durable, comforting alliance of our limbs, past words or analysis or even emotion, this blind thing our bodies knew. It was our version of what people meant when they said, "I would know you anywhere."

"What did you mean," she said after a minute, "in the elevator? '. . . a little early for Schubert.' "

"Oh," I said. "Well, I thought it was Schubert. It sounded like Schubert."

"You thought what sounded like Schubert?"

"The music," I said. "In the elevator."

"Cookie," she said. "It isn't really the kind of hotel that would have music piped into the elevator."

"No, no," I said. "Not piped in. Somebody in another

room was playing. It sort of peaked around the third floor and then faded away again. You must've heard it."

"No," she whispered, starting the familiar leg motion, up and down, under the covers.

"Probably your ears were still clogged from the plane," I said, though I recalled the young Pascal's polite smile, over his shoulder, which told me he'd heard no music either.

CHAPTER

Three

FLORA, THE YOUNG Episcopal priest in El-
len's mysteries, is, like her name, old-fashioned. For the most
part, her habits and her values and her approaches to pastor-
ing are essentially traditional. She is instinctively conservative
in her thinking and emotions. And yet there she is, unmarried

though well into her thirties, female, and a priest. In some ways (and without meaning to do so) she redefines "conservative." It's precisely *because* her reading of the Gospels has a fundamentalist leaning that she is led to a politics of the Left: Helping the poor and needy and refusing to stone the prostitute are what Jesus was all about. Flora is extraordinary in her ordinariness, full of surprises because her nature is so materially unsurprising. Her mother flew the coop long ago, her father is recently dead, and she has no siblings—which gives her a suitable alone-in-the-world quality. Her only known living relative is a great-aunt she has never met, who lives in England. In Ellen's new novel, an unexpected, mysterious summons from this great-aunt brings Flora to London. The woman lives—where else?—in Hampstead, at—where else?—the edge of the Heath.

In a very short time, Ellen was organized and clear-headed about the kind of research she meant to do. It would include trips to Hampstead, of course, but many walking tours, too, of central London, where Flora would spend a good deal of time. First Ellen would go with a walking-tours company and later she would venture out on her own. Her intention over our month was simply to soak up the town, let one thing lead to another, the way it did for Flora, and keep a careful journal.

The weather, it seemed, would cooperate. Everywhere you went, people were talking about how warm and dry it was for October. In Cambridge (Massachusetts), the leaves had already turned and begun to fall. In London, the trees were mostly still green, with only hints of autumn colors here and there. A sweater was required outside at night, but you could go in shirtsleeves by day. My intention was to give myself to Ellen, to be her companion, her collaborator in the broadest sense of the term, and I suppose I'll always wonder how different everything might have turned out had I been able to stick to that original course.

Tuesday is something of a blur, probably due to jet lag. I think we got our bearings, bought some groceries for the flat, dined in a nearby pub. (Our eating options were manifold: there were many restaurants walking distance from the hotel; we could order meals through room service; we could prepare something ourselves in the flat's kitchen; we could eat downstairs in the hotel restaurant.) On Wednesday we took a tour called The London Nobody Knows, which led us through the ancient Holborn-district neighborhood of Samuel Johnson, who was quoted in the brochure as saying, "I love a little bit of secret history." Despite the perfect weather, I suppose we were already into the off-season for walking tours and tourism in general. We were a small group of about a dozen or so—two other American couples, a bit older than Ellen and me, and the odd assortment of blond young people who turn up everywhere in the world, speaking Dutch and German. The Americans kept talking about how clean everything was and about how safe they felt. I recall an old church or two and what was left of a Norman crypt, but I confess I was preoccupied with my own thoughts. Now and then, Ellen would poke me and tell me to take a picture of something, and I would come around long enough to aim and push the shutter release.

I had awakened early that morning and got dressed quietly while Ellen still slept; tea would be sent up to the flat at nine, and I figured I had time for a stroll around the area of the hotel. I had a lovely walk through Belgravia, thinking all the while how clean everything was and how safe I felt. The sight of schoolchildren in their woolen uniforms made me think of Jordie and how I missed her, and I resolved to phone her at the school that evening. I bought some irises in Sloane Square and returned to the hotel.

Pascal was just coming on duty, standing under the canopy, buttoning up his black vest. He saluted and clicked his heels together when he saw me, a surprising antic I didn't quite know how to interpret; I found myself reviewing how much I'd tipped him the last couple of times he'd brought up tea—too much? too little? (It wasn't necessary to tip him anything; a service charge would be appended to our bill.) But as I gained the front steps he was frozen at attention, eyes forward and glazed over like one of the Queen's palace guards; when I spoke to him, he didn't respond but remained silently frozen, and I caught on to the joke. I stopped and passed my hand back and forth before his eyes. I stuck the flowers under his nose. I said boo. I said the French were a bunch of snobs. I said the French were a bunch of drunken sex fiends, and he burst out laughing, turning bright red. He retrieved my key from the gray-haired woman at the desk and, still chuckling, saw me to the elevator, got me closed inside, and waved bye-bye through the little window in its door as I started up. All the pieces of the morning came together then, as I seemingly left solid ground, and formed a wonderfully happy moment: I felt well rested, and the fine weather, the early stroll in cream-colored Belgravia, the flowers, and Pascal's joking all enfolded me in a grand theme of welcome.

Then I heard the sound of the piano again, almost im-mediately, and this time I paid careful attention. It was defi-nitely someone's playing—I heard the pianist stop, back up, and repeat a troubling phrase a couple of times—and it defi-nitely came from the third floor. When I reached our floor, instead of getting out, I pushed 3 and went back down. The elevator stopped, and I pulled back the gate. I could see through the small window a short hallway similar to ours upstairs, white walls, red carpet, but quite well lit, as the several doors along either side of it stood ajar. I also noticed two paint-spattered wooden stepladders, folded and leaning against the left-hand wall. I tried to push open the elevator door, but it seemed locked. I used my shoulder against it, in case it was only stuck, but after failing, I stooped down to the level of the knob and could see, in the crack between door and jamb, what looked like a brass safety hasp mounted on the outside of the door. I closed the gate and returned to the fourth floor.

I'd had no clear plan. I suppose that if the elevator door hadn't been bolted, I would have entered the hall and stood there for a better listen. Here was the odd thing: the music stopped the instant I put my shoulder to the door, and started up again the instant I pushed the fourth-floor button, as if the pianist sensed my presence, or my potential intrusion. I thought to myself that she could have actually heard the elevator stop on her floor—it did make quite a racket—and then I wondered why I'd thought "she."

I found Ellen awake and dressed and cheerful in the bedroom, and this time I didn't mention the music in the elevator. I had some of the same feeling I'd experienced months earlier, the night I got into bed with Ellen right after my fright with Spencer in the backyard at home—a sense that somehow I had participated in something illicit, as if something bad had befallen me on account of my putting myself somewhere I oughtn't to have been. I was sure that Ellen, though she was a writer of mysteries, would disapprove of my attempt at snooping. She would have teased me about hearing things. She might even have warned me not to ruin our holiday with what she called "freakystuff," one word, connoting anything spooky in a supernatural sense. You see, Ellen believes in the old school of mystery writing, the intrusion of disorder (murder) into a world of order (a reliably moral society). If you allow the spectral into this picture, you lose control of its neat device: a kind of amoral disorder is everywhere at all times, behind everything. In the bedroom, I kissed the back of her neck and brandished the irises. Delighted, she got on the phone and asked that a vase be sent up with our soon-to-arrive tea.

Later, during the tour of The London Nobody Knows, part of my distraction was the music itself—the sound of the piano, the melody, passing through my mind, roaming around, waiting to be identified, looking for a place to lodge.

On Thursday I awakened at almost ten o'clock to a still-darkened flat and a note on Ellen's dresser saying that she'd tried unsuccessfully to rouse me; she hoped I wasn't getting sick; she'd gone downstairs to have breakfast in the hotel restaurant; I should join her if I wanted to; if not, she would check in on me afterward; would I like to go with her for a tour of the Old Jewish Quarter (something Flora wanted to do) in the East End at eleven-thirty?

Since getting clean and sober, I very rarely slept late, and no one in the last thirteen years had ever had any trouble waking me. As I washed up and got dressed, I found myself feeling crazily annoyed with Ellen for failing to wake me; I thought she mustn't have tried very hard; I even thought she might not have told the truth in her note. But what possible motive could she have had for lying? And even if she had wanted to have breakfast alone for some reason, she couldn't have arranged for me to sleep late when sleeping late wasn't my natural inclination. In the midst of this irrational thinking I knew it to be irrational, and yet I couldn't seem to turn it off. By the time I was out of the bathroom and sitting on the edge of my bed, bending down to tie my shoes, I was full-blown angry. The evening before, I had wanted to phone Jordie, but Ellen had said Jordie would still be in class and that we should wait and phone after we returned from dinner; then we'd forgotten to phone when we returned from dinner, and I'd woken in the middle of the night and regretted it.

As I was about to leave the flat, the telephone rang. I answered it in the sitting room.

"You're up," Ellen said when she heard my wide-awake voice.

"Of course I'm up," I said. "Where are you?"

There was a brief silence, after which she said, in an overly calm voice, "I'm downstairs, Cook. In the restaurant. I left you a note. Did you not see it?"

Her short, measured sentences of equal length were an insult, a condescension. "I saw it," I said. "Why didn't you wake me?"

"Well," she said, "actually, I want to talk to you about that. Do you want to come down here? They stop serving in five minutes."

I told her to order me something, anything, whatever she'd had, and hung up.

I returned to the bathroom and splashed cold water on

my face. "Get a grip, Selway," I said aloud, and when I lowered my face into a clean towel, something about this gesture reminded me of crying, of sobbing into one's hands, and I felt for a moment as if I would do just that. I think when a person says, "I saw my life flash before my eyes," he means not that he actually saw a narrative unfold at light speed but that he was filled with a sense of his life as a whole story—a beginning, a middle, an end—and in a single moment was able to perceive himself in a way that included everything: all time, all experience, all emotion. That's what happened to me that morning, standing on the white octagonal tiles of a hotel bathroom in London, my face buried in the bleachy scent of a white towel. It passed in a fraction of a minute and was gone, the slippery understanding that everything that had come before led precisely here, and I was left flabbergasted by my arrival, like a man who'd journeyed too far too quickly. I thought of a child on a cattle farm in southern Georgia, a young boy standing on the bottom rail of a fence, arms wrapped over the top rail, staring into a pasture at a bull about fifty yards away—the bull known as Peter Gunn and reputed to be the meanest in the county. The bull stares at me with his death-in-life eyes, and I, unblinking, begin to climb the fence, slowly; keeping my eyes on him, I jump from the top rail onto the ground and stand unprotected, with my hands on my hips. And then, predictably, he's charging, head down, horns foremost, and I just manage to clear the top of the fence as he turns sharply away in a commotion of hoof pounding and snorting and flying dust.

Left with this image of the bull's turning, I first thought how very far I'd come from that life among uneducated country people, untreated neurotic parents, from that farm with its Negro hired help who were roused and collected in the back of a truck at sunrise, dropped off the back of a truck after dark with a five-dollar bill in hand—what my father eloquently called "whisky and pussy money"—an only slightly modified version of bondage. I thought how far I had come, a man severed by sensibility from his roots and always a little

lost as a consequence. But then I asked myself what I'd been
after that day as a child, courting that bull, standing akimbo
on the wrong side of the fence, shirtless, ribs exposed—
visible, goreable heart pounding just beneath the skin. The
answer of course was death—the same thing I'd been after
time and again throughout my life, in various forms, pack-
aged as different dangers: I'd been after death.

What was good about this moment at the bathroom
sink was that it cleared away my irrational anger toward Ellen. I returned to her now emotionally, my eyes opened to
the reality of her love for me (and mine for her), and in
another minute or two I would be able to greet her downstairs civilly, even respectfully.

As I started again to leave the flat, I thought I heard a
sound from the room at the end of the hall, the unused second bedroom, the sound of a human voice, a child's voice, I
thought, and I felt pulled to it as surely as if it were the voice
of my own child. I opened the door slowly, quietly, stupidly,
as if there really were a sleeping child inside who'd cried out
in her sleep. The room was very much like the one Ellen and
I were using—twin beds, two dressers—except that it was a
bit smaller and had a single tall window instead of two; now
there was a chill in the room, of nighttime air. The only light
was what came in through a six-inch part in the drapes, and I
could see that the window had been left open. As I stepped
inside I thought I sensed something odd: not a presence, but
the shadow of a presence, the extremely vague, lingering suggestion of someone's having been there recently—an unsettling feeling when combined with the open window.

Like all the windows in that side of the flat (the street
side), this one opened onto a ledge a few inches deep and a
low stone wall crowned by an ornate molded cornice. The
morning sun was hitting the flat but had not yet found the
street below. I opened the window further, put my head out,
looking side to side, then down. I saw the top of the striped
canopy, the brightest thing in the silent shady street below. A
taxi pulled into the lane, stopped at the hotel, and Pascal

appeared from beneath the canopy. This bird's-eye view of Pascal on the job delighted me; I watched him assist an elderly man from the cab and then lean inside its front window to exchange what I assumed to be some small talk with the driver. In another moment Pascal was giving the taxi a pat on its rear fender (just as he would a horse) as it pulled away, and this cheerfulness of his made me feel warmly toward him too. He stood briefly alone in the street, not moving—was he having a moment of reflection?—and then I called out his name, startling him. He looked up, shaded his eyes with one hand, and began to wave. Just then another cab turned into the street, and I felt a distinct panic. Wildly overreacting, I yelled, "Watch out!" and Pascal, whose bewilderment I could perceive even from five floors up, stepped calmly forward a bit to allow the cab to pull in front of the canopy. I withdrew from the window, embarrassed, and closed it. As I turned to leave the room, I could have sworn I smelled the faintest aroma (unmistakable to me) of Scotch.

The hotel restaurant was simple and bright, one large dining room with a wall of French windows facing a small garden, white tablecloths, a good deal of walnut paneling. It was just about empty of patrons when I arrived downstairs, and most of the tables had been reset for lunch. An older, Asian couple dressed in English-looking tweeds lingered over tea near the entrance, and a young girl about Jordie's age sat alone at a table near the French windows, gazing rather forlornly out at the garden. She had Jordie's blond hair, cut chin length, Jordie's slim angularity, and apparently her world-weariness too; but unlike Jordie, she was dressed like a fashion model, a bit affectedly, in a white and blue sailor-type dress. Ellen sat near the middle of the room at a small table for two. I greeted her in good spirits, kissing her cheek, took the chair opposite her, and began pouring tea into my cup. "M-m-m," I said to a basket of pastries on the table. "Looks good."

Ellen eyed me suspiciously. She'd braced herself for the ogre she'd got on the telephone a few minutes earlier, and now she was encountering a different animal altogether.

"What's going on, Cook?" she said, looking a little more hopeless, I thought, than the situation called for.

"Nothing," I said, tearing open a croissant. Then, "Oh, you mean about before, my grumpiness on the phone. I'm sorry. Sleeping late and all . . . I didn't mean to take it out on you."

"Are you okay?"

"I'm excellent," I said.

"You were strange this morning . . . almost as if you were drugged or something."

"Well, I assure you I wasn't drugged," I said. "Must have to do with the time change."

Over Ellen's shoulder I could see the young girl by the window, and I imagined she was waiting for her mother to return from the washroom. I said, "Let's be sure to call Jordie tonight."

"You really feel perfectly all right?" Ellen asked.

"Yes," I said.

"I thought you felt a little hot this morning," she said. "I touched your brow and it felt a little hot."

"Well, I feel fine now," I said.

She still had her I'm-not-satisfied look on. After another moment, I put down my butter knife and said, *"What?"*

"Something's going on," she said.

"What do you mean?"

"I don't know what I mean, Cook," she said. "You tell me what I mean."

"Well, let's see," I said. "You mean you don't like the hotel. You wish we were staying somewhere fancy."

"No," she said. "I love the hotel."

"You mean this trip was a mistake. You miss Jordie and you miss Spencer and your books and your computer and things and you wish we were back home."

"Cook," she said, "just please don't get weird on me."

"I'm not getting weird on you," I said, shrugging my shoulders. "Did you by any chance leave the window open in the spare room?"

She paused for a moment, surprised by my abrupt question and deciding whether or not to answer it. "Yes, I did," she said finally. "It was stuffy. Now listen, Cook. You called me a name this morning."

"What are you talking about?"

"You called me a name in your sleep . . . when I was trying to wake you. A name I don't care to repeat."

I laughed, and at the same moment noticed, disconcertingly, that the young girl who reminded me of Jordie had left the dining room without my having seen. "Oh, come on," I said to Ellen. "It couldn't have been all that bad."

She leaned across the table, looked me in the eye, and whispered, "How about 'little cunt'? How about opening your eyes, looking right at me, and saying, 'Why don't you let me sleep, you little cunt?' "

Now she sat back very straight in her chair, allowing ample room and time for my astonishment.

"Gosh," I said at last.

"Yeah," she said. "That was my reaction too. Gosh oh gee oh golly."

In order to meet up with our group and tour the Old Jewish Quarter, we needed to take the tube from Sloane Square to Tower Hill station. After breakfast I waited downstairs while Ellen returned to the flat for our old Nikon. Directly opposite the dining room was a sitting room, empty of people now and outfitted with a tea service, newspapers, and lots of rattan chairs and settees. The garden effect that had been attempted in the room—the chair cushions were white and spring green; two small palms stood dying in Japanese urns—was subverted by the presence of a large television (off now, its screen reflecting a dead-gray version of everything). I proceeded to the hotel desk, where I found Hannah, the very well-groomed, gray-haired woman who'd checked us in three days before. She was, as usual, on the telephone, but smiled at me warmly when I rounded the corner. On a tiny video screen behind the desk—a surveillance gadget—I could see Pascal, standing under the canopy out front, leaning against a brass pole, waiting, I supposed, for whatever should turn up. I judged Hannah to be about fifty, and something about her proprietary yet casual manner suggested to me that either she had been with the hotel for many years or it was possibly her family who owned it. She dressed as if for church, very proper and tasteful, a string of pearls, a white blouse, and though she was slightly overweight—what's usually called "plump"—she seemed quite her natural size. She was off the phone in a minute and asked if she could help me in some way. I explained that we were going out, that I was only waiting for Ellen to return from the flat. Then I asked, feigning an air of nonchalance, "Who is it that plays the piano on the third floor?"

Hannah looked puzzled. "The third floor?" she said. "That's been shut off for well over a year. It used to be a flat like yours, but it's been divided into rooms now. Are you saying you heard music from down there?"

"Well, I thought I did," I said.

She nodded. "It's not open yet, you see. The rooms are still being painted, and they've yet to be furnished. I expect one of the painters was playing a radio. I'm terribly sorry if it disturbed you."

"Not at all," I said. "I only heard it a couple of times in the elevator, going up."

Hannah's telephone rang and Ellen appeared at my side at the same moment; Hannah answered the call but asked the caller to hold, cupped her hand over the mouthpiece, and whispered to me quickly, "All the same, I'll have a word with them."

"What was that about?" Ellen asked as we started out the front doors, but before I could answer we were greeted by Pascal, craning his neck from behind an enormous arrangement of flowers; he was coming in as we were going out. Ellen made the "For me?" joke, I realized that I still had my key to the flat in my hand, and I asked Ellen to wait for me and followed Pascal back into the entryway. He headed with the flowers down the hall toward the dining room. Hannah was on the telephone, occupied at the reservations chart on the wall, her back to me, and as I went to drop the key on the desktop, I paused, for the little video screen had caught my eye: Outside on the sidewalk, an old, hunched-over woman in ragged clothes had engaged Ellen. I watched them exchange a few words, Ellen pointed to the woman's feet, the woman looked down for a moment, and then Ellen stooped to the pavement to tie the old woman's shoe. I could see the smile on the woman's face, and when Ellen was done, instead of standing again, she sat back on her heels like a shoe salesman, waiting to see how the customer liked this latest pair. Ellen, too, was smiling—the old woman nodding like mad, clearly overcome with gratitude—and there was something in this moment of charity that so unnerved me, so confronted and challenged my cynic's heart, that I felt sorry for every hurtful thing I'd ever done to my wife, sorry for every failure to protect her and love her as she deserved to be protected and loved. This black-and-white miniature of her on the screen, kneeling at the old woman's feet, restored my faith—when I hadn't even known it needed restoring—that whatever she had come through at my hands and at the larger, more reckless hands of fate, she'd come through with her kindness intact, and it made me hopeful for human nature in general, that there was a life of goodness in people that wanted to prevail, a goodness that died, if it died, very hard.

The old woman was shuffling away when I reached Ellen and took her in my arms. I told her I loved her and hang the Old Jewish Quarter, let's spend the day in bed. She pulled back and looked at me, stunned; she laughed, clearly puzzled, but once she determined that I was serious, she shrugged and said okay.

At the desk, we giggled like kids, asking for a key back from Hannah. I didn't hear any music in the elevator going up, though I did recall Hannah's explanation; shaking my head, I thought, No, not a painter playing a radio.

Ellen, who'd seen me shake my head, said, "What?" but I told her I would explain later.

A young chambermaid was just leaving our flat as we got out of the elevator. We passed in the hallway and said hello; she kept her head mostly down, but I thought she appeared frightened and upset. And I thought I probably only imagined it.

Once we were inside, however, Ellen said, "That was odd."

"What was odd?" I said.

"That girl," she said. "She'd been crying."

CHAPTER

Four

SATURDAY MORNING, OUR first week-

end, I began to want to drink. My urges to drink have noth-

ing to do with a taste for liquor. My urges to drink are the

strong tugs of a compulsion to get out of my skin. (That's

why Quaaludes, Valium, morphine, heroin, cocaine, Percodan, and a number of other things substitute nicely.) Why I should have wanted to get out of my skin that weekend in London is at the heart of what it means to be a drunk. Ellen and I were euphoric, cruising in honeymoon mode, having a great time, but the soul of a drunk is a subversive's soul, the soul of a saboteur. I stood at the bathroom sink in my under-wear, brushing my teeth, thinking how the toothpaste tasted like shit, eyeing with contempt the nearby bottle of ibuprofen, running London's water wastefully, defiantly down the drain, when Ellen came in naked, put one hand on my shoulder, and while kissing my cheek, held her diaphragm under the water to rinse it. This was a buddy thing to do, meaning we were particularly close. She shook it off, popped it into its pink plastic case, and returned to the bedroom. I went in and told her, without any sort of preamble, that I needed some time alone.

My bad timing hurt her, as it was meant to. She had opened the drapes, letting in the sky and our happy view of rooftops. She lay in bed with the sheet just covering her breasts; now she sat up, pulling it under her chin, as if she meant to protect herself. She said, "Is there time for me to dress, or shall I go out wrapped in a sheet?"

When I was a teenager, I'd read the autobiography of Bertrand Russell, and nearly thirty years later, I couldn't tell you a thing about the man, not one iota from the book, except that he'd told his wife once, in a fit of sexual exhaustion, that he didn't love her. The detail impressed me, I sup-pose, because as a teenager I didn't think it possible to be sexually exhausted. Anyway, this odd recollection popped into my head in response to Ellen's question. I was suddenly aware of my nakedness, especially aware of my hairiness, my animal stupidity, my male supremacy. In my hairy ape hand I still held a toothbrush, the little, found object with which—now that I'd mastered the use of tools—I might dig termites out of rotting logs and willfully probe and groom my mate. I said to Ellen, ambiguously, that I was sorry and left the room. I went back to the bathroom and got into a hot shower.

By the time I was out, I understood that what I really

wanted was a drink and returned to the bedroom to apologize in earnest. She was wearing one of the white hotel bathrobes, sitting in a chair by the window, her arms and legs crossed. In the shut-down tone she uses when she's hurt or scared, she asked me if I was finished in the bathroom.

"I really am sorry," I said. "I'm just—"

"What's going on, Cook?" she said. "I asked you before. Now I'm getting anxious."

"Nothing's going on," I said. "I think I just want a drink, maybe."

"Oh, that makes me feel much better," she said. "I won't be anxious anymore."

"Don't worry," I said. "It doesn't have anything to do with you. Or us. It's me. And I'll be fine."

She looked at me, and I could see that there were tears in her eyes, tears, I think (despite her sarcasm), of relief. At least she'd been here before. At least it was something she could recognize.

"Maybe you should find a meeting," she said at last.

"Yeah," I said. "Maybe I will."

"Is there anything I can do?" she said.

"Well," I said, "you could start by forgiving me."

"I do forgive you," she said. "Of course I forgive you."

I have looked back at this small event again and again over the last year—Ellen in an oval of pale light, me in darkness, asking her forgiveness, she giving it, simply, without hesitation. I've returned there with longing, not only because her forgiveness came so readily, but also because, that morning, there was only a hurtful remark to forgive, and I wish I could have kept it that way. The weight of the moment, my wistfulness toward it, was borne (at least in part) on the wings of a childish notion of forgiveness. But I have studied forgiveness the way a speculator studies finance, the way anyone studies what he most wants, and I have learned that it is not a thing owned by one, given to or withheld from another at will. It is actually a change of heart, and knowing this has taught me patience.

.   .   .

The day before, we had left a message at Jordie's school for her to phone us. She called while we were at dinner, and when we returned the call, she was out again. So we deliberately stayed up until midnight on Saturday in order to phone after her dinner hour, when she would be expected to be in her dorm and available to take calls. Apparently, we weren't the only parents who had this idea, for we were told by the school's switchboard operator that the line to Jordie's house had been busy for forty-five minutes. We left another message, asking her to call us on Sunday.

Shortly after falling asleep Saturday night, I dreamed that Jordie and I were on a crowded subway train in New York, somewhere way downtown, standing close together among a crush of people, clinging to a metal pole. I was thinking how grown up she'd become, and I smiled at her sadly. She smiled back, perplexed by my sad face, and then the rattly old train began to squeak and squeal, the lights went out, and all you could see for a few seconds were the naked lightbulbs in their little protective cages at intervals along the walls of the tunnel. When the train's interior lights came back on, Jordie had disappeared.

Just as my panic began to set in, I was awakened from the dream by the telephone, sounding its alien, British double ring on the table next to my head. Ellen got to it before me. I could see by the clock on the nightstand that it was almost 2 A.M. I listened with some alarm to Ellen's end of the conversation—Jordie was upset, but I could soon tell that it was nothing serious. By the time Ellen handed me the phone, Jordie only wanted to apologize for waking us.

"I feel so incredibly stupid and babyish," she said to me. "I knew how late it was there, but I was just missing you so much. . . ."

"Are you okay?" I asked.

"I'm perfectly fine," she said. "I really am. I'm just being a baby. I was feeling homesick, but just hearing your voices has done me a world of good."

A world of good, a phrase I could hear only in a Southern accent, and I knew where she'd picked it up: She'd always enjoyed talking to my mother, because of her knack for focusing quickly on what was difficult in Jordie's life. Whereas Ellen and I tried to bring perspective to Jordie's problems and to point to solutions, Mother's talent was for commiseration. Any difficulty, any manner of struggle, any potential suffering, was Mother's special area. If Jordie mentioned that she didn't like her chorus teacher, Mother would abstract, generalize, and overblow ("There's absolutely nothing worse!") until a prickly teacher in a single subject at school seemed like something requiring survival skills. Of course Jordie loved this approach; it was what was missing in Ellen and me. If Jordie said she was thinking about taking some time off from chorus next term—or thinking about phoning her parents in London, even though it would be 2 A.M. there, and she would most certainly wake them and possibly even frighten them, possibly even confuse and alarm them, interrupting a nightmare in which she herself figured—my mother would say, "Well, it would do you a world of good, honey."

In this case, however, Jordie's call, despite its hour, had done *me* a world of good. A nagging need to talk to her had been at the back of my mind for the last several days, ever since we arrived in England. I kept her on the telephone for a long time that night—long after Ellen had gone back to sleep, and the next couple of days were different for me. I felt no further urges to drink, a great relief that meant I didn't need to find an AA meeting after all, or so I chose to interpret it. (I believed in the healing powers of AA and had attended many meetings over the years, but I had never come along far enough spiritually to lose my aversion to joining the crowd, to taking my proper position as a member of the human race.) I was contented to go places with Ellen, simply to be with her, to be the companion I'd originally intended to be. The mysterious piano, though I think I heard it again once when I was alone in the elevator, was of little interest to me, a curiosity in a quaint old hotel. I had no bad dreams of Jordie. There were no reports of any talking in my sleep. Ellen began to relax, ceased scrutinizing me quite so carefully.

Pascal, who had been off for the weekend, returned on

Monday morning with a black eye, which apparently was the subject of much innuendo and teasing from Hannah and the chambermaids. Monday afternoon, at the front desk, I asked Hannah what she thought of Pascal's shiner. Pascal stood only a few feet away, by the door.

Hannah reacted with great exaggerated affliction. "Can you imagine?" she said to me. "I think our young Pascal tried chatting up the wrong lady, somebody out of his league, if you ask me. I really don't see how we can let him continue to greet guests at the front, do you?"

Pascal came over slowly, deadly serious. "You don't want me to greet guests?" he said to her. "That's okay with me."

"Well, Pascal," she said, winking at me, "we mustn't have you giving our guests a wrong impression of the hotel."

He leaned down with his elbows on the desk and smiled, very close to Hannah's face. "But, Mademoiselle Hannah," he said, "it is not the wrong impression."

The telephone rang, rescuing Hannah, who had turned bright red. She rotated her swivel chair so that her back was fully to Pascal and me. Something in this gliding motion, and the hairpins holding together her perfect French twist, put her for me on a ballroom-dance floor at a social club Friday evenings. Pascal now looked at me and mimicked Hannah's former wink.

I followed him out the front door. Under the canopy, I asked him what had really happened—how he'd actually come by the black eye.

He laughed and said he'd chatted up the wrong lady, somebody out of his league.

And so for about forty-eight hours the world was for me an affable, ordinary place; this corner of it, London, this niche, the Hotel Willerton, were friendly, familiar settings where I felt surprisingly at home. The old city bore no ugly history, no trace of colonial plunder or white arrogance or an excess of hangings and beheadings; no Catholic martyrs, no one killed on account of a king wanting to change wives. Any shameful pockets in my own past were, like London's, overshadowed and silenced by the blessed present, with its autumnal windfall of fine weather, its lingering green parks, its promise of health and wealth and well-being. Tuesday, mid-morning, as we stood at the railing of the topmost gallery on the dome of Saint Paul's, Ellen, in great spirits, passed her upturned hand across the hazy panorama before us and said to me, "All of this could be yours if you will only fall down and worship me."

"But I do already," I said. "You know I do."

On Wednesday, I was shaken awake by this woman I professed to worship. "Cookson, wake up!" she was saying again and again, and when I opened my eyes, I thought her face was the very mask of hatred. I sat up quickly, surprised to be alive. Aloud, I said something like "Wow . . . ," or perhaps "Whoa . . . ," some *w* word that drug addicts are prone to utter when experiencing real-world events.

Ellen was up and away from the bed immediately. From a safe distance on the other side of the room, she said, "What is *wrong* with you?"

I rubbed my eyes. In my mind I composed the question "What do you mean?" though I still felt far from actually being able to execute it.

"You won't wake up," she said, "you're calling me horrible names . . . saying *horrible* things . . . and you're frightening me. What's *wrong* with you?"

The edge of hysteria in her voice I found especially off-putting. I didn't think there was any need to shout when already my head hurt. Surely she could see that I was barely awake and couldn't be expected to answer a barrage of questions. I swung my legs over the edge of the bed, turning my back to her and allowing my feet to touch the floor. I noted that the bottoms of my feet were tender. When I attempted to stand, I noted a similar tenderness all through my body. I sat back down and stared out the open window at the hypnotic spinning of a ventilator on a roof across the way. I was only vaguely conscious of Ellen's presence somewhere behind me. Inexplicably, there was that smell of Scotch I had noticed a few days earlier in the spare room. I sniffed my hands and arms, for the odor seemed to be coming off me. "Do you smell that?" I said in a voice I didn't quite recognize.

Ellen moved around the bed and stood next to me. I held my hand up to her.

She looked at it as if it had recently struck her.

"Smell what?" she said after a moment.

"That," I said, further extending my arm.

She leaned forward hesitantly, her face close to my hand. I saw her eyes fill with tears as she began to move down the length of my arm, sitting next to me on the bed and burying her face in the curve of my neck and shoulder. "I want to go home," she whispered. "Oh, Cook, I want to go home."

"Do you smell it?" I asked.

"Yes," she whispered.

"What does it smell like to you?"

"It smells like whisky, Cook. I don't know what it means, but I want to go home. Let's just go home."

I put my arm around her. "Okay," I said. "I'm sorry I've upset you. I said something in my sleep. Something that upset you."

I suddenly recalled a party we'd been to years before, in Westchester. The hosts—big drinkers, friends we thought we were very close to back then but never saw or spoke to again once we moved to Cambridge—served cocktails before dinner, several wines with dinner, champagne with dessert, and cognac with coffee. Ellen was pregnant with Jordie and wasn't drinking—she never drank much, in any case. On one of my many trips to the bathroom, she waylaid me in the hall and said she was feeling tired and wanted to go home. I was furious and made a scene of saying immediate, abrupt good-byes to everyone, stormed out of the house, and waited for Ellen in the car, leaving her alone to make explanations. Then I drove us—myself and my pregnant wife—the thirty miles to Manhattan in a total blackout. I came to way uptown on Second Avenue, where Ellen was saying, "That was a cop back there . . . you better slow down." The last thing I could remember was lighting a cigarette as I backed out of the driveway in Westchester and dropping the lighter down between the front seats of the car. The coils on the lighter were still hot, and when I reached in to fish it out I burned my finger. I remembered saying, "Jesus fucking shit."

"It doesn't matter what you said," Ellen whispered now. "Let's just go home."

"Okay," I said. "We'll go home today if you want to. I mean, if you're sure."

"I'm sure," she said.

CHAPTER

Five

BUT WE DIDN'T go home.

Ellen remained in the flat to phone the airlines and see

how soon we could get a flight back to Boston, while I went

downstairs—without a shower or a shave—to speak to Han-

nah, to make arrangements for an early departure.

Hannah was occupied at the desk with a German couple who were paying their bill, so I wandered down the hall to the sitting room, hoping to find a cup of tea. It was already after noon, and I could hear the clanking of silverware from the dining room opposite. The tea left in the sitting room's pot was barely warm, but it was better than no tea at all, and I poured out a cup. As I did, I suddenly felt I wasn't alone in the room. When I turned, I saw the young girl who had so reminded me of Jordie recently, the one I'd seen in the dining room gazing forlornly out the French windows into the garden. She wore the same blue and white sailor-style dress as before and was seated in a rattan chair near one of the unhealthy palms, looking at me, not smiling, not frowning exactly, but with a kind of world-weary empathy. I thought the palm must have prevented my seeing her when I'd first entered the room.

She said, "It isn't hot anymore," referring specifically to the tea but in a tone that designated the tea's lukewarmness as but a small emblem for the general state of all things: nothing in the world was quite what it should be.

"Oh, hello," I said. "I didn't see you there."

"No," she said. "I knew you didn't. I should have spoken to you straightaway, but as your back was to me, I feared I should startle you."

In this careful, thoughtful observation there was an unusual degree of distress, and her voice, which was lovely and high, seemed almost to have a small tremor in it. Her accent (though of course I was one with an accent) was refined, schooled, and walking such a high wire that any amount of emotion showed it to waver. I sat down in the chair that was at a right angle to hers. I took a sip of the tea and said, as if to comfort her, "Well, it isn't so bad."

She gave me only the slightest glance, a quick diversion of her gaze (which otherwise stayed dead ahead) that nimbly conveyed her skepticism of my tea appraisal.

"I saw you the other day," I said. "In the dining room, at breakfast."

"Yes," she said. "I saw you too. You were with your wife, I suppose."

"Yes," I said.

"You'd been quarreling," she said.

"Now how in the world did you know that?" I asked.

"I'm frightfully sorry," she said quickly. "That was rude of me," though I could see in her face a hint of pleasure—she was pleased with herself and couldn't quite hide it.

"We did in fact have a kind of quarrel," I said. "Not really a quarrel but a misunderstanding, I guess you'd say."

"Yes," she said. "A quarrel is slightly larger than a misunderstanding, isn't it. Possibly more violent."

"Exactly," I said. "Then of course there's your *spat*, which is always small but often peevish, and your *argument*, which can be any size and even heated."

She smiled pleasantly when she heard this bit of cleverness, though she turned her attention to a pair of white cotton gloves that lay neatly in her lap; she lifted these, realigned them, and placed them carefully back where they'd been. I thought I saw a darkness in the inside of both her wrists, perhaps bruises of some kind, and right away I wondered if the gloves, to which she seemed closely attached, were meant to hide these.

Again she focused on the window, so intensely that I turned to see what might be there: a window, covered with white sheers, nothing to see.

"She's very pretty, your wife," she said at last.

"She would be happy to hear that," I said.

She paused another moment, looked into her lap, moved the white gloves perhaps an eighth of an inch, assessed their imperceptibly new angle, and added, "I think she rather resembles my mother."

"Well, that's very interesting," I said, "because you look something like her daughter . . . our daughter, that is . . . Jordie."

I said this out of a strange allegiance to the fact that it had been true only a couple of minutes earlier; almost immediately upon speaking, this girl had ceased entirely to remind me of Jordie, except in coloring and age. I noted her old-fashioned shoes, brown leather with brass buckles, shoes Jordie wouldn't be caught dead in, the shoes of a supreme nerd. And white cotton gloves?

"Jordie," she said. "That's an interesting name, usually for a boy, I think. Is it G-e-o-r—?"

"J-o-r," I said. "For Jordan."

"Oh, then she's named for the river Jordan?"

"No, no," I said, laughing. "My wife's surname was Jordan."

"I see," she said. "Did you know the river Jordan is the lowest river in the entire world?"

"I think I did know that," I said.

"It's also of course where Jesus was baptized by John the Baptist."

"I think I knew that too," I said.

She took a deep breath and sighed heavily, as if she meant to clear the air of her failure to tell me something I didn't know. "Do I really look like your daughter?" she said. "Because that's rather odd, you see."

"Why do you say that?"

"Because the 'mother' I referred to before is actually my stepmother," she said. "My actual mother died of pneumonia when I was five years of age."

"I'm sorry to hear that."

"Thank you," she said. "I did miss her terribly at first. She was very gifted, as I recall, a musical actress, and quite . . . . quite stylish. I once saw her portrayal of Sophie in *The Yeoman of the Guard*, but I hardly remember it. Actually I can hardly—"

At that moment the light changed in the room somehow—maybe a cloud passed across the sun; or maybe the sun had been behind a cloud all along and now came out—and the young girl's skin almost seemed to glow, her face filled with longing. She'd touched on some real sorrow, the thing, I imagined, her affected world-weariness sought to mask. I suspected that most conversations went this way for her, given the least sympathetic ear. Whatever she was about to say she did not say. She looked at me—for the first time since I'd sat down—and I saw that there was something not right about her eyes; they were extremely cloudy, the whites an almost jaundiced yellow. She of course knew this about her eyes, knew they revealed something painful about her nature or her circumstances, and knew she made herself vulnerable by looking directly at me. And having given herself to me in this way, having invited me in, she smiled and shrugged her shoulders, a moment that projected such breathtaking loneliness I found myself, after speaking to her this briefly and learning this little, wanting nothing so much as I wanted to rescue her from whatever it was that caused her so much injury. I even thought she understood this—that she was able somehow to read this hope (or need) in my face. She'd stopped midsentence, not only because of an emotional difficulty connected to the loss of her mother but because it was simply unnecessary to go on. It was as if she'd brought me into the desired position with such skill and grace that the sheer ease of it had doubly moved her. She *had* me, whatever that meant, and she knew it.

Hannah, apparently having noted my brief appearance at her desk five minutes before, stepped to the door and asked if I required anything.

Our eyes met—mine and the girl's—and she whispered to me one word, urgently: "Go."

But did she mean "Go," or "Go"? Was she giving me leave to speak to Hannah, or urging me to return across the Atlantic? Whatever she'd intended, my resolve (or at the least my willingness) to go back home to Cambridge had deeply waned.

I said to Hannah in the hallway, "What a remarkable young girl."

"Who?" she said.

"The girl in the sitting room there," I said. "I was just speaking to her."

"Oh, sorry," said Hannah. "I didn't see anyone."

"No," I said. "You couldn't see her from the door."

"Well," said Hannah, "if it was a young girl, I suspect it was Emily Davison. You mean a teenaged girl, do you?"

"Yes," I said.

"That would be Emily," she said, nodding. "She's the only young girl here. Lives with her mother in one of the residential apartments on the second floor."

We'd arrived back at the desk, and Hannah had taken her station behind it. We both knew the telephone would ring any second, and if I meant to do any business with her I'd better get started. Hannah flattened out both hands on the mahogany desktop and said, "Now . . ."

I hesitated a moment longer, then put my question to her in a watery form, all subjunctive: *If* something were to come up . . . *if* we were to have to go home sooner than expected . . .

She looked worried and confused throughout my meandering speculation, and then the phone did ring.

"Oh, don't worry about it," I said happily. "Not important. I'll talk to you about it later."

I eagerly returned to the sitting room, but found it empty. I put my head inside the dining-room door; no sign of the girl there either.

Back at the hotel desk, Hannah was free again and gave the appearance of wanting to take up our former, bewildering business. But I said to her, "What did you say her name was?"

"What . . . the girl in the sitting room? Why, Emily Davison. Lives with her mother—"

"If you see her, Hannah, could you tell her my name and say that I was asking for her?"

Hannah seemed more confused than ever—almost, perhaps, suspicious.

"What is it?" I said.

"It's just . . . ," she said, faltering.

"Tell me," I said. "Please." I thought she was about to reveal some grim secret about the Davison family.

"It's just . . . well, frankly . . ."

Here she leaned forward and lowered her voice to a whisper: "I always found Emily a bit odd myself," she said, as if it caused her distress. "A touch sullen, actually."

Going up in the elevator, I heard the mysterious piano music, the same as before. I wondered if I'd misjudged its origin: maybe it was coming from the second floor, from one of the residential apartments Hannah had mentioned. I paid it little mind now, in any case, for I was busy formulating what I might say to Ellen. I didn't think I could tell her that I'd just met a young girl downstairs, a young girl I found so strange and compelling, in some unnameable way, that I no longer wanted to go home. I decided just to emphasize what she, Ellen, would be sacrificing by leaving now: the research for her book; we'd not even been to Hampstead yet. This seemed an especially weak argument when I saw in my mind's eye Ellen standing inside the flat amid our already packed suitcases.

But that wasn't what I found. Instead, she had set two places at the small table by the window in the kitchen and was making us some sandwiches. When I stepped to the kitchen door, she looked at me thoughtfully and said, "I want to talk. . . . I've been thinking."

"I have too," I said, already feeling hugely relieved. I opened the refrigerator and took out two Cokes. I put them on the table and looked out the window. "Another beautiful day," I said. "Can you believe it?"

This was too transparent a remark for Ellen.

"You don't want to go," she said.

"I guess I don't," I said. "But I will," I added quickly, "if it's what you want."

This was a small piece of manipulation: I had no intention of leaving; my feigned willingness was a means of leading her to think the decision was hers.

"Cook, I want you to see a doctor," she said.

"A doctor?"

"Yes," she said.

"You mean because I've slept late two different mornings?"

I sat down at the table. I realized that since arriving at the sitting room downstairs, I hadn't given my physical condition of that morning a single thought. The tenderness I'd felt earlier in my muscles had settled into a kind of general achiness now, but I hadn't once acknowledged it consciously since leaving the flat.

"No, Cook," said Ellen, "I don't mean about sleeping late two different mornings. I mean about sleeping as if you're in some kind of coma, and I mean about my having to shake you awake and about your spouting obscenities the likes of which I've never heard—"

"I was *asleep*, Ellen. . . ."

She took the chair opposite me, pulling it out and up close to me. "Listen, Cook," she said. "I don't especially want to go home. And I don't want to overreact. But don't minimize this. Don't act like I'm the one with the problem here. If all we're talking about is your sleeping late, explain to me why you smelled like whisky this morning when you haven't had a drink in thirteen years. Explain that to me."

"I can't," I said.

"Right," she said. "You can't."

"But I would feel foolish . . . idiotic . . . How am I supposed to . . ."

"Well, what do you think is going on?" she said. "I mean am I the only one here who thinks this is just a little bit weird?"

"No," I said. "I admit it's weird. I just don't think it's particularly serious. Something has happened that we can't explain, but I don't see that the consequences are such that—"

"For *you* maybe," she said. "But I'm frightened by it. I'm the one who—"

"Look," I said. "Maybe it won't happen again. I bet it won't happen again. But—"

"And besides," she said, "you don't even know what the

consequences are. There are all kinds of strange neurological disorders that have all kinds of strange symptoms."

"I don't have a neurological disorder," I said.

"You don't know that," she said. "Foul language, for example, is a characteristic of Tourette's syndrome."

"I don't have Tourette's syndrome, Ellen," I said.

She held up her index finger, close to my face. "Look here at my finger," she said, "and follow it with your eyes."

"Ellen," I said, "a little knowledge is a dangerous thing. I'm not a character in one of your novels."

She was moving her finger from side to side and up and down.

"You're not experiencing any double vision as I'm doing this, are you?"

"No," I said, batting her finger away, out of my face.

"Now do this," she said, wrinkling up her forehead and baring her teeth.

"No," I said. "You look ridiculous."

"Just do it, Cook," she said.

I wrinkled my forehead and bared my teeth.

"Now stick out your tongue," she said.

I stuck out my tongue.

"Pucker your lips."

I puckered my lips.

"Can you whistle?"

"Of course I can whistle, Ellen. Look . . . as I was saying, it probably won't happen again. But *if* it does—and I'm saying *if*—why don't you just go on about your business. Just leave me sleeping and get on with your day. No trouble waking me, no obscenities. I want to go to some of the museums anyway. There's plenty for us to do on our own. If I'm up and about like a normal person, we can do something together, and if not, just get on with your own plans. Get on with your day and forget about me. Let's enjoy ourselves, for God's sake. We're in England."

"Whistle," she said.

I began whistling the melody to "Row, row, row your boat . . ."

She looked enormously disappointed. She sat back in her chair and put her hands behind her head. I suppose she was considering what I'd said. But she remained silent and continued to examine my face long after I'd stopped whistling.

"Well, what do you think?" I said.

"Okay," she said. "You go your way and I'll go mine, that's what you're saying."

"Not at all," I said. "Ellen, I love you. I want to be with you. I can see that this thing has upset you, and I don't want you to have to go home and miss this trip because of it. I feel guilty as hell, and I'm just trying to suggest a workable solution. So we don't have to go home already."

"I don't know," she said, shrugging her shoulders—a gesture that inevitably recalled the young girl downstairs (there was even something of the loneliness). "I'll try it," she said at last. "I guess I'm willing to try it."

"Good," I said.

"But you have to promise me that if things get worse, not to ignore it, and to go to a doctor."

"I promise," I said, and I leaned forward and kissed her.

But I have to say, in the spirit of honesty, that I didn't feel good about that kiss. Something had happened without my specifically planning it. I had not consciously schemed. I had not deliberately misrepresented anything. But walking away from that conversation, over to the kitchen sink to wash my hands, I had managed to get two things I thought I wanted—I might even say, two things that were necessary: to stay in the hotel and to have some time on my own.

That same afternoon, the weather changed. The sky grew dark, the temperature dropped fifteen degrees in an hour's time, and by two o'clock, wind-driven rain was strafing the windows of the flat. The day, so far, had been oddly difficult, and I think we were both a bit worn out by it. We decided to stay indoors for the afternoon, and then, rain or no rain, walk somewhere for an early dinner. Ellen wrote in her journal, read for a while, and soon fell asleep. I situated myself on the sofa in our sitting room and thumbed through some old magazines I found on a shelf inside an armoire. Soon I, too, drifted off, waking minutes later, cold and very unclear about my location. I might have briefly dreamed of being home, for it seemed to me that some hint of my dog, Spencer, lingered with me immediately on waking. Otherwise, I was utterly lost. I lay on my back, my head shoved up against the arm of a deep sofa. The light in the room, dim and diffused, could have been the light of dawn or dusk. The sofa, near one corner of the room, was too short for me, and I discovered that by stretching my legs out straight I could touch the wall with my toes. On this slender, toe-touchable rectangle of wall—formed by the boundaries of the corner of the room and the side of a window—hung the framed reproduction of a painting: a country road lined with tall spindly trees, a vineyard, a farmhouse, a church steeple on the horizon, an enormous summer sky, a man on the road with his dog: *The Avenue*, by Meindert Hobbema, so it was inscribed: a study in perspective, the rutted dirt road widest in the foreground, narrowing into the background, drawing me in. This sense I had of being drawn into the place of the painting, out of an already unknown setting, gave me an odd feeling of vertigo, though I was in fact lying down and in no high spot. As if to grab hold of something, I recalled that my name was Cookson Selway and that I was in England; then that I was the father of Jordie; then that I was the husband of Ellen, the son of Frances and Herman. Soon I knew I was staying in London, in a flat at the Hotel Willerton, and that my wife, Ellen, was sleeping in the bedroom just down the hall.

I could see at once, however, that despite all this being true, something was different. The flat was not quite the same. I sat up. I discovered that the table lamp to my right did not work, and for some reason this frightened me. I called out to Ellen, but she didn't answer. I stood and turned to the corner of the room where the entrance to the hallway should have been, but found it sealed up—no, not sealed up, but simply not there, as if it had never existed. That door, instead, was at the middle of the wall. I opened the door, relieved to find our bedroom (though, again, changed—a large four-poster instead of twin beds), and Ellen under the covers, asleep, her back turned to me. Now I recalled that it had been raining, that it was afternoon, that we'd been resting. I decided to wake Ellen and remind her that we planned to go to dinner early. I sat on the bed next to her. Even before I touched her I noticed that her hair on the pillow was different, curlier somehow, and darker, redder. "Ellen," I said, "darling," placing my hand on her shoulder, which was much too big and rock hard—a shock—and then the bearded man in the bed stirred, turning his face to me, eyes closed, muttering "Sod off" (a stench of stale whisky), burrowing his head down into the pillow, and then quite suddenly opening his eyes, which were gray and bloodshot. Some sound escaped my throat—I'm not sure what; certainly not words—and I was up and out of the room, slamming the door shut behind me. There was a key in the door, which I quickly turned, and then I stood staring at it—the door—trying to catch my breath. From the other side I heard Ellen's voice. "Cook?" she said. "Why have you closed that door? I'm awake. Cook? It's nearly five."

And all at once things were as they should be. I was in the sitting room of our flat at the Hotel Willerton; the door I was staring at was indeed the door to the hallway. I heard Ellen's voice again, calling my name.

I unlocked the door and went down the hall to the bedroom. She had turned on the lamp between the twin beds. She said, "Good Lord, Cook, you look awful. . . . Are you okay?"

"I'm fine," I said. "I fell asleep out on the sofa."

"Come here," she said, reaching out her arms.

I didn't move.

"What's wrong?" she said.

"Nothing," I said, and went to her. She lifted up the blanket for me to get under.

We lay together, entwining our arms and legs ("Did you have a bad dream?"), and, my body convinced that she was she and none other ("No, no, I didn't have any dream"), I clung to her, probably confusing her, I clung to her tightly.

As usual, I was dressed for dinner before Ellen, and I went downstairs alone to see if I could find an umbrella for us to take. Pascal, already off duty, was still hanging around the front vestibule, in a pair of American blue jeans and a baseball jacket. Hannah had been replaced at the desk by the young woman who did the nights—Lois was her name. Passing by, I could see Hannah in the little office behind the desk, pulling on a raincoat. I stepped into the vestibule and asked Pascal if he knew where I might find an umbrella. He happened to be holding one, which he offered me.

"No, no," I said. "I don't want to take yours."

"Take," he said. "I will get another."

He went to a closet under the main stairway and returned with an identical black umbrella. He explained that he was waiting to be picked up by a friend. I asked him (for it only then occurred to me) if he lived at the hotel.

"Yes," he said. "I have a little room downstairs. There is me and two chambermaids live in rooms downstairs. We have little windows high up near the ceiling that look onto the garden. You can see the bushes and flowers if you stand on a chair."

There was something innately comforting about Pascal—he had a sensible nature and was good-humored—and it struck me that I might talk to him. I was going to have to talk to someone, and since that someone wouldn't be Ellen, I thought Pascal might do.

"Pascal," I said, "your eye has turned an interesting shade of orange."

"Yes," he said. "Yesterday it was green. The orange is better."

Hannah opened the glass inner door to the vestibule and said, "Oh, Mr. Selway, Mrs. Davison and Emily are coming down the stairs just now, on their way to the dining room for tea."

I followed Hannah back into the entry hall. "Emily," she said to the girl on the stairs, "this is Mr. Selway."

The girl paused, looking down at me, large and expressionless. "Hello," she said, sullen to the toes, her hair long, brown, and stringy, one side of her shirttail hanging outside her skirt. Her mother, sullen too, but in a better-groomed way, smiled at me with an inquiry in her eye.

I smiled back and nodded pleasantly. I said, "Pleased to meet you," turned, and whispered to Hannah, "That's not her."

"What?" she whispered back.

Hannah and I both smiled and nodded foolishly, awkwardly, and the two of them passed us and went on to the dining room.

"That's Emily Davison," Hannah said emphatically.

"But that's not the girl from the sitting room," I said.

Hannah, belted up in her raincoat, looked down at the floor for a moment, putting her index finger to her chin, as if she were trying to sort out what had just happened. Finally, she looked at me and said, "But she's the only girl we have."

not entirely able to disguise my moods. As we walked back from the restaurant to the hotel, sharing the umbrella Pascal had provided, Ellen mentioned that I had seemed vaguely upset through dinner. Was anything wrong?

It occurred to me to say that I couldn't enjoy myself when she was watching me like a hawk and would she please just lay off for Christ's sake . . . but that would have revealed too much of my hand—I knew I would have to curb these snappish impulses—and so I told her I was feeling a little tired, a little affected by the change in the weather.

We maintained a courteous silence the rest of the way to the hotel. We were silent in the elevator, silent as we entered the flat, still silent as we undressed and prepared for bed. We brushed our teeth together, politely taking turns at spitting into the sink.

The twin beds had been turned down and the drapes drawn by a chambermaid. I had about ten minutes on my own while Ellen finished in the bathroom, and I lay quietly in bed, thinking. I was aware that the flat had permanently changed, my perception of it deepened. It now had a real presence for me, like rooms one has known as a child—and more: a hidden life behind the walls, its odd nooks and trapezoids and triangles formed by the dormer windows, its broad moldings and glossy white panels mere diversions for the eye, bits of interior design, falsely static representations of its true, mutable nature. I felt a strangely familiar ambivalence toward the flat now. Why familiar? Well, I had felt something like this before, felt something like it each time in the past when I tied off my arm with a piece of rubber tubing, each time I saw the swell and rise of the vein, each time I overthrew the youthful fear of injections, touched the tip of the needle to the still gullible skin, and rewitnessed the red prominence of blood surge into the barrel's cold-shaken blow, the *me* mixing with the *it*. Occasionally, dreamily, I would think, at the moment of hitting, of a ceramic novelty we had around my house when I was a kid, a bald-headed man flushing himself ("Good-bye Cruel World") down a toilet.

Ellen came into the room, sat next to me on the bed,

put her hand on my stomach, and said, "Strange day . . . This morning we were going home." Then, after a pause, "I'm sorry, Cook, but you do seem sad."

"I'm not sad," I said.

She looked at me thoughtfully, pondering my answer. Then she smiled and said, "It's so early to be going to bed, isn't it?"

"I know."

She reached across me, turned out the lamp, and got under the covers with me. In the darkness we could hear rain on the windows and, with gusts, one of the windows rattling in its casement. For me, the dark was very alive—rich and auspicious and disquieting. When we made love, I maneuvered her into top position so that I could watch the room, watch the dark, a vigil that proved curiously stimulating. I didn't know how to analyze the man in my vision from that afternoon, the sleeping, bearded drunkard who'd told me to sod off, and I didn't know how to analyze the vision itself (except to know that it definitely was no dream). Nor was I particularly interested in doing any analysis while Ellen and I were making love. What I knew about the thoughts that passed through my mind during sex was that they generally fell into one of three categories—they either contributed to the pleasure, took away from it, or were neutral—and images from that afternoon's vision were decidedly contributing. I could think of it as a man in my wife's bed, or as a man in my own bed, whatever made me happy; but what I couldn't avoid was the certainty that his presence, though terrifying and hostile—enough to scare any reasonable person away—had also been intensely, even essentially, sexual. The curious arousal I felt about watching the dark room while we were making love was the arousal that came from a sense of our *being* watched. And while this sense heightened my pleasure, it also took me psychically away from my wife, deeper and deeper, I felt, into a secret reality, one in which I used her for my purposes as I pleased and withheld from her the truth to which she was entitled. I even felt a strength of purpose behind this experience, that the heat of sex was being used by some power outside myself to burn me away from my attachments, to isolate me. As I said, this stuff would certainly have scared any reasonable person away. But I was not a reasonable person, and I was not scared away.

Afterward, Ellen lay with her head on my chest, stroking with her fingers the muscle in my forearm. "You know, Cookie," she said into the darkness, "I'm aware that I've been too attentive to you so far on this trip. And I know I'm prone to overreact to things. To worry too much. If anything were seriously wrong, you'd tell me, I know that. I think I have some completely normal anxiety about being away from home and away from Jordie, and it just connected to you by mistake. I want you to know that I'm sorry and that I'm really going to try to stop doing it."

On waking, I heard myself whisper, "I have to warn him . . . ," but all details of what I'd been dreaming had permanently left me. It was just past 5:30 A.M. Ellen (on her side, so that I could see her face) slept in her own bed, a few feet away. No sound of rain or wind. Drapes drawn, as before. Furniture the same as before, the door to the hallway in its normal location.

I knew that I'd felt a huge rush of remorse at Ellen's last remarks, after we'd made love—I could recall the evasive little technique with which I'd shoved it, in my mind, to the back of a shelf, to be looked at later; but the wonder drug released into the system by the male orgasm had carried me quickly into oblivion. Now I began to think, not about Ellen or remorse, but about the mystery girl I'd met in the sitting room downstairs. I could recall with precision her constant, central focusing, the way she would plant her attention to a spot directly in front, allowing her eyes to stray only minutely, as if some focal point, invisible to me, were all that prevented her from being carried away; I recalled her loveliness, the air she had of experience beyond her years; and of course her deep well of sorrow. I acknowledged that my strong attraction to her was at least partly a result of missing Jordie, of all the feelings of loss I had about Jordie. Likewise, I acknowledged that the terrifying vision's content, the man in the bedroom, could be a projection of whatever emotional discomfort I harbored about dormant (or lingering) homosexual urges. I told myself I was "man enough" to admit this to myself. And yet the notion of my manufacturing these experiences out of the self struck me as false and egocentric in the extreme. I decided I couldn't trust my thinking in this area, so I might just as well give it up. I decided to see myself as an explorer, an adventurer—which was a way of glorifying my intentions: to get out of my skin, to deceive my wife, to risk her peace and safety as well as my own, to delude myself as necessary in order to get out of my skin.

I recalled a time, years earlier, when I'd come home, twisted, from "work" at my first restaurant in Manhattan. I was never in any way needed in the restaurant and stayed until closing time only in order to drink and snort coke with the kitchen help. After closing, I had gone with some of the waiters to a club and drunk some more. When that bar closed, I went to an after-hours place with one of the guys, way downtown to hell and back, where, as we walked through the door, a contortionist was performing oral sex on himself aboard a small stage behind the bar. At some point later, I was led down some darkened stairs to a men's room, where a head-shaven black man called Silver was tapping out lines onto people's ten-dollar bills. You held out the ten (creased a bit down the middle to provide enough rigidity), he tapped, you snorted, he kept the bill. The place was jammed and very dimly lit, and I was groped by a faceless person while I got high, dispensing with quite a few tens, as the coke was about half baking soda. When I went back upstairs, I discovered that I was in a different bar from the one I had thought I was in. There was no sign of the waiter with whom I'd come downtown. At around dawn, I staggered onto the street and hailed a taxi. In the cab, I decided I was too wired to go to sleep and dropped a Quaalude I had in my shirt pocket. Jordie was a baby at this time. Ellen had probably been up a couple of times during the night to nurse her. Astoundingly, I found my way to our bedroom door, turned on the light, waking Ellen, and said, "I'm sick and tired of being kept on such a short fucking leash."

She looked at me, stunned, and sat up in bed. "What in the world are you talking about?" she said.

"I don't know," I said, and then this explorer, this adventurer, slid down the doorjamb onto the floor and passed out.

Now wide awake at the Hotel Willerton, I climbed from the bed and began to fumble my way through the dark flat toward the kitchen for a glass of juice. I resolved to come clean with Ellen, to tell her everything that had happened, and to suggest we change hotels—a brilliant idea, I thought, since we wouldn't have to go home. As I passed through the sitting room, I heard the sound of a child's voice, a crying sound, very much like the one I'd thought I heard coming from the spare bedroom a few days before. I turned back down the hall toward that room, but before I opened the door, I could already tell that I had moved farther away from the sound rather than closer. I returned to the sitting room. Now it seemed to me that the sound was coming from outside the flat, in the hallway. I opened the door quietly and stood listening for a minute. I could hear the voice more clearly now, though still quite distantly—only its color and pitch, no words; it was a child, a girl, and she sounded as if she was crying. Intermittently, I could hear a young male voice too, as if a young man was consoling the child. I closed the door, went back to the bedroom, and pulled on a pair of jeans. In a minute, I had pocketed the key to the flat and was tiptoeing, barefoot, out into the hallway. I walked toward the elevator, but again found myself farther away from the sound. I moved back along the hallway and stood for a moment by the door to the stairs; this was a door of leaded glass, and when I pulled it open, I could tell for sure that the voices were coming from the floor below, the third floor.

The stairs were garishly illuminated by an Exit sign over the door below. I thought, Of course . . . Though I'd earlier found the third-floor elevator door bolted, the stairs would have to remain accessible in case of fire. I should have realized this before. The voices grew louder, and once I'd pushed open the lower door, I could begin to determine a word or two: "no, no . . . ," "that's not . . . ," "I'm telling you . . ."

There was a strong odor of fresh paint, and the five doors opening onto either side of the hallway all stood ajar. I peeked into three rooms along the way but found them empty—not only empty of people, but empty of everything. I recalled Hannah's telling me that the rooms had not yet been furnished. At the fourth door, I saw the silhouettes of two figures across the room, sitting cross-legged on the bare floor—silhouettes because an enormous window, full of the first gray of dawn, was directly behind them. I was sure in an instant, even in this murky light, that the girl was my girl, the mystery girl, and she was upset about something. When I pushed open the door, she startled, gasping, badly frightened.

"Who's there?" said the young man, whose voice and accent sounded distinctly like Pascal's.

"I'm sorry," I began. "I heard voices and . . ."

"It's okay," the young man said to the girl. "I know him."

"Pascal?" I said.

"*Oui, monsieur.* I hope we did not wake you."

"No, no," I said. "I was already awake. What—"

"This is Melanie," Pascal said. "She is having a dream."

Now I could see, with disappointment, that the girl, though she had a similar haircut, was not my girl but the chambermaid Ellen and I had seen leaving our flat in tears a few days before. She wore a white nightgown and no slippers. Pascal wore a pair of striped pajama pants but no shirt. I had no idea what he meant by "She is having a dream." It seemed to me that surely I was the one having the dream. There was embarrassment all around, so I said, "Sorry . . . I didn't mean to interrupt," and turned to go.

"*Tell* him," I heard the girl whisper intensely . . . and "*No,*" Pascal's reply, just as intense.

"Tell me what?" I said, turning back.

"Monsieur Selway," Pascal said, "it is nothing."

The girl quickly stood. "Nothing?" she said, full-voiced, angry. "Is that what you think? Nothing? I suppose it was nothing done this to me, then?"

She was tilting her head to one side, holding back her hair, apparently showing him something on her cheek. Then she stormed past me, out of the room. Pascal, who was still sitting on the floor, let his head drop to his chest. We could hear the girl's footsteps on the stairs.

"Maybe you'd better—" I began.

"This girl," Pascal said, "this Melanie . . . she is hysterical."

"I didn't mean to barge in on you," I said, for I was feeling somehow responsible for the girl's sudden anger.

"I'm happy you did," said Pascal, and laughed. "She is crazy. A country girl, frightened since she came here. She knocks on my door . . . wakes me . . . walking in her sleep . . . dreaming. Now I have only one hour before I have to get up for work."

"She was walking in her sleep?" I said.

"Yes," he said. "I found her here by this window. Maybe she would jump."

"Jump?"

"She was dreaming," he said. "Maybe dreaming about jumping."

He went on to explain that the girl, who was about eighteen years old, had come down from somewhere in Yorkshire only two weeks before, to work at the hotel. The city frightened her, or so Pascal thought. He laughed when he told me she was homesick and blue almost all the time. When she'd knocked at his room a while earlier, he found her standing outside his door in her nightgown; she said to him something about "the master" being "quite angry about the fire." Then she'd turned and walked away. He thought to himself, *Dreaming . . .* and went back to bed. But he was unable to fall asleep and began to worry about the girl, even to worry about a possible fire. He went to her room, where he found her door open but no sign of the girl herself. He'd gone looking for her and eventually found her here, standing in the open window. When he called out her name, she collapsed to the floor and began sobbing. She'd been walking in her sleep, dreaming, he said again, and now that he'd waked her, she was more frightened than ever. Hysterical. She told him some crazy story about evil spirits.

I asked him what the girl had shown him on her cheek.

"Nothing," he said. "Some scratches. She probably was playing with the cats in the garden. She says *he* did it to her."

"Who?"

"Whoever," Pascal said, widening his eyes. "I don't know. The evil spirit, I guess."

"We saw her leaving our flat the other day," I said. "We thought she was crying."

"Yes, yes," he said. "Don't worry."

"Don't worry?"

"She's crazy," he said. "She should return to Mama. Now I must go, monsieur. I must soon be working."

We walked together to the stairway door. On the landing, he said to me, smiling, "Monsieur Selway rises with the birds," and it took me a moment to understand what he meant—that I was awake very early. He started down the stairs, and I started up.

As I rounded the bend in the stairs, I saw a glove lying on one of the treads, a girl's white cotton glove. Of course I recognized it as *hers* immediately, and I felt elated to see it there. I heard myself say, "Ah!" as if I'd found a lost friend. When I drew nearer and went to pick the glove up, however, it turned out to be some strands of toilet tissue, wadded and discolored and stuck together. Disgusted—almost shocked—I actually held this thing in my hand for a few seconds, refusing the surprise. Then I let it drop and proceeded to climb the rest of the stairs in a cloud of dejection, punished by my own senses and with nothing and no one else to blame.

Back in the flat, I put the teakettle on to boil. I knew I wouldn't be able to go back to sleep. I sat at the kitchen table, looking out the window at the slowly brightening rooftops. In a distant window, a light went on. A pigeon landed on the sill just inches from my hand, then, seeing me, flew away. I thought of what Ellen had said about neurological disorders, that there were all kinds of odd maladies with strange symptoms. I thought about my history of drug-induced hallucinating; once, for example, I'd gone to answer a telephone, and the receiver, in my hand, had turned into a live lobster. I thought about my resolve to tell Ellen everything and to change hotels. Now, more than ever, it seemed the right thing to do.

But when she appeared at the kitchen door, rubbing her eyes and asking me what I was doing up so early, I just shrugged my shoulders. "Woke up," I said. "Couldn't get back to sleep."

"I thought I heard you leave the flat," she said. "I must've been dreaming."

"Yeah," I said. "I guess."

One more day, I told myself. Give it just one more day and see what happens.

CHAPTER

Seven

IF MY CALCULATIONS are correct, that day,
the "day" in "give it just one more day," would have been a
Thursday, a little more than a week after we'd first arrived in
England. Fatefully, it passed without extraordinary event. As I
recall, we took the last of our guided walking tours, this time

through the heart of the old city, a kind of historical survey hung on a schematic of buildings and ruins of buildings, Guildhall and the Roman temple of Mithras. Though the rain had cleared out, it had left behind overcast skies, much cooler air, and an official suggestion that some large progress had been made in heaven and we were all moving on to the next thing. The Hotel Willerton had become for me a kind of five-story Victorian electromagnet: I could escape its walls, but I couldn't quite leave entirely its field of attraction. Now, with the change in the weather, it had added warmth to its drawing powers. Shivering down quaint cobblestone lanes and ancient alleys, I wanted only to be back at our flat, wanted night to come so I might plumb the darkness, the silence of sleeping souls, so I might listen for voices. During the tour, there was a moment when I seemed to "see" us as if from a distance: A small group of people (in the form of a ragged half-moon) stand looking at a plaque on some damp old building; they listen as the guide (surely an aspiring stage actress) explicates the bit of history it commemorates; one man among them has lowered his head and thus seems turned uncomfortably inward; could he be praying? no, he's only studying his wristwatch.

The night passed without incident as well. Late in the afternoon, I had shopped for vegetables, pasta, and lots of garlic, and I cooked dinner in the flat. We went to the theater, the Royal Shakespeare's *Two Gentlemen of Verona*, returned to the hotel, and telephoned Jordie, whom we found in good spirits. She and Ellen talked first, at great length, and by the time I was handed the telephone, she said, "Well, I told Mom everything already. I love you, I miss you, get her to fill you in on the details . . ."

. . . and we went to bed mostly happy and very tired. Absurdly, I caught myself thinking that the Hotel Willerton knew I needed this promised, contingent day to pass uneventfully, in order to justify our staying and not changing hotels. I thought about how the day had begun, about the dreamlike expedition to the third floor and the dreaming, somnambulant Melanie, the frightened chambermaid, the dreamer within the dream. I thought of the illusional white glove on the stairs and the unnecessary lie told to Ellen in the kitchen. (Why couldn't I have said I heard voices in the hallway, went to investigate, and found Pascal and the chambermaid downstairs? What infantile pathology was I acting out by keeping these superfluous secrets from my wife? It seemed—or so I feared—that I wasn't simply lying but that I was losing the ability to tell the truth.) I fell asleep while Ellen was still writing in her journal, with the bedside lamp still burning.

The next morning, sunlight returned to London, and after my twenty-four-hour reprieve, my uneventful day, I'd been blessed (or cursed) with a kind of amnesia; it was as if we'd only just arrived in England and I'd been handed a spiritual and moral clean slate. I think that when, midmorning, I stood at Hannah's desk downstairs, asking her about the hotel's history, I actually had convinced myself that my inquiry was one of healthy, not to say idle, curiosity.

"Dear me, no," Hannah said, faintly distressed. "I don't think anyone has ever prepared a history. I can tell you that we've been a hotel for about fifty years. The two houses served as a nursing home during the war, and private homes before that. Excuse me."

She pulled a pearl hemisphere from her earlobe and answered the telephone. Into it she said, "Yes . . . yes . . . yes . . . no . . . yes . . . good-bye," with the sort of litany-like monotony that could only have been a response to mundane, domestic questions from someone recently left at home.

"You want to talk to the Chopins," she said to me when she was finished.

"The Chopins?" I said.

"The little couple from Hong Kong," she said. "You've seen them, I'm sure. They're generally here every morning for breakfast . . . live in the neighborhood. Have done forever, and know everything there is to know about . . . well, about most everything. *She* does anyhow. I'm afraid *he's* a bit round the bend. You might speak to Pascal, as Pascal's friendly with them. Excuse me again."

The telephone was again ringing. Quickly, I asked, "Where's Pascal now?" and Hannah, answering the phone, pointed silently to the little video monitor. In it I could see Pascal out front, leaning against one of the canopy's brass poles.

It was just after ten. Ellen was still upstairs, taking an even longer than usual amount of time getting dressed for the day. This was to be our first day of separate ventures. Ellen's fictional sleuth-priest (or priest-sleuth), Flora (true to her name), was an ardent horticulturist; Ellen had decided that some significant business was to take place in the Royal Botanic Gardens at Kew and planned to travel down there for a tour. I had elected the British Museum—theoretically at least. (I had never been to the British Museum, and I'd heard that in the King's Gallery there were some famous old manuscripts, English literary masterpieces; I also wanted to see the Elgin marbles filched from the Parthenon, and the Rosetta Stone.) While Ellen finished getting ready, I, great volunteer that I am, went downstairs to see if I could find her a brochure on Kew Gardens. Thus I had arrived at Hannah's desk and, once there, realized there were things other than Kew Gardens I wanted to learn about.

I stepped into the vestibule, which was quite chilly. Pascal stood in the sunlight at the edge of the canopy, his long shadow stretching across the sidewalk and corrugating up the steps at a sharp angle toward me. I was in shirtsleeves, and cold, so I rapped my knuckles against the glass of the door. Pascal, in a woolen overcoat and sea captain's hat, turned, smiled, and came forward, his breath illuminated by the sun.

"Bonjour, Monsieur Selway," he said, once inside, removing his hat and holding it over his heart—a gesture, I thought, of exaggerated devotion.

"Pascal," I said, "you and I have been through some things together already. Please call me Cook."

"Cook?" he said.

"That's my name," I said.

"Cook?" he said again, obviously unhappy. (I suppose my name put me among the ranks of staff, and so I'd come down in his eyes.)

"Yes," I said. "Cook. That's my name."

"Excuse me, monsieur," he said, "but Cook is a person who prepares the food."

"Yes," I said. "I prepare food on occasion."

"You are a cook?"

"Sort of," I said. "I've been known to be. But that's not why I'm called Cook. My given name is Cookson. I was called Cook long before I ever cooked."

"Interesting," he said.

"Pascal," I said, "Hannah tells me you know the Chopins."

"The Chopins," he said, putting more emphasis on the second syllable of the name. "Yes."

"I wondered if you could introduce me."

"Of course," he said. "Come."

"Come where?"

"They are now here," he said.

"The Chopins are?"

"In the dining room. Come."

We were stopped in the entryway by Hannah. "Oh, Mr. Selway," she said. "I was wondering . . . did you ever find your girl?"

"No," I said. "No, I didn't."

"How peculiar," said Hannah. "I wonder who she might have been. I do wish I had seen her. A teenager, was she?"

Impulsively, I wanted the topic dropped right away, so rather rashly I said, "It's okay, Hannah . . . don't worry about it."

"Oh, dear me," said Hannah. "I wasn't worried." She turned her attention to Pascal. "Pascal," she said, "the Davisons need a parcel brought down."

"J'arrive," said Pascal, and continued down the hallway to the dining room.

"Jah-reeve, jah-reeve," I heard Hannah mumbling as we went.

Pascal told me to wait outside the dining-room door. I supposed he meant to prepare the Chopins for my introduction. I stepped into the sitting room opposite and wandered idly over to the window facing the street. I cannot say what, if anything, I saw outside the window; I stood there (the sheer pulled back) looking, as if I were seeing something outside, but completely absorbed, in fact, by my emotions—which were, at that moment, performing some pretty surprising and inexplicable feats. My sense of time and place grew vague, and I found myself at a window (some window somewhere) and looking out with a prisoner's woe, gazing from his cell; I was experiencing a kind of emotional *déjà vu*, suddenly overtaken by deep distress and sadness. As best I can recall, these feelings didn't attach to any event or condition of my actual life, they didn't ride on any detail in the narrative of loss and self-destruction I might have composed out of the threads of my past. Simply, I felt grief-stricken, apart from any clear reference, and I felt I would cry—no, "cry" is too easy and modern a word—I felt I would throw myself onto the carpet and weep. Simultaneously, I had a strong and fearful sense of someone at my back. When I turned, however, it was only Pascal.

"Monsieur Cook," he said, "are you sick?"

"No, no," I said. "I was just having the oddest feeling is all."

Pascal's black hair was mussed. He still held his cap in one hand, and his cheeks were still red from his having stood out in the cold; his eyes seemed to glisten as he continued to inspect my face. He reached for my arm and said, "Come . . . out of this room."

We walked back into the hall, Pascal clutching me at the elbow and guiding me as if I were blind or infirm. He brushed lint or something from my shoulder—he meant to improve my appearance, make me more presentable.

"You feel okay now?" he asked.

"Yes," I said. "I'm fine."

"The air is not good in that room. Very stale."

"Yes," I said, not at all certain that the air in the sitting room was any staler than in any other room.

"The Chopins are just leaving," he said. "They asked me why you wished to be introduced to them."

"Oh," I said. "Well, I—"

"I did not know the answer."

"What did you tell them?"

"I said that you were an American."

"That's an explanation?"

He shrugged. "I told them you were a nice American guy and that you had a beautiful wife. They said I might bring you around to the flat for—"

At that moment, the dining room door swung open, and the older Asian couple I'd seen once before emerged.

"Oh, here they are . . . ," said Pascal.

The Chopins, seeing us, smiled disparate smiles that were in some way to characterize them for me ever afterward—hers reserved, lips pressed together, much more an event of the eyes than of the mouth; his great and unabashed, full of yellow teeth.

"*Monsieur Selway,*" Pascal said, "*Monsieur et Madame Chopin.*"

I realized then, seeing the Asian couple before me, that Pascal was saying not "Chopin" but "Sho-pan."

In this first encounter, the nearly entirely bald Mr. Sho-pan said not a word. (I must say "nearly entirely," with all its botchery, because I did notice a single white hair, approximately three full inches long, sprouting dead center from the crown of his head.) Mrs. Sho-pan did all the talking, and she was very well-spoken indeed, no trace of a foreign accent. Her hair (that is, all her hairs together), jet black, was pulled tightly to the back of her head; she stood two or three inches taller than he, but that may not always have been the case—I had the feeling he'd shrunk a bit in recent years. Neither of them was especially short or frail, as Hannah had led me to believe with her description of them as the "little couple from Hong Kong." They both were dressed as I'd seen them dressed before, in understated, expensive-looking tweed suits. I mean here that she, too, was wearing a man's-style suit (with pants), and a silk shirt beneath, buttoned at the neck. The old man's necktie had a golfing figure in it.

"I've asked Pascal to bring you and your wife round to the flat for tea," she said. "We're only a stone's throw, you see."

"Oh," I said. "You mean today?"

"Yes," she said, blinking her eyes rapidly several times. "Today . . . if that will do."

I noticed that Mr. Sho-pan's face grew inquiring, almost apprehensive, at that moment, and then, in the next, when I accepted his wife's invitation, returned to its previous wrinkled, toothy ecstasy.

"Thank you," I said, genuinely surprised by this immediate hospitality. "Thank you very much."

"See you at five, then?" she said, offering her hand.

"Yes," I said. "Thank you."

"Five-*ish*," corrected Pascal.

"Five-*ish*, then," said Mrs. Sho-pan, and went up gracefully on tiptoe to kiss Pascal's cheek.

Mr. Sho-pan offered his hand to me, a pleasant, silky, malleable thing you might like to hold on to (and even knead) during a court trial or funeral. Pascal and I then saw both the Sho-pans back to the entryway, where Pascal went to fetch their coats.

Though it was apparent that they required no other explanation of me than the one Pascal had given them—that I was American and had a beautiful wife—and that their obvious trust and affection for Pascal was all the entrée I needed, I took this opportunity to explain that I was interested in learning something of the Hotel Willerton's history. This seemed to please Mrs. Sho-pan enormously.

"And a very interesting history it is," she said, smiling.

"Really?" I said.

"Oh, yes indeed," she said. With her index finger, she

touched the corner of her eye and added, "Very much more than meets the eye."

In that moment I noted that the powerful and unsettling feeling I'd had in the sitting room had thoroughly passed and, secondly, that the Sho-pans' attention had shifted from me to someone just behind me. I expected to see Pascal there, holding their coats, but instead it was Ellen, holding *our* coats.

"Oh, hello," I said, and quickly introduced them all. "The Sho-pans have kindly invited us over to tea this afternoon," I said.

"How nice," said Ellen, perplexed.

She had taken Mrs. Sho-pan's hand, and I noticed—in an almost imperceptible tug and surrender of Ellen's wrist—that Mrs. Sho-pan seemed to retain Ellen briefly. Their eyes met, and they exchanged a little inquisitive (I would say almost probing on Mrs. Sho-pan's part) gaze. Then Mrs. Sho-pan nodded and said two words: "My dear."

Pascal reappeared and began helping them on with their coats. We said our good-byes and see-you-laters, and they were gone.

"Tea?" Ellen said, surprise and delight in her voice. "Who are they?"

"The Sho-pans," I said. "Like *S-h-o-*, you know, *p-a-n*. From Hong Kong, I guess. Friends of Pascal's. They live around here. Pascal's taking us over to their flat around five."

"Fun," Ellen said. "How handsome they are. Did you see the way she looked at me?"

I walked Ellen to the District Line train she would take down to Kew. On the way, she asked me if I'd been able to find a brochure about the gardens. I noted a first impulse to lie, to say, No, there wasn't any brochure, but I corrected myself and said, "I'm sorry . . . I forgot to ask."

"That's okay," she said. "I'll get what I need when I get there."

It seemed so simple and rewarding a thing, telling the truth. I decided to remember that fact in the future. As we passed through the square, the flower vendor, a small old man in a striped apron, held up a bouquet of roses and indicated, with movements of his eyes and head, that I should buy these for Ellen. I smiled, declining the flowers, but I thought there must have been something about Ellen and me, about the way we looked this morning together, that suggested romance. Maybe we looked happy together, maybe in love. There was a pleasant crispness to the air, the shadows of the trees in the square made lovely trembling lace patterns on the walkways, and I put my arm around Ellen's waist as we went along. This is how things should have been from the start, I thought. A holiday.

We said good-bye on the sidewalk, outside the tube station. After we kissed, Ellen said, "Are you sure you don't want to change your mind and come with me?"

"Do you want me to?" I asked.

"Only if you want to," she said. "I mean I want you to do what you want to do."

"Well, I'll come if you really want me to," I said.

We both laughed then. She said, "I'm happy to go alone. I just want you to know you're welcome to come."

"I know," I said, and kissed her again. "Have fun."

"I'll be back by four," she said. "I'm looking forward to our tea."

She entered the station, and I stood watching through the open door as she purchased her ticket, went through the gate and toward the stairs. Just before she started down them, something (the intensity of my watching?) made her turn and look back. Over some distance and through the busy counterpoint of the travelers, she saw me in the doorway and waved. Then she was gone. I stood still a moment longer, until a stranger, a woman in a bright-red coat, scolded me for blocking the station door. As I walked away, across the street and toward the square, I did something I'd done from time to time over the years: I recalled Jordie's birth—that is, I recalled Ellen's giving birth to Jordie. It came to me, as it always had, in brief segments, in random order: my touching Ellen's brow with a wet cloth (asking permission each time);

her clutching the front of my shirt; her rapid-fire "I can't I can't I can't I can't . . . ," even as the top of Jordie's head appeared in the broadening portal like a huge lavender egg; the doctor's "Reach down, Ellen, and take your baby"; Ellen's white arms, her Eureka-like, awestruck "My *baby* . . . my *baby* . . ."

By the time I turned the corner into Willerton Way and saw Pascal at his post (at his pole, actually) beneath the edge of the canopy, the memory of Jordie's birth had taken me to a certain insight, to a certain metaphor—not, I'm the first to admit, brilliant by any means, but helpful in an indefinite, comforting way—a view of my years with Ellen (of our years together) as a stream that splits from time to time for durations of various length, some brief, some painfully sustained, into two smaller streams, then reunites, splits and reunites, with a happy recognition, despite any amount of babbling and gurgling, of gained power, of gained breadth and depth in each reunion. This marriage-as-river analogy made me very happy, and it occurred to me (along with about eleven billion Buddhists before me) that all turbulence, all turmoil, occurs in the mind, and all that's ever really needed for happiness is a satisfactory way of thinking about things—or a satisfactory way to stop thinking about things, I suppose. Having forgotten altogether the fleeting "oddest feeling," the deep invading grief of the sitting room, I was happy with my marriage, happy to be in England, happy to have recovered a self that could once again manage life in a reasonable way and be at peace. In short, I felt restored, with the help of a pantomiming flower vendor, to my right mind. My interests in the unusual aspects of the Hotel Willerton were being pursued in a sane fashion at last, a simple course of inquiry, aboveboard, and I wasn't walking around obsessed and ashamed for most of a day.

Pascal had just put someone into a taxi, and now, hat in hand, he waved full-armed at me, as if he were hailing me from the deck of a ship. As I stepped off the curb and began to cross the street, something caught my eye from above, in

the vicinity of the windows to our flat—a quick movement
. . . a change of light . . . something—but when I looked
up, I saw nothing at all; I thought maybe a pigeon had flown
from the ledge outside our windows. The taxi passed just in
front of me. Its passenger was the chambermaid, Melanie,
whom I hadn't seen since our early-morning encounter on the
third floor. As the cab passed by, she looked through the
window at me. I gave her a friendly-greeting kind of smile,
but she pointedly did not smile back. Rather ominously, I
thought, she even turned her head as the cab went along,
keeping her eyes on me for a ways up the street. Staying true
to my sane and simple course of inquiry, I decided, then,
crossing the street, to interview the chambermaid later, to get
the details of whatever it was that had frightened her.

When I reached the canopy, however, Pascal looked at
me in a resigned sort of way, gazed down to the corner where
the cab had disappeared, and said, "This girl had some problems, you know."

"What do you mean, 'had'?" I asked.

"She is going back to Mama," he said.

With disappointment, I told him I'd wanted to talk to
the girl, about what had frightened her.

He dismissed this idea (and my disappointment) with a
smirk and a shake of his head. "She had fantasies," he said.
"Please don't think about it. You know, Monsieur Cook, I
have heard something about young girls like this. They have
the . . . *comment dit-on* . . . the horrormones, you know.
The imagination of a young girl . . ."

Pascal, I should point out, couldn't have been more than
two or three years older than the chambermaid. Her departure—my sudden witness of it—had prompted me to dive
into something I hadn't planned to dive into, not right then
anyway, and the rest of our conversation under the canopy
proceeded with a good deal of self-consciousness on my part,
since in it I revealed myself, in completely conventional
terms, as a looney-tune. I corrected his pronunciation of "hor-
mones" and told him I wasn't at all sure that Melanie's experi-

ences were the product of an overwrought adolescent imagination.

"*Harr*mones," he said. "What do you mean, you are not sure?"

"I mean," I said, "that I've had some strange experiences of my own."

"What kind of experiences?"

"If I tell you, Pascal, I want you to promise to keep it to yourself. I don't want Ellen frightened unnecessarily."

"Sure, okay," he said.

"Well, I know how this sounds," I said, "but I do think there is some kind of . . . I don't know . . . spirit or something living in the flat."

A little laugh escaped him, and then he made a scary face and an *oooooo* sound, antics that were clearly nervous reactions, not intended to ridicule. I thought he was probably regretting having hooked me up with his friends the Shopans, now that I had revealed my true colors.

"You mean a ghost, monsieur?" he said at last.

"Whatever," I said, rejecting the word's pedestrian, storybook flavor. "That's why I wanted to talk to the girl. To see if her experience was anything like mine."

He scratched the top of his head, put his hat back on, and looked across the street. He seemed to be thinking hard, serious now, and then he said, "You are not having me on, monsieur?"

"No, Pascal," I said. "I'm not having you on. I know how it sounds, but I'm not joking. I promise."

He shrugged his shoulders. When next he spoke, he was self-defensive: "She told me an evil spirit had tried to molest her, monsieur. It sounded crazy."

"Molest her?"

"She said he touched her in a bad way and scratched her face. And I—" He gazed sadly down the street for a moment. "I was mean to this girl, monsieur."

"It's okay, Pascal," I said. "It's best that she went home anyway."

He shook his head quickly, as if to say, No, no, you don't understand. "I was mean to her," he said. "I treated her very badly."

About half an hour later, just as I was finishing a sandwich before setting off to the museum, he came knocking at the door. He declined to enter the flat, however, saying that he was wanted downstairs.

"This girl," he said, "she was an artist. I found this in her room."

He handed me a pencil sketch on stiff watercolor paper: a bit crude, the fierce demeanor perhaps a bit exaggerated, but without a doubt a portrait of the bearded man I'd seen in the bed.

Somehow Pascal seemed already to know what it was he'd handed me. And somehow the expression on his face conveyed a perfect and remarkable blend of contrition and skepticism. He said, "I want to meet this spirit, monsieur."

I didn't know what to say, but Pascal didn't wait for a reply, in any case.

When he'd gone, I took the drawing into the kitchen, ignited a burner on the range, held one corner of the drawing over the flame, and set it afire; at the last second I tossed it into the sink, then crushed the ashes with a scrub brush and washed them down the drain.

Throughout this procedure, I had a sense that someone was watching me. I'd felt the same thing a few minutes earlier, as I made and then ate my sandwich. I felt it still as I went back to the sitting room and found my coat. Finally, I left the flat, locking the door behind me.

Waiting for the elevator to come, I thought that my little reformation, my brief hours of being "left alone" by the Hotel Willerton, my convenient amnesia, my decision to pursue my ominous interests reasonably and sensibly—all this— had been a unilateral change on my part; and with some vague fear (and possibly with some amount of solipsism), I thought my presence at the hotel, my eager nurturing of un- usual events, had set something in motion, something that wouldn't necessarily conform to my changing attitudes. I could hear the elevator coming and could see, through the window in the door, the moving cable; I observed with interest that knowing the cable to move was not actually a thing seen but a thing not seen: when it was stationary, you could see the braids in the metal rope; when it was moving, it appeared solid, without any pattern. Impulsively, I patted the hip pocket of my pants and discovered I'd left my wallet inside the flat. Lamenting the fact that the elevator would come and go while I retrieved my wallet, and then I would have to wait for it again, I returned to the other end of the hall, inserted my key, and opened the door.

On opening it, however, I closed it again quickly, thinking stupidly for a split second that I'd entered the wrong apartment; the moment was disorienting and oddly embarrassing, like thinking you're pushing open the door to a men's room, when it turns out to be the ladies'. What I'd seen—all I'd seen, actually—was a room with a gaudy wallpaper, extremely floral, bright-pink peonies or some equally broad effulgent flower on a gray background. Of course I immediately realized it couldn't have been the wrong flat, as it was the only flat on the floor and I had myself opened it with my own key. I pushed open the door again.

Directly across the room, outside the tall window opposite, staring straight at me through the glass, was the girl I'd met in the sitting room downstairs. She was brightly lit by the sun and dressed as before, in the sailor dress. The sight of her so startled me that I cried out loud, just as if I'd been punched in the stomach; I may have even doubled over with the force of it, for somehow I banged my head, hard, on the edge of the door. I quickly shook the little stars from my eyes, went to the window, and threw it open. Breathless, I put my head out, looking right and left along the stone ledge and down into the street. But the street was empty, and she was gone.

CHAPTER

Eight

THE SHO-PANS' FLAT —on the ground floor in one of the cream-colored residential buildings along the narrow street running perpendicular to Willerton Way—was exactly seven hundred and fifty-three steps from the blue-and-white-striped hotel canopy, excluding the two steps leading down into their little slate-floored vestibule. (Why I counted our footsteps as we walked along I can't say for sure. It seems to me that Ellen and Pascal, paired and just ahead of me by five steps, were having a lively conversation and that the conversation was about shrubbery; one of them mentioned a tunnel hollowed out of glossy privet. While counting, I was struck by the fact that their talk was in no way detoured by our meeting a runner, a very fast male runner of middle age and scanty attire, whose face, foremost like a ship's figurehead, wore an almost rabid expression of pain transforming into ecstasy. Admittedly, it was the sort of thing that had always grabbed my attention, like certain wide-angled, narratively irrelevant close-ups in old Fellini movies, but I would have thought the man's face would grab the attention of anyone, especially anyone having a conversation about shrubbery. We met the runner on the five-hundred-and-forty-second step of our walk—five-hundred-and-forty-seventh for Ellen and Pascal—where a corroding iron downspout, with the myriad coloring and pockmarked texture of a Jackson Pollock painting, hugged the building near my right, arthritis-prone shoulder. How do I account for all this trivia-gathering? I had been astonished and badly frightened by the girl at the window a few hours before—as I played it over in my mind, I realized that I'd astonished and badly frightened *her* as well, causing her to teeter on the ledge and fall—and like similar, recent frights, it had remained undisclosed by me to anyone; singled out for private, scary encounters like this, I was distanced from the world, and doubly distanced by my secrecy; now I was clinging to real, though sometimes trifling, physical details, even if I had partly to invoke them, as a means of keeping myself present. This wordy explanation will have to do. It's the only one I have.)

The round drain in the Sho-pans' vestibule, like the ones commonly found in bathroom showers, comprised twenty-two holes; I'd just finished counting them when we were greeted at the door by Mr. Sho-pan—greeted only in the broadest sense of the word: he held the door for us and silently hand-motioned us forward into a dark, wood-paneled hallway. It turned out that Mr. Sho-pan's voice, like the woodwork so prominent throughout their flat, was deep and polished, but he reserved it for pithy remarks—or, more specifically, shorthand references to what were probably pithy remarks. In any case, "Hello," "Welcome," "Won't you come in," and such were not part of his repertoire. Two bright crystal sconces protruded from the wall on either side of the door to a parlor, where, immediately inside, there was the odor of wet wool. (I only name the smell for I was never able to account for it.) We were ushered straight through this room, appointed with much old-world mahogany and bric-a-brac, into an adjacent room, where a table was laid for tea. There Mrs. Sho-pan took charge, and Mr. Sho-pan, his assignment fulfilled, was retired.

The Sho-pans hadn't changed clothes from the morning and were pleasantly recognizable in their nearly matching tweed suits. Mrs. Sho-pan seemed at first a little excited, like a horse just let out of the gate. Glancing round the room rapidly, she said, almost shrilly, "We're so many, I've put us out here at the big table. . . ." Of course we were not so many, only five, but I thought the remark said a lot about the Sho-pans, about how they lived. I noticed that Mr. Sho-pan was viewing himself in the glass panes of the china cabinet, straightening his necktie. "Pascal, be a dear," Mrs. Sho-pan continued, "and take Mr. and Mrs.—oh my word, what am I saying? For once, Pascal, do *not* be a dear and do *not* take anyone's coat. Let me . . ."

And so we were uncoated, the brightness of the chandelier over the dining room table was lowered, and after a brief flurry of who would sit where, Mrs. Sho-pan began to settle down and recover her usual, striking poise. Throughout tea, I fell back, anytime I felt I might be slipping away, on my observer status, collecting data about the food that was served (cold lamb sandwiches, homemade chutney, lemon cookies dipped in chocolate), the china (Shelley of England, Blue Rock 13591), and the sherry (dark-green bottle, white label, from Spain—how could anything so quietly civilized and sweet-smelling embody so ruinous a drug?). Once, Ellen

caught me reading the bottom of my empty teacup and shook
her head at me quickly. But soon I noticed that the data I
collected were almost entirely things to admire—Mr. Sho-
pan's amazing, mute engagement with all that went on, his
subtly changing face conveying every necessary response, his
socks with the identical golfing figure found in his tie; Mrs.
Sho-pan's firm presence, her insistence on eye contact, the
thin gold bracelet she would shake down now and then to
the widening part of her wrist; the resonant chime of the
clock in the parlor, and seventeen marble eggs displayed
(each with its own little carved pedestal) on the dining room
mantel; Pascal's affection for the Sho-pans, theirs for him, and
the fact of their finding each other—and I lost touch with the
oddity of our being together. I began to see our gathering as
simplehearted and lucky. (I began to see it, this next stop in
our London passage, the way Leonard Bernstein once said the
next note in a song should be—fresh and inevitable.) I was
drawn in by the occasion, drawn out of my stupor of fear and
confusion and dark self-centeredness, and despite all that was
to follow in the way of what might be called information, the
mode in which the evening was to live on for me was in a
mode of feeling.

The Sho-pans had come to Britain in the 1920s, when
they both were children. Their two families had left Hong
Kong together, even lived together in this same flat. "There
was great unrest in Hong Kong," Mrs. Sho-pan told us with
the noticeable lack of soul that comes from having used a
phrase too much. "I can remember almost nothing of our lives
there," she said. "Ray can remember some things because he
was a bit older when we emigrated."

Everyone looked at Mr. Sho-pan with expectation, but
he only wrinkled his brow and nodded. Then, after all eyes
had returned to Mrs. Sho-pan, we heard a single word uttered
deep and precise from his end of the table: "China," he'd said,
and at first it wasn't certain which usage of the word he'd
meant; I, for one, looked at the cracks in my dinner plate. A
pause, a silence. Then Mrs. Sho-pan said, "Yes, whatever went
on in China eventually affected the British colony. China was

all agitated with nationalism, and when China was agitated, it wasn't long before Hong Kong was agitated. Would anyone like more tea?"

Meanwhile, Ellen had done some quick math. "It must have been the *late* twenties then," she said.

Mrs. Sho-pan turned to her and smiled. "Why, yes, dear," she said, as if she were very proud of Ellen for having figured that out.

"In fact," said Ellen, "I can't even believe . . . well, I mean, you can't be old enough to have—"

Mrs. Sho-pan, anticipating Ellen's words, and completely delighted by each one of them, interrupted. "How old do you think I am?" she said.

Ellen, embarrassed, said, "I don't know . . . I wouldn't have thought more than sixty."

"I'll be seventy-one in February," Mrs. Sho-pan said, pleased with herself.

"That's impossible," said Ellen.

Mrs. Sho-pan couldn't have agreed more. "Still," she said, tilting her head to one side, blinking her eyes once very slowly, "it's true."

This moment, the revelation of her age, had of course been orchestrated—gracefully orchestrated but orchestrated—and it was clear to me that Pascal and Mr. Sho-pan had seen and heard it all before. In Pascal's sea of affection, a tiny piece of flotsam drifted by (patience, tolerance), but Mr. Sho-pan was way beyond any such impure waters. Looking at him, I thought there were no rating systems still intact behind those half-closed eyes, no panel of judges. He helped himself—reaching toward the middle of the table with remarkable focus—to another lemon cookie.

Once the topic of age had been opened, we were all obliged to reveal our ages, and as far as I know, only Mr. Sho-pan lied: he claimed to be eighty-six, and was corrected, sotto voce by Mrs. Sho-pan, to seventy-six. Pascal, his next birthday, would be twenty-two (the same as the number of holes in the Sho-pans' vestibule drain, a coincidence that made me think briefly of taking up numerology). Pascal had been in England for two years, not having returned home even for a visit, and all of which time he'd been working at the Hotel Willerton.

"I am making perfect my English," he said directly to me.

"You are *perfecting* your English," Mrs. Sho-pan said.

Pascal shrugged, as if to say, "See what I mean." He told us he'd put away nearly all his wages, and soon he intended to take his nest egg back to France and start up an inn with a friend.

"And you'll do very well indeed," said Mrs. Sho-pan. "Pascal has two of the most important qualities for success in the hotel business. He's naturally gregarious and frugal."

"These fancy English words mean nosy and cheap," said Pascal.

"Not at all," Mrs. Sho-pan said. "Gregarious simply means you enjoy people."

"And frugal means cheap," he said.

Mrs. Sho-pan turned to Ellen and said abruptly: "Now tell us what has brought *you* to England."

"Oh," said Ellen, startled, and then, prompted along the way by other inquiries, gave a somewhat more than thumbnail sketch of our lives. Of course, she left out the part about my addiction to drugs and alcohol, and the fact that my overwhelmingly successful restaurant business in New York was founded on the backs of Bolivian peasants who risked their lives and the lives of their children to bring the coca leaves over the mountain. Ellen was not inclined, as I was, to self-mutilation. (Just because The Past always hung there upon its hooks on the game-room wall, you didn't have to pull it down and use it on yourself.) To my complete admiration—I would say almost to my awe—she spun a tale that included the nuthatches and black-capped chickadees and horrible bully starlings that visited the feeder outside the kitchen windows in Cambridge. Somehow, miraculously, it even included white birches and dead poplars and the Head of the Charles Regatta, which I couldn't have given two whits for. Undoubtedly she drew on her writer's powers—her palette held a better-than-average range of colors—but there was nothing false or overblown in her description: this life, her life, full of the world, was one she was committed to, rooted in. My life, on the other hand, full of the great, heavy-heeled self, was like a second or third date: intriguing, but I was still learning the ropes and I wasn't really sure yet that I was going to stick around. I envied Ellen's confidence and her—what's the word?—belongingness, yes, but more than that: her integrity. . . . I envied her integrity. When she got to Jordie and the boarding school, I saw something pass between Pascal and the Sho-pans, the briefest exchange of glances, an almost involuntary nod to some private trouble. And when Ellen was done, it seemed Mrs. Sho-pan had got stuck back at the beginning: she said, "And you're at work on your book even while you're here . . . in England?"

"Well, sort of," said Ellen. "I'm making notes. And I jot down a sentence now and then when it occurs to me."

"Interesting," Mrs. Sho-pan said, nodding. "No doubt someone is in danger in your murder mystery?"

"Well, yes," said Ellen. "Or soon to be. Why do you ask?"

"Nothing important now," she said cryptically. "Now that I understand. Tell me, Mr. Selway—"

"Call me Cook," I said.

Pascal laughed and said, "He wants everyone to call him Cook."

"Well, it is my name," I said. "I don't see what's odd about it."

"Your name is Cook?" said Mrs. Sho-pan.

"Yes," I said. "Short for Cookson. Cookson was my mother's maiden name."

"I see," she said. "I must tell you that all afternoon I've found myself thinking about the Hotel Willerton. . . . What was it specifically you wanted to know?"

I attempted, as best I could, to ignore the look of surprise on Ellen's face. I said, "Anything, really. I'm just curious about old hotels."

"I never knew you were curious about old hotels," said Ellen.

"Well, I am," I said.

Mrs. Sho-pan was looking at her husband, who seemed on the verge of another utterance. But it passed with a wave of his hand, and she said, "I suppose you've already realized that the hotel is actually made up of two houses."

"Yes," I said. "Mid-Victorian, I believe."

"That's right," she said. "And then they were acquired during the war for use as a nursing home. I think that's when they were first joined together. Walls knocked out and such."

"Maternity," said Mr. Sho-pan.

"Yes," said his wife. "It was mostly maternity. The most extraordinary thing . . . Ray and I once met a woman from Whitby, one morning in the dining room at breakfast, who'd been *born* in the hotel—that is, who'd been born in the nursing home. Isn't that extraordinary?"

"You said the houses were acquired," I said. "How were they acquired?"

"Well, purchased, I suppose," she said. "The same people owned both houses. They lived in one and let the other, I believe. Then they sat empty for a while, the houses, before the war came along and . . . Ray, what was their name?"

"Banks," Mr. Sho-pan said. "Shanks. Hanks. Janks. Jenks. *Jenkins.*"

"Something," said Mrs. Sho-pan.

"Two brothers," Mr. Sho-pan added.

"That's right," Mrs. Sho-pan said. "We didn't know them. You see, we'd only been here a few years, and Ray and I were still children, really . . . well, Ray would have been a teenager. The only reason we knew *of* them was because of the accident."

"What accident?" I said.

"There was a terrible accident," she said. She turned to Ellen, whom she sat beside, and placed her hand on Ellen's forearm. "You would be interested in this," she said. "There was a good deal of mystery surrounding the thing when it happened, and as far as I know, nothing was ever really cleared up." She paused for a moment and closed her eyes, thinking.

Pascal, bless him, said, "What *happened?*"

"Oh," she said, "I wish I could remember exactly. It was a frightful thing. Really frightful. Someone jumped out a window, I believe. I want to say there was a fire, but I don't think that's right. I'm very possibly mixing things up."

"He pushed her," Mr. Sho-pan said.

"Who pushed whom?" Mrs. Sho-pan asked.

Mr. Sho-pan, apparently stumped, ignored this question entirely.

Mrs. Sho-pan shook her head. "He doesn't know."

"The girl," said Mr. Sho-pan.

"The girl?" said Mrs. Sho-pan. "Oh, yes, there was a young girl, the daughter of one of the brothers. Was it the girl who jumped, Ray?"

He ignored this question too.

"He doesn't know," she said. "The matter was never cleared up. I believe there was some work done to the houses afterward. The facades were changed in some way. That ledge up top was added, that ornate piece, whatever you call it. I wonder what ever happened to the poor people who'd lived there. It was two brothers. Ray's right about that."

"What about the mother?" Ellen asked. "Wasn't there a mother?"

"I believe the man was a widower," answered Mrs. Sho-pan. "Eventually, we noticed that the houses, both of them, were sitting empty."

She thought for a moment, then raised one eyebrow and said, "You've piqued my interest, Mr. Selway . . . Cookson, I mean. Isn't it frustrating that Ray and I once knew all this? And now, though it's still recorded somewhere inside our heads, we can't get at it."

Pascal, from across the table, held up his spoon, dangling it like a pendulum, pretending to hypnotize Mrs. Sho-pan. Ellen rather overlaughed at this antic.

Mrs. Sho-pan was undiverted. "Well," she said, "there were newspapers back in the thirties, and I've a friend at the library. A very good friend at the library."

A brief silence fell over the room, in which I noticed Pascal looking meaningfully at me; I was looking meaningfully at Ellen, who was looking meaningfully into the few inches of air directly in front of her face. This meant that her wheels were turning: Flora, summoned to London by the old aunt, discovers a quaint little hotel near Sloane Square. Something draws her to the place, something she can't quite explain. She begins lunching at the hotel and soon meets an attractive Asian couple she sees there most every day. She learns through them that . . .

"Ellen's wheels are turning," I said finally, which made everyone laugh and in some way brought an end to that particular conversation.

It came up again a bit later, as we were leaving. Ellen had helped Mrs. Sho-pan with the dishes, and Mr. Sho-pan had taken Pascal and me into the parlor, where he hauled out his insect collection for us to look at. (The Sho-pans had been schoolteachers—he'd taught science, she'd taught history.) When things had finally wound down, the evening come to an end, and they'd shown us into the hall, I noticed a framed illustration I hadn't seen on the way in: a drawing of the human hand, the palm, labeled with all the names of the various lines and segments. While the others were exchanging farewells, I stood studying the names. At last I said, "Who's interested in palmistry?"

Everyone turned. After a moment, Mrs. Sho-pan answered, "Our son was. David. He died a few years ago. It was one of his hobbies."

"I'm sorry," I said.

"Thank you," she said. "He was a lovely boy."

On my way out the door, Mr. Sho-pan touched my arm and whispered, "He pushed her."

At first I thought it was a reference to the dead son, David—I was still thinking about him—but I quickly understood that he referred to the mysterious accident of some sixty years ago. I nodded a kind of confidential, collusive nod, thanked him, and said good-bye one last time.

When we were on the sidewalk, when we'd taken in the fact of the darkness and the fine cold mist that was falling, Pascal said, "It was AIDS. He died only a few years ago, just before I came to work at the hotel. I think it is why they like having me around for company."

A little farther along, Ellen said, "Do you know what she said to me in the kitchen? She said she sensed, this morning in the hotel when we first met, that I was in some kind of danger."

"Really?" I said.

"Yes," she said. "That's why she asked me those questions about the book. She thought she must've been picking up on the danger Flora would be in."

"Interesting," I said, carelessly, distantly, probably insultingly, but I was on overload—too much input. Ellen and Pascal drifted ahead again, just by a few steps, and I took up a mental recitation that went something like: First phalanx, second phalanx, Mount of Venus, Mount of Jupiter, Mount of the Moon, ring of Venus, line of the heart, line of the head, line of life, line of fate, line of fortune, line of health, will, reason, love, line of marriage . . .

deaconry of Lindesfarne (1870), when he wrote: "The walls were standing . . . though not in their integrity." Or to use a more domestic analogy, I mean it in the sense of a completed jigsaw puzzle—no stray piece lost under the couch in the den, all pieces fitting together (none forced) and revealing a coherent, sensible picture that suggests that things couldn't be any other way.

Now why should this be true of Ellen?

That night, while she was in the bathroom, I lay naked under the covers of my twin bed, thinking: She wasn't a drug addict or an alcoholic, but she was that other kind of personality, the one attracted to addicts. Her mother and father were alcoholics, in and out of dry docks before the (suspicious) car crash that killed them, and there were at least two other boyfriends who had (she has allowed) "little substance-abuse problems." And then of course there was the great climax to this tendency, me. As far as I know, this particular habit doesn't kill brain cells—that was in her favor—and then there had been the miracle, Jordie, who, in her baby form, provided an appropriate receptacle for all Ellen's rampant attachment. (I recalled Ellen's telling me, on returning home from a meeting with other nursing mothers, that when she'd expressed concern about her obsession with the baby, the leader of the group had said, "Look at it from the baby's point of view, Ellen—if your mother doesn't obsess about you, who's going to obsess about you?") It was irritating to me that Ellen got to act out her mild insanity, even to deplete it, and all that happened as a result was that she was a good mother. And here, I thought, I'd hit on the problem. I hadn't found the appropriate receptacle. (Since my own not-so-mild insanity was self-destruction, finding an appropriate receptacle might be difficult: if instead of destroying myself I destroyed someone else, would this be progress?) Ellen also had an art, the mystery stories, into which she could channel all sorts of energies, good and bad. I had no art. I had no art and no receptacle. What I'd noticed especially, back at the Sho-pans', was how she'd included the world—she'd actually defined herself using outside elements—me, Jordie, the house, Cambridge, Spencer, the birds in the backyard, for Christ's sake. Whereas I saw the world as a medium, the thing through which the mighty drugged Self plowed, a thing to be excavated and transformed. Despite my rehabilitation over the years, I was still—and I'm trying to say this with humility—the big noisy machine in the landscape. And I was still standing, though not in my integrity.

Ellen came in and climbed under the covers with me. She said, "Are you going to read?"

"No," I said, and she switched off the lamp.

We lay side by side, on our backs, in the dark, the lovely star-gazing arrangement that always made me feel we were about to be cast together down a river or launched into space.

"It's so sad, isn't it," she said, "the Sho-pans. And yet really touching too."

"What . . . about the son?"

"Yes," she said. "That they had this son they loved so much and then he died of AIDS and then sweet Pascal came along and entered their lives."

"Yeah, and a palmist, to boot. A gay palmist."

"You don't know he was gay," she said. "Just because he died of AIDS."

"That's true," I said.

"I really liked them," she said.

"I did too."

"It's amazing that they grew up together."

"And that they've lived in that flat together since they were kids," I said.

"You had asked her about the hotel, hadn't you?"

"Actually," I said, "I asked Hannah, and Hannah referred me to the Sho-pans."

"That's how we got invited to tea."

"Yes."

"You asked because of the weird stuff that's happened . . . the scary stuff. That's why you wanted to know about the hotel's history."

"Yes."

"Because you think whatever's going on is some kind of spiritual thing, lingering from the past."

"Yes. Maybe. I don't know."

"And do you think that's what she was sensing in me? The danger?"

"I don't know," I said. "I hope not."

"You don't think we're in any kind of danger, do you?"

"No," I said. "I don't think so. No."

"Because I don't want to be in any kind of danger, Cook."

"I know," I said.

"I'm not especially interested in danger."

"I know, Ellen. Believe me, I know that about you. I understand what you're saying. You know me to be a person who has been interested in it from time to time. And you're not like that. I understand. Don't worry, okay?"

After a few seconds of silence, she said, "I felt really homesick tonight at the Sho-pans'."

"You did?"

"I felt it earlier today too. When I was by myself at the botanical gardens. I was in one of the greenhouses, and there was this smell. I've no idea what it was—"

"Probably manure," I said. "Probably—"

"No, it was a kind of clean, water and dirt and rock smell . . . you know, a warm air and earth smell. And I longed to be back home."

She paused for a moment, and I suddenly thought she was telling me she wanted to go home. With some surprise, I said, "You want to go home?"

"No, no," she said. "It just pleases me that we have a life I miss that much. You know, when I began to feel homesick, in the greenhouse, it was a lonely feeling. I felt so far away from home. And then I remembered that you were here with me in England. That I'd be getting back on a train in a little while and that you'd be waiting here for me at the hotel. And I thought how very lucky I was."

"That's nice," I said.

"And even tonight at the Sho-pans' . . . just for a moment, I felt it again, that homesickness, that loneliness, and then I thought of this—right now—that in a couple of hours we'd be lying together in our little room, and we'd be together, and once again I thought how lucky . . . how very lucky . . ."

Maybe it was these words of Ellen's that did the trick, but that night, as we began to make love the last time we were to make love at the Willerton—I was of one mind. There was no part of me separated from our togetherness, off in pursuit of a more exotic high. I did no manipulating, no watching of the dark.

Only, as I said before, something had been set in motion at the Hotel Willerton that wouldn't necessarily conform to my changing attitudes:

"Wait . . . wait . . . wait . . . ," Ellen said breathlessly, flattening her hands on my chest, pushing me upward. "Are you okay, Cook?"

"What? What's wrong?"

"Nothing," she said. "Nothing, I guess. Sorry."

Then, less than a minute later, again: "Wait . . . wait . . ."

"What?"

Now she drew me down, pulling my head toward her, so she could whisper in my ear. "I don't know what's going on, Cookie, but do you have the feeling we're being watched?"

"No," I said, mainly because it was the shortest answer I could think of: it was a bad time to be interrupted, and if I considered what she'd said at all, any such consideration was obliterated by a too-late-to-turn-back-now mindlessness—at the peak of which, I happened to catch a glimpse of something, a hint of movement, out of the corner of my eye. At first I thought that someone was in the other bed, the short-fused, hungover visitor I'd encountered before. But when I turned my head and actually looked, he was slouching in the chair beyond the bed and against the wall—shirtless, pants unbuckled, grinning, hands behind his head, just having the best old time.

I did not cry out, but I startled sufficiently to startle Ellen. I sort of collapsed on her, hard, as if a bomb had exploded in the room and I meant to protect her with my own body.

"Oh, God," she said, frightened. "God, what is it?"

"Nothing," I said—truthfully, in a way, for he was already gone.

"What happened?" she asked. "Did you . . . you didn't . . . that wasn't . . ."

"I don't know," I said. "I got a cramp in my leg."

"A cramp?"

"I'm okay."

"Goodness, you scared me. . . ."

"Sorry."

We had in the course of things kicked the covers to the floor. Without really moving off her, I reached down with one arm and pulled them up, over us. There was a significant, transitional moment of silence in which I remained perfectly still, as if I were paralyzed.

Finally, she said, "Which leg, Cookie?"

"What?"

"Which leg? Which leg had the cramp?"

"Oh, this one," I said, shaking my right leg a little.

"Well, has it gone away? Are you okay now?"

"Just about," I said, and slowly, gradually, I became aware of a ringing in my ears, a white electrical hum inside my head, a crude music of sorts, solitary harmony, solitary rhythm, the primordial sound my brain was making.

At some point, Ellen whispered, sadly, "But Pascal's going to leave them too."

I nodded, my face moving up and down in the curve of her neck.

"Honey," she said after another moment or two, "you're kind of crushing me."

. . .

When I awoke, I was alone. The drapes had been opened and one window raised a couple of inches. I could hear a chorus of voices from the street below: male voices and singing, a drinking song, or a fighting song, members of a rugby team, high on winning, strolling with arms around each other's shoulders and singing . . . or so I imagined in my state of dazed reentry. By the time I thought to get out of bed, walk to the window, and look down—and made the first half-hearted movement to do so—the singing had already faded away. I could see by the clock on the dresser that it was nearly eleven in the morning. Even before stirring, I could tell that my joints, especially my knees and elbows, were stiff and achy; there was a tenderness in the muscles of my stomach and a feverish heat behind my eyes. A faint odor of stale whisky seemed to come from under the bedsheet.

The dream from which I'd awakened was calling me back, broadcasting its general, eely flashiness without particulars. Had it been about the British Museum? I lay staring at the ceiling, trying to catch the thing by the tail as it swam in and quickly back out of reach again. No, not about the museum, but the museum was perhaps the hook. I had in fact gone there the previous afternoon, sticking to my plan as a kind of lifesaving mechanism. Of course, the experience of seeing the girl on the ledge, of having been frightened half out of my wits, stayed with me like a kind of persistent nausea, but physically I was there, at the museum. I'd taken myself to the tube, got the Circle Line to Embankment, got the Northern Line to Tottenham Court Road station, walked too far down the Tottenham Court Road to the other side of Bedford Square, but eventually found my way. I recalled passing the open door of a porno shop, in which, as I passed, an entire wall of shelved videos crashed to the floor and two long-haired young men inside began a row about who was to blame. The rest of the afternoon was less specific than this, a grand museum opera with Wagnerian, marble sets and the too-often-repeated theme of . . . what? Parallel lines: the steps outside, the stairs inside, the famous manuscripts,

Beowolf, Morte d'Arthur, Sir Walter Raleigh's autograph note-book for his *History of the World, Jane Eyre, Nicholas Nickleby, Sonnets from the Portuguese,* lines and more lines, the closely packed hieroglyphics and demotic characters chiseled into the Rosetta Stone, the astonishing, fluid crevices of the Elgin marbles, lines upon dark lines . . . lines like the ruts in the dirt road . . . yes, the dirt road in the painting by Meindert Hobbema . . . and the dream came back to me as if I were reading it in a psychology textbook—it was, in fact, a text-book dream: I'm inside the painting by Meindert Hobbema, walking down the rutted country road and thinking about the future. I believe that my dog, Spencer, is with me, though not in any important way. I notice a man working in a vineyard off to my left, and I think he probably has a wife and children back in the nearby thatched-roof house, a family whose safety depends on the toils of his labors, his care and dili-gence, the success of the vineyard. I hope that one day I, too, will have that kind of situation—a wife, some kids, the simple design in which the work of my hands directly provides har-bor for those I love. How satisfying that would be! I look up at the spindly trees on either side of me and allow the vast-ness of the sky to overwhelm me, thinking how like flowers the trees are, with their tall stems and black crowns. When I return my attention to the road, an enormous bull stands dead ahead, head lowered, eyes trained on me, and I think, Don't be afraid, this is a dream . . . but I'm aware, too, of the village in the distance behind me, of how, back in the village, something has gone terribly wrong, and beneath my mental chanting, This is a dream, don't be afraid, is another thought, another voice, which says, You have no future, you have no future; given what has come before, how can you possibly go on? The ruts in the road, deep, black lines, al-ready connect us, me and the bull, and as he begins his charge, I think with horror, This *isn't* a dream, and the horns enter me beneath my ribs and I am lifted by my rib cage into the air—my feet leaving the road, dangling spiritless like a marionette's . . . the last thing I observe, my poor feet, be-fore I die.

I didn't spend any time analyzing the dream—I didn't seem to myself equipped for any such analysis, considering the pounding in my head, though I noted in passing the fallacy about people supposedly never actually dying in their dreams; I'd died maybe a half-dozen times in mine. Eventually, I managed to drag myself out of the bed and down the hallway toward the bathroom, suffused with a feeling of having been severely pummeled, a feeling unnervingly like hangover. I washed my face with cold water. In the medicine chest mirror I saw an only vaguely familiar pair of puffy, bloodshot eyes. Tea, I thought to myself, tea (just as twenty years ago I would have thought, Coffee, coffee), pulled on a bathrobe, and wandered back down the hall to the kitchen.

When I went to fill the kettle, I saw something in the sink that stunned me: In the white porcelain basin was a white porcelain teacup, turned upside down, and in the little recess of its base two large cloves of garlic had been placed, unskinned and still linked together as nature had made them. The spigot had been positioned, and the hot water turned on ever so slightly, so that a steady, steamy needle of water penetrated precisely the crack between the garlic cloves. The thing was decidedly sexual, but insanely sexual, menacingly sexual, arranged, I felt, obsessively. I don't know how long I stood there at the sink, stunned, staring at it. The goofy thought *Did I do that?* passed through my mind, and I began quickly to disassemble it, feeling while I did it that I was destroying evidence.

Rattled, I decided to let Pascal bring up the tea and went into the sitting room to phone down to the desk.

On the table next to the phone I found Ellen's note:

Hi. Didn't try to wake you. Have gone walking. Exploring. Flora's passion for good clothes has got the better of her. She wants to see Knightsbridge and Harrods. Will check in with you later. Hope you're okay. And hope you remember your promise.
XXX,
me

What promise? I thought, annoyed. What's she talking about? What the devil is she talking about? She had written the note on a blank page of her notebook, and for some reason—a kind of lashing out, I suppose—I picked up the notebook and thumbed through it. On another page I read:

> There it was again, the strange music in her aunt's garden. Flora stood only a few feet from the birdbath, the old blue ceramic bowl sunken in the earth, and once again she heard it. It was a piano, Schubert, she thought. She wondered . . .

And something about this pilfering, a thing I should have been used to, a thing that in the past I'd even been amused by, further annoyed me. I supposed she would justify it— stealing from my life without even mentioning it, let alone asking my permission—on grounds that distant, mysterious music was a commonplace in stories. I glanced further through many physical descriptions, paragraphs reflecting our walking tours, then came to this passage:

> Flora shook the old woman by the shoulders, vigorously, but was unable to wake her. She checked her breathing, reassuring herself that her aunt was only sleeping. But was she drugged? Was she in a coma? Just then the old woman's eyes popped open, startling Flora. "Get away from me, you bloody pest," the old woman shouted.

So while Ellen expressed great distress over these anomalies in real life (virtual hysteria, I might say), she was at the same time very busy, secretly using it all.

I changed my mind about having Pascal come up. I didn't feel like seeing anyone. If he were a stranger, as he should have been, a porter in a hotel who would deliver the tea and get the hell out, I could have had him come up. But the way things were, I would have to talk to him.

I went back to the kitchen to start the kettle.

But the kettle, a black cast-iron thing, was already on the stove, over a flame and hissing the way it did when it was about halfway to boiling. The sight of it had stopped me just inside the kitchen door, and now I approached it slowly as if it were a trapped animal. I knew for a definite fact that I had not put the kettle on. I heard myself say, aloud, "Playing with matches now, are we?" and I felt something inside me tear loose: I'd been angry the moment before, but now, oddly, I felt a resignation, a kind of surrender, though I didn't know to what or to whom. I turned off the gas under the kettle, silent, hurting in my head and limbs, trembling a little inside and out, left the kitchen, and started down the long hallway back to the bedroom. I thought, Scotch, a full shot glass (surface tension retaining the amber a fraction over the brim), a few lines of blow laid out on a pull-down shelf in a toilet stall, greasy fast food, all-day TV game shows, drugged, pornographic sex, Xanax and gin, Quaaludes and cheap wine, all my old friends who could help me get to Numbville, the land of Not Me, with its ever-thinning air, its alien buzz, its insect drone of the open-armed lower orders.

In the bedroom, I went to the window and closed it, drawing the drapes without looking out. I removed my bathrobe and got back into bed, beneath all the covers, lying on my stomach, tucking my arms under my chest, and soon I was asleep again.

Right away I dreamed I was back at the chiropractor's office, lying faceup on his padded table, getting adjusted. He stood at the end of the table with each of my feet in one of his hands, pulling me this way and that, Straightening Me Out. He moved to the opposite end of the table and stood over me, looking down, stashing his long beard inside his shirt so as not to tickle my nose. He took my head in his hands, cupping the back of my skull in one palm while probing the nape of my neck with his fingers, feeling the shapes of the bones inside. Kindly, meditatively, he says, "Now just relax . . . just let it all go," and then yanks my head hard to one side.

Something shifts, off kilter.

CHAPTER

Ten

THERE WAS A moment, sometime later, when I'd

awakened but not yet opened my eyes: A sentence took form

in my thoughts, the voice not quite mine but some impatient,

put-out version thereof: *Well, you wanted some time alone, didn't*

you?

I lay on my back (just as I'd been lying on my back in the dream) and when I opened my eyes, I saw the underside of a canopy, dusty white muslin-like material gathered and pleated over several wooden supports, rising away toward the middle and down again at the foot of the bed. A thick drape was drawn around on four sides, enclosing me in a pleasant grayness; I held up my hand before my eyes, counted five fingers. All was very quiet—in fact, more than quiet, more substantial than ordinary silence: it was as if all sound waves had been sucked from the air, leaving the almost palpable no-sound of a tomb. I noted that I felt a good deal better than I had before this useful little nap. I did not feel the least bit afraid. I knew precisely who I was and where I was. I was Cookson Selway, in his middle years, the ugly American on holiday in England; youngest child of Herman (the Violent) and Frances (the Suffering), deeply troubled parents of my three older siblings and myself; husband to Ellen (the Shopping), who would soon push me to execute a promise I'd made her, a promise I couldn't for the life of me recall; father to Jordan, lovely girl lately gone to boarding school, a departure I'd participated in but didn't fully understand; master to Spencer, sturdy Dalmatian, who at least on one occasion had lost his spots, scaring the daylights out of me. As a child, I possessed a small extrasensory gift, a gift put into long remission by my abuse of drugs and alcohol; and thirteen years abstinent, I'd begun to recover it. At the present moment, I was having a paranormal experience in which I seemed to be transported to a former time—I had entered a state of consciousness in which I was being shown my surroundings as they had been many years ago. I'd already glimpsed these surroundings once before; a sitting room would be adjacent to this room, and in it I would find a reproduction of a seventeenth-century Dutch painting entitled *The Avenue*—spindly trees, country road, distant church steeple, man with dog. I was now lying naked in the four-poster bed where on that earlier occasion I'd discovered a bearded man who told me to sod off. I understood perfectly well what was happening. I was not afraid.

Ha!

Why, then, my extreme reluctance to investigate the warm liquid that was now trickling down the inside of my thigh?

I allowed my eyes to stray briefly to a tiny, elongated triangular slit in the curtain just to my right. I decided I didn't want to pull back the curtain. I decided I didn't want to look beneath the covers at whatever was pooling and cooling between my legs. I simply wasn't interested. I squeezed my eyes shut and tried to will myself to "wake up," though of course I wasn't sleeping. This strategy didn't work. I thought maybe, since the heavy silence was so much a part of what was happening, I could shatter the entire illusion with a loud noise. I shouted, as loud as I could (and don't ask me to explain my selection here), "Remember the Alamo!"—words that thudded into the soundproof air about three inches above my lips. Still, something stirred on the other side of the curtain, something changed outside in the room. My heart was racing by now, and I could both feel and hear little whooshing sounds in my ears. I sat up, thinking, What the hell, and pulled the covers down.

While buckets of another's blood has a negligible effect on me, a thimbleful of my own makes me queasy. I've never the least bit minded menstrual blood; Ellen and I have made love many times during her period, sometimes with luxuriant results. Not a problem. But at this moment, when I saw that there was blood on the sheets, blood on my legs clear down to my knees, and blood matting my pubic hair; when I saw the guileless wellspring of this gore, my penis, and the little stream of blood flowing out its tip, I did what any reasonable man in my situation would do. I fainted.

When I came to, I was happy and relieved to be sandwiched between the white dry sheets of my twin bed in a rented flat of the Hotel Willerton, London, last decade of the twentieth century. (Losing consciousness had been like someone's pulling the plug on a movie projector, and I made a mental note to remember this. Not that I thought I could faint at will, but it was comforting to know that there was a built-in governor, a safety switch that would shut things down when things got too hot.) Now I felt I was being given a second chance on this venturesome day. I was better physically than I'd been the first time, a source of new hope. If I were to go humbly to the kitchen and put the kettle on, perhaps there would be no lurid or capricious surprises awaiting me there.

I got out of bed and drew on the bathrobe. I opened the drapes, allowing the light of day into the room. I lingered at the window long enough to look at the sky, which was thinly overcast with a layer of white clouds, and which, in its unvarying color and vastness, consoled me (there was, after all, something bigger and deeper and possibly more important than me and what was happening to me; there was a world outside these walls). I realized for the first time that today was Saturday, Pascal would not be working, I could order tea, and it would most likely be brought up by a faceless porter who would slavishly leave the tray and bow out of the flat.

I phoned down to the desk and got the young woman named Lois who did the nights-and-weekends shift. Once I'd ordered tea, she told me I had a phone message: My wife had phoned to say hello; she was shopping and would try again later.

"Why didn't you put the call through to the flat?" I asked Lois.

"Oh, I did," she said. "About half-past eleven."

"Well?"

"I got no answer, sir," she said.

"You must have rung the wrong room," I said. "I've been here all morning."

There was a brief silence—that classic pause in which one falsely accused but in a subservient position decides not to press her case—and then Lois said, "Sorry, sir." (Whatever you say, sir.)

As before, I walked down the hallway to the bathroom and washed my face with cold water. As before, I examined my bloated eyeballs. Drying my face with a towel, I had that life's-passing-before-me feeling I'd had a few days earlier, and

then I heard the crying sound I'd heard that earlier day too—
the child crying in the spare room at the end of the hall.

At first I had a kind of heart-sinking feeling—wasn't
enough enough? how eventful did one Saturday morning
need to be?—and I thought briefly of ignoring the sound, of
simply walking the other way. But I assumed the voice to be
that of the girl, I'd been wanting to see the girl again, and
after all, I was a father: A child was crying on the other side
of a door . . . how could I not open it? (So what if she
wasn't quite made the same way I was?) I walked slowly
toward the end of the hallway, keeping quiet. Intuitively, I
felt that kid gloves were called for here, that I needed to
make my behavior delicate. I even stood just outside the door
for a minute, listening. Then, surprising myself (but continuing to act on instinct), I knocked gently. The crying stopped.
I waited for what seemed a long time, thinking I'd frightened
her away, and then thinking it was just as well, I'd had
enough for one day, there would be other opportunities. As I
turned to go, leaving the door unopened, I heard the highest,
frailest voice, full of great resignation: "Come in."

I opened the door: I saw the spare room with its twin
beds, nearly identical to the one in which Ellen and I slept,
dusky now, lit through a narrow crack in the drapes of its
single window; on the far side of the far bed, sitting with his
back to me and apparently staring at the far blank wall, was a
young boy, his longish blond hair hanging raggedly over the
collar of a navy-blue coat.

I suppose I was astonished by what I saw—I hadn't expected someone new—but I recall much less astonishment
than a surge of tender emotion. The line of the mattress,
dipping slightly at the midpoint where he sat, flared out with
a suggestion of wings on either side. In this first moment,
when all I could see was the boy's back, I could already tell
from his posture—the rigid spine, the head held deliberately
high—that he was practicing a kind of forced bravery. I
rounded the beds and gained the side view of him: his Adam's
apple moved up and back down once; he kept his eyes on the
wall. I sat on the bed next to him, careful to keep a safe

distance between us, his response a single sharp sniffle, punctuation at the definite end of his crying. I folded my hands in my lap (as his were folded in his own) and stared (just as he did) at the same blank wall.

We sat like that for what may have been a full minute, during which I stole a couple of side glances. I judged him to be about eight. He wore the short pants (matching the navy-blue coat), white shirt and blue tie, blue socks, and black shoes of what was probably a school uniform. I suddenly felt silly and entirely inappropriate in my white terry-cloth bathrobe. The question of who would be the first to speak hung in the air, of course, and I thought I might begin by apologizing for my appearance. But just as I was about to, he said, "If you want visitors, you'll have to dress."

"I'm sorry," I said. "I wasn't expecting to see anyone this morning."

"If you're too ill to dress," he said, "then you're too ill for visitors."

"Yes," I said. "I guess that's true. Tell me, what's your name?"

He ventured a glimpse of me. He said, "You're the American, aren't you."

"Yes," I said. "Yes, I am. You've heard about me?"

"Just a bit," he said. "You're my second American. My first was from New York City. Are you also from New York City?"

"I don't live there anymore," I said, "but I used to."

He seemed to consider this information for a moment, as if he were trying to think how he might best use it. Finally, he said, "Then I suppose you've ridden in a lift or two."

"A lift?" I said. "You mean an elevator? Oh, yes. Many times."

"How many times?" he said.

"Oh, I guess hundreds," I said.

He looked at me, more than a glimpse—grave disappointment on his face—then moved away, down the edge of the bed.

"You don't believe me?" I said.

"Of course I don't believe you," he said.

"But it's true," I said.

The combination of his brass and the frailty of his voice made me smile. He took this in—my smile—then, turning back and speaking directly to the wall, he said, "I suppose you've been to the top of the Empire State Building, then."

"Actually, I haven't," I said, visibly disappointing him a second time.

He crossed his arms and also his feet, at the ankles. "What?" he said. "You lived in New York City but never went to the Empire State Building?"

"I didn't say I'd never been there," I said. "I said I'd never been to the top. And it's not unusual for a person to live in a place and never see the tourist spots. I wonder if you've ever been to the top of Saint Paul's Cathedral, for example."

He uncrossed his arms but didn't answer. He coughed one time, placing a small, very white fist to his lips, then said, "Sorry." A vein, surprisingly wide and blue, bulged on his neck, then receded.

"The lifts in the upper floors of the Empire State Building can travel up to three hundred sixty-five meters per minute," he said. "And they're installed with braking devices—did you know?—that would stop them plummeting should their cables break."

"Really?" I said. "No, I didn't know that. You must be some kind of expert on the subject of lifts."

This remark pleased him—at last.

"Yes," he said. "I am. I've studied them a great deal, because they're very interesting."

"I see."

"And very important. Absolutely necessary in building operations. We couldn't build any really high buildings without lifts, because we wouldn't be able to get the materials up that high, you see."

"I guess that's so," I said. "I never thought about it, but I guess that's so."

"Yes indeed," he said. "Their history goes all the way back to Roman times."

There came a knock at the door to the flat—the porter with the tea. The boy heard it, too, and turned toward the hall, looking over his shoulder, then at me, inquiring.

"That's my tea," I said, "but I don't really want it anymore. Let's just ignore them, and they'll go away."

He looked back at the wall. "Have your tea," he said. "I shan't go away, if that's what you're thinking."

"You promise?" I said. "You'll wait for me to answer the door?"

"I promise," he said. "I shall remain just where I am, here in this spot."

"Would you like some tea?" I said.

"No, I shouldn't like any tea," he said, stifling a giggle.

A young woman I'd never seen before stood outside the flat with a large round tray. I took it from her, befuddling her with my refusal to allow her to enter. I only wanted to return to the spare room as quickly as I could. I poured myself a cup of the tea, which was weak—they'd sent it up so fast, it hadn't yet had time to steep—added milk, and took it back with me, half expecting the boy, despite his promise, to be gone.

The moment I entered the room, he said, as if there had been no interruption, "Vitruvius describes a kind of platform . . . Vitruvius was a famous Roman architect. Are you familiar with architects?"

"Well, only in a general sort of way," I said.

"Vitruvius describes a kind of platform, you see, hooked up to pulleys and capstans. And that's in the first century before Christ."

I asked him if he minded my opening the drapes. He said he didn't mind, curiously adding that the light would do him some good. I must have yanked the drapes open too quickly, however, because he gasped at the sudden flood of light.

"Is that too much?" I asked.

"No," he said, "just a bit too much at once."

"I'm sorry," I said.

"Next time open them slowly," he said.

Again I sat next to him on the edge of the bed, my

weight causing him to rise in elevation a few inches. I noticed that now he held a small pink rubber ball in one hand.

"I still don't know your name," I said.

"It doesn't matter," he said.

"I only want to be able to call you something."

"You may call me Simon."

"Simon."

"Or Patrick."

"Patrick?"

"Or Max."

"Well, which is it?" I asked.

"Maxwell," he said.

"Okay," I said. "Maxwell. That seems like such a grown-up name."

"Call me James, then," he said.

"None of those is your real name, though."

"Father said I mustn't give out my real name," he said. "Call me James."

"Okay, James," I said. "Where's your father now?"

"I don't know."

"Where's your sister?"

"My sister?" he said. "I don't have a sister."

"Oh," I said. "I thought that girl . . . the pretty one with the blond hair . . . the sailor dress . . . about fourteen or fifteen . . . I thought she—"

"She's my cousin," he said. "And she's not so pretty once you know her."

"Where is she?"

"I don't know," he said, shrugging his shoulders. "Around."

"May I ask you something, James?" I said.

He let his gaze fall to his lap, knowing already what I was about to ask. He said, "I wasn't really crying, you see. I only felt a bit lonely. But you don't mind if I was crying."

"No," I said. "Of course I don't mind."

"You think it's all right to cry, if you've got a good reason."

"Or even if you don't," I said. "Sometimes you just feel like crying when you don't even know the reason."

"I've noticed that too," he said. "But Father—"

He stopped himself and lowered his voice to a barely audible whisper. "Father scolds me for crying. He says only girls and sissies cry."

"Is he the big one with the beard?"

"Yes," he said quietly, looking down into his lap. "The long whiskers."

"James," I said, "is this your room we're in?"

"Oh, no," he said. "I haven't got a room."

He emphasized the word "room," as if to suggest that there were other things he had, but a room wasn't one of them.

"I thought this was your spare room," he added. "Yours and your wife's."

"That's right," I said. "But I was thinking about what it used to be, before we came."

He shrugged his shoulders. "Someone else's, I suppose," he said. "Tell me, do you actually know what a capstan is? I'm familiar with pulleys—there's one in the old dumbwaiter— but I'm not quite sure about a capstan."

"I'm not sure either," I said, "but I think it's a kind of spool, or spindle, something to wrap rope around."

"That would make sense," he said. "What about a windlass? Can you describe a windlass for me?"

"Well, that's a kind of crank, I think. You know, again, for gathering rope around as you turn it."

He transferred the ball from one hand to the other, then with his free hand made a cranking motion. "Yes," he said. "That's what I thought too."

Now he turned his little body toward me, pulling one leg up onto the bed and fully facing me. He was strikingly handsome, though I noticed that his eyes were gray and cloudy, like those of a very old person with cataracts. He openly searched my face, and there was something about his scrutiny of me—partly that mixture of handsome child and very old person; but also some dim trace of hope against hope, some stubborn faith—that greatly moved me. It was as if, for that moment, I completely forgot the circumstances of our visit, that the circumstances of our meeting had any aberrant quality whatsoever, and I was wholly taken instead by the human thing between us.

At last he said, "You won't tell Father you found me crying, will you?"

"No," I said. "No, I won't. You know, James . . . I imagine your father doesn't want you to cry because it upsets him. He just wants you to be happy."

He looked at me with surprise.

"What?" I said.

He turned away, dropping his leg and facing forward. "I thought you understood that much," he said, using the tone of resignation with which he'd earlier invited me in.

"Understood what?" I asked.

He seemed to go extremely pale. He looked straight at the wall, squeezing the rubber ball with the fingers of both hands. He whispered, "I thought you understood . . . he doesn't want me to be happy."

I should have paused there, to take in what he was trying to tell me, but I did what adults generally do when children say things that make them uneasy—I offered the foggy adult viewpoint.

"Oh, I think all fathers want their children to be happy," I said. "Even if sometimes it seems they don't."

He looked at me with about as much fatigue in his face as I deserved. He said, "Did your father want you to be happy?"

"Well . . . ," I said.

He shielded his eyes (rather dramatically, I thought) with a milky forearm, and moved as I was, feeling that I'd failed him in some fundamental way, I practically fell all over myself getting to the window to adjust the drape.

With my back to him, I said, "To tell you the truth, James, I don't think my father ever gave my happiness much thought, one way or the other."

And when I turned around, it took me a couple of seconds, in the restored semidarkness, to see that he was gone.

Disappointed—so much so, it almost felt like grief—I went to the bed and sat where I'd sat before.

"James," I said aloud, but in the very next moment I was no longer thinking about him. I was no longer thinking about him or his father, or my father, or about anything that had happened that morning. I felt extremely tired, almost winded. My thoughts were not really thoughts at all, but images, sort of refined images of nature, and if there was any language attached to them, it was a primitive, monosyllabic, Iron Age language: water, bird, sky, smoke, woman, rose . . . as if my consciousness had been boiled down, and this was the residue. I'm not sure how long I sat there in this odd condition, but at some point I realized I was staring at a blank wall like an overly sedated patient in an asylum and, with a great effort of will, pulled myself up.

In retrospect, I believe I was in an altered state during visits such as this one with James (and the earlier one with the girl), some form of what paranormalists would call the "medium state." It's the only way I can account for my composure, my words and manner; I spoke with the children in a down-to-earth, respectful, and even affectionate way, almost as if they were my own. It seemed that once I entered their world, I lost awareness (to the necessary degree) of mine, so I didn't think of the nature of the encounters as phenomenal—not while they were happening—and the two worlds didn't in any way seem to clash. In any case, the arrival of James on the scene led to a change in my thinking, and fairly immediately. I began to consider seriously the possibility that what was happening at the Hotel Willerton was in fact some kind of psychic projection emanating from me. This notion (popular among amiable skeptics), that all these events could have me and only me as their source, had seemed at first a kind of drug addict's delusion of grandeur. But after meeting James, I couldn't avoid noticing that the three "personalities" manifested did in fact seem to represent something vital in myself:

the red-bearded reprobate, the crude, self-indulgent drunk (my at-present remissive, dark self); the adolescent girl (my loss of Jordie); the precocious, troubled James (the father-needing little boy with worries about his manliness).

It's ironic that I became truly frightened once I began to think that what was going on was going on only in my mind. It could be that the sheer volume of events that Saturday morning pushed me into fear: the garlic arrangement in the kitchen sink, the atoning kettle on the range, the decapitation nightmare, the transport to a previous time, the bleeding, then James: a virtual sideshow of supernormal phenomena right there in my hotel suite.

In the afternoon, having still not heard from Ellen, I went for a walk—I needed air, and besides, the chambermaid wanted to get into the flat. Of course I was entirely preoccupied with my incessant thinking; and paying little attention to my surroundings, I turned into a narrow, tree-lined lane about two blocks from the hotel. It was very quiet, absent of people. The shadows of the trees lay over the pavement, creating an interesting pattern of sun and shade, and yet there was something not quite right about this pattern.

I stopped walking and gazed down the lane, confused by the sudden realization that the day was overcast, no sun shining, and therefore no shadows.

Apparently, there had been a sprinkling of rain only a few minutes before. The rain had darkened the pavement in the spaces between the trees but not penetrated the trees themselves, leaving the pavement beneath the trees dry. So what I'd first taken for sun and shade was actually only the chiaroscuro of wet and dry pavement. What had been "not quite right" with this picture was that it was in reverse, like a photographic negative.

This small misperception—my actually seeing the opposite of what I first thought I was seeing—seemed to reinforce my sense of myself as unreliable witness.

I ended up eventually on the King's Road and walked all the way to Beaufort Street and over to Battersea Bridge, where I stood for a minute looking upriver at the waters of the Thames. A strong October breeze, hardly noticeable in the streets, dominated here in the wide, gray openness. A tourist boat, one of those modern bullet-shaped things that look something like the pupa of a giant insect, passed under the bridge, traveling upstream, perhaps to Hampton Court. The passengers on the decks were bundled in coats and huddled together in little knots, looking for the most part miserable. As the boat churned the waters and droned farther and farther away from the bridge, I could have sworn I heard someone call my name. Considering all that had happened today, and my narrowing conclusions as a result, I doubted my ears along with my other senses. But I heard it again, more distinctly—"Cook . . . Cook"—and then spotted an arm waving in slow broad arcs from the stern of the tourist boat. I began waving back even before I knew who I was waving to, before I was able to single out the ever-diminishing face in the jumble.

It was Pascal, on his afternoon off, having himself a river trip, beaming up at me now, amazed—I could see even at this distance—by the improbability of the moment. We kept waving to each other until he was so far away it no longer made any sense to continue. Maybe it was hearing my own name called into the vast bog of my anonymity; maybe it was the sight of him, his happy face, his brightness on the water; maybe it was the simple wonder of that kind of luck; but the way we waved and waved as if to make the thing last as long as possible, our shared unwillingness to let go of something so singular, thrilled me in a commotion of joy and sorrow, discovery and loss, everything at once and unexamined. Though I knew the name of the bridge, I didn't know exactly where I was, I'd walked so far; I couldn't have pinpointed myself on a map. And when the boat's cargo was hardly distinguishable as human, and all that was left were the remnants of its wake, the most distant ripples of which waned toward either bank of the Thames, I lowered my arm and wiped tears from my eyes.

Well, obsession doesn't really work that way, does it? The very soul of obsession is its handy self-perpetuating feature: it doesn't diminish with use, it snowballs; acting out an obsession doesn't provide a purging effect but, rather, brings new life. Which means that Ellen must have understood—maybe she grew to understand as Jordie grew—that the great opus of raising a child was a slow, attenuated release; and that she gradually corrected this thing in her character (the refusal to let go, or the tendency to refuse anyway) without my noticing. Or maybe she didn't correct it so much as learn to contain it, which would account for her lines (cracks in the containment walls) of chronic worry.

I thought about this that Saturday afternoon as I walked back to the hotel from Battersea Bridge—the degree to which Ellen had changed over the years from a person attached to the needs and weaknesses of others into someone who actually loved: she defined herself and her life in terms of the world, not because she was overly attached to the world's needs and weaknesses, but because she actually loved the world.

As for me, I didn't love it so much as I depended on it for stimulation. (A gentle rain had begun to fall, producing a colorful show of bobbing umbrellas along the King's Road, a worldly display, a kind of found art, I almost loved; and my reverie was probably to blame more than any stranger's clumsiness, but I nearly got poked in the eye a half-dozen times; I also got quite wet.) I revisited the morning, many years before, when I'd showed up at our apartment in Greenwich Village, woken Ellen, said, "I'm sick and tired of being kept on such a short fucking leash," slid down the bedroom doorjamb, and passed out. Ellen's reaction was not that of a person attached to a drunken husband; it was the reaction of someone who had transferred to her new baby whatever attachment she may have once had to a drunken husband; it was the reaction of someone who'd been freed by actual motherhood (achieved beyond the hurdles of two sad miscarriages) from an earlier tolerance for drunks. She didn't struggle with my leaden body, dragging me piecemeal into the bed, removing my shoes, and tucking me in. She left me on the cold, hard floor. When I awakened hours later, into the dreamlike white noise of nobody-home, the back of my head was pressed up against a baseboard and my right arm was twisted painfully beneath me. (Along the King's Road, it occurred to me, for the first time ever, that in Ellen's elaborate preparations for leaving me, she must have stepped over my apparent corpse a dozen times.) Pinned to my shirt—I guess she couldn't quite resist this one infantalizing gesture—was a sheet of white typing paper, and on it were two words: "Do something."

When I'd dragged myself into the bathroom, I saw that her makeup was gone from the medicine chest. I went to her bedroom closet and found a gap where her clothes should have been. In the nursery, the crib had been stripped of its sheet and blanket, and all the stuff was missing from the changing table—diapers, wipes, powder, and lotion. Ellen hadn't just gone somewhere with the baby; she'd taken the baby and *gone*. I went back to the bedroom, to her note, as if to discover in it the key to this baffling turn of events. "Do something," it stubbornly read, or, more precisely, as I experienced it, "Do something . . . do something . . . do something . . . do something . . ." I wadded up the paper and threw it, hard, against the bedroom wall; it bounced off the wall, hit me in the head ("Do something"), and fell at my feet ("Do something"). I bent to pick it up from the floor, so I might throw it again, harder, but my head seemed to fill with fluid and I was pulled over by the sheer weight—that is, I toppled. Dazed, I returned to the nursery and looked again at the stark crib, with its chilly, waterproof mattress; I stood with my hands on the side of the crib, and then I began to shake it, as if a good shaking of the crib was all that was needed to make the baby reappear. I made quite a racket shaking the crib and then returned to the bathroom (the third point in my private little Bermuda triangle), where I briefly viewed the hooded eyes and blanched kisser in the medicine chest mirror and busted it with my fist.

A shard of broken glass lacerated the side of my hand, just at the root of my pinkie finger, rather deeply. I could recall vividly everything that preceded the blood; and I could clearly recall the exotic and desultory Sunday afternoon in the emergency room at Saint Vincent's Hospital. My memory of getting there was vague. I'd lost consciousness a couple of times leaving the apartment, which was on West Twelfth Street, two long blocks and one short one from Saint Vincent's. But this was all that mattered: The technician who stitched up my hand, a young man with the high polished brow and courtly style of an African diplomat (I'll forever remember his nameplate: Lovett Olango) must have seen something in my face, for as he worked with the needle and thread, he said, "What's the mahttah with you, mahn? You could have lost this feengah. You should be hoppy."

I asked him if the hospital had a detoxification unit.

He stopped to look at me for a moment, comprehending. Then he went back to his sewing and said, "Yah, we have one. I will draw you a mop."

In a way, Ellen's "Do something" was responsible for our future together. It was no accident that on my rainy walk back to the Hotel Willerton I pondered the nature of her attachments and replayed the memory leading to Lovett Olango's hand-drawn map to Detox. Inspired by the spare-room appearance of the little boy, James, I'd decided (again) to tell all, to come clean, to reveal what had really been going on at the hotel, and I felt oddly at risk, as if I were about to disclose my most secret shame. I reminded myself that Ellen already knew something of what I had to say; it wouldn't be a complete surprise. But I didn't want to be treated to her severest clarity, to her cleanest prose—I didn't want her to shrug her shoulders and say, "So . . . do something." Truthfully, I'm not sure what I did want. In my heart of hearts, I knew there was something dangerous and unhealthy about the degree to which I'd been swept away by the supernatural events at the Hotel Willerton—I was drunk on them—and I probably wanted to be comforted, told I wasn't crazy, and given permission to continue my binge.

. . .

But during the walk from the bridge to the hotel that Saturday afternoon, after I'd been virtually hammered and lashed in the morning by the antics in our rented flat, I was quietly commanded away from this worrisome mood by a heightened sense of the ridiculous—possibly a delayed reaction to the sight of Pascal waving from the stern of a tourist boat in the Thames. In a shop window, some bright-gold, headless female mannequins (with hard, pronounced nipples) caught my eye. At the curb, a cabbie's "Ta, gov'nor," shouted to a smartly dressed gentleman already out of the taxi and breaking into a trot across the street, struck me as Dickensian in the extreme. When I reached the hotel, climbed the steps, and entered through the beveled-glass doors, the lobby seemed most like a theatrical set, not quite a part of the real world. For the first time since he'd said it, I thought of Tony Rosillo's remark ("You'll love this place . . . it's like something out of *Masterpiece Theatre*"), and Lois's pinched face behind the hotel desk (she was understandably angry about the peremptory tone I'd taken with her earlier) caused me to giggle a little as she handed over the key to the flat. When I asked her if Mrs. Selway had come in, she said, "I think so," not about to commit herself.

Moving toward the elevator, I whistled the *Masterpiece Theatre* theme music. It used to be, during the credits on the old *Masterpiece Theatre*, the camera would pan an array of books and knickknacks in Alistair Cooke's study (a kind of video collage the British seem fond of), and among all the odds and ends was a brass snake (semierect, about to strike, or having recently struck). In bed on Sunday nights, when the familiar theme music (Jean-Joseph Mouret's "Rondeau") began, I would ask Ellen to identify the composer; for some reason, she could never ever remember the word *Mouret*. She would say, "Jean-Joseph . . . Jean-Joseph . . . Rameau, no Reynaud . . . no, Mornay . . ." Then, with the snake's entrance, I would grab her and yell, "Snake! Snake!" I did it every Sunday night, which was the only thing that made it the least bit funny, my dogged repetition of it. Now, riding up in the elevator, when I heard the mysterious piano music through the walls around the third floor, I yelled, "Snake! Snake!" and laughed. I liked this new mood I found myself in, a buoyancy on which I might ride my confession.

The dark sitting room, however—and the utter quiet of the place—was like a bucket of cold water. In fact, the sense of foreboding was so strong, just inside the door, that I stood still and called out Ellen's name.

"In here," she called back, with a kind of crime-scene tone.

Moving down the hallway, I thought how absurd we were with our several rooms: the rarely used sitting room, the only occasionally used kitchen, the dining room in which we'd never set foot; and a spare room? They were all spare rooms, for the most part . . . the moneyed Americans with their cravings for more more more.

The bedroom, too, was dark. Ellen sat on the side of her twin bed, still wrapped in her khaki-colored raincoat, hands folded in her lap (much as James had sat earlier, only Ellen was facing the other bed rather than the wall).

I said hello and walked between the beds, sitting on mine so that our knees were nearly touching, and creating a symmetry that made me think of us as little boy-and-girl figurines on an ornamental clock.

"Your mother called," she said flatly.

"My mother?" I said. "What's happened?"

"Nothing's happened," she said. "She just wanted to give me her critique of our 'sending Jordie away to that school.' And our 'traipsing off to Europe' right afterward."

"You're kidding me."

"She said Jordie was unhappy but was afraid to say so because of how she'd begged us to let her go. And that Jordie needed us now but was afraid to tell us she needed us because she knew how important this trip was to us."

I took Ellen's hands in mine. "You know how Mother is," I said. "She's a complete hysteric. Jordie probably mentioned a hangnail or something . . . a paper cut. Now she's miserably unhappy and needs us to be there. That's my mother's way. She blows everything out of . . . Look, we'll just call Jordie and—"

"I talked to her already," Ellen said. "She's fine. I made her promise me that she was okay. I told her exactly what Frances had said, and she said it was Grandmother who didn't like the idea of her being away at school. She said she'd had a squabble with another girl over some silly thing and she told Grandmother about it. Maybe she cried a little. But everything was fine now, and we didn't need to worry."

"You see," I said. "I knew it was something like that. Some small thing that she just blew—"

"But your mother's right about one thing, Cook."

"What?"

"It was selfish of us to put Jordie in school and go away right afterward."

"What are you talking about?"

"I planned this whole thing, you know. The timing of it. It was all about me, about how lonely I was going to be, about how empty the house was going to feel. I planned this trip so I wouldn't have to face that big house without Jordie in it."

"And it was a good idea," I said. "The house did seem lonely with Jordie gone. It was a good idea."

"It was selfish," Ellen said. "It was all about us, without giving a thought to . . . well, what if she did need us? Here we are, halfway around the world."

"That's Mother's phrase, isn't it—'halfway around the world'?"

Ellen didn't answer, didn't need to.

"Look," I said. "Do you want me to call her and give her a piece of my mind?"

"No," she said. "That would only make things worse."

"I'll do it," I said. "I would enjoy doing it. I'm still angry with her for throwing that flyswatter at me when I was eight years old. This would be a good time to bring that up."

"She threw a flyswatter at you?"

"When I was eight," I said. "For sassing her. She also threw a head of lettuce at me once. Iceberg lettuce. Why don't I just call her and—"

"No," Ellen said. "Please don't."

"I'll tell her to mind her own business," I said. "I'll tell her to stop calling Jordie and to butt out of our lives."

"That wouldn't be fair to Jordie."

"I'll tell her to keep her opinions to herself. I'll tell her to go jump in the lake . . . or, you know, the reservoir. I'll tell her to go jump in the reservoir."

She gave me a kind of friendly-exasperated look—why did I have to make a joke of everything?—and said, "Did you go to the doctor today?"

"The doctor?" I said, taken aback.

She looked at me, allowed me my gradual dawning, and slowly withdrew her hands from mine.

"Oh," I said at last. "I feel perfectly fine. Really."

"You promised, Cook," she said. "I couldn't wake you again this morning."

"You mean you tried?"

"Well, no," she said. "But I made plenty of noise. A normal person would have woken up. And you were talking in your sleep."

"What did I say?"

"I don't know," she said. "Gibberish. But it was very weird. You used the word 'rapscallion.' "

"What's so weird about that?" I said.

"It's like something out of a former period, Cook," she said. "And we agreed. If it happened again, you would go to the doctor and get checked out."

"Actually," I said, "if we were to consult a transcript of that conversation, I don't think it went quite like that."

"What do you mean?"

"I mean I think we said if things got worse, I would go to a doctor. That's not the same thing as 'if it happens again.' "

She stared at me, narrowing her eyes. It was immediately clear that I would win this on a technicality, but for a moment I thought I saw in Ellen's face a hint of relief: she wanted me to win; she might protest, but secretly she wanted me to win. Perhaps she so admired my precision here that she thought I deserved to win.

"That's splitting hairs," she said.

"One of my specialties," I said.

If splitting hairs was what we were about, things had got worse of course. Ellen, however, didn't know it.

"And what about the drinking?" she said.

"What drinking?"

"Are you still feeling like you want to drink?"

"No," I said. "That passed as quickly as it came."

"And how are you feeling in general?" she said. "You haven't been feeling ill in any way?"

"I feel excellent," I said.

"Well . . . ," she said with a sigh, again that odd mix of defeat and relief.

After a pause, she stood and began to walk away toward the closet, untying the belt of her coat. She'd gone down her checklist of worries, and though she'd got no real satisfaction, nothing like actual comfort, she'd decided to make do.

I stood and moved behind her, took her in my arms.

She turned, putting her head on my shoulder, and said, "Do you think we're terribly selfish people, Cook?"

"You know what I think?" I said. "You know what I honestly think? I think we're terribly hungry people. I think we need a home-cooked meal. What about if I run out and buy a few things and make dinner?"

She pulled away suddenly, wiping the side of her face with her hand. "I think you're a terribly wet person," she said. "Have you been walking in the rain or something?"

It just wasn't the right time to tell her. She was already a little upset. I would have to wait for a better opportunity.

I ran around like a maniac in the rain for about forty-five minutes, from one market to another, finding the things I needed to make one of her favorite dishes, eggplant cannelloni. Back at the flat, I peeled the eggplants, sliced them thin, lengthwise, laid the slices out on paper towels and salted them (to draw out the moisture), flipped them and repeated the procedure on the other side; I made sauce with fresh tomatoes (seeded and skinned, of course) and lots of garlic; I breaded the eggplant slices with flour and herbs and corn-meal, then fried them in olive oil, drained them, and rolled them up with ricotta inside, like cannelloni; laid the little rolls in a buttered pan, smothered them with the sauce, moz-zarella, fresh grated Romano cheese, and more herbs, and put it in the oven; I made a spinach salad (rich in calcium) and set us up for the first time in the dining room. I lit candles.

The whole thing had taken hours, and Ellen wandered into the dining room like a stray, pale and wearied. Once she began to eat, she perked up a bit and began telling me about her day in Knightsbridge. She'd found a beautiful little church on a side street off Brompton Road, near Brompton Square, and she'd sat inside for a while, waiting out a rain shower. An elderly couple, who'd been kneeling in a pew near the front of the church, finished praying and got up to leave; she said they resembled her own dead parents so much it nearly took her breath away. She said she thought the couple had come to the church to pray because they were going through some especially difficult trial—a sick child, or perhaps severe money problems. She said the woman had looked at her on their way out, had smiled sadly, and that Ellen had wanted to follow them, tell them how they resem-bled her parents—she'd wanted to, but of course she couldn't, and it had conjured for her dozens of similar hesitancies, failures to connect out of some vague fear, out of shyness. She was sure that this identical thing would happen in the new book, to Flora, and that it would be significant in some way, be the thing that pushed Flora to some important re-solve.

We were startled during dinner by the telephone. Ellen looked at me, disappointed, apprehensive. Having already brought back to the cave the slain eggplant, I was sure I could also strong-arm a small electronic nuisance; rising from my chair, I said in my most virile voice, "I'll get it."

It was Mimi Sho-pan, saying she had something she thought we would be interested in seeing and could we possibly join her and Ray tomorrow morning for breakfast in the hotel restaurant. They planned to attend early church services and would be downstairs at around ten-thirty. I accepted at once.

"What do you suppose it is?" Ellen said, back at the table.

"I imagine she's found out something about the accident they were telling us about. Whatever it was that happened here at the hotel."

"Oh, yes," Ellen said, quickly, oddly formal. "You're probably right."

"What?" I said.

"What what?"

"What's wrong?"

"Nothing," she said. "I'm just suddenly, totally exhausted. Do you think we could maybe just rinse these things and leave them till morning?"

This was Ellen's way of signaling, after a romantic dinner, that making love wasn't in the cards, and I felt an enormous reprieve. The intrusion of Mimi Sho-pan had recalled for me the whole, huge specter of The Strange Business at the Hotel Willerton, and I felt wasted. With all my designs to cheer Ellen, I'd forgotten for a short while this darker thing at the heart of my present life. As I glanced at the tall black rectangle of the dining room window, I thought of the creature features of my youth, and I recalled a little boy, alone (albeit gratefully) on a Saturday morning, sprawled on the living room floor of a farmhouse, rapt, transported by the exotic magnetism of his close friend Bela Lugosi, all white-powdered and slick-wigged, intoning, Sleep . . . sleep . . . sleep.

CHAPTER

Twelve

SUNDAY MORNING, I awoke with a little
movie playing in my head, in which a man (me) thinks he
hears voices coming from somewhere on a lower floor of his
London hotel and goes down to investigate. I saw myself
pulling on a pair of jeans and quietly leaving the flat, saw

myself on the stairway, luridly lit by the Exit sign, pausing for a moment to listen again to the voices. In the lower hallway, I peered into three different rooms along the way, and because I'd been told by Hannah that the third floor was being remodeled and hadn't yet been furnished, I saw what I expected to see—empty rooms. But now, as I replayed all this as if I were watching myself in a movie, an image took hold in my mind's eye, the image of something I'd seen in one of the other rooms: pushed into an alcove, a large square-shouldered object of some sort, covered with a paint-speckled dropcloth.

Ellen was still asleep. Though she'd claimed exhaustion last night after dinner, she'd got into bed with her notebooks and briefcase, pulled out a red pencil and a map of London, and begun the kind of methodical review that usually produced a chart or two and sometimes a time line. Her lamp was still on when I fell asleep. I dreamed of elevators—specifically, a thrilling kind of elevator without walls or ceiling, a rapidly moving platform called a "Vertigo" (or "Verti-Go"), purported to have been designed by a young boy. Two different times during the night, I felt what I assumed to be Ellen, in bed with me, starting to fool around, but then I would wake up and see her across the great divide, asleep in her own bed. And once, before I went back to sleep, I heard her trying to call out in a dream, the eerie, reedy wail trapped in the back of the throat.

Now I actually climbed from under the covers and pulled on a pair of jeans. Like the man in the little movie, I did indeed slip out of the flat and down the stairway to the third floor; I did indeed find a room with an alcove, a large, bare, beautiful room, with white walls and a blond wood floor and two tall, bright windows; a stepladder stood dreamily against one wall, and at the edge of an alcove, beneath the alcove's long, graceful arch, was something covered with a dropcloth. Feeling oddly obedient (though I'm not clear about what or whom I was obeying), I moved slowly near. I took a corner of the cloth between my fingers and began to tug. It was a Bechstein, an upright, aged wood, so dark it looked almost black, with the kind of cracked, yellow-edged ivories that seemed to suggest a need for dental work.

I felt something like exhilaration—I guess it was because the piano was the first solid object, the first material prop, in my secret melodrama. It literally brought substance to these events, and now, in the telling, there was something to point to, something to show.

Or so I thought, quite temporarily. Doubt began to set in as soon as I started back up the stairs to the flat: What did the real existence of the piano prove? I was still the only person who'd heard the music. In fact, its actual existence only confused matters further, for if the piano was being played—whether by normal or by supernormal forces—shouldn't anyone with normal ears be able to hear it? The Bechstein proved nothing, it was evidence of nothing.

On the upper landing, I turned, descended the stairs again, and returned to the third floor, doubting now my having seen the piano only moments before.

But there it was, standing across the white room, grinning dumbly. I went over, closed the fall-board, and covered the piano again with the dropcloth. As I did so, I experienced that deep sadness I'd felt days before in the sitting room opposite the hotel restaurant downstairs. I was drawn to the window, and I went and stood by it, looking out, though there was nothing particular to see: other houses, other windows, early-morning fog, no people, some pigeons on a granite sill across the way, a small, bike-cluttered courtyard below. And once again, my sense of time and place grew vague—there was nothing to anchor me to a specific identity, to a specific life—and the window's appeal seemed that of an escape hatch, an exit; standing there, I felt the prisoner's woe I'd felt before. There was the same invisible presence at my back, the same impulse to weep. I was suddenly, decidedly grief-stricken, without knowing the parent of my grief.

After about a full minute of this, I shook myself free and left the room.

Back upstairs, inside the flat, I went to the kitchen to put on the teakettle. But the teakettle was already on. My friendly helper, my extra pair of hands, was up to his (or her) tricks, and I took the recurrence of this little event as an apt beginning to the story I meant to tell Ellen.

I went to the bedroom, where I found her still asleep. I sat next to her on the bed. As soon as I touched her shoulder, she rolled over and looked at me. "Morning," she said sleepily.

"Could you come out to the kitchen for a minute?" I said.

"Why?" she said.

"Just come, okay? There's something I want to show you."

I led her by the hand down the hallway, through the dining room, through the sitting room, and to the kitchen doorway. She was wearing her tiger-print nightie, and her hair hung down in her face; she looked like somebody out of *La Dolce Vita*. We stood gazing into the kitchen. I still held her hand. I pointed to the kettle, which was beginning to make its halfway-to-boiling rumble. "Look," I said.

"Look at what?" she said.

"The kettle."

"What about it?"

"It's on," I said, "and I didn't put it on."

Now she brushed the hair out of her eyes, dropped my hand, and began what appeared to be a medical examiner's scrutiny of my face—she was looking for signs of foul play. After a moment, she said, "What are you trying to tell me, Cook? I know you didn't put the kettle on."

"That's what I'm trying to tell you," I said. "The kettle's on, and I didn't put it on."

In a voice reeking of pathos, she said, "Cook. *I* put the kettle on. What's your point here?"

"You put the kettle on?"

"Yes."

"You were asleep."

"Well, I woke up. I woke up and put the kettle on."

"When?"

"When you were in the bathroom," she said.

"I wasn't in the bathroom," I said.

"You weren't?" she said. "Then where were you?"

"When?" I said.

"When I put the kettle on, just five minutes ago."

"Let me get this straight," I said. "You were asleep. You woke up. You put the kettle on. You went back to bed."

"That's right," she said. "I thought you were in the bathroom. I don't understand what you're trying to tell me."

I shrugged, completely thrown. "Nothing," I said. "Never mind."

She leaned near me and sniffed around my neck and shoulders. "Are you feeling okay this morning?"

"Yeah," I said. "I guess I'm just not quite awake."

She kissed me on the cheek, went into the kitchen, and took down the box of tea from a cabinet. As I turned back toward the hallway, I heard her whispering something to herself, but I couldn't make out the words.

CHAPTER

Thirteen

WHEN WE ARRIVED, the Sho-pans, along
with Pascal, were already seated at a large round table in the
corner of the dining room farthest away from the garden
windows. I wasn't particularly apprehensive about this visit—
on the contrary, I was eager for it—but (perhaps in a

Pavlovian spirit) I did absently count the number of diamond shapes in the elevator's lattice gate (ninety-four) and the number of doorways (six) Ellen and I passed through on our trek from the elevator to the dining room. Right away, I saw that Pascal, like me, had worn a suit and tie to breakfast. A real Frenchman, he was exceptionally good-looking in his clothes, and I wondered if, like me, he'd dressed with the Sho-pans in mind (they were the kind of people you dressed for). As we approached the table, Pascal beamed at us from across the room, though he continued listening, head slightly cocked, to something Mrs. Sho-pan was saying into his ear. It was only when he rose to his feet that the Sho-pans became aware of our presence; seated side by side, they turned their heads simultaneously, as if their heads were connected to one mechanism, and they seemed flabbergasted to find Ellen and me standing so near their table. I noticed that Mr. Sho-pan struggled getting up, attaining his full height a moment after Ellen and I were already seated. He seemed very pleased with Ellen and her cream-colored cashmere sweater—as did Mrs. Sho-pan, who continued gazing at Ellen so persistently after we were settled that Ellen leaned forward, stretched her arm across the table, offering her hand, and said, "It's wonderful to see you again." The two women discovered that they couldn't quite reach each other, and only touched fingertips and laughed.

As Mrs. Sho-pan poured out tea for Ellen and me, she said, "Ray has a headache."

She said this with such finality, I almost thought it the answer to a question we'd all previously discussed and that it expressed the purpose of our get-together.

Mr. Sho-pan was extremely pale when we looked at him, but then I observed that everyone was extremely pale— something about the dining room's huge bank of French windows, something about that great wall of natural light and the garden full of fog.

Ellen said, "Oh, I'm sorry," as if the headache were her fault, and Mr. Sho-pan scrunched up his face and urgently shook his head in a way that appeared painful. I suppose he meant to dismiss his headache as a topic, but Mrs. Sho-pan wasn't quite ready to let go.

"There's nothing for it," she said. "You just have to wait it out. He gets it every Sunday morning at church, and it generally goes away soon after breakfast."

Ellen suggested that Mr. Sho-pan eat something before church, and Mrs. Sho-pan said that he always did eat a little something, that the solution to the problem was not as simple as that; Ellen wondered whether incense was used during the church service, and Mrs. Sho-pan said that sometimes it was and sometimes it wasn't and that Ray got the headache no matter what; Ellen asked what kind of wine was used for Communion, and Mrs. Sho-pan said it was sherry but that sherry at home never gave Ray a headache, and so forth.

I thought this a lousy beginning and resented my wife's part in it. Also, I sat next to Mr. Sho-pan, which made him and me a pair between the two women, who were discussing him as if he were invisible. Maybe for this reason (because we were paired and both male), I felt I should defend him against this female belittling, but when I turned to him I saw that he was like a cat in a cartoon, watching a tennis match, completely fascinated. (Both his hands still rested, pawlike, on the edge of the table, where he'd placed them a minute earlier, as he'd lowered himself back into his chair.) I looked across the table at Pascal, whose face had glazed over; the muscles of his neck bulged as he swallowed a yawn, and at that moment, we were rescued by the waiter, who took our orders for breakfast.

Happily, once the waiter was done and gone, Mrs. Sho-pan brought out her surprise without further ado. She reached down into what must have been a bag on the floor and retrieved a large sheet of paper, folded in half. Without unfolding it, she passed it across to Ellen—not to me—saying, "There now. Isn't this lovely?"

"Oh, Cook," Ellen said, beginning her inspection of the paper, "it's just what you thought. Look . . ."

"My librarian friend sent me out to Colindale," said Mrs. Sho-pan, leaning forward with enthusiasm, directing her remarks to Ellen. "That's where they keep the newspapers, you know, in Colindale. I spent most of yesterday there, and I can't recall when I've had as much fun. And only fifty pence per page. Isn't it remarkable that they come out actual size like that?"

What had come out actual size and cost fifty pence was a reproduction of a page of the *Daily Mirror*, from July 1936. I could see that Mrs. Sho-pan had drawn a red, lopsided circle around the boldface heading above a short column midpage—"Puzzling Fall Leaves Two Dead"—but from my second-class vantage, I couldn't read any copy.

Mr. Sho-pan reached all the way across me, tapped his index finger three times inside the red circle, and said, "You see—he pushed her." Then he sat back up straight in his chair, took a sip of tea, replaced his cup in its saucer, and added, "Just as I said."

"Yes, Ray, you did say," said Mrs. Sho-pan quickly, "but there's no evidence of any such thing. You also said their name was Jenkins, when it was Jevons. Now let them see it for themselves."

Pascal and I got out of our chairs and huddled around Ellen, each reading over a shoulder. After a moment, Pascal, stuck in the first paragraph, pointed to the page and said, "What does this mean, 'dry *goods*'?"

Ellen explained that "dry goods" meant textiles, ready-to-wear clothes, and such.

This first reading at the breakfast table was hurried (not to say ravenous), but of course I had occasion later to study the item. The writer described the incident as an "early-morning tragedy," a "bizarre accident," and a "hideous blow" that had left neighbors "stunned and baffled." An adult man, identified as Walter Jevons, 41, fell to his death sometime near 5 A.M. on a Sunday, outside a home in an "inconspicuous" section near Sloane Square. Alongside the man, the body of a child was found, also the apparent victim of a fall from the same fourth-floor window. The child was identified as Victoria Jevons, 14, Walter Jevons's niece. The bodies were discovered a bit after 6 A.M. by a railroad worker on his way to duty at Victoria Station, and there were no witnesses to the incident. The house out of which the victims had fallen was owned by H. E. Jevons, the dead man's brother and father to the child. A merchant in dry goods and a widower, H. E. Jevons was away at the time of the accident, in Liverpool on business. The grief-stricken father, summoned back to London, told authorities that he shared the house with his younger brother Walter, in whose charge he customarily left the girl whenever he himself traveled. But otherwise, Jevons had been unable to shed any light on the circumstances of the accident.

The various responses of neighbors were reported, including one woman who claimed to have heard what she took to be a woman's scream just before 5 A.M. She looked out her window, on the street side of her own fourth-floor flat, directly across from the Jevons home, but, seeing nothing unusual, went back to bed. Another neighbor said the Jevonses' was an "unlucky house," apparently alluding to a fire that had destroyed two rooms on the third floor only a year before. Several neighbors (forming the usual Greek chorus that attends such tragedies, reciting the commonplace lines) described the Jevonses as a quiet family who kept to themselves. No one, it seemed, knew them well. The "lamentable incident" was under investigation by police.

And that was it. I returned to my chair. Pascal continued reading over Ellen's shoulder for a moment, and then she smiled up at him, passing him the paper, allowing him to take it with him back to his seat.

Ellen looked at me, waiting, apparently, for my response. Mrs. Sho-pan, too, seemed to be waiting, but more aggressively, her eyebrows pitched very high.

Finally, I shrugged and said, "But there must have been a follow-up article, surely."

At which Mrs. Sho-pan, more of a showman than I'd imagined, produced a second, identical-looking paper, identically folded in half, and passed it across to Ellen.

I was on my feet again, reading over Ellen's shoulder, and joined there after a minute by Pascal.

A full four days had passed between the two reports. Little was known, still, regarding the gruesome occurrence of last Sunday near Sloane Square. A few new physical details: at the time of her death, Victoria Jevons had been dressed for bed, while her uncle was dressed in street clothes; the girl wore a locket on a chain around her neck, containing a likeness of her dead mother; on this same gold chain was a small gold key, like that fitting the lock on a jewel box, but no such jewel box had been found. In the girl's fourth-floor bedroom (out of which the victims apparently fell), the police had discovered some evidence of a struggle—an overturned electric lamp, a crumpled carpet—and some smudge marks on the frame of the open window, which, alas, were, according to police, "inconclusive."

H. E. Jevons, when interviewed, had characterized the relationship between his brother and his daughter as affectionate and described Walter as "like a second father" to the girl. But several neighbors (some reluctant) had portrayed Walter Jevons as a drinker. Patrons of a neighborhood pub recalled a recent row between Jevons and an unknown Scottish tourist in which Jevons, drunk, had become "violent without merit."

No evidence had been found indicating the presence of any third person in Victoria's bedroom, of any intruder. The only persons who could "reliably disclose" the exact circumstances of what had happened were dead. Police were "not hopeful" for further revelations.

Once again, Pascal, lagging behind in his reading, returned to his seat with the paper to finish. And once again, I took my seat and observed the expectant silences of Ellen and Mrs. Sho-pan. I noted that Mr. Sho-pan, throughout and now, appeared far away in thought, his eyes closing and opening slowly, as if he were keeping one foot in the here and one in the darkened there, wherever *there* was. (It could have been simply that he was in some way ministering to his headache.) I also noticed that Mrs. Sho-pan held her husband's becalming, kneadable hand in her lap.

This time, Ellen was first to speak. "Well," she said, "the key, obviously, was to a diary," and Mrs. Sho-pan actually threw back her head in delight.

"Of course it was to a diary," Mrs. Sho-pan said, again leaning toward Ellen. "A diary, I daresay, that was destroyed before the police could find it. Yes?"

"And who do you think destroyed that diary?" Ellen asked with the singsong inflection of a children's riddle.

"Why, the father, of course," answered Mrs. Sho-pan.

"Right you are," said Ellen.

"The father," said Mr. Sho-pan, nodding and showing an abundance of yellow teeth.

Pascal looked up from his reading and said to Ellen, "What did you say? The father?"

"The key," said Ellen, "the little gold key they found around the girl's neck . . . it was to her diary, don't you see. And the reason the diary was never found was that it had been destroyed by the father."

"How do you know that?" Pascal asked.

"Because she knows," said Mrs. Sho-pan. "Because I know too. It's the only key a young girl would guard so carefully. Her innermost thoughts. Her most painful secrets."

"But why would the father destroy it?" asked Pascal, serious and literal-minded.

"Because something in it reflected badly on his family," said Ellen. "Because he wouldn't want whatever was in it made public."

"Ah," said Pascal, "I think I see. And what was this thing . . . this thing he did not want to be public?"

"Well, that will require some thought," said Ellen, looking to Mrs. Sho-pan.

"Of course the poor girl was being mistreated," Mrs. Sho-pan said without a pause.

"By the uncle," said Ellen.

"He—" Mr. Sho-pan started to say.

"We know, Ray," interrupted Mrs. Sho-pan. "You think the uncle pushed her. Yes," she said, turning to Ellen again, "mistreated by the uncle. And perhaps by the father as well."

"That would certainly be my first guess," said Ellen. "But what if it was something more unexpected, more surprising, than that?"

"Excuse me," I said, thoroughly revolted by this little game. "Is that it?"

"Is what it?" Ellen asked, the only one who could have detected any upbraiding tone in my voice.

"I'm asking Mrs. Sho-pan whether or not there are any other reports."

"Oh," said Mrs. Sho-pan. "No. I found nothing further. Nothing other than a brief mention of the incident in an article about something else. A burglary in the same neighborhood a week later. Unrelated. The article simply pointed out that it was the same neighborhood. As if to suggest that a lot of bad things were happening lately in the neighborhood. It was *our* neighborhood, wasn't it, Ray? *This* neighborhood. Amazing to think. It was the flower shop that was burgled, on the corner, Ray, do you remember? I can actually recall there being a flower shop on the corner. All those many years ago. There used to be a bright-red hibiscus tree in the shop window. In a ceramic pot. Bright-red papery blossoms, beautiful when I was a girl. And long, long stamens jutting out like little trumpets. Now it's a sandwich shop there. And it's been many different things in between, too."

"Mistreated?" said Pascal. "You mean beaten."

"Perhaps," said Mrs. Sho-pan, dreamily, possibly still thinking about hibiscus blossoms. "Perhaps beaten."

Then she seemed to shake herself free and added, "No; no further reports. But don't you see, it's much better this way. It's the best thing about it, really. For now it remains a mystery. A mystery to be solved." Then to Ellen: "I knew *you* would find it intriguing."

"You didn't come across any mention anywhere of a boy?" I asked.

"A boy?" she said. "What kind of boy?"

"A boy in the family," I said.

Mrs. Sho-pan looked at her husband, turning to him and clutching his hand, now with both her own. Her expression was as if I'd said something unpleasant. "I don't recall any boy," she said at last. "Do you recall any boy, Ray?"

"A boy?" he said.

"A boy in the family," she said to him. "A boy in the Jevons family."

"Jevons?" he said.

"Yes, Ray," she said. "In the Jevons family. A boy. Mr. Selway wants to know."

Mr. Sho-pan closed his eyes. I suddenly became aware of the clattering of silverware and china and human laughter in the dining room. We were all looking at Mr. Sho-pan, and there was this dining room noise going on. And behind him, very much in the background, past all the other tables and diners, the fog in the garden. Inside the fog, virtually imperceptible, two figures, stirring, almost like prisoners circling in a walled recreation yard.

Mr. Sho-pan began, slowly at first, then more rapidly, to shake his head.

"No," Mrs. Sho-pan said. "He doesn't know about any boy."

"What boy, Cook?" Ellen asked me. "What are you talking about?"

"Well, it's just—" I said, choking up, clearing my throat.

I looked at Pascal, whose brow was ridiculously knitted. He sensed, I suppose, that I was entreating him in some way.

"Monsieur," he said to me. "You want me to—"

He clearly had no idea where his question was going (though it could have traveled miles on its earnestness), and therefore he stopped himself.

"Cook?" Ellen said, placing her hand on my forearm, and as much to my own astonishment as to anyone else's, I found myself sitting in a public restaurant in a foreign land, a middle-aged man among strangers for the most part, tears flowing down my cheeks.

I can't explain why I began to cry. I'd shed a couple of tears the day before, on Battersea Bridge, seeing Pascal on that boat. I suppose it was in the air, my need to cry, irrepressible. If I were a psychiatrist I would probably say it was some little bit of regression. At the table, I did feel like a misunderstood child, I did feel the misunderstood child's loneliness and sense of isolation and despair. (During the period of my life when my mother was dressing me as a girl and playing dollies, I cried a great deal; I couldn't have said then why I cried so often, though I see it now as the outward signal of an inner, secret trouble, a child's involuntary public appeal for help.) I have as much difficulty crying as most grown men, and I believe I feel the conflict that most grown men feel about it—an appreciation for the clarifying effect of tears, the way tears somehow make you feel restored to your true self, and how being restored to your true self, for a man, is humiliating. It's my personal theory that most men spend most of their lives pretending to be someone they are not, because they've been made to feel that there's something intrinsically debasing about being who they truly are. In any case, when I began to cry at the table, I thought I felt some of this clarifying, restorative stuff, and the echo of all past crying, but in addition, I felt an emotional connection to the distress and anguish I'd experienced across the hall in the sitting room and, later, upstairs in the empty third-floor apartment.

Ellen had removed her hand from my forearm, somehow a respectful gesture. Through my tears, I was able to take in everyone's reaction at once: Ellen embarrassed, concerned; Pascal confused; Mr. Sho-pan completely unaffected; Mrs. Sho-pan engrossed.

Ellen started to pass me her napkin, but I raised my own to my face.

"I have something to say," I said. "Since we arrived at this hotel, I've been having some experiences. Very definite experiences of . . . I don't know . . . people. People who used to live here. And of the place itself, the way it used to be . . . the walls and doors in different places. Two of the people I've met seem to fit the description—"

"Met?" Ellen said, laughing nervously. "Met?"

"Yes," I said. "Met. Two of the people I've met . . ."

CHAPTER

Fourteen

ODDLY ENOUGH, ONCE I got started with
The Strange Business at the Hotel Willerton, it came flu-
ently—I told about the piano music in the elevator, about my
meeting with the young girl in the sitting room, about the
inexplicable changes in the flat, the teakettle, the bearded

drunk in the bed, and finally about James; I made no mention of my comatose sleeping, of sex or blood or garlic arrangements in the kitchen sink—and no matter how much I tried to shape it into the form of a confession, no matter how many opportunities I took along the way to point out my extreme defects of character, my obsessive nature, my shameless secrecy, all anyone cared about was the story itself; they weren't the least bit interested in *me*. This of course is what every storyteller ultimately wants, to be upstaged by his material, yet I couldn't help but feel a little slighted. As perverse consolation, my agile mind provided, stuffed into every breath and pause, a recurring intrusion for my private enjoyment, snatches of a kind of fretful cabaret ballad, full of wishes: I wished I'd been born to physically attractive, educated parents who lived someplace like Philadelphia or Georgetown, who read books and went to plays and gave dinner parties; I wished my father had been, instead of a farmer and a murderer, a college professor and a civil rights worker, and that my mother, instead of crawling around on all fours in a farmhouse bathroom, scrubbing out the tub and the toilet with Ajax, groaning with the pain of her arthritic hips and shoulders, had played the violin and cultivated roses; I wished we'd had a summer place on a lake, and a boathouse; I wished that as an adolescent I could have come in from the fields with my butterfly net over my shoulder without feeling I was a foolish disappointment to my whole family; I wished I hadn't got drunk before the senior play (*Death Takes a Holiday*) and performed my role (Eric) from start to finish in a total blackout; I wished I hadn't thrown up in my brother's borrowed Camaro on the way home. These, I understand, were not the wishes of a child but the wishes of an adult man who had failed in some significant way to grow out of childishness. To what degree this wistful theme affected the tone of my account at the breakfast table I can't say for sure. I do recall looking repeatedly to Pascal, for his encouraging loyalty, and I recall one pathetic bit near the end, which went something like: "I know you're probably all thinking I'm crazy, that I need to see a doctor, that there's

"He wanted not to frighten her," Pascal said, glancing at Ellen.

"Yes," I said directly to Ellen. "I wanted not to frighten her."

"I *knew*," she said at last, put off by my self-consciousness and maybe trying to save face. "Of course I knew. You as much as told me, Cook. I just didn't have all the particulars."

"Ray knows something about ghosts," said Mrs. Shopan. "Don't you, Ray?"

"No," Mr. Sho-pan said. "Not quite yet."

"He didn't understand me," she said to us. Then: "About *ghosts*, Ray, I said you know something about *ghosts*."

"Oh," he said. "Yes, ghosts . . . well . . ."

"Give him a moment," she said. "The thing that so interests me is how you speak about them as if they were ordinary human beings. How you were able to converse with them just as freely as we're conversing now."

Pascal said, "You overpassed the girl, Melanie," and I realized that in all my anguishing over what was "real" and what was only inside my mind, I'd completely forgotten that the young chambermaid who'd fled the hotel in fear not only had encountered Walter Jevons in the flat but had sketched a picture of the man.

I quickly told this part of the story, and Mrs. Sho-pan said, "How exciting! What have you done with the picture?"

"I burned it," I said, and she looked at Ellen with a kind of perfect poker face, concealing sympathy, I suppose.

"The man with the gladstone," said Mr. Sho-pan suddenly.

"Oh, yes," said Mrs. Sho-pan. "Where was it, Ray? In Cornwall? On that field trip to Cornwall?"

"No, no," he said. He'd tilted his head far, far back, eyes closed tight. "Gloucestershire it was. Not Cornwall. Nowhere near Cornwall. Not Cornwall."

"All right, Ray," said Mrs. Sho-pan. "Not Cornwall, but Gloucestershire. It had to be twenty years ago at least."

"Gloucestershire it was," he said. "We'd booked into an hotel in the spring."

"Not me," said Mrs. Sho-pan. "He was traveling with a small group of his students."

"A peaceful weekend for me and my students," he said. "Hot for spring, quite hot for spring. There was an old man sitting in the hall in a smart gray suit, just sitting there on a courting seat all alone in the hall. Staring straight ahead kind of sad like."

At this point, Mr. Sho-pan did an imitation of the old man sitting on the courting seat, staring straight ahead kind of sad like—and a convincing imitation it was, not, apparently, too much of a stretch.

Mrs. Sho-pan had to prod him out of it. "Do go on, Ray," she said sweetly.

"Oh," he said. "Yes, well. We were to visit our rooms, get settled, you see, and meet back up in the hall before going in to dinner. So we did that, and I was the first to return, before any of my students, and the old man sat right where I'd seen him earlier. I went over and asked him was he waiting for someone, and he said to me, 'They've kept me bloody waitin' for a bloody table all this time.' There was a young lady behind a desk in the hall, the hostess, I guessed. I inquired of her whether or not this gentleman's table was soon to be ready. She says to me, 'What gentleman?' And I said, 'Why, that gentleman there, right there,' and she says, 'Excuse me,' and fetches some redheaded fellow, the proprietor, I guessed, from out of his office. This redheaded fellow takes me aside, whispering, very hush-hush. Whispering, he says, 'Now don't make a fuss . . . ,' and all the while I'm watching the old gentleman out of the corner of my eye." (Mr. Sho-pan repeated, briefly this time, his imitation of the old gentleman, staring sadly.) "He was alive as you or me, he was. The proprietor says to me, 'Now don't make a fuss . . . ;' and in the blink of an eye the old gentleman's gone. Just like that, gone in his gray suit. Had a gladstone with him, and a black umbrella."

This was far and away the most I'd ever heard Mr. Sho-pan say at once, and it did seem to tire him out. With a shaky hand, he reached for his teacup but found it empty. He passed his fingers all around his bald head, as if he were bolstering himself with the memory of his hair, or as if he'd made some connection between its absence and the empty teacup. Mrs. Sho-pan, very proud of her husband's narrative performance, poured out more tea into his cup, saying, "That's right. Ray's always been quite definite on those two points: he had a black umbrella and a gladstone bag." She paused for a moment, then added, "So you see, Cookson, you're not the only one at our table who knows something about ghosts."

I couldn't tell whether this last remark was meant to welcome me into respectable ranks or if she was upbraiding me for thinking myself so special.

"I never saw one," said Pascal. "I don't think we have ghosts in France."

"Don't be ridiculous," said Mrs. Sho-pan. "What, with all those guillotines? I should think you have the most frightening in all of Europe, poor headless things roaming the countryside."

Pascal looked sheepish and said, "I forgot."

"Excuse me," said Ellen abruptly, and stood to leave the table.

I took her wrist, pulled her close to me. "Do you want me to come with you?" I whispered.

"To the powder room?" she said, loud enough for everyone to hear.

We at the table seemed to have some tacit understanding that the subject at hand should not be discussed while any one of our members was away. A tea-sipping silence ensued, which may have felt awkward only to me. Surreptitiously, I turned my eyes to the garden, to see what, if anything, was going on there. The fog had grown brighter—it seemed in fact to be reaching some peak of brightness in which it would no longer be fog but be pure light—and the only figures I could make out inside it were those of a stone bench and a small ornamental tree. The waiter came and put down our breakfasts, a happy event to my thinking, for though I had no appetite, I would have something to do besides sip tea. Pascal, behaving like a cranky customer—an in-joke between him and the waiter—said haughtily, *"Et bien alors,* this is not what I ordered." The waiter, a middle-aged man with white sideburns, tweaked Pascal on the ear, they shared a belly laugh (of which Mrs. Sho-pan seemed to disapprove), and then we all began to eat. Ellen soon returned, apparently having come to some resolves in the powder room. Pulling out her chair, she gave me a sharp, arctic once-over.

"Oh," she said, surprised by the food. She sat down but took up no knife or fork.

"Eat, dear," said Mrs. Sho-pan with an air of confidentiality.

"Yes," I said. "Eat, dear."

"If Cook can talk to these . . . ," Ellen began, "whatever they are . . . presumably he could ask questions. We could learn what really happened that night."

"Precisely," said Mrs. Sho-pan.

"We could find out who pushed whom," Ellen said to Mr. Sho-pan, a remark he let go unnoticed, though it seemed to delight Mrs. Sho-pan utterly.

Mrs. Sho-pan cupped her hand to one side of her mouth, the side away from her husband, and said, "He already knows."

"We could get to the bottom of a couple of things," Ellen said.

She'd brought a rehearsed stoicism back with her from the powder room and was attempting to cuddle up inside her little utilitarian refuge. Any minute now, she would strap a visor to her head, pull out a clipboard and red pencil, and get busy with her charts and checklists. I'd just dumped this big scary animal in the middle of the breakfast table, and Ellen was trying to take control of it; her taking control was familiar enough to me, but suddenly I was aware of the judgment and superiority beneath this impulse. I didn't think she gave a damn who pushed whom. I didn't think she was temperamentally inclined to giving a damn about anything that was truly mysterious. Wasn't her very career a means of managing the *illusion* of mystery, mapping out with color-coded charts and graphs where people were going to be and where things were going to happen, methodical, extremely complicated, without any emotional center? Wasn't it all a big, elaborate strategy for harnessing a beast she deeply feared: the great unknown?

"Precisely," Mrs. Sho-pan said again.

"We could find out if we're right about that key," said Ellen.

"And we could learn who the—" Mrs. Sho-pan began.

"Wait wait wait," I said. "You all don't understand."

My wife and Mimi Sho-pan, who seemed increasingly like birds cackling away at feeding time, fell silent. I was right in what I'd said, but I wasn't entirely sure, yet, what it was they didn't understand.

When it became clear that I wasn't going to elaborate, Mrs. Sho-pan said, "I think I do: you're emotionally involved, and Ellen and I are not being delicate enough."

A fair enough assessment, even accurate, but I perceived inside it something else: she'd articulated the alliance between her and Ellen, against me.

I immediately regretted having told anyone anything, and I wanted to take it all back, to restore it to the privacy it deserved, to erect a shrine around it and barbed wire around that. Hadn't the children and all the rest been given into my care, and hadn't I now bungled my stewardship? (I didn't notice, there at the breakfast table, that my thinking was taking an odd turn toward the paranoid. In my secrecy, I had been alone; now that I'd told the secret, I needed to find a new, more complicated way of being alone.)

"It's not a question of delicacy," I said. "It's not a question of my being emotionally involved."

Another pause: Everyone stopped eating, then continued eating.

At last, Pascal said, "What *is* the question?"

"The question is . . . ," I began.

Then a little explosion occurred inside my mind. I wouldn't have called it an insight, but something grander than insight, more three-dimensional than thought, an almost

sensual thing, and it came in the physical form of a picture—
the painting I'd seen of the man walking his dog down the
country road. It seemed to me that I could smell the vineyard
alongside the rutted avenue (does a vineyard have a smell?),
the tall trees on either side comical in their extreme spindli-
ness, and that I could feel the warmth of the summer air on
my skin. I'd seen this painting in a vision and in a dream—
possibly I'd seen it, too, in real life, without taking much
notice; in the dream, I'd actually got inside it; and now it
seemed it had got inside me. I heard myself say, without
having the slightest idea what I meant, "It's a question of
fate."

"Fate?" said Ellen.

It felt like a dare.

"Yes," I said. "Fate."

And then I went on, blindly: "Fate," I said again. "Right
here at this table. This ridiculous conversation. This plotting
you're attempting to do. This amusement with old newspapers. This rather cheap excitement, if you don't mind my
saying so, over what was an actual tragedy in actual people's
lives. We have some choices to make here, and yet it's as if
we're just acting out choices that have already been made by
somebody else. We're just the next link, don't you see, in this
chain, this line of fortune that includes these children and
their untimely deaths. I mean this is a story about somebody's
child lying dead in the street, even if it did happen sixty years
ago. She was somebody's child, and she had her whole life in
front of her. Somewhere in this story there's a grieving father.
Somewhere there's a—"

I stopped there (not soon enough), for Mrs. Sho-pan
had reached again for her husband's hand and was looking at
him as if to say she was deeply sorry he had to endure this
hopeless American buffoon, and I did see Mr. Sho-pan's eyes
go misty as Ellen whispered, ambiguously, "Oh, Cook," and I
felt stupid and crazy and brought back to earth, briefly at
least, by the sight of the old man, with his white napkin
tucked inside his shirt collar, missing his son.

CHAPTER

Fifteen

AFTER THAT BREAKFAST, my descent to calamity was essentially laid out; all the necessary positions had been assumed (affectively at least), save one—Pascal's replacing Ellen as my companion:

Despite further noble orations on the need for respectful handling of my ghosts, the group decided that I should coax them out and pump them as best I could. I should simply think of myself as getting to know them better—after all, wouldn't I be giving the poor things an opportunity to unburden themselves? Since Mr. Sho-pan had proved himself to have the "seeing eye," he should pay the flat a visit or two. I should report any unusual events as soon as they occurred, and perhaps Ellen could write everything down. Under Mrs. Sho-pan's leadership, it all felt a little like starting up a club, The Sloane Square Ghost Society.

Feigning an air of diplomacy, I remained uncommitted without rejecting the plan outright; I waxed increasingly purple (sometimes in iambic pentameter) and, Pilate like, publicly washed my hands, putting the matter into those of Fate; I said I wouldn't be able to do any coaxing, but if there were any future *chance* encounters ("should Fate see fit to cross our paths again"), I would see what I could learn of Walter and H. E. Jevons and the girl. Secretly, I thought James, whoever he was exactly, the most likely one to tell me. I said that naturally Ellen and I would welcome a visit from Mr. Sho-pan anytime, for any purpose.

We said our good-byes in the front hall of the hotel. Mrs. Sho-pan's last words to Ellen were, "Of course you must come and stay with us, dear." I overheard this remark, though it was spoken softly (almost conspiratorially) and though Pascal was saying something to me at the time, and I watched out of the corner of my eye as Ellen thanked Mrs. Sho-pan and kissed her on the cheek. Then the three of us, Ellen, Pascal, and I, stood briefly lost in the hall—it was a sudden intermission, when no one had thought ahead, the Sho-pans were gone, and we had to imagine on the spur of the moment what would be next. I thought, Okay, now that's all settled, I suppose I should go upstairs and get to coaxing out my ghosts. I thought that both Pascal and Ellen were looking as if this was what was expected of me. Pascal handed me the two copied pages of the *Daily Mirror*, smiled, and shrugged his shoulders. I said, "Oh," and, "Thank you." Someone came in the hotel's front door, and we all turned to see who it was, quite shocking the poor old woman greeted so intensely by six wide eyes. Finally, Ellen said, mock-cheerily, "Well . . ." Pascal looked at his watch and said he would go change out of his dressy clothes. He kissed both Ellen and me, walked to the door beneath the staircase, which presumably led to the staff quarters below, and waved at us before disappearing through it.

We rode up in the elevator in silence. It seemed to me, perhaps overgloomily, that the metallic clanking made at each floor was like the sound of another iron door being latched. When we reached our floor, I went to pull back the lattice gate but couldn't. Ellen said, "What's wrong?"—two words, a glint of alarm, a sawtoothed edge of blame. I said the gate seemed to be stuck. Then the car suddenly bounced up another inch, scaring both of us, and I found I could now slide the gate open. As we walked down the dark hallway toward the door to the flat, Ellen's last words—"What's wrong?"—echoed in my ears.

Inside, she went straight to the bedroom. I followed her and found her lying on her bed, staring up at the ceiling. By now I had no feelings to speak of, only an almost prurient curiosity about what she was going to say. I took off my jacket and sat on the inside edge of my bed, facing her, wrapping my tie around my index finger like a window shade, letting it fall open, rolling it up again.

After a while, without looking at me, she said, "You didn't tell them about my not being able to wake you . . . or about the smell of the whisky and the obscenities."

"That's true," I said. "I guess I left some things out."

Another long pause.

Finally, she said, "I'm not sure how I feel about all this. I'm not even sure I want to sleep here tonight."

"I understand," I said. "It's a lot to take in at once."

She closed her eyes and sighed. "Is that what I'm supposed to do, Cook?" she said. "Take it in?"

I had no answer to this question. I supposed it was rhetorical. She turned her head and looked at me intensely. She continued doing this until I said, "What?"

"I'm just thinking it seems like a long time to have known someone without really knowing him," she said.

"What do you mean?"

"You know exactly what I mean," she said.

"Isn't that a little melodramatic?" I said. "Just because this stuff is a bit unusual, it doesn't mean I'm suddenly a different person."

"I want you to see a doctor, Cook," she said.

"What for?"

"What for? Because something's happening to you. Isn't it obvious? You're getting worse and worse, and you seem to have this notion that no matter how outrageous you become, it's just something I'm supposed to 'take in.' It's the story of our whole life together, if you want to know the truth."

"Wait a minute," I said. "Before we go into the story of our whole life together, I need to get something straight. You're saying you think everything I said down there at the breakfast table is the result of some kind of mental illness?"

She rose from the bed abruptly, moved to the chair in the corner of the room, and sat, rather like a fighter taking to his stool. "Something is happening to you, Cook," she said. "That's all I know. Something's been happening to you since we arrived here. This was supposed to be a trip . . . a chance . . . an opportunity for me to soak up atmosphere for my book. Instead, I'm soaking up—I don't know—whatever new weird, incredible thing you come up with. Since we've been here, I'm worried about you half the time, concerned that you're going off some deep end, concerned that you're sick, and now we have this deal where I'm supposed to wander around London by myself because you're back in the flat in some kind of coma and can't wake up. I know—"

"I don't think you can complain about atmosphere," I said. "There's been plenty of atmosphere."

"I know you're interested in spiritual stuff," she said, ignoring me. "And I'm not particularly. That's okay. But you're having auditory hallucinations, Cook, talking to spirits like some—I don't know—like some Hungarian person in a tent somewhere. Being transported to other time periods . . . it's like something out of the *National Enquirer*. I mean, what's next? Astral projection? Stigmata? Are you going to start writing mysterious messages on the walls, channeled from an entity in outer space? Why don't you get *really* out there, Cook? Good old Ellen, she'll just take it in."

"The Sho-pans believe me," I said, trying not to sound too much like a sulking child.

"The Sho-pans are *English*," she nearly shouted. "They'd believe anything that had a ghost in it."

"Actually, they're Asian," I said.

"Actually, they're English," she said. "To all intents and purposes. Listen, Cook, you didn't describe these spirits to me and then we went and found the newspaper reports. You read the newspaper reports first and then said you'd met these . . ."

She held out her hands, palms up, as if she were pleading. "Don't you see, Cook? I just think it's possible that you—"

"I'm confused," I said. "At breakfast, I thought you were as interested in this as Mimi was. You were as enthusiastic—"

"I was trying to make the best of a bad situation, Cook. My guidebook doesn't say anything about what to do if your husband goes psycho while staying in London. What was I supposed to do? Besides . . . I don't honestly know what to believe. I don't think this is as simple as who believes in ghosts and who doesn't. I don't think it makes any difference, frankly, whether this stuff is in your head or actually happening—it's still making you weird. It's still affecting you. I can't believe it's good for you. Do you think it's good for you?"

"I don't think I have any choice," I said.

"Oh, great," she said. "I get it now. We're going to be like those couples in horror movies where something horrible and scary is going on in the house, and for some strange, inexplicable reason they can't just get in the car and leave.

They have to stay in the house so a movie can be made about it. I guess we should start hanging up crucifixes all over the flat and wearing strings of garlic around our necks—"

"That would be to keep away vampires," I said calmly.

"Maybe we should scatter human hair around our beds at night—"

"That would be to keep away deer."

"What do you mean, you have no choice?" she said. "Of course you have a choice."

"No," I said, "I don't think I do. What did you mean, it's the story of our whole life together?"

"What I mean is that for the last sixteen years I've accommodated one thing or another, whatever *phase* you happen to be going through. And I'm not just talking about pills and booze, though God knows that would have been enough to deal with. I'm talking about your gun-collecting phase, when you know I hate having guns in the house. I'm talking about your chanting-at-sunrise phase, when every morning Jordie and I were awakened at the crack of dawn by some mysterious moaning in the house."

She stood and walked out into the hallway; I heard the sound of the medicine chest in the bathroom opening and closing. Then she was back.

"I'm talking about your sending Jordie off to school," she said, "with black-bean-and-alfalfa-sprout burritos for lunch when every other kid's got a peanut-butter-and-jelly sandwich, because you didn't think she was getting enough calcium in her diet. I'm talking about your bringing home morbid pictures for her to look at of old women bent over with osteoporosis, to get her to drink her milk. I'm talking about your low-fat, low-cholesterol, health-and-fitness, work-out-at-the-gym-twice-a-day-every-day and your fear-of-asbestos, fear-of-lead, fear-of-*radon* phases."

She sat back down in the corner chair.

"And what was it last year?" she said. "The mysterious child's face that nobody could quite see but you? How do you think it made me feel, your bringing out an X ray of your pelvis every time we had people over for dinner? How in the world do you think that made me feel?"

Somewhere near the midpoint of this long, excessive speech, I was distracted, charmed, and strangely comforted by the sight of a face in the window just over Ellen's left shoulder: leaning in from the side of the frame, the face—the eyes and better part of the nose—of the girl I now assumed to be the young and lovely, possibly victimized, Victoria Jevons. She looked directly at me, in what I took to be a show of sympathy for the poor man so unfairly subjected to these ravings of a harridan.

It was for this reason (and for this reason alone) that I smiled when Ellen was finished, and continued smiling as I said, "I don't know how it made you feel, Ellen. How did it make you feel?"

"I'm glad you find this amusing," she said.

She stood, went to the wardrobe, and took out her beige all-weather coat. She draped it over her arm and moved to the hall door.

"I'll tell you how it made me feel," she said, beginning now to pull the coat on. "It made me feel tired," she said. "Which is how I feel now. I feel very, very tired. I don't know why I've accepted every quirky, idiosyncratic behavior you've dreamed up over the years. I don't know why I've accommodated everything and everybody who has come my way my whole life long. I don't know why I seem to push aside my own needs in order to meet everyone else's. But I'm very tired. And I'm not doing it anymore."

I continued to sit, unmoved, on the edge of my bed and held the gaze of Victoria Jevons at the window, listening first to my wife's footsteps in the hallway and then to the sound of her leaving the flat. When I heard the door close, I turned for a moment toward the sound—it had a hard-edged, briefly painful tone of finality—and the thought of following her, catching her at the elevator (which I surely could have done), passed quickly through my mind. But I remained still. And when I turned back to the window, the face was gone.

At that moment, sunlight flooded the room, so abruptly it was almost startling, then faded away. I stood, walked to the window, and looked out. I seem to recall a faint, lingering moon up there in the now unfogging, pale, blue-white dome of the sky, but it's more likely that I saw some haze-screened version of the sun. I'm not entirely sure what I saw. That night, however, I would stand at the same window, alone, and actually see the moon as it was overwhelmed and extinguished by charcoal-colored clouds. Pascal would phone, to see if I was all right, to see if there was anything I needed. Then I would return to the window and stand for a long time, rather empty-headed, brooding without a definite subject (if that is possible), and staring at the browns and grays and blacks of the jigsaw rooftops, the yellow domestic lights of other lives, the amberish-pink city glow that hovered over it all, and I would wait. I would wait, and in a while, rain would move in, and stay. It would rain every day until we left England.

successful cottage industry sewing curtains and drapes. By the time Pascal came along, half the children were already in their teens, so there were lots of helping hands—lots of *bosses*, from Pascal's perspective—and he sometimes felt that the entire world was in authority over him. Very early on, he discovered that by staying out of the way (something he seemed to have a natural gift for), he could avoid the exercise of most of this authority, and he soon earned a bittersweet status: he was often forgotten. He had been especially attached to the oldest sister, Catherine, but she was already nineteen when he was four, and at twenty she married and had her own child, making Pascal an uncle at the age of five. Catherine continued to live at home with her new family, and what little attention Pascal had got out of his baby-of-the-family rank was transferred to the infant grandchild. Almost nothing had ever been demanded of Pascal in the way of chores, everything being done by older siblings, and even before starting school, he found himself assuming an independence that was apart from the family yet nearly always in some way focused on them. His "office" was beneath the massive oak table in the dining room. There, behind the folds of a long damask cloth sewn by his mother, he hid for hours, unmissed, and the boisterous home (which attracted plenty of outsiders) became something heard and smelled, surrounding him but tangibly distinct from him. There was the clatter of pots and pans in the kitchen, the hum of the washing machine, music from the radio upstairs, garbled commentary from the television downstairs, the frequent doorbell, pieces of conversations as his brothers and sisters passed in the hall with their friends; the kitchen aromas, the scent of the oil soap used on the wood floors, and the girls' perfumes, eventually distinguishable one from the other. (There was also the always amusing appearances of feet beneath the hem of the tablecloth.) When, at the age of fifteen, Pascal took his first part-time porter's job at a small Paris hotel, he found something oddly comforting and familiar about the setting—in ambience, a virtual replica of home, except that now he was conspicuously, happily useful. He felt, at the hotel, the surety of a bird in flight, and when he left the Géricaults right out of high school to make his own way and began working full time, it was a fairly easy change. (He recalled pictures he'd seen, in school, of galaxies shaped like raggedy pinwheels, and imagined himself as one of those last trailing stars, spun out at high speed from the tail end.) Once he'd gone to England, his sister Catherine remained his primary link to the family and wrote him brief but regular letters, apologizing for not writing more often and for not having more to say.

I gathered these details from Pascal himself, and from Catherine. When I asked Catherine about her and Pascal's father, she told me the father was a silent type and had for the most part silently opposed Pascal's leaving home and going to England; he had in fact declined to say good-bye to Pascal the night Pascal left. She also told me a curious, seemingly irrelevant story about the father's hair—that the man had been bald almost all his adult life, but when he'd stopped drinking coffee, at the age of forty-nine, his hair had astoundingly returned. Perhaps it was the most remarkable thing about the father that she could think to convey. I asked her what Pascal's relationship to his father had been—had they been particularly close?—and she shrugged her shoulders and used the French word *inaperçue*, "unnoticed."

Catherine added that I resembled the father somewhat, but when I met him, an impassive, swollen-knuckled man in his late sixties, I failed to see what she'd meant.

My first night in the flat alone, without Ellen, passed uneventfully, as I've said, except for the emergence of rain and Pascal's phone call. In our brief conversation, neither Pascal nor I mentioned Ellen by name: it was understood that I knew where she'd gone and that I knew Pascal knew too. Pascal's tone was studiously absent of sympathy, which I interpreted as his restraining himself—there was plenty of implicit sympathy in the fact of his phoning. I said, "Don't worry; I'm not worried." In response, Pascal said, "I'm not worried," and for half a second I thought he was mimicking me. But he only meant to assure me that whatever had happened between us, whatever had prompted Ellen to leave, she was safe with his friends. He said he would come see me the next day, which sounded a little overly cheerful, like a promise to visit a sick friend. It could be that another man would have felt embarrassment, his wife abandoning him in a hotel and bunking in with people she hardly knew a block away; but when I thought of the talk that was surely going on behind my back—the Sho-pans, Pascal, and Ellen consulting one another about my condition—I felt vaguely important, or at least at the center of something important. I went to bed with the brave preparedness of a secret operative on an assignment of highest danger, deepest gravity; I felt that all obstacles had been removed at last and I was finally going to get down to business.

But all that happened was that I slept more soundly than usual and woke up late, around nine-thirty, feeling well rested. I thought, dimly, that I'd been awakened by something, and as I lingered in bed, the hotel below me seemed full of new presences, creakings and bangings and thuds, and perhaps even voices. More eager than ever for the show to begin, I pulled on a pair of jeans and went barefoot and shirtless to the hall door, opened it a crack, and listened. I heard the percussive ignition of the elevator's electric motor, and its whir, and then, distinctly, a male voice, coming from the floor below. I moved to the stairway, pushed open the door, and began to creep down the stairs to the third floor. I stopped midway, when I heard the sound of the piano.

This time, it was not Schubert but something schmaltzy, the florid intro to a popular song. I continued down, and the moment I set foot in the hallway, a lovely tenor, his diction exaggeratedly precise, began to sing, "There was a young man from Montrose/Who could diddle himself with his toes . . ."

The door to the room was wide open: I saw two men in the alcove, both about my age or a little older, both wearing navy-blue coveralls; one sat on the round piano stool, playing and singing; the other listened, smiling, his folded arms on the Bechstein lid as a chin rest; crumpled at their feet was the white canvas dropcloth that had earlier cloaked the piano. The one man sang to the other with a kind of mock passion: "He did it so neat/He fell in love with his feet—"

The one doing the listening saw me in the doorway, stood upright, and stopped the other man's playing with a backhanded tap to the shoulder and a quick nod in my direction; then, as if he'd been caught naked and meant to cover himself, he bent down and began gathering the dropcloth from the floor.

We stared at one another for a moment, all three of us, during which time I noticed out the corner of my eye a new dressing table, angled against the left-hand wall in such a way that I could see my own reflection in its mirror. The man who'd been singing remained seated on the stool, twisted severely around so he could see me, and smiled, beet red in the face. "And christened them Myrtle and Rose," he said finally, tilting his head to one side, smiling. "Sorry. We didn't mean any harm." He patted the lid of the piano with one hand and added, "Nice old thing here . . . Still got a good quality, though she's way out of tune."

The men looked at my bare feet (had the very same Myrtle and Rose just shown up at the door?), my bare chest, and my bare feet again, as if, now, it was my turn to explain.

At that moment, the elevator door opened to my immediate left, and two more men, these much younger but identically dressed in blue coveralls, began to worry a chest of drawers out over the bumps, upended on a padded dolly. They got it out, closed the lattice gate and the door, sending the elevator back down again, then stopped short, startled to see me in the hall; one of them, a fellow with a menacingly pointed chin and wearing a kind of red skullcap, said, "Hallo . . . ," but with a scrappy inflection, as if *I* were the trespasser. Without a word, I turned, went back through the fire door, and climbed the stairs.

Inside the stairwell, I thought I could hear the patter of rain on the roof of the building, and it seemed to me that my entire life had been a drunken ramble down a long blind alley; that I was doomed never actually to arrive, and if I did arrive, all it would amount to was a bunch of jokers sitting around a room in overalls, singing bawdy lyrics, and everybody looking at me as if to say, What are *you* doing here?

Just before I reached the top landing of the stairs, I heard a chorus of male laughter from below—muffled through the walls and floor—which sounded something like thunder.

Back in the flat, I phoned Hannah at the front desk and asked her what the devil was going on below.

"Oh, dear, the movers," she said, taken aback by my territorial tone. "I've asked them to be especially quiet up there, but you know how they can be. What with so much furniture, Mr. Selway, and only the one elevator, I'm afraid it's going to be a bit noisy most of the day."

"Does this mean *guests* will be moving in as well?" I asked, as if it were an outrageous proposal for a hotel.

"We've no one booked in there till next week," Hannah said.

"Good," I said, and hung up, astonishing even myself with my rudeness.

There came a knock on the door, and I opened it angrily. Pascal stood in the hallway with a tea tray. "Good morning," he said, "I've brought your tea."

"I didn't order any tea," I said, and Pascal's eyebrows went up.

"But I thought you might appreciate—"

I apologized and let him in. I explained that I was out of sorts on account of the movers' waking me.

"I know," he said, putting down the tray in the parlor. "I have just now come up in a Louis Quatorze chair."

He poured out a cup of tea, then said, "It's very dark in here, yes?"

He went to the windows and yanked back the drapes. The tall windows were rain-bespeckled, and what I could see of the sky was a smooth, unvaried gray; still, the light was bright and sudden. Pascal turned, touching his fingers to his temples, saying, "Oh . . . what is happening?"

He did appear very pale, but I thought it was the light;

then he teetered a bit, and I began to move toward him, but he put up his hand. "It's okay," he whispered. "I am okay."

He took one step back, put his hand up again, and said, "I am okay."

I went to help him into a nearby chair, but he pulled away from me. "No, no," he said. "It is okay. I was only dizzy for a moment. I am okay."

Even as he spoke these words, he was already sidling around me toward the hall. "I will come back," he said quickly, and was out the door.

I opened the door, calling to him, but apparently he'd taken the stairs and was already gone.

When, over time, I have recalled this first morning on my own—the encounter with the singing movers, my rudeness to Hannah, Pascal's strange behavior—what comes to me most vividly is Pascal's face: in his moment of dizziness, his eyes were closed, and when he opened them, they were full of fear. During his urgent leaving, he never once looked at me. I have said that he was a strikingly handsome young man, and yet as he uttered his parting words, "I will come back," he appeared so gruesomely transformed, his face ugly with fear—fear and something else . . . revulsion, loathing—his words sounded almost like a threat.

I didn't see him later when I went out.

Hannah was at the front desk, on the telephone, and swiveled in her chair, pointedly putting her back to me as I dropped off my key.

I had decided to take a walk in the rain and had hoped to borrow an umbrella from Pascal's stash under the stairs. As he wasn't around, and as Hannah was snubbing me, I simply reached into the closet and took one.

Once outside, I saw at the curb the van that had brought the new furniture for the third floor. I also saw that I hadn't dressed properly for a walk, the air much colder than I'd anticipated. Under the circumstances, a gallery or museum seemed in order, and I began to make my way toward the tube station at Sloane Square. In passing, I recognized my conduct this morning as peculiar—rebounding like a pinball from one encounter to the next without design, entirely dependent on luck for the outcome—and I even noted, in passing, how this peculiar conduct was probably meant to avoid thoughts of Ellen. But it seemed to me (near the flower vendor where two weeks before I'd bought her irises) that it was my *situation* that was peculiar and not me myself. When I thought about this, I felt slightly disoriented; I'd entered the shade trees and crisscrossing walkways of the square and was suddenly struck by the absurdity of being in England at all, and the further absurdity of knocking about alone because my wife had abandoned me for the company of an ancient, oddball couple from Hong Kong. (I was also cold, which made me a little miserable.) At this point, contemplating luck and absurdity, I of course had no notion that in a very few minutes—having taken the Circle Line to Embankment, changed for the Northern Line to Charing Cross, got out, and walked into the National Gallery—I would be standing, in abject awe, before Meindert Hobbema's original painting *The Avenue at Middelharnis*, the painting I'd seen in my visions and dreams of the last several days.

I came up on it (as people say in the South, usually referring to a snake or other dangerous animal) in an already mildly bemused state: Instantly, on starting my walk through the halls, I'd felt that museum claustrophobia in which too much art is thrown at you with too little air to breathe; I'd stopped briefly to watch a class of schoolchildren, sitting cross-legged on the floor of the Sunley Room, before De-troy's painting of *Time Unveiling Truth* (the teacher, a lovely, exuberant young African woman, explaining allegory, pointing in turn to various female figures representing the virtues of Prudence, Temperance, Justice, and Fortitude, while the boys in the back row giggled over Truth's exposed boobies); as I walked away from this scene, with an illusive emotional ache of some kind—something about how susceptible the children looked, knotted together on the polished wooden floor in their matching plaid woolens—I'd begun to think of the singing movers again, and suddenly I imagined myself walking through the museum bare-chested and without shoes; I turned a corner, and there was *The Avenue*, with its haunting rutted road and increasingly sinister spindly trees.

It was very, very beautiful, this painting, and it appeared to be developing its hold on me with a good deal of vigor. There's no telling what degree of lostness I would have achieved had a batty old gentleman in a black suit and smelling strongly of lavender soap not moved in alongside me and whispered, "It's not actually very good, is it? . . . *You* may think it's good because you're impressed by a certain amount of decorative skill, but it's not actually very good."

I looked down at him—he stood only a couple of inches over five feet—and as he turned his wet eyes away from the painting and upward onto me, he whispered, "Well, am I right or am I wrong . . . what do you think?"

This question thus detonated, he remained locked on me for my answer.

At last, I said, "You're entitled to your opinion is what I think."

His shrunken face with its day's growth of white whiskers registered disappointment, review, and acceptance in the span of about three seconds, and he walked away with an almost enchanted air, as if his being entitled to an opinion (or any other thing) was a fresh idea, something that had never before occurred to him. I thought I knew this old man's story: He'd started out as a romantic youngster with an ardent desire to become a painter; he'd ended up dotty in the National Gallery, whispering to strangers his grievances against the Dutch masters. It seemed a familiar fate, a pattern I recognized, and somehow it made me think of the moment a few days earlier when I'd watched Ellen on the surveillance monitor at the hotel desk, tying the old woman's shoe: suddenly, it seemed tragic that we were apart, and stupid that I'd allowed it. I resolved to return to the hotel, phone her at the Shopans', and say whatever was necessary.

Though it was only around one o'clock when I stepped back into the outdoors, the day had grown darker and, I thought, even colder. It was darker still when I emerged from the tube station at Sloane Square. Drivers had turned on their headlights, and in the Sloane Street stores, lights burned bright; the late lunch crowd on the sidewalks rushed along with collars turned up, beset by the violent, wintry bent of the weather. When, from the corner, the Willerton came into view, with its cheery canopy and its doors of beveled glass lit gleaming from within, I felt I'd been rescued at sea. The furniture van was still at the curb, but it was shut up tight now—lunchtime for the men in the blue coveralls, I guessed. Pascal stood in a long coat inside the vestibule; he smiled and pushed open the door for me.

"Hello," he said with a little bow, and though he seemed mostly restored to himself, there was a lingering restraint. He followed me into the front hall.

"I borrowed this," I said, passing him the umbrella. "Hope you don't mind."

"No," he said. "Of course not."

With this slightly formal exchange, we went our separate ways—he to the closet, I down the narrow passage to the elevator—on opposite sides of the stairway. But before the elevator was ready, he was beside me again.

"Do you have a moment?" he asked.

"Sure," I said, and followed him back around the stairway to the little door under the stairs that led to the staff quarters below. I looked for Hannah as we passed the desk, hoping to put in a quick apology, but she was gone from her station.

On our way down the creaky stairs (the treads smoothed and round-edged with wear), Pascal said, "I want to show you something."

His room was rather like a monk's cell, complete with crucifix over the cot—gooseneck reading lamp, washbasin in the corner with shaving mirror, small set of shelves with a dozen or so books; clean as a pin, very little light, colorless. He directed me to sit in the only chair, which he pulled up alongside the cot, a ladder-back chair with a cane seat. Then he placed in my hands a roughly eight-by-ten photograph of a woman, framed in an inexpensive gold frame, the kind you can buy in a dime store. The frame's glass was broken, cracks splintering out in a kind of starburst design, but still contained by the gold metal around the sides. The woman herself looked something like Pascal—she had his fine-tailored features and dark coloring; she appeared to be in her thirties, very pretty, with short hair and wearing a light-colored turtleneck.

"My sister Catherine," Pascal said after a moment. He'd taken a seat close to me, on the cot.

"Very pretty," I said.

"Yes," he said. "Thank you."

"You should replace this glass," I said.

"That's just it," he said. "I have replaced it."

"What do you mean?"

"In six days," he said, "I have replaced this glass two times already. When I have returned to my room, it is broken again."

"Where do you keep it?" I asked.

"There," he said, pointing to the bookshelves. "I do not find it fallen. Each time, it stands just as before, but with a broken glass."

"Pascal—" I began

"Three times," he said.

"Pascal," I said again, "Tell me what happened to you this morning, in the flat."

"This I can not explain," he said. "I am sorry. I opened the drapes, I am blinded by the light, then I am dizzy. Then I am very afraid. I can not explain it." He pointed to his chest. "In here," he said. "In my heart. I am very afraid."

"But what were you afraid of?" I asked.

He shrugged his shoulders. "This is what I can not explain," he said.

I passed the photograph back to him.

He looked at it for a moment, and continued looking at it as he said, "I can look at this photograph of Catherine and I am home. I am a little boy again, hiding under our big table. All the sounds and smells of home are with me again. I can smell my mother's cooking. I can hear the radio and television, my brothers and sisters talking with their friends in the hall. I can smell the soap my mother uses on the floors, and my sisters' perfumes. But no one knows where I am. No one is thinking about me. I will show you something else. Not spooky."

He stood, put the photograph away, and returned to the closet, where he took down something from the top shelf. "This," he said, "is my hotel as I imagine it."

He placed on the cot a breadbox-size model of a simple frame house, fashioned out of balsa, painted a slate-blue color with white trim, and a cloth canopy out front, with broad blue-and-white stripes; it all rested on a flat board painted green (for grass, I supposed), and there was a remarkable amount of detail—porch railings, shutters, stairs, mullioned windows covered over with clear cellophane, and even individual roof tiles—but the really amazing moment was when Pascal reached down between the bed and the wall and plugged in an electrical cord leading away from the house: in his subterranean real-world chamber, with its spartan, chronic twilight, Pascal's little hotel came to life, bright and promising.

"Look," he said to me, pointing to one of the windows on the front. "Inside here you can see me."

I had to get out of my chair and go down onto my knees. I put my giant's face close to the window and looked inside, where I saw—standing next to a matchstick table with a red bucket of sunflowers—a tiny young man in a tuxedo.

Seventeen

PASCAL SAW ME to the hotel lobby, where the furniture men were back on the job, holding open the doors and letting in the cold, and where Hannah was in a dispute with the pointy-chinned man concerning the lorry's position, directly in front of the canopy. It was quickly clear that I would be waiting a long time for use of the elevator, so I said farewell to Pascal and started up the stairs.

Getting from the street level to the fourth floor meant climbing one set of stairs, entering the hallway, and walking to the other end for the next set of stairs. Thus I was fated, on the third floor, again to run into the musical movers of the morning; we smiled and said hello as I passed along the corridor, and I wasn't sure they recognized me in my clothes. I got all the way to the fourth floor without realizing I'd forgotten to bring up my key from the front desk—which required my going back down, getting it, and climbing all the stairs again. On my way down, I encountered the same movers in the third-floor hallway, and this time they did give me the fish eye. Downstairs, I took the opportunity of saying sorry to Hannah at last, and she dismissed my apology with a wave of her hand, as if she hadn't even noticed my earlier rudeness. I ran into the musical movers yet again on my way back up; the two of them were uncrating something just inside the door to one of the rooms, and as I passed, they stopped what they were doing, stepped into the hallway, and watched me go; I turned and waved with my fingers as I went through the fire door to the last set of stairs. I was quite winded by the time I inserted the key into the lock and flung open the door to the flat.

The place had been tidied by the chambermaid, my tea things cleared away, and the sitting room was freezing cold. I saw that one of the windows had been left all the way open. I crossed the room to shut it—thinking I would phone Ellen immediately and say what was needed to reconcile us—and when I turned back around, Victoria Jevons sat primly on the settee against the far wall.

I wasn't especially startled this time—I only jumped a little, silently, my reaction tempered maybe by my already being winded. The girl, dressed the same as always (complete with white gloves folded on lap), seemed to wince when she saw me and then compose herself, as if *she* needed to accommodate *my* presence. It had the (perhaps intended) effect of making me proceed gently.

"It's freezing in here," I said after a moment.

"I know," she said, again in that tone she had of extreme sympathy, of extreme sensitivity to the world's always coming up short. "I'm afraid that's my fault," she added, focusing on the narrow strip of wall between the two tall windows. "I quite forgot about the window."

I wasn't sure exactly what she meant by this—had she come in through the window and left it open? had she found it left open by the chambermaid but neglected to shut it?—but I let it pass. "I've been hoping to talk with you again," I said.

"Yes," she said. "I know."

"You know," I said.

"Yes," she repeated. "By the way, your wife was here a bit earlier."

"She was?"

"Yes," she said. "She took a few things. And left you a note."

She extended her hand, which held a white envelope, the hotel stationery. She did this with immense sadness, as if the note she was giving me contained the particulars of my death sentence.

I thanked her and opened the envelope. Ellen's handwriting:

Dear Cook,
I'm off to Hampstead today, with Mimi. I miss you, and I feel afraid. Can we have dinner tonight? We'll be back by four. Here is the number at the Shopans' . . .

"She's very pretty, your wife," said the girl. "As I'm sure you know."

"Thank you," I said. "Were you actually here when she was here? I mean, did you see her?"

"Oh, yes," she said. "But she didn't see me, if that's what you're wondering."

It was, of course, precisely what I was wondering. "I almost wish she had," I said.

"That wouldn't be possible," she said.

"Why not?" I asked.

"I'm not sure," she said. "I only know it wouldn't. You and she have had another quarrel."

"A big one," I said.

"I'm afraid she's left you," she said.

"Only temporarily."

"Yes," she said. "That's what I thought. Tem-po-rar-i-ly. 'My wife has left me, but only temporarily.' "

"Very good," I said.

"It's my only real strong point," she said, smiling almost imperceptibly, "a gift for good spelling. I inherited it from—"

"Don't tell me," I said. "From your mother, the musical-stage actress."

Now she faced me for the first time—and smiled genuinely, openly. "Well, no," she said. "From my father, actually."

"Would it be all right if I sat down over here?" I asked, indicating the sofa that was at a right angle to the smaller settee.

"Yes, of course," she said.

The settee had a hard, wine-colored cushion and arms and a back of black wood that looked something like wrought iron, an edgy piece of furniture, somehow suited to the girl's uncompromising posture. I sat at the far end of the sofa, farthest away from her.

"May I ask you a question?" I said.

"So long as I may ask you one," she answered.

"Okay," I said. "I think your name is Victoria Jevons. Is that right?"

"That's right," she said.

"Well, tell me, Victoria," I said. "Why is it that you stare so intensely at the wall?"

"That's two questions," she said, "but I don't mind. I'm anchoring myself, to avoid dizziness, you see."

"Anchoring?" I said.

"Like a dancer, when she twirls," she said. "Otherwise, she might become dizzy and fall. It's the only way I can be here with you. Now it's my turn to ask a question."

"Okay," I said.

"Those newspapers over there on the table," she said. "Where did you get them?"

She referred to the pages of the *Daily Mirror* that Mimi Sho-pan had had copied.

"They're from the library," I said. "They're Xeroxes."

"Zeeroxes?" she said.

"Copies," I said. "A kind of photograph of the actual page."

"I see," she said.

"Did you read them?" I asked.

"I do hope you don't mind," she said. "I didn't think you would mind. It's just that they've got it all wrong."

"In what way?"

"In any number of ways," she said. "To begin with, they've said the dead girl in the street was me, when it was my sister Iris. It was Iris fell from the window, not me."

"I don't think anyone knew you had a sister," I said.

"It couldn't have been me that fell," she said.

She continued staring at the wall—anchoring—and apparently thinking. At last she shook her head and said, "No, it couldn't have been me. People frequently confuse us, you see, Iris and me, though we're quite different. Still, you would perhaps expect the newspapers to get it right."

She began to draw on her gloves.

"You're not going?" I asked.

"I'm afraid I must," she said wearily. "I'm beginning to feel a strain. And besides, that boy is at your door . . . that *French* boy."

There was a knock, and in the second it took for me to turn my eyes in the direction of the door, she was gone.

Pascal, standing in the hallway, declined my invitation to come in (a bit skittishly, I thought), held up the tiny ceramic miniature of a Dalmatian puppy that had been a parting gift from Jordie; he said, "Does this belong to you?"

I reached out and took it from him. "Where did you find it?" I asked.

"On my bed," he said. "In my room. Perhaps it fell from your pocket?"

"Thank you, Pascal," I said.

Then, handing me a message slip, he said, "Hannah forgot to give this to you," and left quickly.

Tony Rosillo, my stockbroker in New York, the man who'd described the Hotel Willerton as "something out of *Masterpiece Theatre*," had phoned.

I put the message slip and the Dalmatian on the table with the copied pages from the *Daily Mirror*, went to the bedroom, and lay down, feeling, I imagined, a strain similar to the one Victoria Jevons had mentioned. I looked up at the ceiling and thought of the moment, a few days earlier, when Ellen had asked me to whistle and I'd begun whistling "Row, row, row your boat . . ." It seemed a random thought at first, as I lay on the bed recalling it, but in the next moment, when I got to "Life is but a dream," I saw its subliminal message: Certainly, life, at the present time, had the elusive nature, and the nonsense, of a dream.

Grace, I thought, had touched me in Ellen's note. Just when I was about to relent, there she was, folded inside an envelope, relenting. Grace was a funny, ironic, and perhaps dangerous thing to a narcissistic, non-drug-taking drug addict like myself; though grace was by definition unmerited, the fact of its bestowal could make you feel deserving. In the heart of every drug addict (even while he lay in the gutter) was an ember of pride, ever smoldering, and all that was needed to make it burst into flame was a bit of luck.

Briefly, I considered some of the questions I should have put to Victoria Jevons but didn't. For starters, What are you doing in my flat? What do you want from me? Who the devil is James, and why is he not mentioned in the newspaper accounts? I was completely bewildered by Victoria's mention of a sister, Iris. I also recalled that in our first meeting, in the sitting room downstairs, she'd told me she had a stepmother. The *Daily Mirror* described H. E. Jevons as a widower (as did Mimi Sho-pan). But I discovered fairly quickly that this kind of thinking—this kind of analysis—required a mental skill no longer available to me, and over the next few minutes I experienced that same boiled-down, imagistic consciousness I'd got into right after my encounter with James.

Eventually, however, a good deal later, I began to think of food—it would soon be four o'clock, and I'd had nothing to eat since my single scone with jam that morning—and I noticed that something about going without food was suddenly very appealing; the hollowed-out feeling beyond hunger seemed just the ticket, an essential part of my readiness. I decided not to have dinner with Ellen after all but to propose tea, where she could have whatever she liked and I would forgo (as inconspicuously as possible) any solid food.

I waited until exactly one minute past four and phoned the Sho-pans. Mimi answered, and with her crisp, club president's manner, said, "Cookson, hold the line . . . she's just here."

"I'm sorry," I said when first I heard Ellen's voice.

"I am too," she said. "Do you want to have dinner?"

"Let's get together around five for tea," I said. "Can you make it that soon?"

"Yes," she said. "Where?"

"What about here?" I said. "Downstairs."

"Okay," she said. "I love you."

"I love you too."

And that would have been that, simple enough—we would have patched up, and that patching up would have led us to a better destination—had I not replaced the white telephone in its white cradle, rolled over, and fallen asleep.

I dreamed the chiropractor dream again, in which I'm lying faceup on his padded table, he says to me (kindly, meditatively), "Now just relax . . . just let it all go," and then twists my head from my body. This time, however, in his panicky efforts to correct his mistake (in his overzealousness), he additionally drops my head on the hard tile floor; I feel a thud at the base of my skull, the treatment room spins a few times,

I'm suddenly looking at the chiropractor's enormous black shoes, and then, shifting my eyes up a bit, at the underside of the table.

The dream didn't seem nearly so unpleasant as before. Inside it, I recognized that I'd had this experience previously, and I solaced myself with the knowledge that it was in fact only a dream and that I would be waking from it at any moment. This enabled me to detach from the chiropractor's panic (it was his panic that had been most frightening) and even to enjoy to some degree the perspective issues raised by sudden decapitation. Beneath the table, looking at the chrome crosswise braces on the underside of the treatment table, I could feel myself growing philosophical, a proper and logical direction, I thought, for a head without a body to take. But had I a toe (which of course I didn't), I'd have barely dipped it into these waters before I began to awaken.

I say "began to awaken" because I passed from dreaming to not-dreaming as a kind of slow fade-in: the chrome braces on the underside of the chiropractor's table became the mahogany braces on the underside of a muslin canopy. I lay on my back, under the covers, and I noted that somehow I'd lost the clothes I'd worn earlier that day to the National Gallery. The room was dark now, though nearby, somewhere down around my right hip, a stripe of light ran up from the bed to the top of the canopy (a part in the side curtain). I thought it interesting that on waking from the severed-head dream I should be made so extremely aware of my bodily conditions: I ached in my joints (particularly my knees and elbows), I reeked of whisky, and I could feel a heat behind my eyes, as if I were running a fever. There was a dreadful familiarity to this—I'd seen and felt it before—but there was something else too, something new, a kind of heavy pressure all along the length of my left side, as if I were wedged up next to a hard wall. This wall, pressing against me and seeming almost to bulge and recede as if it had life and breath, was the new focus of my fear, the thing that kept me perfectly still so as not to disturb it, the thing that made me close my eyes and begin my litany of who I was, where I was, and no need to be

afraid. But this time, as I began silently to recite to myself my
various relational claims—husband to Ellen and so forth—it
seemed an abstract of the hopeless shambles I weakly per-
sisted in calling my life: Cookson Selway, son of disordered,
murderous, hick parents, deserted by a skeptical wife, abandoned by a spoiled, head-in-the-clouds daughter, dragged by
unknown powers to a foreign country, an impressionable,
self-extincting player in one of Fate's nasty little subplots. No
comfort there. I had achieved what I meant to achieve: I'd got
myself alone on Terror Island. I recognized the place from
earlier visits, back in the days of hallucinogens. (Long before,
coming on to an especially intemperate dose of acid—I'd dissolved a laced sugar cube intended for four people in a glass
of water and drunk the whole thing down—I sat on a red
Naugahyde ottoman in somebody's house, and—middle of a
conversation, lots of people and activity around me—the entire world fell away, rapidly, leaving me dumb with fright,
isolated a mile high on my ottoman.) Once again, the silence
in the room, inside the curtains of the four-poster, was absolute, tomblike. Once again, I felt my heart racing and could
hear little whooshing sounds in my ears. Then I heard—huge,
reverberant, as if from an echo chamber—the slow clop-clop
of horse hooves outside in the street, beginning faintly, growing louder, stopping entirely, beginning again, fading away.
The wall that was pressed against my left side began to shift,
to slide downward like a rotating drum even as it renewed its
hard pressure, and then a muscular arm fell across my bare
chest, a mass of red curls emerged from the covers, a beard
brushed up hard against my chin, nuzzling, a gravelly sigh, a
dead stench of stale Scotch.

A second later, I landed on the floor, hitting it hard at
the base of my skull, precisely in the spot where I'd thudded
against the chiropractor's treatment-room floor a minute earlier in my dream. I actually experienced a moment of free fall
on the way down from the high bed. Immediately, Walter
Jevons poked out his head from the side curtain like a jack-in-
the-box; he looked down at me, pathetic and naked on the
cold hardwood floor, made a kind of irascible grunt, and

withdrew his head, snapping shut the curtain, good riddance to bad rubbish.

I would have thought that the impact of my body against the floor might have broken up the illusion (for lack of a better word), that things would have been restored to their natural state, but no: I lay naked on the floor of a room very much like the bedroom of our flat at the Hotel Willerton—there was a recognizable pattern in the panels set into the wainscoting, but instead of cream-colored plaster walls, we now had a wallpaper depicting (perhaps seven hundred times) a pastoral scene (a dell, a stream, a bridge, three swaying poplars) in beiges and golds and olive greens. Heavy floral drapes covered the windows, the cornices covered in the same fabric. I'm not sure how long I lay stunned on the floor beside the enormous bed, but I do recall shivering at some point for cold, and I do recall a complete, childlike loss about what to do next. Should I crawl out of the room naked, on my hands and knees? Should I part the side curtain and strike up a conversation?

There was about a three-inch space between the floor and the hem of the bed's dust ruffle, and when I turned my head I could see straight under the bed to the other side of the room. Piled on the floor, way over there on the other side, I saw what looked like my clothes. One errant sock lay a few feet away from the pile, like a little adventure craft recently embarked from the main island, and something about this sight gave me a sense of hope and purpose: if I could just get my clothes, I might be all right, I might survive. I decided that hands-and-knees really was the best mode of travel and quietly began the journey to the other side. There was a wool rug at the foot of the bed, a welcomed cushion to my knees, but beneath it a squeaky board that let out a caw into the silent room, causing me to freeze. I heard a stirring in the bed, the curtain parted again, and I received a blow to the back of the neck that flattened me.

This seemed grossly unfair. I didn't mind so much being frightened—that was a consequence of my expanded consciousness, it came with the territory of giftedness—but why should I be abused? I'd done no one any harm.

I stood quickly, grabbed my jeans off the floor, pulled them on, yanked back the side curtain, and began to say, "Wait—" (righteously indignant, I was going to say, "Wait just a minute"), but something (Walter Jevons's head?) struck me in the stomach with the force and heft of a cannonball, taking my breath and knocking me back against the wall. In the next moment, I found myself wedged, legs splayed like a rag doll, in the right angle of the wall and the floor. Some brief blackness, no more than a blink, and I was back in the bedroom with the twin beds, this last blow, which I could still feel deep inside my stomach, having returned me to the Hotel Willerton.

Surprising myself—though I now acknowledge the slapstick quality of what had just happened—I began to laugh out loud, and I think I may have had some little bit of trouble stopping. The room was quite dark, somehow darker than it had been only a moment earlier. I felt nauseated, and all the other symptoms—the achiness, the feverishness, the smell of stale whisky—were still with me too. Eventually, I rose from the floor, finished dressing, and started out into the hall on my way to the bathroom.

As I went through the bedroom door, another fright awaited me: a pink rubber ball came bouncing down the hall, unnaturally high, passing in front of my face, hitting the closed door of the spare room, and rebounding back up the hall into the sitting room. It came to rest in a corner next to the dining-room door. I went into the sitting room and picked it up. I knew at once that it was the ball belonging to the little boy I'd encountered in the spare room. I took the ball with me into the bathroom, where I placed it on the sink; I turned on the light over the medicine chest, and viewed myself in the mirror. I had changed: Even now, I can't say explicitly how it was apparent, but the man I saw in the mirror had a different past and a different future from my own; this culprit with the hooded eyes had pulled out all the stops and taken some of the hairier paths not actually taken by me; this was the unlucky wretch, for example, who'd gone on to develop a career in smack, the one who'd driven one night from a party in Westchester to New York in a blackout, lurched the car off a bridge, killed his pregnant wife, and lived to talk about it. I could see about twice as much detail in my face as I wanted to see—every line and black and white whisker and purple blemish and reddish blotch.

To my great relief, I was saved from dwelling there by a familiar crying sound coming from the spare room. "James," I said aloud, and picking up the rubber ball, I went into the dark hall toward the door.

As before, I knocked gently.

As before, I heard the high resigned voice: "Come in."

As before, I saw a young child, blond in the dimness, sitting on the bed with his back to me. I took a few steps toward him, stopped, and said, "I've found your ball."

The child turned slowly to face me. It was not James but Victoria—a transformed Victoria Jevons, instantly harder and bolder—who smiled severely at me and said, "Fooled you, didn't I?"

Eighteen

ON THE NIGHTSTAND between the two beds was a digital display clock, the older kind, with little flaps that fall down to change the numbers, and as the girl smiled at me, the minute and hour changed—inexplicably— to nine o'clock. I must have startled visibly. Somehow the rubber ball fell out of my hand, bounced sluggishly a couple of times on the carpet, and rolled under one of the beds. Victoria Jevons, with her new demeanor and new voice (a good perfect fifth lower than before), cocked her head, raised one eyebrow, and said, "Feeling a bit jumpy tonight, are we?"

The only light in the room was what spilled in from the bathroom via the hallway, but when she cocked her head I caught sight of her eyes, got a good look at them. They were bluish and extremely cloudy (like James's), as if they were stuffed in sausage casing. She lingered on me long enough to achieve her wily, taunting effect, then turned back to face the wall—apparently "anchoring" herself there. She was dressed as before, in the sailor dress, with two significant changes: she went barefoot, and the white gloves were gone. I asked her if she minded my turning on a light.

"I'll do it," she said, and rolled back onto the bed, extending one slender white arm to switch on the nightstand lamp. She covered her eyes for a moment, then slowly moved her hand away. "I do wish you had candles in here," she said. "They're ever so much more agreeable." She remained stretched out on the bed, drawing her legs up and smiling, an awkwardly seductive maneuver I couldn't begin to imagine of the girl I'd originally met in the sitting room. She said, "Your lovely wife dropped by again."

"Yes, I know," I said. "You told me before."

She'd chosen a new anchor, a spot on the ceiling, and until I caught on to this, I thought she was rolling her eyes at my remark. She said, "I couldn't have done. I'm saying she was here tonight."

"I don't understand."

"You'd best sit down," she said, patting the mattress beside her, but I took a seat on the other bed. As I did this, she rolled her eyes back so severely I thought she might be starting an epileptic seizure. "She was here tonight," she said at last. "And very upset, I must say."

"What was she upset about?"

"She wanted into the flat, didn't she?" she said with a

hint of a smile. *"Somebody had fastened the chain lock. That chain lock's a bit controversial around here . . . a regular bone of contention. But you've never heard such banging and bellowing from a civilized woman. I think you were supposed to have tea?"*

"Yes," I said. "I'd better phone her."

"I don't think that would be very useful now," she said. "She's quite aggravated."

"But I never heard her," I said.

"Of course you didn't," she said. "You were with Walter."

"I was asleep," I said.

"Yes," she said, "in a manner of speaking."

"What do you mean by that?"

"I'm sure I don't know what I mean," she said. "Your wife's a rather aggravated sort, if you don't mind my saying so."

I felt confounded by this young girl curled up kittenish on the bed, physically recognizable as Victoria Jevons but unrecognizable in any other way. I suppose I felt challenged by her. I said what I'd meant to say earlier: "What do you want from me?"

She appeared genuinely shocked by the question. "Whatever do you mean?" she said.

"What are you doing here, in my flat? What do you want?"

"Oh, dear," she said. "You Americans do have an edge, don't you? I only meant to be sociable. I only meant to be hospitable."

"Where is the boy?" I said. "I want to see the boy."

"You mean James?" she said. "It's a bit late at night for little boys, don't you think?"

"And where are your gloves?" I said.

"What gloves?" she said. "Oh, you mean Victoria's gloves. I'm afraid they've gone and got themselves soiled. That's the trouble with white gloves, isn't it? So clean, Victoria. Such a good *clean* girl. Not at all like the rest of us."

"Then you're not—"

There was a knock at the door to the flat. She looked up at the ceiling for a moment, then shook her head quickly and dropped her shoulders with exaggerated disappointment. "What a pest that one is!" she said.

"Wait," I said. "Don't go. I'll just—"

The knocking came again and more insistent. The girl sat up, swung her legs off the bed, facing the wall as before, and turned to look at me one last time; when she did, I saw in her face Victoria's fragility, and when she spoke, it was in Victoria's high, delicate voice. "Could you do me an enormous favor?" she said with great poignancy, pulling down the hem of her dress.

"What?" I said.

"Could you possibly see to that door?"

She winced when, at that moment, the knocking came a third time. She closed her eyes and touched the bridge of her nose lightly with two fingers.

"Okay," I said. "But don't go."

She only looked at me sadly, then turned back to face the wall. By the time I reached the door and let in Pascal, she was of course gone.

"What has happened?" Pascal asked, just inside the dark sitting room. "You are ill?"

Ellen, having failed to rouse me, had asked him to look in on me when his shift was done. I explained—I think with some impatience—that Ellen was making a mountain out of a molehill, an analogy that confused Pascal. I went on to say that I'd only been sleeping, that Ellen couldn't have tried very hard to wake me. I said that I would phone her.

Then I had an idea. "Pascal," I said, "what are your plans for the night?"

"Tonight?" he said. "I have planned a very exciting evening for myself. I will have a bath, watch the telly, and go to sleep."

"Good," I said. "I want your help."

He shrugged his shoulders.

"I wonder if you would mind sleeping here tonight," I said. "In the spare room."

His face lit up, all trace of earlier skittishness gone. "We will chase the spirits?" he said.

"Something like that," I said.

"Okay," he said. "I will help. Tell me what to do."

About an hour later, as I lay in bed poring over the copied pages of the *Daily Mirror*, the phone rang—Ellen, quite emotionally shut down and guarded. I said I'd been just about to phone her (a lie: I'd not felt like phoning her and had decided to put it off until the next day). We replayed a composite of former conversations. She wanted me to see a doctor. I said there was no need. She wanted me out of the flat. I said I had no choice but to stay. She said that was ridiculous. I said I agreed, but there it was. We decided to meet for breakfast, to continue our tedious conversation. I said I would come around to the Sho-pans' at nine the next morning.

Pascal was settled into the spare room, having gone down to collect what he needed, returned, bathed, and tuned in a television show he was accustomed to watching on Monday nights. My idea was simple enough: I would use Pascal as my own sort of anchor—if I found myself transported to the flat's other world of four-poster beds and abusive miscreants, I would remember that he was somewhere nearby and call out to him. (I was anxious to see what effect the intrusion of another person might have, and I was interested in acquiring a witness as well.)

In the *Daily Mirror*, I'd been searching for some detail I might have missed, some overlooked particular that might be of use. I hadn't found any. Given the style of reporting that seemed to be typical of the paper—a very terse, tabloid format—it didn't surprise me that the reporter might have botched some of the data. (The articles were without bylines, though reports from far-flung locations began "From Our Own Correspondent.") In general, the flavor of the paper was more prurient than earnest, meant to entertain more than to inform. On the same page with the story about the Jevons tragedy were reports about a man who'd hoaxed over a hundred of his fellow visitors to Loch Ness by swimming about the loch with an artificial serpent's head protruding from the water; Queen Mary's wedding gift (an antique dressing case) to the Duchess of Kent's lady-in-waiting, who was about to marry the Duke of Kent's equerry; a psychic who'd painted a picture of a man from over three thousand miles away; and a man who'd fashioned himself a set of false teeth out of the melted-down aluminum crankcase of his motorcycle. (There was also a very brief mention of a German speaker at an International Trades Union Congress in London, who warned that behind Hitler's peace speeches, preparations for war were quite far advanced.) It occurred to me that my own story, the story of my recent experiences at the Hotel Willerton, was just the sort of thing that would interest the *Daily Mirror* and that this was precisely what it had all come to—my life would make a good feature in a tabloid newspaper, something to read in the checkout line at the grocery.

I could hear Pascal's television down the hallway, and though the sound was welcome, I was struck once again by the extreme abnormality of the situation; my wife had abandoned me, and now the porter at the hotel was sharing my flat. I ached all over. I felt feverish. I was exhausted, though I'd slept for hours. I switched off the bedside lamp, and as my head sank into the pillow, I smelled the odor of bleach on the fresh sheets; the crispness of the sheets was a comfort, and then something like compassion for myself crept into my feelings. I saw myself as a poor fool, alone in the darkness, desperately clinging to his ghosts. My ghosts seemed all I had left. I thought there was something deeply wrong with me—there had always been—some deep need for relief that I'd tried to answer with drugs and drink and any number of other dubious pursuits, and that still sang to me from its black hollow: sang quietly of adventure and importance, but mostly sang an atonal air about nothing at all, nothing specific anyway, only a suggestion perhaps of *more*—more than what was, more than met the eye, more than usual, more than average, more than most.

I fell asleep for a short while, and immediately on waking, I thought of the rubber ball that had rolled under one of the beds in the spare room. At first I made a mental note to retrieve it in the morning, but then I found I couldn't let go of it. I couldn't get back to sleep, and every path my mind took circled back to the pink rubber ball. I thought of it in the little boy's hands, how he'd moved it uneasily from one hand to the other, how he'd squeezed it during our visit, the way Greek men play with their worry beads. I thought of the way it had bounced so unnaturally high, out of nowhere, startling me in the hallway, and how it had hardly bounced at all when I'd dropped it on the carpet in the spare room. After a while, the ball seemed to be growing, swelling under the bed to the size of a basketball, wedged and trapped against the slats. And I found that when I thought of the ball's swelling, I had difficulty breathing, as if it were swelling inside my own chest, crowding out my lungs. I thought of the air inside the ball, its soft smell of rubber, and soon I was cupping my hand over my mouth and nostrils—it seemed to me that my own breath smelled of rubber. Now and again I dozed for brief intervals, in which I dreamed of the ball—my coming upon it in the midst of a forest stream; Ellen opening her purse, lifting it out, and saying, "What's this?" In short, I was Obsessed in the Night, and after quite a long time of this, I decided to steal into the spare room and get the damned thing.

Pascal had left his door open, as I'd asked him to. I stood for a moment in the doorway and shivered; it was chilly in the flat, and I wore only my undershorts. I tiptoed into the room and into the narrow space between the twin beds. Pascal slept in the right-hand bed, looking rather cherubic in the dark. I got down on my hands and knees and searched under first one bed and then the other. As I didn't spot any ball right away, and as it was pitch black under the beds, I flattened myself out on the floor so I might reach an arm under, to feel around. There was a stirring, above me as it were, and when I raised up, again on my hands and knees, I

came part of a ludicrous dream in which my wife had left me for an old couple from Hong Kong, and the head porter of the hotel where we'd been staying had now moved in with me. When I fully awakened, about two hours afterward, I felt rested, not nearly so ill, but also disappointed that there had been nothing for Pascal to witness other than the oddity of my searching under his bed in the middle of the night for an alleged rubber ball. (I never found the ball, and later in the morning, when I looked again, it was not there.) After I'd dressed (not showered, not shaved), I had about forty-five minutes before it would be time to go see Ellen. As I took a seat on the sofa in the sitting room, folding my hands in my lap, glancing about, the extra time seemed a burden, an unwieldy, unwanted obstacle to my peace of mind, and this concern quickly grew into an awareness of my great anxiety about seeing her. At first I thought I just didn't want to deal with her, didn't want to have to explain myself again, and didn't want to feel the guilt and shame about having to explain myself. But as I began to imagine the task step by step—going downstairs, leaving my key at the desk, walking the seven hundred and fifty-three paces to the Sho-pans', and so forth—I saw that I was feeling anxious simply about leaving the flat. I tried to make the fear specific, tried to think of what it was precisely that frightened me so, but the images that came to mind were all small and mundane, memories of paltry, innocuous moments—dropping coins into a chocolate machine in the underground, struggling with the coins, finally getting it right, only to read in the machine's display, "All Out, Make Another Selection"; ordering a cheese-and-chutney sandwich in a shop, the counterman's saying, "Take away?" and my requiring a moment to grasp what he was asking (did I want the sandwich "to go"). Now these moments seemed fraught with panic (the train was coming into the station; people were waiting in the sandwich line behind me), and I dreaded repeating them, dreaded other moments like them. Most absurdly, it also occurred to me that everywhere I went, perfect strangers would stop me and ask if I was ill.

I did manage to abandon this line of thinking, eventually, and went into the kitchen to brew a pot of tea. After the tea, I decided just to go ahead and go . . . what difference would it make if I was a bit early at the Sho-pans'?

Out in the hallway, I could hear the sounds of workmen on the floor below, getting the new rooms in order, and more than anything, I hoped to escape the hotel without having to see any of them. I had to wait a long time for the elevator, but when it did come, I rode all the way down to the lobby, blessedly alone. (And I heard no piano music.)

When I dropped off my key at the desk, Hannah smiled naughtily and said, "You almost got me in trouble last night."

I experienced a flutter of panic ("Make Another Selection"), in which I racked my brain for what terrible thing I might have done in some altered state last night that I couldn't now remember. Hannah quickly explained—while the telephone rang—that she'd got on a bus going home the night before and seen a passenger whom she took for me; she gave the man a big friendly smile, the man returned a look of shock, got off the bus at the next stop, and then, only then, as Hannah watched him walk away, did she realize the man was not me after all.

She answered the ringing phone, and I took back my key, mouthing the words "I've forgotten something."

It was an innocent enough story, of course, but I thought it had a sinister edge; as I rode up in the elevator, I didn't like thinking of this man who looked like me, my double, out there in the world, in London, riding buses, taking offense at women's smiles, doing all sorts of things, acting out any number of dark impulses with my face stamped on them. When I got back into the flat and closed the door, I leaned against it, breathing deeply, as if someone had been chasing me and I'd got to safety just in the nick of time. I decided to phone Ellen and say I wasn't feeling well; then I thought the better of that—she already wanted me to see a doctor. I would simply say I was running a bit late and could she come to the flat instead; then I thought the better of that—I didn't especially want her in the flat.

This small dilemma of what to do and what to say to

Ellen seemed enormous to me, insurmountable, the sort of lose-lose situation that prompted ritual suicide as the only honorable course; but since I had no intention of disemboweling myself with a sacred shiv, the only thing I could think to do was to return to bed, perhaps even to pull the covers over my head. Returning to bed was unacceptable too, for it would only cause Ellen to phone the flat, then I'd be faced with the smaller dilemma inside the larger one of whether or not to answer the telephone. (I thought of those dreadful Russian nesting dolls, with their horrible little shrinking pageant.) If I answered it, then she would ask me what was wrong, and we would again pursue the familiar ground of previous conversations. If I didn't answer it . . . well, you get the picture. Ridiculously, yo-yo-like, I left the flat again, went back downstairs and, this time, out into the street and on to the Sho-pans'. I rang the doorbell at exactly nine o'clock.

Ray Sho-pan greeted me and let me into the dark hall. The effects of my recent adventures must have shown on my face, for he kept staring at me curiously, studiously, as if he might push a giant pin through my thorax and mount me on a piece of corkboard. Soon he began to nod—he'd apparently grasped all there was to grasp about me—and I began to nod too, agreeing with whatever unspoken conclusion he'd reached and smiling. Thus we were discovered by Mimi Sho-pan, in the hall, nodding at each other in the near dark like a couple of lobotomized diplomats in a psych ward.

She got us both into the light of the wet-wool-smelling parlor and settled on a couch. "Ray is worried about you, Cookson," she said, passing me a cup of tea she'd just poured.

"Yes," said Mr. Sho-pan. "You see—"

"He's concerned that you . . . may have lost perspective."

"That's right," he said. "You can get quite—"

"Caught up," she said.

"You can lose," Mr. Sho-pan said, "sight of . . ."

There was a long silence, in which he continued thinking about what word he wanted, Mrs. Sho-pan smiled at him, keeping her eyes focused intensely on his bald head (as if she were telepathically recharging his brain), and I felt the strong pull of the Hotel Willerton. I only wanted to get back to the flat, and my desire was beginning to have a little jungle beat of desperation inside it. I concentrated on a blue-and-white ginger jar that rested on the mantel, then on a sterling-silver baby rattle next to it.

At last, Mr. Sho-pan said, ". . . *yourself*, yes. Lose sight of yourself."

"Ray doesn't think you should be alone," Mrs. Sho-pan added.

"Well, that's what I want to talk to Ellen about," I said, though nothing could have been farther from the truth. "Where is she anyway?"

"She'll be right down," Mrs. Sho-pan said. "I'm afraid she's had some trouble sleeping."

I happened to notice that her eyes had settled on a large standing photograph on a table across the room, a picture of a handsome young Asian man with thick black hair, a wool scarf around his neck, and holding in his hand a white cockatiel; the young man was a full-of-life, bright, smiling, slightly exotic apple of someone's eye who could only have been the dead son, David. The frame was especially fine, broad and woven with amber-colored straw, chosen, I imagined, with love.

"I see," I said.

Mrs. Sho-pan looked at her wristwatch, and I realized that they, too, were waiting, waiting for Ellen to appear and for us to leave so they could proceed to the hotel for their breakfast, as they were accustomed to doing, and it seemed to me that I was steeped in a long, clogged-up history of waiting for Ellen, waiting for her to finish dressing, waiting for her to get out of bed, to come out of the bathroom, to set the table, waiting for her to get her period, to shed her grievous mood, and (cruelest thought) waiting for her orgasm. At the same time—in this cool room of dark woods and burgundy-colored satin pillows and porcelain litter and irretrievable losses—I continued to feel the increasing tug of the flat; the analogy that came to mind had to do with ocean currents, with tides, and I saw myself as pulled inexorably by an undertow, or riptide, that, if I fought against it, would exhaust and drown me; if, on the other hand, I simply let it take me, stopped resisting it (as I was resisting it now by sitting in the Sho-pans' parlor), it would eventually deposit me safely back on dry land. (I didn't know if this was true, this stuff about rip-tides, but I'd heard it all through my youth, growing up driv-ing distance from the Gulf Coast.) I believe each of us—Ray and Mimi and myself—had departed one another's company for a private daydream, and suddenly, having entirely lost awareness of the teacup in my hand, I let it drop into my lap. A great commotion ensued in which, after a moment, I found myself alone in the entry hall, having been instructed to make a right turn for the washroom, but impulsively, throwing cau-tion to the wind, I turned left instead, and so out the door and onto the street.

At the hotel desk, Hannah said, "You must be freezing."

It was quite damp and chilly out, and now I stood be-fore her in my shirtsleeves, my hands shoved into my pants pockets. Certainly I was vaguely aware that some component of my current misery had to do with body temperature, but no remedy for that condition (such as a jacket) had yet oc-curred to me. "Yes," I said in a dazed tone of self-discovery, "I am," and proceeded to the elevator.

The telephone was ringing as I entered the flat. I had no idea what I was going to say to Ellen, but I picked up the receiver anyway, with the same abandon with which I'd ducked out of the Sho-pans'.

The voice I heard was a man's, and though it was dimly familiar, and though he was familiar with me—"Cook, my man," he said, cheerfully, "how's it going?"—the surprise com-pletely threw me. I made a long, tongue-depressed "ah-h-h-h . . ." sound.

"Tony," the voice said. "Tony Rosillo. How's it going, Cookson?"

"Tony," I said. "Fine, fine."

From where I stood, I could see the kitchen door, which now framed a kind of surrealist picture of a small café table and two chairs, a window, a bright chrome toaster, and on the right side of the frame a pair of small bare legs protruding into the picture, swinging in midair, the legs (in short pants) of a child who must have been sitting on the kitchen counter.

"What'd I tell you?" Tony said. "Just like *Masterpiece Theatre*, right? What'd I tell you?"

"Yeah," I said, moving around, the better to see into the kitchen, stretching the phone cord taut. "Just, Tony. Just like it. Aren't you up awfully early?"

"This is normal for me," he said. "Got to get a jump on the day, you know. Early bird gets the worm, I guess, or some such baloney. Insomnia, more like it, if you want to know the truth. Hey, Cookson, listen . . . I really hate to bother you on vacation and all, but a little something's come up—"

Now, from my new position, I could see the little boy sitting on the counter. He was paying me no mind whatsoever, but simply tossing a pink rubber ball into the air, catching it in his hands and tossing it again.

Tony Rosillo went on about some global market thing that had a deadline he'd let slip up on him. I'd heard maybe half of what he was saying, and when he actually began quoting figures, I interrupted. "Tony," I said, "I'm going to have to get back to you—"

"But that's what I'm saying," he said quickly. "To get in on this thing—"

With a composure that impressed even me, I calmly explained that I couldn't talk right now, and urged him to take care of business, to do whatever he thought was right.

As soon as I hung up the phone, it began to ring again, this time most assuredly Ellen.

At the same moment, someone knocked on the door.

I stood in the middle of the room, looking from the boy in the kitchen to the telephone to the door. The boy was still seemingly oblivious of me—certainly oblivious of my quandary—and at last I reasoned that he might stay put if I let the phone go on ringing, answered the door, and got rid of whoever was there.

It was Pascal, standing in the hallway with tears in his eyes even now, though from the swollen, blotchy look of his face, he'd been crying for some time. In his forearms, like a drowned child, rested his model hotel, now smashed to bits.

is vivid in some of its particulars, there are many gaps—blank spots—and I've had to improvise a chronology based (mostly) on reason. My experience of this passage was episodic and dreamy; I was kept asleep a lot of the time, taken out now and again and played with, then put back. (I could sometimes be roused by a banging at the door or by a ringing telephone, but apparently not every time, and usually, on coming round, I found myself in some bed or other, supine on a couch, or even prone on the floor.) I didn't leave the flat (except once, to go as far as the elevator) during those three days and three nights; I didn't bathe or shave; if I ate (and I suppose I must have), I ate what I could scrounge from the kitchen cabinets and the fridge—at least once, Pascal, concerned for my health, brought up a sack of scones with currants. Pascal was the only hotel employee for whom I would unlatch the chain lock, the only one allowed to cross the threshold. Lucky Pascal! How good of me to choose him! He, for his part, was out for revenge from the time he discovered the smashed hotel; rightfully, he blamed my ghosts, though I was never clear about how he thought he might punish them. No chambermaid was admitted into the flat to clean. Once, a young girl in a black and white uniform overrode the Do Not Disturb sign I kept hanging in the hallway and actually knocked at the door; I opened it a narrow slit, put my face there, and snarled ghoulishly one word: "No." That seemed to do the trick. You see, I had decided that my "problem"—the reason I didn't seem to be getting anywhere with my ghosts, the reason things didn't seem to be developing satisfactorily—was due to the persistent muscling in of the outside world, due to all the confounded interruptions. What I needed, if I meant to get anywhere, was to give myself over, utterly. I'm not sure where, exactly, I thought I was going to "get." I suppose I thought I would draw out the ghosts, learn their story, and, from my advantaged, still-incarnate state, help them in some way. I was, after all, a man with a gift, brought by fate to this place of tarrying souls so that I might perform a necessary mission.

As for Ellen—the love of my life, the woman to whom,

even in her now-exiled state, I actually owed my life—she arrived twice at the narrow slit of the door and was ignored by me the first time, let in briefly the second. The Sho-pans came only once but were, effectively, turned away.

Because Victoria Jevons had a nasty little habit of appearing out on the ledge and putting her face at the window, never failing to startle me, I soon kept the heavy drapes drawn in the flat, and the usual, helpful distinctions of night and day dissolved. Now and then I heard the sound of rain spattering against one of the windows, the cooing of pigeons on the sills, a car horn or police siren in the street, but these mild intrusions were far away and only reminiscent of a life and world to which I *used* to belong. A gamy odor claimed the flat, an odor I affectionately referred to once as "the essence of things," and the odor, in truth, wasn't completely off-putting, but was rather like a taste that had to be acquired—a very yeasty dough beginning to mold, or some exotic cheese; even, perhaps, something left too long in the smokehouse . . . well, like most odors, hard to describe with words, but it did have, inside it, a hint of something burning, or having burned. The odor (like the more temporary whisky fumes) claimed *me* too—weeks afterward, many baths and showers later back home in Cambridge, I fancied I could still smell it on my skin, and I began to think of it as my "damned spot." The other thing that would linger—and here I mean linger as a bur lingers beneath a horse's saddle, as a stone lingers inside your shoe—was something James said: Once, in that surprising manner he had, actually by way of a greeting, he said, "The fog in Green Park has condensed on the leaves of the plane trees, and now, when the breeze blows, it falls like rain"—a reference to the natural world, a young poet's nod, in hell, to unforgotten beauty, a reference whose future bedeviling, the way it would goad me, proved (somewhat, at least) remedial.

That Tuesday morning, as James sat on the kitchen counter tossing his ball in the air, as the phone rang and rang, and as a tearful Pascal stood in the doorway with his wrecked dream in his arms, I couldn't under the circumstances send

Pascal away as I'd planned to do. I invited him in. He wanted me to relieve him of his burden (apparently, now that I'd been given a private viewing of it, I'd become a kind of godparent to the dream), and as I went to take the thing from him, I somehow let it slip from my hands; it crashed to the floor in a heap of balsa rubble and electrical wires, insult to injury, and Pascal's response to the absurd length to which things had gone was to stomp it with his right foot and kick some of its timbers halfway across the room. He muttered something in French. I bent down to retrieve the little man in the tuxedo, brushed him off, and passed him to his life-size counterpart, saying, "Sorry, Pascal." The telephone stopped ringing.

Then we were both down on our hands and knees, gathering up the pieces and piling them all together on the green-painted platform representing a grass lawn. Before going, Pascal said, as he'd said on an earlier occasion, "I'll be back," and this time it really did sound like a threat.

The minute he was out the door, I stepped to the kitchen, where I saw James, sitting on the counter, swinging his legs and tossing the ball back and forth from one hand to the other. Without looking at me, he said, "I didn't do it . . . I swear."

"I didn't say you did," I said, and then he trained his cloudy eyes directly on me: I couldn't have said honestly at that moment whether I thought he'd done it or not; but there was something boundless in his eyes, a suggestion somehow that whatever was true about him, whatever was dominant (be it injury, deceit, or malevolence), it was essentially unlimited.

"I *didn't*," he said. "It was that girl."

"You mean your cousin?" I said. "Victoria?"

"Oh, yes," he said, as if he'd forgotten that Victoria was his cousin. "Well, Iris, actually," he added. "She did it . . . said you'd think it was me."

He seemed to be using a cabinet knob across the way as an "anchor."

"James," I said. "That's your real name, isn't it?"

He looked at me again, surprised. "I didn't think it would matter if you called me James," he said, "as long as you didn't know it was my real name."

"That was clever," I said.

"Not clever enough," he said.

I asked him who, exactly, Iris was.

He glanced past me, over my shoulder. "She's just there," he said, and when I turned I saw the girl, crouched outside on the ledge, looking in at us.

Of course I startled. "But isn't that Victoria?" I said when I'd caught my breath.

"They're the same," he said. "Only she doesn't think so. Sometimes she goes as Victoria, you see, and sometimes as Iris."

"You mean like a split personality?" I asked.

He appeared confused, thoughtful. "I suppose you could say that," he said at last, uncertainly. "Yes."

I went to the window, pushed it open, and invited in the girl, who at first only gazed inside one way and the other, as if to see who else might be present. After another moment, she tentatively climbed in and lingered near the sill, smoothing down her dress.

"We're talking about you," James called from the kitchen with some small amount of venom, and it did seem to be just what the girl had been worried about, out on the ledge, looking in, trying to see if we might be talking about her, talking about something she'd done. James came into the sitting room and sat on the sofa, staring defiantly at her. He looked down at the floor for a moment, focused on something there, then back at the girl. "We're talking about *you*," he said again, more aggressively.

"Whatever do you mean?" she said at last. Then, with a tremor in her voice, she said, "What have I done?"

"You smashed that man's model is what you've done," said James. "And you meant to blame it on me."

"But I didn't," she said. "I couldn't. I would never—"

"It was Iris did it, you stupid girl," James said.

"Iris?" she said.

"You're a . . . don't you know anything? You're a . . . split personality, you stupid girl."

She looked at me, as if to enlist my aid. She appeared to be on the verge of fainting. She went over to the sofa and sat next to James, a surprising move at that moment, I thought. She sat primly with her knees together, angled slightly in James's direction; her white gloves had been restored to her, tucked into and folded over the belt of her dress; she took these out now and placed them neatly in her lap, smoothing them down into place, a nervous ritual. She didn't look at the boy but instead seemed to focus on the same spot on the rug he was apparently using. When she spoke, it was still as Victoria, politely, but with more firmness than I'd heard before.

"James," she said, "you are being rude, and I'll not have it. You may not stay unless you apologize at once."

The boy glanced quickly at me, to see if I was observing the situation. His head bowed, he said, almost inaudibly, "Sorry, then."

"Good," she said. "There now. If Iris has smashed that boy's model, I'm sure you couldn't care less. So stop pretending."

"Just what he deserves is what I say," said James.

"Exactly."

"But she meant to blame me," he said. "It's not fair."

"Of course it isn't fair," she said. "You let me take care of it, will you?"

The boy glanced at me again, as if he'd saved some face here and wanted to be sure I'd noted it.

"Yes, all right, then," he said quietly, continuing to hold my eye.

"Good," said the girl. "Now where is your ball?"

"Here," he said, producing it from out of his trousers pocket.

"Good," she said. "Now please go."

"But you said I could stay if I—"

"And I want you to stay out of that grimy motor room, do you hear me? You'll soil your clothes and—"

"But I—"

"James, as you can see, is a good boy," she said to me. "But he needs a bit of discipline." She placed her hand to the side of her mouth and whispered, "Motherless."

"It's not fair," said James, rising and walking out of the room, into the hallway.

"*And* fatherless," whispered the girl. "An orphan."

"But I thought Walter was his father," I said.

"Walter?" she said, apparently stunned. "I assure you Walter is nobody's father."

James reappeared at the hall door. "I never actually said he was my father," he said to me. "I only agreed with you that Father had long whiskers."

"Go," said Victoria. "*Shoo*," and the boy retreated.

"I don't understand," I said. "Is James not your cousin?"

"Oh, no," said Victoria. "I have no cousins. James is a floater."

"A floater?"

"Yes," she said. "He came with you."

"With me?"

"Yes. He has no actual place to be, you see. He came to us when you came to us. He's a dear, poor James, but he really must try harder to get along with Iris. Has anyone ever mentioned to you, by the way, your strong resemblance to Stanley Baldwin?"

"No," I said. "Stanley—"

"Younger you are, and you've a great deal more hair," she said, "but quite strong, quite noticeable. I saw it straightaway. Father says that Stanley Baldwin is a relative of Rudyard Kipling, but I don't know whether or not to believe him. Father likes Stanley Baldwin, you see, because he says that Stanley Baldwin keeps the workers in their place. But I'm not sure it's such a good thing, keeping the workers in their place. It seems . . ."

She allowed her gaze to stray to the window; midsentence, she appeared to have lost her train of thought, to have accidentally changed tracks, and her face nearly crumpled under the weight of whatever she'd moved onto.

". . . it seems somehow . . . cruel," she added, "somehow . . . bullying."

"Victoria," I said. "Are you sure you didn't fall from that window?"

Without looking at me, she said quietly, "Sometimes I think I might have done. Oh, dear . . ."

"What?" I said.

Her eyes appeared to roll back into her head, then she focused again on the spot on the rug. "It's nothing," she murmured. "It's just . . ."

James suddenly reentered the room, walking deliberately over and standing with a very straight spine next to me. We stood side by side for a moment, looking at the girl, who seemed to have fallen asleep, though she remained neatly on the edge of the sofa, her head lowered now as if she were praying.

At last, smiling, James said, "She does that sometimes— nods off, just like that, in a wink. This is funny. Watch this."

He bent forward and shouted, *"Giddyap,"* startling the girl full off the sofa and onto the floor, which sent the boy into gales of laughter.

Finding herself on the floor, the girl smiled and pulled her legs under her, leaning back against the sofa, feigning a poise she couldn't quite bring off, as if she'd all along intended to sit there on the floor. She chose a spot on the wall behind James and me, focused there briefly, getting her bearings, then looked at me and said, in her lower, harder voice, "Well, I see you've found your little friend at last, the little sodomite."

"Smelly twat," said James, shockingly in his short pants.

"Piss off," said the girl.

"Simpering shit," said James.

"Bug-eyed little ponce," said the girl.

I suddenly felt nauseated, and drained, as if I'd run a mile up a hill in a heat wave; I even felt my heart pounding. I moved to a nearby chair and sat down, aware that the children, having fallen silent, were watching me. I must have gone pale.

"Now see what you've done," said the girl to James.

"What *you've* done," he said, "with your carrying on like some kind of bloody lighthouse."

I closed my eyes, for I really was feeling faint. I thought a cold rag in the face would do me good, and when I opened my eyes again, both children had vanished.

Sometime later the same day, I opened my eyes and noticed that the drapes in the flat had been drawn, though I had no memory of having done it. The drapes, as best I could make out in the darkness, were thicker somehow and of a different pattern, a maroon color with what looked like a tropical vine winding through the folds. I lay on the couch in the sitting room, my feet close to the wall where hung the reproduction of my old Dutch friend, *The Avenue*, which I'd construed to symbolize Fate—the man on the road with his dog and his burden of longings—and I recollected that somewhere at the National Gallery (was it right next to the painting?) I'd read that Hobbema's own fate, after his having rendered many tranquil landscapes, water mills, and ruined castles, was to die unappreciated, a pauper. The wall behind *The Avenue*, like all the walls of the room, was very dark, charcoal gray with huge blossoms like radioactive peonies exploding all around. It hadn't yet occurred to me to be afraid, though I was aware of a churning dread (a form of fear) in my solar plexus; I was also aware of a churning regret, and in that way I resembled the man on the road with his burden of longings, wishing he could change the past, wishing he could determine the future. This, of course, was only how I had tortured what was otherwise a lovely lesson in perspective: the actual man on the road had been hunting, I think, with his dog, in fine weather, and is probably walking happily back home now, where he'll no doubt be greeted at the door with hugs and kisses from his one true love.

Physically, I felt better than I did before; I'd begun to

feel better immediately after the children were gone. The nausea had passed; I must have lain on the couch. I recalled now the curious thing James had said about the girl's carrying on like a "bloody lighthouse," a quaint expression I never heard before (or since) and that faintly amused me; maybe he meant to refer to the switching the girl did, from Victoria to Iris—was that something like the intermittent beacon of a lighthouse? Suddenly, my sense of dread and regret seemed to attach to the children themselves, to some nascent disappointment I felt about my "young" ghosts—James, a foul-mouthed impostor in knee breeches, Victoria, a narcoleptic with multiple personality disorder—and I found myself laughing out loud. Though my laughter was halfhearted, and certainly fleeting, I suppose it must have provided some relief, for I dozed off briefly. When I awakened again, it was to the sound of voices—or the sound of a voice.

I noted quickly that the peonies still graced the wallpaper in the room, that I still lay on my back on the too short couch, that the painting still hung on the bit of wall near my feet. That would mean that the flat had changed (or remained changed) to its former constitution. The voice was coming from the next room, which would be the room with the four-poster. Briefly, I praised my levelheaded analytical skills and shifted onto my side, and when I saw that the door to that room stood open, I was abruptly afraid, like a child frozen in his bed at midnight by a sharp noise. No light came from the other room—everything a study in dark gray, with only suggestions of shape and color—and then Walter Jevons appeared, staggering, propping himself up against the doorjamb, entirely naked, unpleasantly hairy from head to ankle. Even from this distance (twelve feet or more) I could smell his odor, a stench of whisky and tobacco and human rot. As a reflex, I sat up on the couch, and though I couldn't see his eyes clearly, I could tell that he was staring right at me; I actually felt the hairs on the back of my neck bristle.

Never averting his eyes from mine, he belched and idly scratched his belly, and it occurred to me that he was using me as an anchor. (It further occurred to me that to use a human being as an anchor would most likely be, in ghostdom, a lapse of decorum, a delicate sphere whose tangents Walter Jevons had escaped absolutely.) "There was always a great roll in the Mediterranean," he growled, as if he were merely continuing a conversation we'd been having. "We was just a . . . we had this . . ."

He went into a long, phlegmy seizure of coughing, then wiped his mouth with the back of his hand. "That fucking dog, that yellow hound, got so fucking seasick," he went on, ". . . sat around with his tail between his legs, moped about at all hours of night and day, eyes turning bright red-like . . ."

He seemed to go blank, then glanced at the ceiling, as if he were looking for his lines up there. "And we had a monkey once," he said then, returning his eyes to me. "Some of the men called it an ape, but it was an overgrown monkey . . . used to catch colds a lot, that one." He slid down the doorjamb into a shadowy crouch, huddling as if for chill. "The good thing about the animals," he said after much apparent thought, "was they was anti-officer, you know. We dearly liked that about 'em, anti-officer."

Jevons was silent for a moment, during which I sat very still, breathing very quietly, hoping he would go away if only I sat very still and breathed quietly. Then, to my surprise, James walked up behind him, shirtless, and peered at me over the man's head. Something about the boy—his sympathetic gaze, his vigilant bearing—seemed to suggest that he'd been seeing to Walter in some way and that at any minute he would reach for the man's hand and lead him back to bed.

"Once," said the man, with renewed energy, "some star-crossed sailor went overboard . . . at Nouméa it was . . . and in a flash they was sharks swimming all around him like buzzards circling a carcass . . . nine of 'em they was, nine sharks with their sharp fins sticking up spelling death in the water. . . . We stood there watching along the rails as they got the ship's dinghy launched . . . and we seized lumps of

coal and played Aunt Sally with the sharks . . . played Aunt
Sally, you see, till they could haul the man in to safety. . . .
Saved that sailor's life with fucking lumps of coal. . . ."

And then Walter Jevons raised his hand, pointing his
index finger straight at me—he was about to threaten me—
but James, much as I'd anticipated, stepped forward and
wrapped his own small, pale hand around the man's still-
pointing finger. Walter at first appeared surprised to see the
boy and regarded him as something he'd never before confronted; then in the next second, recognition washed over
him, a slow dawning that seemed, once it had started, to go
far beyond James and the actual situation, passing him
through *scolded, contrite,* and on to *grateful,* as, after a moment,
he rose, using the doorjamb for support, and allowed himself
to be led away.

"Got that fucking overgrown monkey in Gibraltar," I
heard the man mumble, though I could no longer see either
of them, only the empty open doorway.

Eventually, I would understand that Walter and James and
Victoria (in both her personalities) were dependent on me for
energy—that somehow they were using my power in order to
appear in a form visible and audible to me—and that was why
I felt sick so much of the time and needed to sleep. ("Emerging," as Iris would once refer to it, was, apparently, enjoyable
to them, and they needed me for it.) But in the beginning,
without any clear explanation, I thought perhaps I was being
drugged—an interpretation no doubt based mostly on my
past experience. I'd been very eager for the show to begin
and taken quite some pains to set the stage, and now that it
had begun, now that I'd isolated myself so the ghosts could
adequately have at me, I kept nodding off, a great annoyance.
Understandably, I was also (despite my remarkable willingness to offer myself up) made vulnerable by this sleeping,
endangered by it. I didn't know why Walter Jevons seemed to
want to harm me, why he seemed so angry at me, but no
matter—I couldn't stay awake to protect myself.

The next thing I recall after Jevons went back through

the doorway with James is James's face, close to my own: I'd opened my eyes and there he was, standing over me, gazing carefully. "It's darker here," he said, "but better, you know, because we don't require quite so much of you."

I had no idea what he meant by this remark. With great hopelessness, I said, "I don't know what you mean."

"It doesn't matter," the boy said. "Just rest now and try to—"

And I suddenly thought that *I* was the one whom James had led back to the four-poster; *I* was the one whom James attended, standing by the bed and looking down at me now.

"—try to sleep," he said, pulling the side curtain shut, and I was utterly lost inside this fabric chamber. That indeed was the phrase that took root in my mind: *utterly lost*. Apart from the white pulsing of blood in my ears, there was only silence, the silence of a mossy well, and as I began to drift off again, I thought that I must find Pascal. Pascal, I thought, could help me, and surely he was somewhere near, if only I could find him.

When I awoke, I was still in the four-poster, the folds of the side curtains like the pleated satin lining of a coffin, my only heaven the bowed canopy with its dirty muslin and wooden braces. I'd had a horrible dream, a version of the dream where I am the man on the road in the painting. This time, I could see a farmer operating a harrow in the rainy fields, his horse's black coat shining wet like the harrow's blades. The ruts of the road were filled with rainwater. The bull stood in the middle of the road, head lowered, horns dripping, and I thought, *I have accepted my fate, my relinquishing of the regular world in service of a higher cause.* There was only the silent rain and the deep silvery lines connecting me and the bull, but as the bull began to charge, Pascal appeared in the side road, waving to me full-armed as he'd done from the stern of the tourist boat in the Thames, calling my name, full of wonder at our extraordinary luck, our curious chance encounter, and the sound of my name, "Cook . . . Cook . . . ," a noun and a verb, sounded for an instant like a confusing imperative—

there was something I must *do*—and I tried to warn him about the bull in the road, flailing my own arms, tried to caution him back out of the road, but unseeing, he stepped between me and the charging animal, paused for a moment, and said cheerfully, "I'll be back. . . ." He meant to continue across the road on his own course, but the bull lifted him from behind, beneath the rib cage, into the air, Pascal's feet leaving the road, dangling spiritless like a marionette's. . . .

I seemed to know that I would be awake for only a minute, and vaguely I wanted to make the most of it, but my poor physical condition overtook me, subdued me. I hurt all over. My eyes burned. My knees and elbows throbbed. An odor, like smoky cheese or a ripe, yeasty dough, pervaded the air, crowding the more familiar stench of stale whisky. I made a sound, a low moan, and the curtain parted at my right side, revealing the girl, who tilted her head in a kind of mock compassion.

"Now, now," she said, "you don't need to look so sad. What's the matter?"

I began to cry then, for under the sheets I was naked and all wet between my thighs.

"I'm bleeding," I said to the girl, who smiled.

"That's the least of your worries," she said. "Walter's—"

James appeared at the part in the curtain, shoving the girl aside and saying, "Leave him be, you smelly twat . . . get away from him."

Surely it was the middle of the night, and yet some fool was pounding at the door. Didn't they know I was too sick to be disturbed at all hours of the night? Couldn't they just leave me alone? I dragged myself out of the bed and to the door, where I could hear a female voice on the other side calling out, "Housekeeping"—an interesting, earthbound word, a word with some warmth in it, and one I would probably have been curious about if it hadn't been the middle of the night and if I hadn't been so sick. I opened the door about two inches, put my face up to the crack, and saw a young woman standing outside in the hallway; she wore a black dress under a white apron. In her arms she held a stack of bath towels. My Do Not Disturb sign hung on the outside doorknob, but apparently this young woman could not read English. Smiling, she said the word again, "Housekeeping," then her face quickly changed—she looked uncertain, perhaps even afraid.

I said, "No," that was all, and closed the door.

I'd found the chain lock on, though I didn't believe I'd latched it myself, and now, thinking of Pascal, wanting to be sure Pascal could get into the flat when he arrived—he would arrive, wouldn't he?—I unlatched it. As I walked away from the door, I noticed that I was stark naked.

Housekeeping, a word with some warmth in it. I was stark naked. Utterly lost. I lay prone on the floor behind the sofa in the sitting room. I heard rain spattering the windows, a sound that made me very cold; vaguely, there was a desire to move, to get up, find a bed, find covers, find warmth . . . but that would have required more strength than I had. A truck horn blasted outside in the street, and more distantly the siren of a police car, identifiable, urban noises for which I felt a hint of nostalgia—not longing, exactly (for I had now accepted my fate, my relinquishing of the regular world in service of a higher cause), but rather a kind of detached affection. I was definitely awake, though I kept my eyes closed, the better to listen to the rain and the traffic and to contemplate my noble departure, my voluntary crossing-over, my inestimable courage. I thought I could lie there for a long time—I felt a quiet, solid peace—though I wished I weren't so cold.

A new sound, immediately recognizable, *someone else* at the door, and from my position on the floor behind the couch and in my limpid state of mind, it seemed I could hear the smallest detail: the sliding of the key blade into the lock's keyway (could I even hear the action of the key's serrations against each tiny pin tumbler?), the slamming back of the dead bolt, the drawing in of the latch bolt, the brief creak of the door hinges, and then the surprising yet somehow satisfying *Wham!* as the chain lock caught.

"Cook!"

It was my wife's voice from the hallway, a sound, like the horns and sirens outside, that filled me with a sensible fondness, a love of what used to be, but moderated by a surrender to what was now.

Requiring nothing of me but silence, the kind thing.

"Cook, I know you're in there," said the voice in the scolding tone of a schoolmistress. "Come and open the door."

But her words were only sounds, absent of content, absent of meaning: the stops, fricatives, approximants, trills, taps, and laterals, the frequencies and harmonic structures of the million-year-old music of human speech.

"*Cook!*"

And of course the intensities.

Pigeons were cooing on the windowsill, trills and harmonic structures. "Now that's better, isn't it," she said, looking down at me, her face pure kindness, the girl I met so long ago in the hotel sitting room, with its browning palms and pot of tepid tea.

I heard myself grunt out a reluctant agreement, though I wasn't sure what we meant, *better.*

"Yes indeed," she said. "Much improved."

The side curtains on the bed were pulled back to the posts; the room was bathed in a gray eternal dusk, but somehow not quite so gloomy as before. The girl took a seat in a chair by the bed now and looked rather comical there: the bed was so high, I could see only her slender neck and shoulders above the mattress's horizon. She smiled at me, genuinely, her cataractal eyes trained on mine briefly, then turned her head and faced away, focusing on something across the room. I dimly recalled some horror about bleeding from my penis, and I thought I must have had a nightmare. Generally, I was feeling better now—that's what *better* meant!—not so sick, not so despairing, not so frightened, though I was still very weak; if I'd had to move, had to get out of the bed, I wasn't sure I could have done it. But I was comfortable at least, and dry, thank God, beneath the sheets.

"Did you know," the girl said cheerfully, "that Rudyard

Kipling died only last January and right here in London? The most popular author of his day, he was. And the first Englishman to win the Nobel Prize for literature."

Though in that moment I surely couldn't have recited even a fraction of the specifics of my situation, there was something loathsome about the girl's launching into this extraneous chatter. I'd had enough. "I don't give a shit about Rudyard Kipling," I heard myself say.

She didn't seem surprised by this remark; she didn't even blink her eyes. "Oh," she said, still cheerful. "Well, many don't care for him. He's come in for a good deal of criticism, you know. My stepmother says on account of his imperialistic attitudes. You're certainly not the first. My stepmother—"

"I don't give a shit about your stepmother," I said.

She was silent for a moment, and though I could see only her profile, she appeared to grow pensive. "I quite understand," she said at last. "I shall stop babbling and let you rest."

"Victoria," I said quickly, "if you are Victoria—whoever you are, whatever you are—what the devil am I doing here? What are *you* doing here?"

She bowed her head briefly, then gazed forward again. "I don't think I know what you mean," she said.

"What's the purpose of all this?" I asked. "I think I'm here for some purpose, but I don't know what it is. Can you help me to understand?"

Now she remained silent for quite a long time, during which I concentrated on my breath, trying to safeguard my energy. Soon, and to my enormous frustration, it became clear that the girl had nodded off.

"Victoria!" I said, startling her awake.

She stood and walked away from the bed, toward the door. I had a sudden moment of panic at being left in the room alone—alone with this terrible sense that nothing had any particular value, everything was of equal insignificance. She stopped, almost as if she sensed my distress, turned, and came back to the chair, resuming her previous position exactly.

"I think," she said after another moment, "that perhaps I can help you."

She cleared her throat, like a student about to give an oral report in class.

"You are here for us," she said, nodding rhythmically with the cadences. "You are here for Iris and me, and Walter, and even for James."

I expected that this was the beginning of an explanation and that she would continue after a pause; but evidently she considered this to be the entirety of it—she was finished.

"But to what end?" I asked at last.

This question caused the girl to laugh, though sweetly. She sighed and said, "I'm afraid Iris is the one with the brains. My spelling's first-rate, and I'm clever with a needle and thread. I'm not bad at memorizing—I can quote you a good deal of verse, if you care to hear. 'Now winter nights enlarge/The number of their hours;/And clouds their storms discharge/Upon the airy towers.' Thomas Campion. 'While youthful revels, masques, and courtly sights/Sleep's leaden spells remove.' I love that, 'Sleep's leaden spells remove,' don't you? Oh, I could never write anything as beautiful as that. I could never even think it. You see, I can memorize almost anything, but reasoning has never been—"

"I'll tell you what I think," I said. "I think you fell out that window over there in the next room about fifty-some-odd years ago and that you haven't a clue about what actually happened. I think you've refused to face up to what actually happened, that you've repressed it because you can't deal with it. And you're stuck here in this stinking limbo or whatever it is because you haven't understood things well enough yet. That's what I think. And maybe I'm here to help you sort things out. So you can move on."

She laughed again, still sweetly, and shrugged her shoulders. "I'm sorry," she said. "But when you say things like 'move on,' it makes me feel giddy. I don't know what to make of—"

"Then let me talk to Iris," I said.

"No," she said, standing abruptly. "She's not here now."

She moved toward the door again, turning just before she reached it. "I can tell you one thing for certain," she said with exaggerated kindness. "We do not 'move on.' "

"Please don't leave," I pleaded. "Stay and talk some more. Help me understand. What do you mean, you don't move on?"

"We *are* . . . ," she began. "We are precisely, you see . . ."

"What?"

"We don't 'move on,' " she said finally. "Don't you see . . . that is who we are."

CHAPTER

Twenty-One

IN ANOTHER DREAM, I'm like the man on

the road in the painting, but everything about the landscape

has changed. Trees no longer line the road, though I can see

three tall poplars up ahead; the road itself doesn't cross flat

tilled fields, as before, but descends to an old stone bridge and a stream. It must be autumn, for everything is rendered in beiges and golds and olive greens. There are no people anywhere, not even any animals. I cross the bridge, climb the gentle hill on the other side, and at its crest I see an exact duplication of the scene I just passed through—the descending road, the bridge, the stream, the three swaying poplars. As I descend this new hill toward the bridge, I can hear the sound of the wind in the trees, the delicate gurgle of the stream, and a rapping sound in the distance, perhaps a woodpecker. Once again, I climb the hill on the other side of the bridge, gain the crest, and see an exact duplication of the dell with its stream and bridge and three tall trees. The rapping sound has grown louder—continues to grow louder and louder as I walk toward the third bridge—and it suddenly hits me: I'm not in the painting at all . . . I've somehow got myself into the *wallpaper* now. . . . I'm wending my way through the repeating pattern of the wallpaper in the room with the four-poster bed. This perception frightens me—I feel a sudden terror of flatness, a great dread of two-dimensionality—and I awaken to the rapping sound of the woodpecker.

It took me a few seconds, but eventually I understood that I'd been dreaming again, that I was in my twin bed, in my flat, in the Hotel Willerton, London, England. (I could see the empty bed where my wife used to sleep.) And the rapping sound was the banging on the door of someone who wanted into the flat.

I pulled on a bathrobe and staggered to the door. (I say "staggered" because it seemed, once I was up, that I hadn't walked for quite a long time and that now I had to reacquaint myself with the process on rubbery legs.) I found Pascal peering in from the hallway through the narrowly opened door.

"Pascal," I said, virtually overjoyed to see him. I quickly slid back the chain lock and let him in. "I've been wondering where you were."

"Sorry," he said. "You are already sleeping. I have brought a key, but the chain was latched."

"Yes," I said, and was about to add that it seemed someone kept latching it, but he handed me a white paper sack of scones.

"Some food," he said, closed the door, and turned the dead bolt.

I thanked him for the scones.

"It is dark here," he said. "You have already gone to bed. I will slip down the hall quietly."

He headed down the hallway for the spare room. Once inside it, he switched on a lamp and the television, then turned and seemed surprised to see that I'd followed him into the room.

"I'm fine," he said to me, almost irritated. "There is no need. Return to bed."

He'd changed somehow—there was a new guardedness in his attitude, surely a distinct, deliberate distance he was putting between us. I couldn't think what I might have done to cause this, and though I had no right to be, I felt hurt. I suppose my feelings were all the more pointed because I was so extremely glad to see him and the sentiment was decidedly not mutual. He stared at a cooking show that had materialized on the television—a man had sliced fresh salmon paper thin and sautéed it, and now prepared a dill sauce so thick with butter and cream it nearly made me gag.

"How about a little salmon with your sauce?" I said, but immediately regretted it, for I could see that Pascal was eyeing the dish with obvious appetite—appetite and something else: he remained grounded in the world in which such things as the preparation of food still mattered; it had value to him, his engagement a sign of his flesh-and-blood nature.

Again he seemed surprised to find me in the room, but looking at me, scrutinizing what must have been a goofy expression on my face, he wearily said, "I am sorry . . . you said you have been wondering where I am?"

"Well, I knew you must be here somewhere," I said. "I could sense that you were near, but I've been too weak to find you."

Muting the sound on the TV, he said, "You look . . . how can I say? Very white. You are ill?"

"I suppose I am, in a way. I think I may have been running a fever."

"Do you want a doctor?"

"No, no," I said. "No doctor. I'm already much better. Pascal, I'm so glad you're here. . . . I've missed you."

He appeared confused and a little embarrassed at this remark. At last he shrugged his shoulders and said, "Nothing happens."

"What do you mean?"

"I come here, I sleep," he said. "That is all. Nothing happens. And *you* sleep. Sleep and sleep. I have tried ringing you today. Your wife tries ringing you too, but no one answers. Why do you not answer? You are asleep. It's crazy. What's the point?"

He stood still before the television, at a loss. I did think I'd heard the telephone ringing from time to time, but distantly, like a phone ringing in someone else's apartment. Then a kind of logistical reality began to filter through my fog: I didn't even know what day it was or how many days had passed since I last saw Pascal; he was frustrated at a lack of results, and now he was trying to tell me he didn't want to sleep here again tonight.

"Something happens, Pascal," I said. "Believe me, a great deal happens. It's just that it isn't always clear to me *where* it happens. Or when, exactly. And when it's happening, I don't know how to reach you."

He shrugged his shoulders again, very tired of the game.

I asked him to tell me what day it was.

"It is Wednesday," he said patiently.

"Wednesday," I said, struggling to do the arithmetic. "Then you've slept here . . . what? Two nights?"

"Yes," he said. "This will be number three. And still nothing happens."

"I don't recall having seen you, Pascal."

"You have been *sleeping*," he said. "You are asleep. I let myself in. You are asleep. I let myself out. You are asleep."

"And have you actually seen me sleeping?"

"No," he said. "Your door—the bedroom door—is closed. I didn't want to disturb."

For a moment, I tried to recall what I'd had in mind when I first asked Pascal to stay with me in the flat. I imagined I'd been thinking of him as a kind of "designated driver" (alcohol abuse) or "guide" (psychedelics)—someone who'd stay straight and steer the course for the whacked-out. But now it occurred to me that I only wanted a reference point, or safety net, someone made of flesh to fall back on if things got too kinky for me to handle. Clearly, having him in the spare room wasn't sufficient. "Pascal," I said, "I wonder if you would consider sleeping in the same room with me?"

He did consider it, but only for a moment, then he shrugged his shoulders a third time, reached behind him to shut off the television, and said, "*Oui*, sure. Why not?"

But for Pascal it was the end of the day, and for me it was the start. Long after he'd fallen asleep in the twin bed next to mine, I lay awake, staring in the dark at the ceiling. Earlier, as he'd walked out of the spare room ahead of me, I'd noticed that he'd missed a belt loop in the back of his pants, and something about the sight of the missed belt loop called up paternal feelings in me, an acceptable, even worthy emotion, and for a brief time afterward the situation at the Hotel Willerton—Pascal's replacing my wife in the twin bed and all the rest—seemed more remarkable to me than absurd, more colorful than frightening.

I did eat one of the scones he'd brought me, in bed, with a glass of milk.

Pascal had taken a bath and returned to our room wearing a handsome plaid flannel robe and slippers. He climbed into bed, situated himself on his back, smoothed down the covers over his chest, and closed his eyes like someone hellbent on sleeping. "If something happens," he said, keeping his eyes closed, "wake me."

I said okay, and a long silence ensued. Then I heard him sniff the air and say, "There is an odor here, no?"

"The essence of things," I said, mysteriously (still riding

high on my "remarkable" assessment), but Pascal was too near sleep to question or appreciate my response.

What kept returning to me now, again and again as I continued staring at the plain white ceiling, was the word he'd used in the spare room—*crazy.* "It's crazy," he'd said, and "What's the point?" In the dark, I closed my eyes and attempted to meditate on this subject, accompanied by and matching my own breath to the comforting sound of Pascal's breathing: It's crazy . . . what's the point? Breathing in, It's crazy, what's the point? Breathing out, It's crazy, what's the point?

I've no idea how long I lay there, not asleep, but after a while I began to feel another's presence in the room with us. I opened my eyes and saw a not-at-all-pleased James, standing at the foot of Pascal's bed. Without looking at me, continuing to stare at Pascal, the boy whispered, "What's he doing here?"

"He's keeping me company," I whispered back.

"Get him out," said James.

"No," I said. "I want him here."

"Get him *out,*" he repeated.

"No."

James then turned on me a face of such bottomless pain and fatigue it nearly took my breath away. It was the face I'd seen the day we sat together on the bed in the spare room and talked of high-speed lifts and windlasses and capstans, the day I'd finally won him over by acknowledging that he was a real elevator expert; at one point, then, I told him I imagined his father only wanted him to be happy, and he asked, "Did your father want you to be happy?" At the time, I thought he was only challenging the truth of what I said, but now, as the question revisited me, I heard in it a kind of wonder, a curiosity about a possible marvel this boy had never before entertained. Now he turned quickly and headed for the door.

"James," I called to him. "Wait . . ." But he didn't even pause.

I got out of the bed, grabbed a bathrobe, and followed

him; just as I entered the hallway, I both heard and saw the door to the spare room slam shut. I waited outside it for a moment and could hear the whimperish quavers of his weeping. I tapped with my knuckles on the door, gently, trying already to atone with my repentant knocking style. After a few seconds of silence, I heard exactly what I'd heard that first day: a high, frail voice, full of resignation: "Come in."

But this time the door opened into a room I'd never before seen. It was very much the size and shape of the spare room at the Hotel Willerton—the window was in the right spot—but there were no twin beds inside, no matching dressers, certainly no television; instead, it appeared to be a sewing room, with tan walls, a satin-covered chaise longue, a coatrack, a dry sink, a dress dummy, a wooden ironing board, and, in one corner, an old black and gold sewing machine with a filigreed foot treadle.

James sat on the chaise longue, with his back to me. I went over and sat next to him. He scooted down the chaise longue, putting space between us.

"James," I said. "Please don't be angry."

"Get him out," he said, staring at the wall.

"I need him."

"You don't need him."

"Yes, I do. I need him to help me understand what's going on here."

"That doesn't make any sense," he said. "There's nothing to understand."

Then he looked at me, pleading this time: "Get him *out.*"

His desperation made me very uneasy; I stood and looked about the room, shoving my hands into the pockets of the robe, avoiding James's harrowing gaze. It wasn't only his desperation that made me uneasy; it was also the sway he seemed to have with me. For a moment, I thought perhaps he was right about Pascal—there was something irritating about Pascal's attachment to his future, his precious hotel, his sophomoric passion for the material world—and that we should get him out from a place in which he didn't fit. But the irritation, the sway, was passing, and soon I was thinking this: If the spare room had become a sewing room, did that mean the whole flat had changed again? And if the flat had changed, then where was Pascal now?

"Excuse me," I said to James, and moved back to the door, stepped into what had been the hallway (now a wide passage with closets that connected the sewing room to another); at the next door, I saw the room with the pastoral-scene wallpaper, the four-poster bed, the side curtains drawn shut.

Of course I had to open the curtain and see what horrifying thing awaited inside, see what terrible thing had befallen Pascal. As I approached the bed in darkness, I thought I heard someone breathing somewhere in the room, and just as I reached for the curtain, something heavy and hard as a brick connected with the side of my head, exploding my right ear; it seemed to me there was a cacophony of hysterical voices then; I was struggling across the floor to get out of the room, and could it be that feathers were flying everywhere? I made my way, pitching, stumbling, and crawling, to the middle of the dark sitting room, where once again I was struck on the head, harder, rolled by the blow onto my back, and this time I was quite sure I witnessed a blizzard of white feathers lofting, swirling, drifting down all around before my lights went out.

"Well . . . ," I heard the girl say, "the patient finally comes round."

She leaned in close, her cloudy eyes peering into mine; briefly, she seemed to examine my right ear.

"Walter, of course," she said. "There's nothing he enjoys so much as bashing people in the head. That and marrowing them whilst they sleep."

She stood next to the bed, alternately staring down at me and doing the anchoring thing with a spot on the opposite side curtain: Iris, her demeanor less world-weary than worldly wise. She was dressed as always, in the sailor dress, but now she'd tied a white handkerchief around her head so it looked as if she were wearing a nurse's cap. This observation, like all "reality," came to me in the form of deep reverberant pulses as my cranium seemed to expand and contract.

"Marrowing . . . ," I said, shocked at the feeble remnant of my voice.

"Sitting on them whilst they sleep," she said. "Drawing out their muscle and marrow. I daresay you know something of that, having spent so much time with Walter."

"Yes," I said, uncertain of what I meant, trying to push myself past the pain in my head.

"But now I'm afraid you've quite upset the boy."

"The boy . . ."

"Young James," she said. "He doesn't much fancy your young intruder."

"Intruder?"

"Your French lad," she said.

"Pascal . . ."

She laughed and added, "You're thinking he's no more an intruder than you are, but you're wrong. He's quite different from you. Not nearly so given to us as you are. We've had quite a row or two over that chain lock, I can tell you that. James keeps fastening it so your French lad can't get in, you see. He's insanely jealous. I for one am interested in seeing what develops."

"I must find Pascal . . ."

"Oh, he's gone now," she said.

"Gone?"

"Gone to work, I imagine."

"But—"

"He's perfectly all right," she said, shaking her head at me as if I were a child distressed over a trivial matter.

"What the devil did he hit me with?" I asked, touching my ear, wincing.

"A feather pillow," she said, smiling. "Made quite a mess of the place too."

"A pillow?" I said. "It felt more like a brick."

"Well, it had a brick in it, didn't it," she said. "He put one down inside the pillow slip. One of his inventions, a brick inside a pillow slip. He's very keen on slinging it about, whirling it over his head like Christ driving out the money changers from the temple."

"And where's James?"

"He's around," she said. "Sulking somewhere over your French lad. Plotting against him, I imagine. If I were you, I wouldn't have him back anytime soon, your French lad. It's not entirely safe for him here. James may be a little boy, but he's a bit of a monster, take my word for it. He's capable of a good deal more than you would expect."

"Iris," I said, "tell me the truth about what really happened here."

"I've already told you," she said. "Walter bashed you over the head with—"

"No, I mean about the window. About the fall from the window. How did it happen?"

"Oh, that," she said. "Well. That's a rather complicated matter."

"Tell me."

"Aren't you the curious one, barely conscious."

"I need to know."

"And why would that be?"

"Because I do," I said. "There's got to be some reason . . . some purpose . . ."

"Oh, I know all about that," she said, "you and your reasons and purposes. I've heard about how you're sent down to save us from ourselves, to help us sort things out. But you've got it all wrong, Mr. America. You and my sister are of the same kidney, the two of you . . . both so deluded. Has Victoria told you about our stepmother? We haven't any stepmother, mind you. Some children have imaginary friends, Victoria's got her imaginary stepmother. Meanwhile, our real mum grows more exotic and glamorous every hour. An actress on the musical stage indeed! Mummy would have considered the theater of any sort beneath her. Victoria doesn't even bother to get her facts straight. Taken lately to saying Mummy came from someplace called Edmund Island. Ever heard of it, Edmund Island?"

"No," I said.

"Of course you haven't," she said. "Because it doesn't exist. Walter told me it doesn't exist."

"What about the window?" I said, steering her back around. "What about the fall?"

She sat down in the straight chair next to the bed, chose a new anchor somewhere across the room, and grew intensely solemn. At last she said, with great petulance, "Of course, it was all about money. Nothing was ever about anything in this house but money." Then her voice softened, returned to its more usual urbane tone. "He didn't mean for me to fall," she said. "Well, actually he did. But he didn't start out that way. And he was sorry. I suppose that's obvious, how sorry he was."

"Walter . . ."

"Of course Walter," she said impatiently. She sighed, exasperated with so dull a student. "I'm very tired," she said. "This takes a toll, you know, all this *emerging*. It's a great pleasure in its own way, but it does take a toll."

"What do you mean, he 'let' you fall?"

"Well, he was gripping me, see . . . look at these." She held up her arms, turning them so I could see the dark bruises on the inside of her wrists, the bruises I'd only glimpsed the first time I met Victoria. "That's how tight he gripped me whilst he thought about what to do," she said. "It was quite a long time, actually, him dangling me there five stories high."

She lowered her chin, staring into her lap briefly, then looked straight ahead again. "And you know," she said almost wistfully, "whilst he was doing his thinking, I was doing some of my own. By the time he let me drop, I didn't really mind."

"You didn't mind?"

"No. I'm not sure why, exactly. I suppose I'd reached some peace with myself. It was summer, you see, July, and quite near dawn. The air was intensely pleasant, and the sky had begun to turn the palest shade of pink. I'll never forget that color. I don't think I'd ever seen it before. Like heavenly water, so pale and clear, with just a whisper of rose in it. I had that feeling you get when you've completed something . . .

something very hard and tedious. You may not be entirely pleased with the results, but at least it's done and you can be proud of that. You get very caught up in the fact of its being done, you see, its being over, and then, having hated it enduringly, you find yourself thinking perhaps it wasn't so bad after all. That's how it was. I reached some peace. The sky was that truly incredible shade of pink, and I felt very glad of being done. And I didn't really mind, that's all."

"But why did he do it?" I asked.

"He was drunk, of course," she said. "Daddy was away; in Liverpool, I believe. He was in the habit of leaving us with Walter. A real father would never have done that. Anyone could see that a girl shouldn't be left with the likes of Walter. He came back from the pub—Walter, that is—cocked to the gills and squiffy-eyed . . . and we had a row."

"About what?"

"Well, not what you're thinking," she said. "Oh, he'd tried that once or twice with Victoria. If it hadn't been for me, he would have had his way with her too. Victoria can't fend for herself, poor thing. She's very delicate, as I'm sure you've noticed. But Walter knew better than to try anything like that with me."

"What, then?"

"*Money*," she said. "I already told you. Oh, God, I'm exhausted now. Aren't you feeling very tired?"

"Tired," I heard myself say, and it did seem like a label attached to the pounding in my head; I gingerly touched the base of my skull, feeling the tender lump left by Walter's brick; I closed my eyes . . . perhaps I even dozed briefly. I expected she would be gone when, sometime later—half a minute? half an hour? half a day?—I came to again. But the first thing I saw as I opened my eyes was her head, wrapped in its comical nurse's-cap facsimile. The sound of rain on the windows seemed to rattle at the edge of my attention, poor limping mole that my attention was, and grasping, in a kind of raspy, drugged awe, I whispered, "Tell me . . . what does the garlic mean?"

Her head pivoted slowly round to face me, with a bit of

a jagged struggle, as if it were a mechanical thing whose batteries were running down.

"Mean?" she said. "What . . . Walter's little creative arrangements in the kitchen sink?" She rolled her eyes, this time having nothing to do with anchoring. "It doesn't *mean* anything," she said, and laughed down at me through her nose. "It doesn't mean anything."

Sometime later, I was summoned to the door by knocking and the sound of Mimi Sho-pan's voice. Not quite awake, I stood leaning against the door for a while. "Cookson," I heard her say. "Everyone's terribly worried about you. Open the door, Cookson. Let us come in . . . please."

I opened it then, but only as far as the fastened chain lock would allow. Mr. Sho-pan stood just behind her, peering over her shoulder.

"Cookson," she said, smiling compassionately, but also a little shocked at my appearance. "Are you ill? Pascal tells us you sleep night and day."

Mr. Sho-pan whispered something in her ear.

"Ray thinks you've lost perspective," she said to me very quietly, creating an aura of intimacy. "Have you, Cookson? Is that what's happened? Have you lost perspective?"

For a moment, her sympathy worked on me like voodoo—I felt something tear loose inside me, a breach in the dam of my isolation and willfulness, and I watched my hand go up to the chain lock. I was about to unlatch it when, behind the Sho-pans, at the end of the hallway, the little window in the elevator door ignited with the golden interior light of the mahogany-paneled car; I could see, through the window, two or three of the black diamond shapes of the lattice gate; I expected that someone would open the door, emerge from the car, but no one did. Suddenly, the glass went dark again, and I thought I heard the howling of wind inside the shaft. Something about this so frightened me that I felt all the blood leaving my face; the Sho-pans both turned to look behind them, to see what had frightened me, and I seized this moment to close the door. As I walked away, scattering with each step the feathers on the sitting-room floor, I heard Mimi Sho-pan's voice in the hallway. "Cookson," she called out, "please come back. Ray wants to tell you something, Cookson. Cookson . . ."

I'd been sleeping on the sofa in the sitting room again, and now James stood at my feet, having slipped into the narrow space between the end of the sofa and the wall. He smiled very sweetly when he saw that I was awake. "The fog in Green Park has condensed on the leaves of the plane trees," he said, with a note of sadness in his voice, "and now, when the breeze blows, it falls like rain."

"Is that so?" I said.

His eyes appeared swollen, and his nose was bright red. "James," I said, "you've been crying."

"You think it's all right to cry," he said.

"Yes," I said, "that's true. James, I'm sorry I've upset you, but—"

"You mustn't let him back in, you see. He mustn't sleep here anymore. You don't need him. You don't need him at all when you have me."

He looked at me intensely now, and I thought I saw, through the remnant of the child, a weathered, unyielding corruption. "James, I—"

"My father thinks only girls and sissies cry," he said, "but you don't mind. I can't help it, you see, crying, and the really nice thing is, you don't . . . you don't disapprove of me."

"No, James, I—"

"You don't judge me."

"No, I—"

"You don't give me a girl's task and say it's all I'm fit for, not like him."

"What?"

"You don't give me a girl's task and say it's all I'm fit for."

He slid out, to a door on the other side of the room— the door, I thought, to the hallway. Before he went through it, he turned. "It's *not* all I'm fit for," he said.

. . .

"The place is a mess," I heard myself saying at the door, surprised at the degree of shame I felt and suddenly imagining myself an inmate, awkward on the occasion of his wife's first call at the visitors' room.

"I don't care if it's a mess," she said. "Let me in, Cook."

"I can't," I said, though, almost involuntarily, I widened the crack in the door another inch. "I'd like to, but—"

"What's happened to your ear?" she said. "There's blood."

This small voice of concern awakened me to how lovely she looked in the darkish hallway, a woman who'd simplified, simplified, simplified, prompting one to the shine of her eyes, the shape of her mouth, the graceful slope of her neck. Her raincoat had fallen open, revealing the hollow at the base of her throat, the slight medial dip of the clavicle, and maybe I only imagined it, but I thought I saw an anxious pulsing there, a faint admission of her heart.

"Cut myself shaving," I said (a ridiculous lie, since it was obvious I hadn't shaved in days).

"Cook," she said, "I'm going home this evening. I want you to come with me."

"I can't."

"You can. Why can't you?"

"I just can't leave now."

"I want you to come home, Cook. I don't want to go without you. I don't want to leave you here alone. Things have gone all wrong with this trip, and I think we should cut our losses and just go back home. Today. This evening. Please, please come with me."

"I can't."

"Cook," she said, without a pause, without even the slightest sag in her composure. "Do you remember when we were first married and we went down to visit my parents? We had that awful dinner of Mother's, what she called her mixed grill—awful things like tripe and . . . what was it? What was the other awful thing?"

"Tongue," I said.

"That's right," she said, "*tongue*. And Dad drank so much

during dinner that he went upstairs right afterward and fell asleep, and Mother, who'd also drunk too much, began to cry and say that no one had enjoyed anything she'd prepared. . . . Do you remember this? Do you remember what you did?"

"No," I said, honestly.

"Well, you were kind to her, Cook. You told her you'd enjoyed the dinner 'enormously.' I remember that was the word you used, 'enormously'—you'd been drinking too, of course. And you began to ask her questions about how she'd marinated the meat, and you praised her on several points. And later, when we went up to bed, I asked you about all the lies you'd told my mother about her cooking, and you just shrugged and said that she'd wanted so badly to impress you: she'd been trying very hard to impress you, you said. The meal was so awful that that simply hadn't occurred to me. And I fell asleep in my childhood bed, thinking how happy I was that I'd grown up and married someone who cared about other people."

She waited for a few seconds, giving me time to let this sink in, and it seemed to me that the hallway, where she continued standing patiently, grew a shade darker. I had a headache that would have registered on a seismograph, the enduring aftershocks of Walter's "invention."

"We didn't leave until after lunch the next day," Ellen said. "Do you remember how you spent the morning? My parents' house was the classic home of drunks. Full of broken things, things that didn't work properly. You went to the hardware store in the morning, and when you came back, you replaced the dimmer switch in the dining room. You repaired the leaky faucet in Mother's kitchen and unclogged the drain. You mended the screen door that wouldn't close right; you even rotated the tires on Dad's station wagon. All before lunch. I remember a specific moment when the three of us— Mother, Dad, and I—were standing at the picture window in the living room, looking out at you in the driveway: you were jacking up Dad's car. Dad turned to me and smiled and said, 'You got yourself a real live wire, sweetie.' We were all three astonished by you—Mother, Dad, and I. You were an astonishing person, Cook. You were caring and capable and astonishing."

She waited another moment, giving me a chance to let *this* sink in. At last I said, "I also glued a lamp back together."

She smiled and said, "That's right. . . . I'd forgotten about the lamp."

Then I did the only thing possible for me to do: I slid back the chain lock and let her come in.

Inside, she took a seat on the sofa in the sitting room. She purposely did not glance around the room or make obvious note of the feathers on the floor. She did not remove her coat. I took the chair opposite her, the tea table between us, and after some silence, she said, very calmly, "What's that strange smell?"

"I don't know," I said. "The chambermaid hasn't been in. Probably the trash in the kitchen."

My swift desire for her made me aware of my own undesirable status: unwashed, unshaved, crazed in my soiled bathrobe.

"Can we open the drapes?" she asked.

"I'd rather not," I said.

"Can we turn on a lamp, then?"

"I can see you," I said. "Can't you see me?"

"Yes," she said. "Actually, I can see you fine. You look like hell, Cookie."

"Do I? Well, you don't."

"What do I have to do to get you to leave this and come home?" she asked.

"Ellen," I said, "there's so much I want to tell you."

She leaned forward, solicitous. "What, Cook?" she said. "What do you want to tell me, darling?"

"Well," I said, "I feel like I'm making some real progress here at last."

"What do you mean?"

"I feel like I'm finally getting somewhere," I said. "They're starting to open up to me a little bit. I'm beginning to get things sorted out."

"What things?"

"It's been pretty rough, if you want to know the truth," I said, and suddenly I was filled with a sense of the great enchantment of my story, revved up by it, ready to tell all, ready to cast its net over my errant wife and draw her back to me forever.

"I've been lambasted a couple of times," I said, "and frightened and sick to my stomach a lot. Nauseated. You see, they seem to run on my energy. I'm like a battery to them, their electrical charge. They drain me, and then I have to go to sleep to recharge. But even while I'm sleeping, Walter—that's the uncle . . . well, never mind about Walter. The point is . . . James, the little boy, turns out not to be related to the family at all. He's a kind of wandering soul. I think he's become overly attached to me at this point. I don't know what went on here, exactly, Ellen—not yet—but I think it must have been pretty grim. The girl, Victoria, has an alter ego, you see, another self she uses to face things that she wants to avoid: she kind of lives in a fantasy world where she imagines things to be better than they really are. She doesn't even admit she fell from the *window*. But Iris—that's the other personality—says that—"

I stopped talking then, suddenly taken aback by the sight of tears streaking Ellen's cheeks. "What's wrong?" I said, genuinely baffled.

This question, this honest, simple inquiry, seemed to shake her even more, and now she was crying hard, putting me at a complete loss.

I thought I would move next to her, comfort her—that was what a husband usually did when his wife cried, when something he'd said upset her—but just as I was about to make my move, I was delayed by another feeling: What was it that was so familiar about this scene?

I looked at her, sitting on the sofa, weeping in her raincoat, and though I knew I was actually witnessing this, it almost felt as if I'd read about it somewhere.

And indeed I had read about it somewhere: I recalled a scene in one of her mystery stories, in which Flora, the priest, visited a parishioner whose wife had recently died; the wife, a woman in her thirties who suffered breast cancer, was one of Flora's closest friends in the church. The bereaved husband has got himself lost in a long, isolated funk—he won't go out, he keeps the drapes in the house drawn, keeps the lights off; he receives Flora in darkness and refuses her requests to open the drapes or turn on a lamp. It's been raining out, and she wears a beige raincoat, which she hasn't removed. She sits on a sofa opposite him, a coffee table between them, and listens as he attempts to tell her the dimensions of his loss. And finally, unable to control herself, Flora—the one who's supposed to do the comforting—begins to weep. The man goes to her, tries to console her, apologizes for having upset her so, and then, moved by the sight of the priest's grief, he walks at last to the window and opens the drapes . . . the beginning of his return to sanity and to the world.

It struck me, with spectacular disappointment, that Ellen was only playing a role, that drawing on the contraptions of her fiction, she meant only to manipulate me. She'd manipulated her way into the flat, and now she meant to manipulate me out of it.

As she began to compose herself, I said, "I see what you're up to."

She appeared stunned.

"Cook," she said.

For an instant, she seemed ready to take me on—to challenge me directly—but she gave that up quickly, upturning her palms, and pleading instead.

"Please, Cook," she said. "You need to get out of here. Let's pack your things and just leave right now. We'll go over to Mimi and Ray's and spend the afternoon, and then we'll go to the airport. Come with me now. Please. Won't you please come with me?"

"No," I said.

"Please," she said.

"No."

She rose from the sofa and began to move around the

tea table. I was quickly out of the chair and standing behind it, a defensive maneuver that stunned her anew.

Then she drew herself up and spoke to me in her famous short, simple sentences—as if I were some kind of imbecile. "Cook," she said. "I'll be at the Sho-pans'. I leave for the airport in four hours. You have four hours to change your mind. This is important, Cook. I'm going home. Back to Cambridge. Do you understand that? You need to come home too. Please do this for me."

She turned for the door, and though she'd seemed virtually glacial in this last bit, I thought I saw, in her eyes, just as she turned, a definite fracture in her confidence.

And then she was gone.

I felt a dim, passing worry about her safe descent in that rickety lift, with its idiosyncrasies and howling winds, but I dismissed it as ill placed. My hands still gripped the back of the chair—a huge, tall, winged affair that might have come with an optional team of horses—and mostly, the sound of my wife's retreating footsteps in the outside hallway was a great relief.

CHAPTER

Twenty-Two

I WANT TO say that Ellen's visit left me completely

shot, and it does seem that there was some special physical

exertion required in order for me to make the zigzagging

emotional tour from without-her to with-her to without-her

again. But of course I was in a general state of wastedness

before she ever showed up at the door. I also want to say that this last evening and night at the Willerton was like an alcoholic binge, with blackouts. But it was better organized than that: my recollections are nearly as absolute-seeming as the neat vacuums between them. I can recall with precision the sounds of Ellen's departure—her footsteps in the hallway, the arrival of the elevator, the opening and closing of the lattice gate—and then a silence that prompted me to take a deep breath behind the barrier of my wing chair. (It was as if I'd not fully breathed for the duration of Ellen's visit.) But I have no memory of leaving the sitting room or of any other event that might connect her departure with the next thing— Victoria, in darkness, speaking: "Daddy told us he was never quite right in the head after the navy," she said. "Something happened to him, you see, but I'm not sure what it was."

"Where am I?" I whispered, for I could see only the girl's face, peering out of what appeared to be a black liquid.

"Wait," she said, her face now vanishing behind the surface, leaving ripples on blackness.

I found myself thinking, *Silence, silence* . . . and all my symptoms arrived at once: the throbbing in my head, the heat behind my eyes, the aching in my joints. After a moment, I heard her voice again. "There," she said, and in the emerging, more familiar dusk, I saw that we were in the sewing room. I lay on my back, on the chaise longue where earlier I'd sat with James. I'd been restored to my customary nakedness, beneath a knitted wool coverlet spread over my stomach and legs. Victoria sat at my feet, gazing down at me with her usual wounded goodwill.

"Better?" she said. "Yes. As I was saying, he was always rather . . . well, rather irrational. He'd come back from the navy that way. Quite incapable of really getting on in the world. If he hadn't had Daddy, I don't know what would have come of him. That was how Daddy was, you see. Very, very generous with Walter. Indeed, with everyone. He was the kindest, most caring father a girl—"

"But he would go away and leave you alone with Walter," I said, propping myself up on my elbows.

This sudden remark took her aback. She wasn't surprised by its content—I could see that right away: she accepted the truth of it at once—but she was apparently
shocked by my knowing it and by my saying it aloud. She
was also able to see instantly how I knew it, for after a moment she sighed and said, "You have to understand . . . Iris
has always blamed Daddy. Iris contends that Mummy's . . ."

She faltered, as if she'd taken a direction she didn't
mean to take, or as if she was unexpectedly too weary to
continue.

"What?" I said. "Tell me."

"Iris thinks Daddy was responsible for Mummy's death,"
she said at last, shaking her head as she said it. "So I suppose
it's only natural—"

"How did your mother die?"

"She drowned," she said. "We used to live by a river,
you see, far away from London. Daddy couldn't have possibly
. . . well, you see, he loved her very deeply. He couldn't
have possibly—"

She stopped abruptly and appeared to be listening to
something I couldn't hear, something inside her head, perhaps. Then she stopped listening and glanced about the
room, her eyes pausing for a moment, fixing on an object
behind me. With a burst of energy, she said, "What a lovely
room this is! My very favorite in the house."

Touching the decorative stitching on the broad collar of
her dress, she said, "I made this shift, you know. Designed it
too, with a little help from a picture in a magazine. Daddy
brought me down the fabric from Wakefield . . . do you
know it, Wakefield? An ancient town once part of a royal
estate, owned by Edward the Confessor. Daddy often
brought home short pieces from all over. And there was very
little Mummy couldn't do with a needle and thread. An excellent seamstress. I suppose I take after her in that. She taught
me everything, of course. It was from her I learned to—"

And then she was gone—not gone, but asleep.

She woke almost immediately and said, ". . . crochet

. . . crochet as well. Oh, she had many talents. As a girl on Edmund Island, she—"

And she was asleep again.

Poised on the edge of the chaise longue, she leaned forward a fraction more with each breath, a course that, if continued, would topple her headfirst onto the floor. The fact that I found this possibility irresistible caused me to examine the exact nature of my particular altered state at this particular moment: I thought that if I was to be lied to, deliberately confused, manipulated, beaten about the head with bricks inside pillow slips, reduced to the role of passive observer and frustrated detective, there was nothing lost in my being amused, too, from time to time. I could hear the sound of the girl's breathing. As she continued her slow arc in regular, rhythmic increments (something like a wheel in a clockwork), the springs in the chaise longue squeaked ever so discreetly. Soon her hair had fallen forward, covering her face; soon she was doubled over, her shoulders nearly touching her knees. But alas, she stopped there, steady on the edge. I quietly slipped out from under the coverlet, putting my feet to the floor; I was extremely thirsty, and I meant to find running water. Just as I stood up, however, the girl awakened.

"Gracious," she said, tossing me the coverlet, "have you no modesty, man?" Then she patted the cushion of the chaise longue, inviting me to sit down.

I noticed that in the brief journey to her knees and back up again, a gold chain had fallen out of her dress collar; it was the first time I'd seen it, the chain with the oval-shaped locket and the little key.

"I wouldn't go wandering about if I were you," she said. "Walter's in a frightful rage. He's likely to hurt you again."

"Why is he in a rage?" I asked.

"There's no *why* about it," she said with a familiar impatience. "That's who Walter is. It's what he does. He rages. He hurts people."

"I see," I said.

"No," she said, smiling. "Actually, you don't see."

"No," I said. "I suppose I don't."

"But you want to see," she said.

"Yes."

"You're caught up in something quite grander than your-self," she said. "Your wife is angry and upset with you . . . not that it's rare for her to be angry and upset. And you think you can do something to help us poor restless souls who need to . . . how did you put it to Victoria? 'Move on.' You want to help us sort things out so we can 'move on.'"

"Yes," I said, sitting on the chaise. "What's that around your neck?"

A bit surprised, she touched the chain, then quickly tucked it back inside her collar. "Victoria's," she said.

"A picture of your mother in the locket."

"That's right."

"But what's the key?"

She gasped, widening her eyes—mocking me. "Ah," she said. "A mysterious key. What do you suppose it opens? Per-haps it unlocks the door to our salvation. The door to our 'moving on.' What do you think?"

"I think maybe it opens a diary," I said.

This made her laugh, exaggeratedly, throwing back her head.

"It winds Victoria's table clock," she said at last. And laughed some more.

For a reason I couldn't begin to understand at the time, this small thing—the key, thought to be crucial, turning out unimportant—caused in me a rush of anxiety, almost as if it were in fact a "key" to understanding the larger picture in which it figured. I suddenly felt my heart racing a bit, and it occurred to me that my poor tractable heart was the machine that powered the whole shooting match here—the girl, James, Walter, the furniture, the four-poster bed, the dress dummy in the corner, the very grain in the wood of the floorboards. I saw that the girl had gone even paler than usual. "Are you okay?" she asked me. "You're not having a heart attack, are you?"

"No," I said. "I'm fine."

"You're under a strain," she said. "You'd better get some sleep."

"I thought I'd just waked up."

"Well, you'd best get some *more* sleep," she said. "And do try to stay out of the way. Walter's in a rage. He's never quite known when to quit. Such a bother he is, such a . . . such an obligation. Pure evil . . ."

She paused, tilted her head to one side. "That's a funny turn of phrase, isn't it," she said. "Pure evil. Hadn't thought of it before."

"Iris," I said, "you said that you and Walter fought about money the night you fell from the window. But in what sense, money?"

"A silly one-pound note, actually," she said, shrugging her shoulders, laughing a little. "He'd been on one of his late-night pub crawls, and he'd run out of money. Daddy was away, and Walter came upstairs expecting to find Victoria, who would have given him some. She was always doing that. He had none of his own, you see. He always had to come begging." She smiled impishly and added, "But he found me instead. Woke me up. Demanded I give him some money and began to root around in my things, making an awful mess, calling me perfectly terrible names. I happened to know that Victoria had a pound note in her little white cloth purse, which was in the bottom drawer of the dresser. So I got out of bed, I found the purse and went to the open window. It was July and quite warm. I held the purse in the air, out the window, and I said to Walter to come and get it if he wanted it so badly. I meant to snatch it away, you see. I certainly wasn't about to let him have Victoria's pound note. But he . . . well, he got hold of me somehow. He was very resentful of the money situation, always having to come begging like that, and I'm afraid I made him more angry than I'd intended. He was always a loose cannon, Walter. Never knew quite when to quit."

Apparently, she was finished. She smiled at me, almost

as if she took some pride in what she'd just narrated. I said, "Victoria told me you think your father was in some way responsible for your mother's death."

"In some way responsible?" she said. "He bloody drowned her. I saw him do it. I watched him . . ."

She pulled back, looking at me askance. "There you go again," she said. "Trying to help us sort things out, are you? Trying to help us move on?"

"I can't believe it's an accident that you and I are here together this way," I said. "That I can see you and talk to you this way. That I found my way to this flat in the first place. I can't believe that all this is for nothing. I can't believe—"

"Oh, it's not for nothing," she said quickly. "It's for sport, don't you see? It's just sport."

"Sport?"

"We've *already* been sorted out," she said. "That's who we are."

She smiled at me in a naughty, would-be-seductress way, not quite successfully. "It's sport," she said, lifting one eyebrow. "And I suppose that makes you a sportsman."

She bent down and straightened the buckle on her shoe. "By the way," she said. "Thought you would want to know . . . it *was* James smashed your French lad's doll-house."

Silt, a stirring of sediment: everything a study in dark gray, with only suggestions of shape and color, the windows rattling in their casements. Middle of the night; Walter Jevons, staggering, props himself against the doorjamb, entirely naked, hairy from head to ankle, and even from this distance I can smell his stench of whisky and tobacco and human rot; "You were an astonishing person," says Ellen. "You were caring and capable and astonishing . . ." Abruptly afraid, a child frozen in his bed at midnight, I think I must find Pascal; Pascal, I think, is here somewhere, if only I can find him; "You may not be entirely pleased with the results," says the girl, "but at least it's done and you can be proud of that. . . ." In my dream, the farmer operates a harrow in the rainy fields, the horse's black coat wet, shining like the harrow's blades, the ruts in the road filled with rainwater, and back in the village, something has gone terribly wrong; "Ray thinks you've lost perspective," Mimi Sho-pan says very quietly, creating an aura of intimacy. "Have you, Cookson? Is that what's happened? Have you lost perspective?" I have accepted my fate, my relinquishing of the regular world; I hurt all over, and Pascal, vulnerable, leaving the spare room, has missed a belt loop. . . .

I turned my head on the pillow, having swum up from the depths of a coma-like oblivion, and actually saw a young man, Pascal Géricault, head porter at the Hotel Willerton, safely asleep, looking rather angelic in the other bed, his plaid flannel robe folded neatly at the foot. I didn't recall his arrival at the flat. I didn't recall seeing him or speaking to him, yet here he was again, loyal, patient, a willing would-be witness, wanting to help.

With a menacing grace, a single, actual white feather seesawed slowly down from the ceiling.

Soon I was fully awake, and I'd become fully awake so I might sample the pungent loneliness the night was currently serving up; I felt a sharp loneliness and something else too . . . a feeling that something had changed. . . . Of course I have carefully examined the sequence of these events again and again, and I have noted with remorse the number of warnings I was given, the number I ignored. But for now, I only had a dim sense that I'd moved willy-nilly (or *been* moved, for despite all my foolhardy appetites, despite all my imprudence, I couldn't help but feel misused) past some point of no return, past some point of too-lateness, and that the boy, James, had somehow been neglected by me, underestimated by me somehow, not taken carefully enough into account.

I was famished. I quietly climbed out of bed, found my bathrobe, and made my way through the sitting room to the kitchen. There was no curtain over the kitchen window, so for the first time in a long while I saw London, the jagged roofscape obscured by a low sky of fog and drizzle. It was deep night. I turned away from the window, vaguely afraid of the vastness outside the window, the vastness behind the vastness behind the vastness . . . a childhood terror, the curve of space, infinity . . .

In the kitchen sink, cloves of garlic had been arranged in a circle around the drain, an assemblage of megaliths resembling Stonehenge with an abyss at the center, and I thought, It really is only sport, fun and games. . . .

Whatever hunger I'd felt a minute earlier had now turned into queasiness. I was queasy and suddenly weak. (By now I'd learned to take this as a sign of the nearness of my ghosts.) I heard sounds from the sitting room (a hoarse rhythmic moaning, actually), and when I stepped to the doorway, I saw Walter, naked from the waist down, sprawled on the sofa, openly, that is to say obliviously, masturbating. The girl sat next to him, posture perfect, pointedly averting her eyes but otherwise peaceful, primed to hold forth on the imperialist attitudes of Rudyard Kipling, the anti-labor policies of Stanley Baldwin, the musical pleasures of Elizabethan verse— entirely overlooking what was going on inches away.

Walter's head was so far back he would have been gazing at the ceiling if it weren't for some kind of cloth covering his eyes and nose. As I began to move closer, I recognized this "cloth" as a pair of my wife's panties, and my knees buckled beneath me—a purely physical drain having little to do with this recognition. At the same instant, both he and the girl fixed on me, he drawing down the panties from his face, she quickly shaking her head, as if to caution me away, and I was reminded of that first day we met, when she whispered to me in the sitting room downstairs, "Go." Walter Jevons's face was suddenly twisted with rage, and he appeared quite ready to hand over one pleasure for another: he lowered his head, glaring at me from under his brow, from under his red curls. He lunged forward, off the sofa, the girl let out a delicate little yelp, and then, outrageously, the telephone rang.

It had to be two in the morning, and the telephone rang. All three of us froze, Walter on his hands and knees, and stared at it, the alien, ivory-colored instrument on the fanciful Regency secretary in the corner.

Inside this strange moment there was another one, the smallest, densest version of the moment, the version inside which there was no other. I was acquainted with the moment already, from my history of self-abuse—it was when, having allowed the fire to grow out of control, you were tested regarding what else you would be willing to throw onto the thrilling blaze. The questions asked (from a voice whose origin remains a mystery) are no longer about you or your ambitions or any material thing. They are about what you love most deeply, about what you have the fewest real rights to or powers over, about what's most given to you in trust. Are you willing to throw your wife on the fire? Are you willing to throw your child? And I was forced in this moment to behold my lifelong ambivalence, my thirst for drama and ruin, my great and sad spiritual poverty. The telephone continued its urgent, twentieth-century, twin-ringing signal. I could not summon the will to answer it. I was extremely nauseated by now—I thought I might collapse—and yet I seemed to watch my own caveman's legs from a distance as they moved, carrying me toward the desk. It was necessary for me to turn my back on the room. When I lifted the receiver to my face and managed to get out some desperate variation of "Hello," I heard the voice of my daughter, high and clear as the polestar, saying, "Daddy, what's wrong? Are you okay, Daddy?"

I said her name—no, I sang it quietly. The nausea passed, the pulsing of blood inside my ears abated. She reiterated her two questions. I turned back to the room and saw that Walter and the girl had gone. Then Pascal appeared from the hallway, headed for the door, wearing his pajamas and robe; I could see right away that there was something deeply wrong in his appearance, even terrible somehow; his robe hung open, its belt dangling on either side, and looking at me (but not quite looking at me), he put his finger to his lips and said, "I'll be back," unlatched the chain lock, and left the flat.

Something about his eyes . . . they were open, but he

was definitely not awake. Now Jordie called my name again and again from across the ocean, but I heard myself say, "Oh, God, no," evenly spaced words from ancient history, and the telephone fell from my hand.

By the time I got down the hall, by the time I reached the elevator, there was only silence and more silence, though I have surely wondered from time to time, unsleeping, about the sounds Pascal may have made, the sharp notes of his surprise. The elevator door stood open, the shaft empty. At the edge, I looked down, but it was too dark to see anything below. The air inside was cool, and smelled of oil and metal and dust. On the right side of the doorframe, some fabric had snagged on the protruding lip of the striker plate and moved now quietly in the gentle updraft, the belt to his flannel robe, whole, intact, a wide ribbon of cloth.

Twenty-Three

GAZING DOWN INTO the empty shaft and standing for a minute in its faint and slightly acrid currents had the effect of infusing me with absolute composure. (Looking back, I believe I was in a state of psychogenic shock or, more accurately, a state of "aftershock"—my blood vessels dilated, my trusty heart rising to the occasion and filling in the new regions, things quickly correcting themselves, the system purged.) I had seen nothing but darkness; I'd heard nothing; but I knew that Pascal had fallen and that he hadn't survived the fall. I returned to the sitting room in the flat, where the telephone receiver lay on the floor. Jordie was crying at the other end, apparently very frightened. I spoke to her calmly, but also as if she were about five years old.

"Jordie," I said, "Mommy and I are okay. It's just that someone has had a bad accident here at the hotel. Now Mommy's already on her way home, and she'll—"

"On her way home?" she said.

"Yes, and I'm sure—"

"But I spoke to her a few hours ago. . . . She didn't say anything about coming home."

"Well, she's on her way now," I said. "She may even be there by now, and I want—"

"But why is she coming without you?"

"We'll explain everything to you later, Jordie," I said. "Sweetheart, somebody's had an accident here, and now I need this telephone to call for help, okay?"

I promised that Ellen or I would talk to her the next day, and I made her promise not to worry about anything. Then I phoned down to the hotel desk.

A young man answered, someone I didn't know. Again I spoke very calmly. I told him who I was and said that Pascal had fallen down the elevator shaft.

There was quite a long pause, after which the young man said (and I will forever remember his exact words): "Are you quite sure?"

I told him that I was sure.

Under the circumstances, what I did next didn't entirely make sense, though the composure and facility with which I did it probably would have lent it (had anyone been watching) an air of good judgment: I went into the bedroom, got dressed, and packed my things. While I was doing this, I willfully closed out the possibility of ghosts; I kept my eyes focused on the very small details of my tasks, almost as if I were doing a kind of "anchoring" of my own—zeroing in on the buttons of a shirt, the bristles of my toothbrush. Still, I could not entirely avoid the general affect of the place, its lingering theme of something monstrous having been birthed here—the disarray, the smell. I left the flat, not looking back, not quelling any urges to look back, and carried my bags down the four flights of stairs to the ground floor and to the desk, where I intended to ask the young man I'd spoken to on the phone to prepare my bill. But the man (surely Hannah's grown son, a young male version of her) was already busy leading a firefighter down the narrow corridor on one side of the staircase, to the elevator door.

Five members of the fire brigade's Knightsbridge station (A-26) came to the hotel in a matter of minutes and got Pascal out of the elevator shaft. When Pascal had fallen, the lift cage had been in the basement, which meant that he fell a full four floors, a survivable distance (I was told), depending on the particulars of the fall, depending on how "controlled" the fall happened to be. The fire brigade forced open the door on the first floor, then winched up the lift cage manually until its top was at floor level, giving themselves safe, easy access. (The procedure of winching up the lift cage was particularly interesting to me: a firefighter on the first floor communicated by radio to another firefighter, doing the winching at the top of the building—in the "motor room," the "grimy" place Victoria had told James to stay out of for fear of soiling his clothes.) It was easily determined that Pascal was dead (though despite this he was moved onto a spineboard), and he was taken by an ambulance service directly to the city mortuary. He had not had a very controlled fall—his neck was broken—and one of the medics told me he'd most likely died instantly.

I had imagined that the police would become involved, but they never did. It was generally assumed that the lift had malfunctioned in some way, enabling Pascal to open the door on the fourth floor when the cage was not present. I answered some questions asked me by a female firefighter, the young woman who would write up a report for the coroner, and I was extremely discreet (in keeping with my newly acquired composure), answering entirely within the range of the specific questions she put to me; the only information I volunteered was that Pascal, when I'd seen him leave the flat and go into the hallway, had appeared to be sleepwalking. Though I was made to endure any number of raised eyebrows—what was the hotel's young porter doing sleeping in my flat while my wife was away?—there was nothing, apparently, to suggest foul play. When this question was posed explicitly, at the end of the interview, I gave a slim variant of the truth: I'd been hearing some strange noises in the night; I'd told Pascal about it; we'd thought the noises might be of a supernatural origin; Pascal had offered to sleep in the flat in order to investigate. This account comprised only one plain lie, the business about Pascal's *offering*, but it was taken no doubt as wholly contrived to cover over a more randy actuality.

In the street, as I watched Pascal slid on his spineboard into the ambulance, I noticed what looked like a rope burn on his left cheek; I saw the same apparent burns on the upturned palms of his hands; his pajamas were soaking in the groin area, and a clear liquid flowed out of his nose and ears. Otherwise, he looked, in his pajamas and flannel robe, as if he might have been only sleeping. I gave the ambulance driver the belt to Pascal's robe, then my "French lad," in less than three-quarters of an hour after he'd looked in my direction and said, "I'll be back," was simply gone.

The ambulance disappeared down the block, the fire brigade departed too, and I was left standing in the street, in the dark, in a fine falling mist that had coated everything with a grotesque sheen. The young man whom I took to be Hannah's son was coated with a grotesque sheen as well; he stood looking at me now from the curb. "What then?" he said to me after a glance at my bags beneath the hotel canopy. "Are you leaving *now?*"

Yes, I told him, I would leave now; the hotel had an

imprint of my credit card, and would it be all right if I settled my bill by mail?

"Of course," he said, "but where will you go at such an hour?"

"I'll just walk a bit," I said (which didn't alter the very worried look on the young man's face), and I gathered my bags and headed down the lane.

Seven hundred and fifty-five steps later, I stood in the Sho-pans' sunken vestibule, ringing the doorbell.

I pushed the button only once, not overly briefly, not overly long, and though it was quite a while before I heard any sound that could be taken as stirring inside, I somehow knew that one ring would do. Through a small oculus window in the door, I saw a light go on, and when the door opened, the bald Mr. Sho-pan stood in the hall, wearing brown leather slippers and a silk robe of midnight blue over bleachy-white pajamas buttoned at the neck. He said not a single word when he saw me, but reached for my arm, gripping me just above one elbow and pulling me inside as if he were snatching me from imminent danger. He closed the door, took my bags, setting them down right there, then steered me into the parlor and onto the couch. Under this sure, unexpected influence, I gained an immediate rag-doll nature, physically and spiritually, welcoming the sense that someone else, someone far more decent and reliable than I, was now in charge. He switched on a small lamp with a green-glass shade, instigating in the dark-wooded room a dim, theatrical atmosphere that seemed to say, Abomination, three in the morning.

His first actual words were, "I won't be a moment. . . . I'll just put on the kettle."

Once I was alone, David, the Sho-pans' dead son, smiled from across the way, accusing me exotically (cockatiel in hand) within his frame of woven straw. And then Mimi appeared from the hall, rounding the couch, taking a chair opposite, and scrutinizing my face. She wore the white pajamas and the silk robe too, hers a dark maroon, and she seemed already to know at least the magnitude of what had happened. She crossed her arms, hugging herself and leaning forward, resting her elbows on her knees, bracing herself. I tried for a moment to determine what had changed about her, a diversion maneuver on my part—her hair was down— and then it seemed that I must do the thing I could not do: speak. It was not that I couldn't form the necessary words— that was simple enough—but that the words themselves, already formed and lodged in my heart, wouldn't submit to utterance. I suppose I must have looked altogether hopeless. Mimi said, "Cookson," and emerged from her self-protecting attitude long enough to reach for my hand. Under the circumstances, I couldn't very well take it, could I? Mr. Sho-pan returned to the room, went behind the chair in which his wife sat, and placed his hands on her shoulders. They both continued looking at me, unblinking, and they seemed, for the first time, mostly old; when at last Mimi spoke again, there was the slightest hint of anger in her voice: "Just *say* it, Cookson," she said.

"Pascal is dead," I said. "He fell down the elevator shaft at the hotel."

They clenched their eyes tightly shut, and then there was a horrible shifting of their bodies, a kind of grievous choreography in which he sank toward the floor, bearing himself now with his hands on her shoulders, her own hands flew up and clamped down over his, he bent forward as she arched back, and together they seemed to crumple into each other, but exactly as if they'd been doused with acid. It was truly one of the most terrifying things I'd ever seen, accompanied only by the ticking of the mantel's clock, but I had little time to dwell there, for in the next moment, the teakettle wailed its shrill alarm, and my wife stood across the room in a white nightgown, saying, "Cook, my God, what's happened?"

Twenty-Four

HAPPINESS INTRUDING IN that terrible moment was nearly as stunning as the sight of her itself. It wasn't pure happiness—I felt that anything pure had passed out of my life for good. (Emotionally, the moment was something like the one at the beginning of the story, when I'd crawled into bed next to her, back home in Cambridge, still trembling from the fright delivered me by the dog with the albinic eyes. . . . I'd wanted comforting that night but didn't seek it because I was curiously ashamed.) The spectacle of the Sho-pans, a crushed little heap swelling and heaving between us in the room, was the powerful evidence against me; now that it had been witnessed by her, I would never be able in any future accounting to leave it out. Part of me, the unhappy part, felt caught by her sudden presence, and I dimly seemed to rehear the sound of her retreating footsteps in the Willerton's hallway, as if I might grasp after that earlier sense of relief. I suppose it was this astonished split in me (and a sovereign, persistent selfishness in spite of everything) that made her question—"Cook, my God, what's happened?"— seem aimed at something closer to home than Pascal's sad fate. It was, to me (teakettle still shrilling), What's happened to our life together? What in the world have we come to?

I remained, I think, reasonably engaged throughout the ensuing disbelief and desultory journey of the next ninety minutes or so; Ellen needed answers of the sort that had earlier been sought by the firefighters; Mimi pretty much confined herself to painful remarks about Pascal's dashed dreams, and how hopeful and handsome he'd looked the first time they'd seen him, and what a sweet, congenial boy he was. Throughout, I withheld any mention of my ghosts and any suspicions I had about James's involvement in Pascal's "accident." I provided virtually the same report I'd given to the others, at the hotel, adding only that it was too soon now for anyone to know how or why the lift had malfunctioned. In the context of the Sho-pans' very worldly grief (and what I was beginning to see as Ellen's torn condition), the ghost stuff would have seemed vulgar (as of course it inherently was). But the ghosts and my role in their unfinished melodrama were exactly the tensions that colored everything and created an odd social awkwardness when you would have thought we might all have been well past such things: no one mentioned the ghosts because no one wanted to implicate me outright, to my face.

As for Mr. Sho-pan, he never uttered a word, and it was perhaps his enduring silence that was hardest for everyone to bear. I believe that tea was made and poured out but that no one drank any. And when at last Mr. Sho-pan drew himself up and began to move silently toward the door to the hall-way, Mimi said, "Ray, darling, wouldn't you like to go back to bed?" though surely that was what he was already doing. He stopped, turned, and nodded very deliberately: that was just what he was going to do, go back to bed.

Lowering her voice to a whisper, Mimi said to us, "I think I'd better go with him," and followed her husband into the hall.

Once they were gone from the room, Ellen explained that when it had come time to leave London, she hadn't been able to—she hadn't been able to leave me there alone. The Sho-pans had encouraged her during the afternoon hours to stay and have another go at persuading me out of the flat. "Mimi had a plan," Ellen said. "I was to come to breakfast with them in the morning—*this* morning—and then the three of us were going to call on you at the flat. We were determined to get inside and then stage a kind of sit-in. We would simply refuse to leave until you came with us."

She said all this with irony, but with a sad kind of irony, not the least bit bitter.

I said, "What is that you're wearing?"—referring to the long white thing she had on, a gown that went straight down from the shoulders to the floor, buttoned at the neck and made from some kind of heavy material that was hard to imagine sleeping in. "I've never seen it before."

"It's Mimi's," she said.

There was nothing left for me to say but that workaday word that conveyed the burden of remorse over the whole range of human events, from a sneeze to genocide—*sorry*, sorry for everything.

She waited for quite a while, and then said, without judgment, with full acceptance, "I know you are."

We sat opposite each other in the room, I on a couch,

she in an armchair, a distance of about five feet between us, unobstructed by any other piece of furniture, and though we held each other's gaze for a few seconds, neither of us moved.

That morning, around dawn, I took a taxi to the Hilton. Ellen had suggested I stay at the Sho-pans', but when I said I thought it best that I go to a hotel, she said, thoughtfully, "Well, maybe that would be better."

Then she said, "I think I should stay with them, don't you? I don't think they should be left alone right now."

"No," I said. "They shouldn't. You stay and I'll phone you later, when I'm settled. We'll make some plans."

Checking in at the Hilton was something like going to Mars, exactly the breadth of change I was looking for, and I don't know if spending three hundred dollars a night was a form of pampering or a form of penance. I only knew I didn't want to stay at the Sho-pans'. I was consumed too much by shame to wallow under the eyes of those who knew me for what I was, and like an animal, I meant to lick my wounds in private.

The plans we eventually made were for my going to Paris on the third day thence, a Sunday—I was in touch with Hannah, at the hotel, who was in touch with Pascal's family—and for Ellen to return to Cambridge on Sunday too. She wanted to see Jordie—she was worried about Jordie—and in a very fundamental way, she simply wanted to go home. Friday night, as I drifted to sleep in my room at the Hilton, I recall envisioning a parchment-colored map of Europe on which, out of London, my trail, in red, headed toward France, Ellen's, in blue, toward America. We also planned to spend Saturday together before going our separate ways.

To some extent, I was glad to have these different trips with their opposite directions ahead of us, glad to delay the hour when we would have to see what things were actually going to be like between us at home. I was also glad to have the intervening day alone, a transitional day. I knew that if I was going to thwart a more substantial and lasting separation between Ellen and me, I would have to present myself honestly on Saturday as a man reformed, as a man with a clean slate. In that case, there was something I still needed to do, a last bit of business concerning my ghosts.

It wasn't as if I walked out of the Hotel Willerton and simply never thought about them again; I thought about them over and over during the next few days, but I thought about them with a new kind of detachment, the difference, say, between thinking about water while drowning in the ocean and thinking about it while sunning on the shore. I went on for a while, still trying to put meaning to everything, the sort of foolishness that had made Iris laugh at me so: There was the coincidence that the girl's father (if we were to believe Iris) was a murderer, like my own father; there was the great representative of all that is self-abusive and escapist and raging and destructive in the world, Walter—a walking (sort of), talking (sort of) *end* I might have reached, unimpeded by grace, in my own life; there was the coincidence that James felt abandoned by his father (whoever that may have been) and had been left—like another version of me, taken to its extreme—with some unnatural, overblown hungers. Privately, I continued experiencing the frustration of someone who'd been given only some of the pieces to a puzzle; I didn't get it, what the girl had been trying to tell me: that they were what had been left behind. I wanted answers, the missing pieces in their stories that, rightly placed, would make a coherent picture—a picture with meaning.

On Friday (the intervening day), having looked up the location in the phone book, I stopped by the offices of Lohengrin Lifts, on Fulham Road; I entered the building, which might have once been the stone rectory of a church, and climbed a dark, narrow stairway, creaky and crooked (an irony, I thought, in an elevator company). Once I'd entered an outer office through a door with a panel of frosted glass, I introduced myself to a receptionist as a friend of the young porter who'd fallen down the shaft at the Hotel Willerton. The receptionist, a beautiful black woman with seven silver earrings arranged all the way up the helix of one ear, looked stricken when I said who I was. Briefly, she spoke into a telephone, and then a fair-haired man in his thirties invited me into another office and asked me to take a seat. He regarded me suspiciously at first and deflected whatever questions I'd come to ask by asking some of his own—what part of the States was I from? what brought me to London? and so forth—then telling me more than I could possibly want to know about a recent visit he'd made to Boston with his wife and two young girls, to attend an elevator convention. He asked me if I'd ever been to a certain discotheque in Jamaica Plain. But small talk aside, he proved, having warmed up sufficiently, to be, like another person I'd met on this trip to London, very keen on lifts and unable quite to pass up an opportunity to hold forth.

"The lift checked out in perfect working order," he said. "We replaced some parts anyhow, just to be on the safe side, but there wasn't any accounting for the malfunction."

He said his company was required to inspect the lift and issue a report every six months, but the lift had been inspected and maintained by him more frequently than that—in fact, once a month, on a regular basis. (Indeed, it had been checked out only three weeks before.) With great care and attention to detail, he explained about the retractable ramps that trigger the rollers that release the locking mechanism on the door as the cage passes a given floor. "But there's a problem with that scheme," he said. "A person could yank open the door, you see, whenever the cage goes by."

"Maybe that's what happened," I suggested.

"No," he said. "You couldn't've done it on the top floor—there's no going by there 'cause it's the end of the journey, you see. Besides, that's only how things used to be. Now we've added electrical contacts to the mechanisms. You can't open the door unless the cage has come to a stop."

I asked him if the locking mechanism could be defeated by someone who had, say, got onto the top of the lift cage.

"Why would you ask such a question?" he said.

I shrugged and said I was baffled by what had happened and was simply fishing.

"No," he said. "You couldn't do it from atop the cage. You'd have to gain access to the motor room."

From the motor room, he told me, one could, theoretically, short out the circuitry for a particular floor, open the door, then put the circuits back to rights.

"But you could only do it from the motor room," he said. "And you'd have to know what you were doing."

So there I had it: This, as you can imagine, was the sort of talismanic bit of science you think is going to make a significant difference of some kind, change the way you feel, change the way you understand things . . . but once you actually have it in your hand, you realize how useless it is. Not only was it, on its face, preposterous that a young ghost had sabotaged the lift, contriving the death of his perceived rival for paternal affections, but now that I'd proved to myself that there was indeed a way to bring about such a thing, how could I possibly use it? To what purpose could this knowledge possibly be put?

As an act of mercy to myself, I'll bypass the particulars of my being alone in the hotel room, watching from my high picture window the endless rainfall in Hyde Park: my inability to eat, my fear of sleeping, my fear of dreams. Suffice to say I saw dawn arrive in the sickle mirror of the Serpentine. Ellen and I were to meet below, in the café, for breakfast at ten, and I did some lugubrious hovering, from about six to nine, over the question of what to wear. I couldn't help but notice that each time I imagined myself sitting in a restaurant amid food aromas, I felt queasy—and there was an odd little thing going on with my skin: If I came to a complete rest, a tingling sensation, beginning at the top of my scalp, emanated out and down my face and the back of my neck and then continued into my arms and chest and legs; it was interesting, but very unsettling, and when I attempted to lie on the bed, the widening tingle grew so agitated as to shake the bed. I decided I would phone Ellen, tell her I wasn't feeling great, suggest we skip breakfast and go for a walk. (I liked the idea of outdoor air.) But just before I was about to do that, she phoned me—this was around nine—and suggested we skip breakfast and go for a walk instead. I mentioned that it was raining out, but she said she had an umbrella. I said I had one too.

It was ten-thirty before she got to the hotel and phoned me from the lobby. I told her my room number and asked if she cared to come up, but even as I said the words, it seemed an odd invitation, oddly timed: I'm not sure what I meant to express—probably a desperate desire magically to put things right, to put us in a hotel room together again, normal, safe, as if the spectacular view from my picture windows and grand Georgian-style furnishings could redeem us, could possibly redeem me. In any case, she was confused, speechless; I jumped into the silence and said, "Bad idea. . . . I'll be right down. . . . We'll go for a walk."

Downstairs, I didn't see her at first, and when I did see her, I experienced an ambivalence similar to what I'd felt at the Sho-pans'—part of me elated to see her, another part unhappy at *being seen* by her. She was wrapped up tight in her raincoat, legs crossed, arms crossed, looking sideways into the empty part of the love seat where she sat. When I moved alongside and said hello, she brushed her fingers over the seat cushion and looked up at me; I recall feeling nearly assaulted by the neutrality in her eyes. Her first words to me were, "Look, there's a little rip here in the fabric. . . ." Then she stood and smiled (some sadness there, some kindness, some letting down of the guard), and on my initiative, we embraced—not an altogether repulsive ordeal for her, but more intimacy, I think, than she was quite ready for.

We went out, sharing my umbrella. Instead of entering Hyde Park, we turned southeast and headed down through Green Park (and eventually on through Saint James's Park and toward the Thames). It was a light rain, and not windy, not too chilly, pleasant enough, and the fresh air was everything

I'd hoped it would be, steadying somehow. We walked an uncomfortable distance in silence, after which I asked whether she'd spoken with Jordie.

"Twice," she said, paused, then added, "She sounds okay . . . a little worried about us but happy I'm coming home tomorrow. She's in a skit Tuesday afternoon."

"A skit?"

"Yes. I thought I'd drive down there Tuesday morning and stay overnight."

"What kind of skit?"

"Something to do with Eleanor Roosevelt, I think."

I suggested she have the house-sitters stay until she returned from Connecticut.

"Oh, no," she said. "I don't want anybody in the house after I'm there. I've already phoned and told them I'll be there tomorrow. Besides, I'll have Spencer to keep me company."

"But what will you do with him when you go down to see Jordie?"

"I'll take him with me," she said.

"Aren't you afraid you'll have trouble finding a place to stay?"

"What do you mean?"

"I mean a place that will take dogs?"

"I've already checked, Cook. The inn in town takes dogs. Don't worry."

A lengthy list of domestic concerns had sprung to my mind—having to do with paying bills, starting up the newspaper delivery, phoning the post office, changing the filters in the heating system, and so forth—and I imagine I could have continued this kind of domestic dialogue for at least an hour, but I restrained myself; in this initial exchange about the dog and exactly how long Ellen should keep the house-sitters, there had been just enough subterranean tension to back me off. I asked her how Ray and Mimi were doing, and she seemed glad of the change in subject.

"They seem . . . ," she began, and then appeared to think better of what she was about to say, as if she'd reminded herself to tread gently.

"I think they're still stunned," she said at last. "They haven't gone to breakfast at the hotel these last two days. Nothing was said about not going; they just didn't go. And Mimi's developed a sudden penchant for small talk. She rattles on about the weather, clothes, food, the good old days . . . everything but her feelings. I'm not sure what it is I expect her to say."

"What about him?"

"It's hard to tell," she said. "This morning he brought a click beetle to the dining-room table—out of his collection— and began to tell me all about its many fascinating habits. Including its ability to produce light. He explained about its luminous organs and how a certain enzyme interacts with some compound or other to make light. It was very interesting, but Mimi came into the room and asked him to put it away. It's strange, because they're actually more talkative than usual . . . but in this weird way—emotionally, I guess—they're much more withdrawn. Everything they do feels like a substitute for the thing they're not doing. Everything that's said feels like something that's not being said."

This, of course, was a lucid enough description of *us*— and I think we both sensed it. "What about tomorrow?" I asked quickly. "What about when you leave?"

"Well, I've asked her to get in touch with some people at their church—to let somebody know what's happening— and she said she would. But I don't know if she will. I think they're afraid to let themselves feel how grief-stricken they really are."

"Because of the son," I said.

"Exactly. It would have to be like opening an old wound."

We'd taken a turn somewhere along the way that led us to a small white-painted pavilion—a bandstand, I guess— where we climbed the steps and sat inside on the peripheral bench. She asked me if I'd spoken to anyone in Pascal's family.

"No," I said. "I've only spoken to Hannah, at the hotel.

She told me his sister, Catherine, has come to London. They had to do a . . . you know, because it was an accident . . ."

"Postmortem," she said.

"Yes," I said. "Catherine's going back to Paris with . . ."

"The body," said Ellen.

"Right, and the funeral's Tuesday."

"Are you sure you want to do this?"

"What . . . go to Paris? I have to."

"Are you planning to introduce yourself to the family?"

"I don't know," I said. "I'll probably just play it by ear. I could go anonymously. It's really for me that I'm—"

She looked away.

"What?" I said. "What is it?"

"What is what?" she said.

"What is it you disapprove of?"

"I don't disapprove of your going to Paris," she said. "I understand completely. I was thinking it would be good for you to meet the family. To tell them who you are."

I said that I probably would, and another of those where-do-we-go-from-here silences ensued. I found myself watching some kind of black-bellied ducks scrapping on a nearby lawn. Then I studied for a while the peeling paint on the floor planks of the bandstand.

"How's your new room?" she asked finally.

I wasn't sure if she'd thought the question over, realized it was impossible for it not to be loaded, and asked it anyway—or if it had just popped out of her. I evaded its subtler implications and said I had a bathtub big enough to accommodate a Volkswagen.

"And how are you feeling?"

"Feeling?" I said (feeling my most hated misery, estrangement from my wife). "I'm not sleeping much."

"Well, *there's* a change," she said.

"I don't blame you for being angry," I said. "I went crazy and spoiled your trip."

"It wasn't my trip," she said. "It was our trip."

"Anyway," I said, "I don't blame you for being angry."

She didn't respond to this for a long while, and I decided to let her have her silence if that was what she wanted; then, at last, she complained of being cold—said she was cold, sitting there—and so we moved on.

When we'd left the park and reached the street, a truck sped by, splashing a puddle and sending up a spray of dirty rainwater. I pulled her back from the curb, yelling, "Watch out!"—loud enough to attract the attention of a few fellow pedestrians and, I think, embarrassing Ellen. Her coat was splashed, and my face must have been registering a high level of distress (in fact, my heart was racing), for she said, "It's only water. . . ."

Once that was behind us, a block or so more, she said, "Cook, my anger or disappointment or . . . even my worry about you—about what's wrong with you—whatever else I may be feeling pales in comparison to the terrible thing that's happened, don't you think? Something terrible has happened. I just want to go home. I want to see Jordie. I want to sleep in my own bed. Eat my own food. The Sho-pans are lovely, wonderful people . . . but what am I doing there? How did I get there? It's as if I'd climbed onto a merry-go-round, something that looked like fun, and then it spun out of control, and when it stopped I was separated from my husband and staying with these two nice old people from Hong Kong. I can feel it, right here in my chest, this fear. . . . I don't think I'll believe I'm home until I'm actually inside the house. No . . . I won't really be all right until I'm holding Jordie in my arms."

She'd said all this while we continued walking, looking straight ahead, not looking at me. Down the street, Westminster Bridge had come into view, and I was struck by what little consequence it had: it was recognizable only as foreign, and we could have been anywhere in the world; the fact that we were in rainy London was about as significant as it might have been to Ray Sho-pan's impaled beetles. I said to her, "Is that what we are? Separated?"

"I don't know," she said. "What would you call it?"

"Apart, I guess. I'd say we were apart."

"I'm not sure I understand the distinction," she said, "but okay. Apart."

"You see, the one thing's like a decision, and the other's just . . . circumstances. It could change. It will change. It doesn't have to mean—"

"I just need to go home, Cook," she said. "Maybe I can sort all this out, but I have to do it on dry land. I have to do it at home."

"Do you still want to go to the airport together tomorrow?" I asked.

"Yes," she said, with just a tinge of exasperation. "Of course."

Something terrible had happened: It lingered behind the rest of our time together, which—because of the vague way in which our time together was not going well; because of how it was vaguely painful, being together—we cut short. Soon after we reached the river, she said that she was cold and suddenly very tired and wanted to go back for a nap. She said she had a long trip ahead of her the next day, and she didn't want to begin it already tired. I think she used the word "tired" maybe a half-dozen times in different ways, and when I looked at her that was finally all I could see: she was tired. She wanted to take the tube back (because it had been a long walk, and she was tired), and I opted to continue walking on my own for a while. I saw her to the station, bought her ticket for her, gave her another (somewhat knotty) hug, and watched her get onto the escalator that would take her far below the ground. She didn't look back at me, and I watched her body disappear from the feet up, legs, hips, shoulders, head, gone. It was awful.

I did in fact keep walking—out of the station, aimlessly, in a funk. I walked away from the river, away from openness, making random turns; it was near enough the lunch hour that the sidewalks were crowded, and the narrower the street, the more abandoned it was, the more eagerly I chose it. At the end of a certain block-long lane (something like Willerton

Way), I went down some stone steps and soon found myself lost on a sloping bit of London, the backsides of some buildings looming above on my right, a tall chain-link fence on my left, enclosing a long and narrow path of cobblestones. Through the fence I could see the unpopulated green of an esplanade and the river beyond; opposite this was a colonnade, a part of the substructure of the buildings above. Under the shelter of the colonnade, dozens of homeless people huddled in many encampments against the inner, recessed wall. My pace slowed in the lane as I moved past these people, framed iconically now and again in the pillared archways of the colonnade, and I felt almost as if I'd entered another world—the world behind and beneath the world, a neat, hidden arrangement, the invisible, inhabited underpinning of things. I couldn't entirely look away, though I tried to, and somewhere near the middle of this single-sided gauntlet, I began to have trouble breathing. The day had grown quickly darker, it had begun to rain hard, and there was something disagreeable in the snappish blossoming of my umbrella. With some effort I pushed past to the end, where there was another stairway of stone steps, leading up and, I hoped, out. The steps were flanked by the high brick walls of the buildings on either side and thus deprived of much light; one long flight up, there was a landing and a sharp turn to the right, where I met with a dead end, a black steel door, and the acrid stench of old urine that universally defines such places. A child crouched amid the stains on the pavement floor in one corner, his long blond hair smeared with what looked like grease from a crankcase, and he wore dark ragged clothes, short pants, his bare legs covered with the soot of exposure and neglect; over his head, scratched into the paint on the metal door, were the words "fuck me til i bleed!" I felt a familiar queasiness, a speeding of my heart, smelled a burnt scent inside the other odor, and then the child, whose face had been buried in grimy hands, looked up at me, locking his yellowish eyes to mine.

It was James, leveling a glare of such indictment I experienced a moment of partial blindness. Then I simply turned, took the steps down two at a time, and got the hell out.

By the time I'd found a tube station and was back at the Hilton, I was in a state that brings obsolete vocabularies to mind: *racked, wretchedful.* Though it had been forced on me, though Pascal had paid the price of my readmission, I'd taken a certain amount of false comfort in quitting the Willerton and taking up the "real" world again. Without putting it into so many words, I imagined that I had escaped, and effectively erased the "unreal" past. Encountering James that way, *outside*, had the symbolic effect of waking me to what I'd been evading these last three days—the laboring of my remorse, a version of what people call "living with yourself." It was, I could see right away, a remorse that reached way past the Hotel Willerton.

Faced with this prospect, my first tack, back inside my "new room" (as Ellen had put it), was to go to sleep.

A perk of being married to a writer of mysteries: you know some of the details of autopsy. I dreamed of Pascal, cold and white and naked, supine on a metal table, gullied with the infamous "Y" incision (diagonally from each shoulder, meeting below the sternum, and on down the abdomen to the pubis). There was something here of the ambience of the recurring chiropractor dream, but this time the table was icy stainless steel, with a shallow rim and a drain hole, and I was the practitioner; the oddest thing—I experienced myself as a *cook*, blind (nearly) to the exact nature of the dish I was preparing, though somewhere in the back of my mind I knew the truth, and this made for a good deal of uneasiness as I proceeded. I had recently cut through the ribs and cartilage to expose the heart and lungs and was now removing these, along with the esophagus and trachea; on a cutting board near Pascal's feet (the big toe of one foot tagged with an identifying label), I cut the heart free from the other organs and placed it in a spring scale (the kind at the grocer's). It weighed nearly eight pounds, and, smiling at the play on

words, I thought what a heavy heart Pascal had. I took it out
of the scale and sliced it in two with a favorite Wüsthof
Trident carving knife and set it aside. I next removed the
liver, spleen, kidneys, stomach, pancreas, and intestines, cutting here and there where necessary, but also pulling where
pulling would do the trick. (More than once I had to push
aside Pascal's perpetual erection—it was getting in my way—
and faintly I recalled reading somewhere that priapism was a
sign of spinal injury.) I placed all these in a large colander
where they could drain, then moved on to the head. I made
an incision all the way from behind one ear, over the cranium
to the other ear, bearing down hard, making sure to hit bone;
then, leaning in close and whispering, "Sorry," I peeled the
scalp forward down over Pascal's face. I was about to find the
tool required to saw through the bone, when I realized I
would need to aspirate some of the clear liquid that was leak-
ing through a fracture in the skull; I found a bulb-type turkey-
basting syringe for this task, and as I set about it, the surprising familiarity of the clear liquid was what turned the so far
unsettling dream into a full-blown nightmare. I thought,
Tears; then, No, not tears: the water-like fluid I'd seen coming
out of Pascal's ears and nose as he was loaded into the ambulance. I "awakened" inside the dream, finding myself up to my
elbows in blood and knee-deep in entrails, and I wildly began
trying to put things back, tossing and stuffing organs into the
enormous gaping cavity, and crying all the while, "Oh please
God, please please please God . . ."

So much for my escape. I woke worse than ever. My next
tack was to phone room service and order a bucket of ice and
a bottle of Glenlivet. It seemed to me, as I surveyed (however
myopically) my interior landscape with its bleak vistas, that
thirteen years was long enough, and that enough was enough.

I had slept in my clothes, and I now stripped down to
my underwear and undershirt—a proper drinking ensemble
(for a certain kind of drinker)—opened the drapes wide, and
propped myself in bed.

A knock came at the door with amazing dispatch. I pulled on a robe, grabbed some coins, and answered it.

Ellen stood in the hall, bags in hand and looking resigned, younger than I remembered her, beautiful. "Mimi kicked me out," she said. "Okay if I stay with you?"

This time I experienced no ambivalence. The sight of her, the fact of her, here, now, humbled me. I tearily took her bags, got the door closed, and helped her off with her coat. (I did all this rather hurriedly, fearing a sudden reversal.) The first thing she did—probably the first thing anyone did entering this room—was to go to the large picture window. She took in the view, breathing deeply, then turned and took in the room. "My, my," she said. "No skimping on the old family recipe."

"No," I said. "Mimi kicked you out?"

"It was a kind of old-world frenzy," Ellen said. "She said I belonged here, with you, and that she didn't want any argument about it."

"A woman among women," I said.

"Yes," she said, looking unsure.

"Can I get you anything?" I said. "Are you hungry? You want something to drink?" (Of course it was here that I thought of the Glenlivet en route, but basking in the mystery of her arrival, I had no room for panic of any sort.)

"No, thank you," she said, turning back to the window, no doubt thinking, Have I made a mistake, coming here?

After some moments, she said, "But I wouldn't mind a peak at that bathtub you mentioned."

When the Scotch did arrive, she was in the bathroom, door closed, water running. I gave the porter a generous tip, asked him to return the bottle, and once that was taken care of, I went around tidying the room, picking up my clothes, switching on lamps, straightening the bedcovers. Then, in an entirely unfocused way, I kept trying to think of things to say to her. Occasionally, I could hear the faint splash of her bathwater as she moved an arm or a leg. I went to the bathroom door and stood outside it. I heard her sigh, then another stirring of the water. I thought I wanted to tell her about the nightmare I'd had, and about my encounter with James in that stinking hellhole at the top of the stairs; I wanted to tell her about the Scotch I'd ordered (would I have drunk it? I'll never know for sure); I wanted to say that I thought it was finally hitting me—the truth and hugeness of the terrible thing that had happened, Pascal's pointless death, and the truth and hugeness of the various injuries I'd handed down in this life; I wanted to say that I knew that changing my habits wasn't enough, would never be enough, and that the problem, my problem, was inside the spiritual bedrock, my soul; I wanted to say that I had no idea how to go about changing *that*, yet it felt right somehow, not knowing. But standing there outside the door, listening to the quiet stirrings of the water, I also knew that words, too, would never be enough, that she had to be shown—slowly, over time, she had to be convinced by what she saw with her own eyes. I gently tapped on the door. "Ellen," I said, "can I come in?"

There was a pause, then, "Okay."

Inside, the mirrors were fogged, and even the walls seemed dulled with mist. When she looked up at me I could see she'd been crying. I began to undress, a simple task since there was only the robe and the underwear. She watched me, tentatively. She said, "What are you doing?"

"I want to get in," I said. "If that's okay."

She looked very uncertain but after a moment drew her knees up to her breasts and slid back against the wall of the tub, making room for me. She seemed to know it wasn't sex I was after, only nakedness. I got in, duplicating her knees-up position, facing her. "Do you mind if I add a little hot water?"

"No," she said. "Please do."

The faucet was located on the wall behind the tub, so that when I opened the tap, a stream of water fell between us. Soon the water was deep and extremely hot. Soon she had turned very red, very raw-looking, and I suspected that I must have looked the same. Soon we were both crying, red and raw and crying. It was the prevailing kindness in her eyes, I think, that undid me, and the willingness I could see there to forgive, despite the great maze that had grown up between us.

We did quite a lot of weeping together that late afternoon, for a long time in the tub, and now and then one of us would try to say something, but each time we tried, only the hard squawks and sputters of heartbreak would come. Some silence would ensue, some calm—I thought it was the silence of knowing that everything that ever was would ever be: I would not be able, even with my duplicitous skills, to make any of what had happened never have happened—then one of us would look at the other, and the crying would start up again. She was enormously kind throughout, and there was an inherent hopefulness for me in the nostalgia of her naked body and in the way we seemed reduced (or restored) to our red and raw child selves there in the hot water; but in spite of all that—in spite of her kindness and our grieving together—she was in some way lastingly pulled back, withdrawn deeper and deeper into the core of the maze and its cold marble fountain of tears. I could tell, right from the start, that she hated the way things were—this peak of untended resentment we'd reached, this ugly outpost in the odyssey that had led to an innocent's death; and she hated also the ambiguous state it left us in. I could tell that she wanted to forgive, that she had now, and would continue to have, the will to forgive, but that forgiveness, being a change of the heart, didn't answer to the will. When, eventually, she stood in the water and stepped out of the tub, I watched with longing as steam rose off her shoulders and arms.

CHAPTER

Twenty-Five

IT IS APRIL, about six months later, and for the last

little while I've been lying on the leather couch in the library,

midafternoon, thinking of Jordie. (On a hike early this morn-

ing, I twisted my ankle, and I'm trying to give it a rest.)

Jordie, home for spring break, is upstairs somewhere, probably in her room, and perhaps doing some thinking of her own, though hers, I imagine, is spring centered and surely less nostalgic than mine. I was recalling a time when she came with us one night to a dinner party given by a stuffy salt-and-pepper-haired couple (the man a critic, the woman a poet, both fellows of some sort at Harvard) who'd decided to take one of Ellen's books "seriously," as reaching past the boundaries of its feeble genre, and to invite Ellen on those grounds into what was apparently a revered fold, complete with view of the Charles. There were twelve of us altogether, Jordie, just shy of three, the only person under the age of thirty. (Jordie's inclusion by the party-givers had been a reaching past some boundaries of their own, possibly one of those futile stabs in the dark at becoming in a single gesture somebody you wish you were but never could be.) Mostly, the other guests variously admired, throughout dinner, one another's works and conducted an ongoing contest to see who could drop the most literary names in a single sentence. Jordie and I weren't expected to participate, of course, and we were reduced to an equal, toddler status by the whole table's falling silent anytime either of us ventured to speak . . . then crinkly-eyed smiles all around, and a resumption of what we'd so charmingly interrupted. Somehow, in spite of the vulgarity of all this, the atmosphere accrued a nearly parodic-seeming good breeding. I noticed, late into the evening, that people were beginning to refrain from the use of contractions, and one man (whom I knew to have grown up near Revere Beach) strangely acquired a kind of British-Pakistani accent. Just when I'd begun to think that everyone had taken leave of his senses, Jordie climbed down from her chair and (in the spirit of sharing newly acquired knowledge) began going around the table announcing which guest had a penis and which a vagina. A couple of minutes were required to get to everyone (here and there a splendid moment of hesitation), and I wouldn't in a million years have dreamed of stopping her until she was done. It was just the blast of tropical air the cold night needed, and to her great credit, Ellen didn't make any attempt to stop Jordie either.

"No," I said. "I meant I hope that someday soon you'll explain how things are to *me.*"

"You know as well as I do . . . ," she said, and turned, and went back inside the house.

I suppose I was intrigued by the ambiguity of her remark: unemotionally, I returned to my raking and took up an analysis of the phrase itself: "You know as well as I do . . ." Was it intended to be the full answer to my request, or was it only the beginning of an answer she'd thought better of? I couldn't possibly know, but I did notice an awkwardness in her turning away, as if she was trying to cultivate a parting-shot tactic she couldn't quite bring off. Her awkwardness was vastly important to me. It suggested that she hadn't changed so much as she was only behaving differently—a *temporary* condition—and it showed me how hurt and grief and disappointment and mistrust can take people into all sorts of shabby behaviors to which they may not be naturally inclined. What I really suspected was that her new habit of truncating scenes like that was a simple, fearful refusal to engage. Engaging had become a complicated enterprise of risks and unintended implications and retreats.

Since frozenness and a need for thawing were the issues between us, it was unfortunate that we were embarking on winter, an especially icy and snowy one at that. In truth, my own question, that day under the chestnut tree, affected more heart for our marital troubles than I really had. I wasn't anywhere near being ready for Ellen to explain to me how things were at home (that is, I wasn't really ready to *hear* her on the subject). I was still much too soon released from the malignant spells of the Hotel Willerton, and too soon back from Paris, where I'd gone and met Pascal's family and attended my one and only Catholic funeral mass. I'd lost fourteen pounds and was still having difficulty eating. I was having nightmares nearly every night, sometimes several in a single night, often interspersed with drunk dreams. Because I was waking almost every morning with a craving for a great variety of substances that might give me some relief, I'd begun sitting in on a lot of

AA meetings. (That's how I preferred to think of it, as "sitting in.") I was trying not to allow myself the indulgence of active self-loathing, for self-loathing felt too much like pleasure. But because I'd become host to the parasitic remorse that had begun overseas, I couldn't avoid replaying London contrari- wise: I'd kept no secrets, pursued no paranormal highs; we'd changed hotels; I'd stayed by Ellen; failing all that, I'd left with her that afternoon in the flat when she begged me to; we flew home; Pascal didn't die.

When I thought of Pascal's people, it was as if I could see them only at a distance, their grief somehow lacking clar- ity; when I thought of the Sho-pans (whom I could hardly bear to think of), I of course saw them crumpled in a heap in their parlor, heaving between me and Ellen, though even that was somehow at some distance; but when I thought of Pascal himself, many times in a given day, I saw him up close, al- ways up close: He has seen me to the lift and now waves to me, his face at the little window in the door.

There was never a moment when I considered telling anyone in authority the "real" story, the whole story of the events at the Willerton that led to Pascal's death. Even if I could have found anyone to believe me, which was unlikely, what purpose would it have served? (And in the truest sense, there was no "real" story, certainly no whole story. In Paris, I did venture to tell Pascal's sister Catherine a pared-down ver- sion of the "real" story, and she rather abruptly ended our visit; I don't know if she did this because she believed me or because she didn't.) Sometime in late November I received by mail a request from a coroner's officer in London to supply, as an "interested party," any information I had regarding the circumstances surrounding the death of Pascal Géricault; I wrote down the details I'd already given the fire brigade. (Some ten weeks or so later, we would learn from Mimi Sho- pan that the coroner's finding was "death by misadventure," a finding I thought to be at once both true and untrue.)

I have never learned exactly what Ellen said to Jordie the day in November when she brought her home from school. It was clear to me that some briefing was necessary, because Jordie would have sensed right away that something had changed between her parents, that something was wrong between us. But during her visit home, she pointedly did not ask me any questions about England. She was full of school, drama club, new friends, and obviously very happy. While she stayed with us, only five days, there actually seemed to be more light in the house—I'm not sure if there is a practical explanation for this. Ellen seemed, off and on, almost reachable, and she and I slept together for the first time that weekend; I mean not only did we make love for the first time since England, but we also slept in the same bed. I'd been camping on the daybed in the "snoring room," my study. But when Jordie returned to school, we were restored to our sad and seemingly exclusive plights.

Jordie's homecoming at Christmas had the same happy effect as before. For all her life, you see, we were accustomed to focusing on Jordie—it was something we knew very well how to do, something we both believed in, very nearly like a mutual faith, and I almost imagine its effects were similar to what religious married people get out of worshiping together on Sundays. Over the holidays, I moved back into our bedroom, and some vague progress was made, but a progress, again, that didn't seem to have any roots. What I noticed was that Ellen seemed to come up against a wall inside herself whenever *she* noticed me acting as if nothing had changed between us, as if things between us were pre-England. I don't necessarily believe that time heals anything, but it does dilute, if drop by drop, and I simply consoled myself with hope. One consoles oneself with what's at hand, and hope, for me, was what I had.

Meanwhile, I was coping with my own private torture chamber inside my head, complete with state-of-the-art audiovisual equipment, quite apart from concerns about my marriage. Off and on, I would lose the seeds of clarity that began to sprout for me in the aftermath of Pascal's death; occasionally, it seemed I'd only brought my body back home, my body which still stank, unwashable, of the Willerton's flat; I found myself thinking too often about my ghosts. I felt duly ashamed of thinking about them—hadn't Pascal's death been enough to make me give it up? But there were so many unanswered questions, so many pieces of the puzzle missing (their story and, by affiliation, mine lacked integrity). Mid-February, a very fat envelope arrived from England, covered with a profusion of stamps. It was addressed to Ellen, an extraordinarily long letter inside, written to her by Mimi Sho-pan, a letter I have never read and that has never been read to me. Folded inside that letter, however, was another, shorter (though also long), meant for me. Here it is, reproduced in its entirety (all the ellipsis marks Mimi's own):

7 February

Dear Cookson,
That afternoon in October . . . when Ray and I came to see you but were not allowed into the flat . . . Ray wanted to tell you something he thought might be of some use to you . . . something he'd learned about the Jevons family. Following my lead, he'd spent a good deal of time at the library, consulting ancient records of many sorts, and learned that the Jevons family, before coming to London, had lived in a small country town near the Welsh marches, in Herefordshire. Ray thought this little shard he'd unearthed might be the beginning of something . . . that you might want to use it as a starting point for tracing the family's history. Ray also thought it might get you out of the flat and get you involved in something . . . well, forgive me, Cookson . . . something less dark.
Since Pascal's tragic accident . . . which was found last month by the coroner to be death by misadventure . . . Ray and I have made the London libraries our second home. We have made the Jevons family history our special project, beginning with a visit back to Colindale, and taking up where Ray left off. We have stopped breakfasting at the hotel, at least for these many weeks . . . it is simply too

painful . . . too many memories. Our special project has been a diversion in our sadness . . . something to do, a way to spend our days, and most helpful to us. I don't think I exaggerate when I say that
our task has been Herculean. It has required an incal-
culable number of hours, not only spent in the libraries, but making telephone and written inquiries of all
sorts, examining court files, and many other things. I
imagine, Cookson, that you have agonized over Pascal's death, and Ray and I send you the fruits of our
research in the hope that it will help you in a way
similar to how it has helped us. I realize that the
connection between Pascal and this bit of archaeol-
ogy is oblique, but, as I said, it has helped us and it
might help you too.

In Colindale we learned that the mother, Elizabeth Jevons, née McGlame, of Lincoln, drowned in
1927. The family was very well-to-do in Herefordshire, apparently prominent in the little town situated
on a river. The brother Walter lived with them even
then and was thought very little of by the towns-
people . . . he was an immoderate drinker and a
ne'er-do-well. The circumstances of the drowning
were suspicious. The husband, H. (amilton) E. (llery)
Jevons, was in a boat with Elizabeth when she fell
into the water. He claimed to have made attempts at
saving her but was a poor swimmer himself. Ray and
I have been unable to find any reason given for the
woman's falling out of the boat in the first place. It
seems that people's suspicions were based entirely on
the fact that Elizabeth had not long before inherited
her own deceased mother's fortune . . . and it was
thought that Jevons had everything to gain by his
wife's death. There was a thorough inquest . . . as
thorough as these things are in small towns . . .
and though Jevons was generally thought to have
had a hand in the drowning, nothing was ever
proved and he was never brought to any trial.

But a stigma attached to the brothers, who

were assumed to have profited by the woman's death. Worst of all, the little girl, Victoria, aged 5, suffered an hysterical muteness following her mother's death, disabling her starting school, and it was rumored throughout the town that the child had witnessed her father murdering her mother from her high bedroom window overlooking the river. Under these conditions, the Jevonses sold the house in Herefordshire, moved to London less than a year later, and nothing more was heard of them until 1936, when the gruesome defenestration . . . well, you already know, don't you?

As you also know, Ray believes that Walter Jevons pushed Victoria from that window in London. Jevons would have been very foolish indeed to have done so, but if in fact he did, there would have been much to recommend his flinging himself down after her. Namely this: Mrs. McGlame, Elizabeth's mother, was already quite old when Elizabeth married Jevons, and she greatly opposed the marriage. She didn't like Jevons, and she didn't like his strange brother. She got up an extremely complicated will, leaving everything to Elizabeth, but leaving it in trust and delineating every possible contingency . . . she wanted to make certain that none of her money ever wound up in the hands of the Jevons lot. Should Elizabeth die, Victoria became beneficiary of the trust. If Jevons did murder his wife, he might well have thought he would have better control over his daughter . . . being her legal guardian . . . than over his wife. It turns out that Jevons's business was scarcely paying, and that the family were living in London for the most part on Victoria's income. According to the stipulations of Mrs. McGlame's will, however, should Victoria die before marrying, and childless, then the Museum of Lincolnshire Life . . . which boasts among other things locally built steam engines . . . would become beneficiary. Which is what happened. We found no mention of H. E. Jevons after he departed London . . . he was simply never heard of again. And we never found any mention of any boy attached to the family, the boy you mentioned that morning at breakfast.

And there you have it, all we learned. One last item, Cookson. I fell into conversation with Hannah in the street recently. She told me she recalled a woman from New York City who'd booked into your flat sometime back in the seventies. The woman had left the flat, and the hotel, shortly after arriving . . . complaining that her rooms were haunted.

Yours,

Mimi S.

I did not show Ellen my letter, for all its remarkable spoken and unspoken compassion—not spitefully, not because she didn't show me hers, but because I didn't think she would want to see it. Aside from reading the letter, alone, closed in my study, refolding it, and putting it away in the locked drawer of my desk, I've done only two very small secret things along these lines, which I think of as "slips." One frozen day in March, I drove in a blizzard to Tower Records and purchased every compact disc I could find of Franz Schubert's piano music. When I had the chance to listen undetected, I listened. Spencer seemed to be very taken with this music, and he dropped whatever he was doing anytime I put it on, came into the room, lay down, sighed heavily, and struck a sphinx-like pose on the carpet, eyes at half-mast. Eventually, I found the piece I wanted (the middle movement of the A-major sonata), listened to it straight through once, and have not sought it out again since. (I suppose I'll never know who I heard playing the piano at the Hotel Willerton, or why I was able to hear the music when no one else could.) And I made a trip of my own to the Cambridge Public Library, where I looked up the libretto to *The Yeoman of the Guard;* I learned that in that operetta there is no character named Sophie.

. . .

Because she's home for the spring break, I've made beef stew for Jordie, one of her favorite dishes. At sunset, I stand at the stove trying to fish out with a spoon the twelve peppercorns and six whole cloves that are buried inside this pot, somewhere beneath the brown-red gravy. I've found eight of the peppercorns and five of the cloves. We had the windows open today—it was just warm enough for it—but we were too slow to close them, and it got cold in the house; the kitchen is altogether the best place to be. Ellen hasn't yet returned from . . . where? I'm not sure where, not sure she told me where she was going. Memories of Jordie have continued to visit me all day, and I've been thinking, here at the stew pot, about my teaching her to throw and catch a baseball when she was about ten. She got quite good at it and played two years of Little League, the only girl on her teams; later she took up touch football at the middle school, trailblazing for the girls in her class. What I recalled was her telling me that she wasn't sure she was interested in football but that she hated the way it made her feel to watch the girls standing on the sidelines, watching the boys.

Now she comes through the kitchen's swinging door and goes limp, very dramatically, closing her eyes, letting her jaw drop, leaning against the wall for support, completely done in by the smell of the stew. I think that this enactment expresses all she needs to say on the subject of the stew. Spencer, who has followed her into the kitchen, likewise expresses all he needs to say on the subject of stew, by standing three feet away, stock-still like a statue, head hung down just enough so he can stare penetratingly at me from the very top rims of his eye sockets.

"You fell asleep," I say to Jordie.

She moves to the table, pulls out a chair, and sits down. "How did you know?"

"Well," I say, "there are some very red creases on the left side of your face."

"Oh."

My back is to her, and after some silence I feel her eyes

boring into my shoulder blades. "What?" I say, not turning around.

"There's something I need to know," she says.

"What?"

"Am I supposed to never mention your trip to England?"

"What do you mean?"

"I mean it's been six months already."

"You can mention it," I say.

"I'm mentioning it," she says.

I turn and face her. For just an instant, she looks like Ellen. Throughout her growing up, people have been re- marking how she resembles her mother, and until this very moment, I've never seen it. My noticing it now could have something to do with the fact that everything she's wearing belongs to Ellen—the jeans, the sweater, a vest over the sweater, the earrings—but it takes a while for me to take that into account. "What do you want to know?" I say.

"Well," she says, "are you sure it's all right if we talk about it?"

"Of course," I say. "Yes. It's all right. What do you want to know?"

"Nothing, really," she says, shrugging her shoulders.

She has taken all the oranges out of the fruit bowl on the table, and she's arranging them in the shape of a triangle, racking them with her forearms to look like the unbroken balls on a pool table.

"The truth is," she says, "I don't think I really want to talk about it. Besides, Mom says things are getting better between you. I just needed to know, you know, that it was all right to talk about it, all right for it to come up."

"Did she really say that?" I ask.

"Say what?"

"Did Mom really say things were getting better between us?"

"Yeah," she says. "I just feel creepy if I think I'm sup- posed to not talk about something."

"When did she say it?"

"*Recently,*" she says, impatiently. "It makes me nervous,

like it's going to slip out by accident and everybody's going to be mad at me."

"I understand," I say. "I think that's a good quality to have."

"What quality?" she says.

"Feeling creepy," I say.

"Gee, thanks," she says, getting up, moving to the broom closet. "Where did you go so early this morning?"

"I went exploring," I said. "To an ancient vista point. Way upriver."

"You mean like up the Charles?"

"Yes," I say. "I mean specifically up the Charles. Did a little exploring."

"Cool," she says. She has unscrewed the stick from a push broom and is headed for the table with it. "But I was wondering," she says. "Have you hurt yourself or something? I noticed you're walking kind of funny. . . ."

Jordie has lit a tall cream-colored candle at the kitchen table, where we sit finishing our stew. When Ellen finally shows up, entering the kitchen through the door from the garage, she appears flustered, as if she's been hurrying to get home, almost as if she'd been chased through the door by the big bad world. She actually leans her back against the door once she gets it closed. "I'm glad you two didn't wait dinner on me," she says, and for a fraction of a second I think, mistakenly, that she's being ironic. "What is with the traffic?" she says. "Is something going on in Cambridge today I don't know about?"

"You didn't hear?" says Jordie.

"What?" says Ellen, still barricading the door.

Jordie means to pull a prank, to come up with some outrageous event that might have drawn a crowd to town, but now that she's started the joke, she can't finish it, can't think of a punch line. She looks to me, widening her eyes, as if to say, "Say something."

The only thing I can think to say is that there's been an

Elvis sighting, so I say, "Elvis was sighted on the Anderson Bridge today."

Jordie groans, making a thoroughly disgusted face, disappointed beyond words. Getting up from the table, she says, "Come sit, Mom."

Ellen protests, insists that Jordie not trouble herself, to go on with her own dinner, but Jordie helps Ellen off with her coat and steers her by the shoulders to the table, pulling out a chair and forcing her down into it.

Now Ellen sits directly across from me as Jordie brings bread plate and drinking glass, silverware and napkin. Ellen looks like a young girl somehow, very upright and trusting, waited on in her ladder-back chair. As Jordie dishes up the stew for her mother, our eyes meet for a second, mine and Ellen's. I don't know how she spent her day, she doesn't know how I spent mine. With just the smallest alteration here—I'm not sure exactly what: the right word, a perfect gesture—we could be in each other's arms, I know it. I can feel it. I even think she feels it too, for she glances at our daughter, over at the stove, then back at me, and smiles. She cups her hands around the top of the candle as if to warm her fingers and stares into the flame. I can read in her face, at the very least, that she's happy to be home.

I've come across a book, a book about the Charles River, entitled *The Charles River*, written by a man named Ron McAdow. In it, the author has mapped out the river valley, dividing the Charles and five of its canoeable tributaries into about two dozen sections, starting at its source on a high hill in Hopkinton and ending at Boston Harbor; he takes the river a section at a time, gives a bit of history, identifies access points, suggests walks and canoe outings, describes the surrounding land, the flora, the fauna. So far I have learned that the impressive darner (a big dragonfly) can produce up to sixteen hundred wingbeats per minute, and I have learned about the red-tailed hawk's clever method of soaring, unflapping, on columns of sun-warmed air. I am learning to recognize greenbrier, arrowwood (note its handsome trinity of double letters), buttonbush, bladderworts, kinnikinnick, and bur reed with its three-foot leaves. To date I have already taken five of the suggested walks, and now that the river is thawed, I plan soon to be putting in a canoe. I hope to take Jordie with me, when she's out of school, as often as she will come. I suppose it's overly obvious, the form my atonement takes here, a jilting of the supernatural for the natural, my "gift" put back to sleep, this time by deliberate benign neglect: the river is close to home, and I imagine the spirits of the Transcendentalists hover over the waters (allow me at least this!), and the spirits of the native Algonquin-speaking Nipmucks, Penacooks, and Wampanoags long before them. From cooking I've found that you can be more rhapsodic than most people would lead you to believe, and with only a little instinct for discerning what absolutely won't work, you can combine in a dish the ideas of many cooks; unpredictable connections are made between flavors, just as unpredictable connections are made between human experiences. I mean (no surprise here) to take every one of this book's suggestions and to explore the full, nearly eighty-mile length of the river, on foot, on water, mile by mile.

This morning I took a hike to a spot called King Philip's Lookout, in the Sherborn Town Forest. I twisted my ankle on a root along the trail, but not too badly, and continued anyway to the vista point. It was very early, and I met with no other person. From the top, I could see miles of the river valley and acres of forest and field. Did I feel a kinship with the humans who'd dwelled along the river for nine thousand years before me? No, I fretted over the pain in my ankle and worried about getting back to my car. But precisely because of the pain, I lingered there in that high place, soon discovering myself without expectations, soon forgetting my ankle; there on that wall of bedrock a hundred feet above the river, I closed my eyes and saw the afterimage of the panorama before me, saw the spectacle of the earth for the massive resplendent grave that it was, and I thought I wanted to live a useful life. I even thought that perhaps this was in the range of possibilities, that it wasn't too late. I didn't feel like taking any leaps of faith; for once, I didn't feel like taking any leaps of any kind. Mostly, I was filled with sorrow, if you want to know the truth, but I imagined sorrow as the arable soil of faith. From what I had observed, albeit through my various hazes, that seemed to be the case.

Epilogue

IF YOU BELIEVE that dreams are the psyche's at-

tempt to purge itself, to rid itself of what's not needed or

wanted, then my ghosts were dreams, self-proclaimed residue,

what didn't move on, suggesting that some undamaged core,

perhaps, of goodness—I like to think, of goodness—is what

did move on. (I should say that, technically, they were not *my* ghosts but anyone's, with the possible exception of James, the floater, who may have attached to me by design.) Happily, there is sometimes something to be learned from alluvial dregs. There's nothing elegant about the human mind; it's a scatterspray organ, hoping in its gusto to cover what needs to be covered by covering everything in sight; there's bound to be a lot of waste. And surely all residue is not equal in substance. Recently I dreamed I was among white academic types and playing a parlor game called Millennium Madness, in which players were challenged to come up with a work of literature and pair it with a reader—someone who would read it aloud—and in the pairing, capture the flavor of the twentieth century, now that the twentieth century is winding down. In the dream, I chose "The Wasteland," as read by W. C. Fields. (Don't ask me to explain it.)

Some residue—two last observations, lest anyone think I didn't notice:

(1) the remarkable number of times, in this tale, in which I either bashed my own head or had it bashed.

(2) I am aware of a gun in the "first scene" of this drama, and students of the stage will be expecting it to go off before the curtain falls. Well, it won't. However: One long, troublesome night in November, when I couldn't sleep, couldn't find any peace, when anguish seemed to crouch at the end of every path, I went into my study, took my Ruger semiautomatic out of its locked drawer, laid it on my desk, and sat staring at it for maybe a full hour. The next morning, still alive, I phoned my gun club buddy and asked him to keep my pistol at his house for a while.

More residue, a scene that didn't seem to fit as effectively anywhere else, composed of some reminiscences I collected while in Paris:

Pascal's father objected to Pascal's going to London, but in the man's laconic style, he would never tell Pascal why. The evening Pascal was to leave his childhood home and catch a train to Calais, his father was at the dinner table—not the big table in the dining room where Pascal used to hide as a boy, but the smaller, round one in the kitchen. M. Géricault was finishing his meal and couldn't be bothered to come into the hall and say good-bye to his son—his youngest and, in that sense, last child. Finally, dropping his bags on the stoop outside the front door, Pascal went back into the house, into the kitchen, and sat at the table next to his father.

The father went on eating, silently.

Pascal looked at his wristwatch. He asked his father if he wouldn't at least say good-bye. (*"Tu ne me diras pas au revoir, Papa?"*)

M. Géricault went on eating, silently.

At last, Pascal sighed and said, *"Si tu me défends d'y aller, je n'irai pas."* (If you tell me not to go, I won't go.)

The father looked at his son, and to Pascal's astonishment, there were tears in the man's eyes. Could it be that all along the father's objection was on account of his not wanting to be apart from his son? But M. Géricault, driven by his own failings, and human in his ignorance of consequences, said nothing and returned to his meal.

In the end, Pascal stood and stepped to the door, resigned, ready to go. At the last minute, before crossing the threshold, he turned, moved to his father's chair, and wrapped his arms around the man, embracing him from behind. Catherine, who'd come to see Pascal off, and who entered the kitchen with her camera at that moment, snapped a picture. (When the photograph came back from the developers, it would appear that Pascal was trying to prevent his father—who held a knife in one hand, a fork in the other—from eating.) Pascal kissed his mother again in the hallway, and then the mother went into the kitchen to scold the father.

Catherine followed Pascal out onto the stoop of the house. From there they could see the evening star, just piercing through a lilac sky. Pascal was full of wishes, like anyone in the early steps of a journey, but Catherine imagined that some of these wishes were about the past as well as the future. A truck went by in the street, causing a great racket, and when Pascal lifted his suitcase, the bag fell open, scattering its contents down the steps. For some reason, this small mishap made Catherine burst into tears. Later, she would write her brother and tell him that their father had gone out after dinner and sat on the front steps, in the dark, alone, for most of the evening. Catherine, who'd stayed and visited with her mother for a while, found him there as she was leaving, staring down the gloomy street.